Terence Strong was brought up in south London, after the Second World War. He has worked in advertising, journalism, publishing and many other professions. His bestselling novels (which have sold more than one million copies in the UK alone) include *Rogue Element*, *The Tick Tock Man*, *Wheels of Fire*, *Cold Monday* and *White Viper*. He lives in the south-west of England.

Visit www.twbooks.co.uk/authors/tstrong.html

Acclaim for Terence Strong

'An expert miasma of treachery and suspicion building to a thrilling climax' *Observer*

'Belongs to the action-man school of writing, backed up by hands-on research' *The Times*

'Tension ratchets up wickedly – a strong sense of reality is reinforced with powerful emotion and gritty characters' *Daily Telegraph*

'An edge-of-the-chair thriller with the chilling grip of authenticity' *Independent on Sunday*

'Well plotted and genuinely exciting' *Sunday Telegraph*

'An extremely good topical thriller' *Jack Higgins*

'The storylines are skilfully intermingled – the writing is fluid, the action furious and the political premise entertaining' *The Times*

TERENCE STRONG

White  Viper

POCKET
BOOKS

LONDON • SYDNEY • NEW YORK • TORONTO

First published in the United Kingdom by William Heinemann, 1996
First published in paperback in the United Kingdom by
Mandarin Paperbacks, 1997
Reprinted by Arrow Books, 1997
This edition published by Pocket Books UK, 2007
An imprint of Simon & Schuster UK Ltd
A CBS COMPANY

3 5 7 9 10 8 6 4 2

Simon & Schuster UK Ltd
Africa House
64-78 Kingsway
London WC2B 6AH

www.simonsays.co.uk

Simon & Schuster Australia
Sydney

A CIP catalogue record for this book
is available from the British Library

ISBN-13: 978-1-84739-033-2

Printed and bound in Great Britain by
Cox & Wyman Ltd, Reading, Berks

For
EL VAGO PEQUEÑO
He's still out there, somewhere

Author's Note

This book is inspired by real people and real events.

The full true story can never be told, simply because, as with all professional covert operations, no one knows the full picture – or would *want* to know it. At least no one who will ever tell. This is my fictional interpretation of what happened.

Suffice to say that the character of Kurt Mallory is real, only part invention. Some would say he offers a light of hope in the darkest of shadows. Others would disagree.

The organisation that has no name? An international network of 'the great and the good', whose family members have been gravely traumatised or suffered as a result of narcotics, forming a self-help network to fight back against the 'untouchable' traffickers who seem beyond the law? Rich and poor, black and white, Jew and Gentile fighting alongside each other. Politicians, judges, bankers, industrialists, Freemasons, policemen, soldiers, and businessmen joining forces in a secret battle. Is that really so fanciful? Perhaps, yet it exists.

Because I cannot know the extent of local corruption and involvement more recently in Colombia, I have substituted the names of Santa Maria and Adoración for Malaga and Concepción in my fictionalised account; my characters there are again pure invention.

But *los gringos malos* were there and they were the perpetrators of the events described in the chapel at Cruz de Oro. Their later fate in the *cuchillas* was as described, as were events on the road to Madrid and the end to which the trail eventually led. So, so close to home.

And that *should* give food for thought.

Terence Strong
London 1995

This book could not have been written had it not been for a chance encounter on the island of Crete with the 'real' Kurt Mallory and the help that he subsequently gave. I thank him for sharing at least part of his story with me and for allowing me to 'steal' much of his life and personality, for reading and advising on the manuscript, and for his patience with the embellishments necessary in the writing.

Many others kindly gave of their time and expert knowledge to help fill in the gaps or to point me in the right direction and my thanks go to:

IN LONDON: 'Des' for his encyclopaedic knowledge of Colombia and the international narcotics scene and for putting me right; Neil; old friend and journalist Mark Urban and his brother Stuart; TV producer Alma Taft; Father Pat Browne; Colin Harding of the Independent; Jim Ferguson of the Latin American Bureau; Frank Kennedy of Justice & Peace; Fabianne Warrington of Oxfam, and former mercenary Peter McAleese (author of No Mean Soldier) for their advice and contacts.

Special thanks go to a 'fan', Gary Davis who works as a long-distance lorry driver in Europe and who kindly dreamt up a 'foolproof' smuggling system for me.

IN VENEZUELA: Friend and task master Roy Carson for arranging everything and his lovely wife Victoria for a memorable high tea; my hijacked and uncomplaining chauffeur Egon Koopmans and Linda Sonderman for getting me to Puerto Ayacucho; British Ambassador HE James Flynn and the DEA's Country Attaché Leopold Arreguin and special agent David Lorino for their highly informed briefings.

IN COLOMBIA: The prettiest, wittiest and most fearless (even when the bomb went off) guide and companion one could hope for, Luz Stella; Simon Strong (author of The Shining Path and Whitewash, the Escobar story) for finding her and for so much good advice; photographer and journalist Tim Ross; journalist Ignao Goméz, Hernando Villamizar and his family for their hospitality in the cuchillas; David Davies for being there and British Ambassador HE Keith Morris with my apologies for being a party-pooper.

IN BOLIVIA: British Ambassador Mike Jackson and his very talented artist wife Mollie for their most welcome hospitality; Robert Gray and local DEA chief Gene Castillo (now retired) for explaining how it all worked.

IN MADRID: Manuel Jiménez of the General Direction of Police and journalist Bill Bond.

IN HUNGARY: British Ambassador HE Sir John Birch and journalist Julius Strauss for putting the final pieces together.

Prologue

Vic West was never late, but today he was.

Eight o'clock at the beach bar, he'd said. Before the weekend crowds arrive from the city and before the Caribbean sun makes the sand too hot to walk on. They serve some of the best coffee in Venezuela at the bar; we can sit in the shade and talk undisturbed for a couple of hours. Watch the sea and the girls walk by. West liked watching the girls.

But it was gone nine now and Colonel Oliver Maidment still sat alone with a half-eaten *cachito* croissant and his third cup of *café negro*. High-octane caffeine that would set his pulse racing for the rest of the morning.

Something big has come up, West had said. Real important, he'd emphasised in that secretive way of his. But no details, not over the phone. So the chairman and chief executive had cancelled the board meeting of Portcullis Industries and Procurement plc and taken the next available flight from Heathrow to Caracas, flying via Miami.

A total of twenty energy-draining hours without sleep to get to the rendezvous and then West doesn't show.

For the umpteenth time, Maidment scanned the roadway and the beach. At least there could be worse places to wait.

A strengthening sun was breaking up the high haze of cloud, the sea becoming bluer by the minute and sparkling like a floating bed of sapphires as each wave shrugged towards the shore. His eye caught the movement of the lone jogger as he ran along the waterline where the breakers foamed up the deserted strip of sand.

Deserted? Not quite, Maidment realised. The music was carried on the offshore breeze from the multicoloured parasol some fifty metres away. An upbeat bossa nova number. He looked and saw the garish towel and the splay of pink legs half hidden by the circle of shade.

All right for some, he thought, and beckoned the morose barman. In his poor Spanish, Maidment said: 'I am waiting for a friend. I wonder if you saw him here earlier, before I arrived?'

The man grimaced as he tried to understand, as though the effort were causing him physical pain. 'What is his name?'

'Victor West. Mid-fifties, stocky and balding with a heavy moustache.' It sounded almost like a betrayal to describe his old friend in such unflattering terms. Especially an ex-Royal Marine. He added: 'He's a regular here. Drinks King of Scots and Coke. Likes to chat up the girls.'

Black lifeless eyes appraised this tall lean Englishman with his panama hat, linen suit and kidskin loafers. The barman looked directly at the sunburnt face and the head of crinkly brown hair that had given way to a receding crown, then met the cool green eyes. At length he said: 'Your friend, he is a gringo?'

Maidment shook his head. 'No, not American. He is English.' There was a fine distinction.

The barman finally grunted in recognition. 'Ah, yes. He comes most weekends. In fact he was here yesterday evening when I closed up.'

'I suppose he didn't leave a message?' He knew he was grasping at straws, but West had been adamant that they should meet urgently. 'A message for Mr Maidment or the colonel perhaps?'

A shake of the head, irritated by this waste of time when he could be sitting down in the shade of the bamboo awning doing nothing. 'No message. Your friend was with two other men, talking. Maybe he comes here tomorrow.'

Maidment ordered a *batido* fruit juice and watched the man go.

Sure, *mañana*. That was a South American's answer to everything. Appointments were flexible things. Arrange a meeting and you could expect to wait half a day for someone to turn up without a word of apology. As though it were the most natural thing in the world. If you invite guests for supper, Vic West had once told him, don't be surprised if they turn up a week later expecting to be wined and dined.

But West himself was never late.

Something must have happened, something unavoidable. For all he knew, his friend's car had broken down – very likely, given the state of repair of most vehicles in this country. Or some unexpected and urgent meeting had been called by an important client. There would be a good reason. No doubt the man would show by lunch.

In the meantime Oliver Maidment had no intention of wasting his time. Collecting his briefcase from the hired car, he settled down to catch up with his paperwork. The company of which he was now chairman and chief executive had invited him to join the board soon after he'd stepped down from his parliamentary seat before the General Election of 1987. His spell as a junior defence minister had been followed by the poisoned chalice of a parliamentary undersecretary post at the Northern Ireland Office. Clearly he had been banished to the political wilderness. That he would not return became evident when his daughter Sophie accidentally killed herself with a cocaine overdose at a society party in London. He was devastated by the loss and by the lurid stories splashed across the front pages of the tabloid press.

Life at Portcullis Industries and Procurement suited him. He was back amongst old military friends, many of whom he'd known from his days as colonel of one of the infantry line regiments. Out of the media gaze in all but the financial pages, he enjoyed working for the highly respected public company in a field that he knew well. Arms procurement – preferably of British manufacture, but not necessarily – was the name of the game, selling to governments and police forces worldwide. Training was also given to foreign armies, together with security advice. The company was also involved in the highly specialised manufacture of related products, from surveillance equipment to one-off weaponry. And all with the matronly blessing of Her Majesty's Government.

On joining the company, he had been surprised and delighted to find that Vic West was their sales representative in South

America. The paths of the two men had crossed during the Falklands War. Then West, a former Royal Marines officer, was attached to the Secret Intelligence Service, while Maidment was a junior MOD minister. West's father, an English Jew, had been an engineer and had spent most of his life working in the Venezuelan oilfields. He married the daughter of a wealthy Peruvian businessman. Therefore the young Vic West spent his formative years in either Lima or Caracas and his late teens and early twenties travelling the South American continent in search of adventure. By this time he had become a fluent Spanish speaker.

In 1964 at the age of twenty-five, West had decided that the military life was for him and joined the Royal Marines. Later he passed selection for the Special Boat Squadron which brought him into contact with the Intelligence Corps to which he later transferred.

By the time Argentina invaded the South Atlantic islands, West had already served in several South American SIS stations as an acknowledged expert on the area. Maidment appreciated West's explanations of the Spanish American psyche and the two men became close acquaintances, if not yet good friends.

That was to develop five years later when the minister resigned his parliamentary seat after the tragic loss of his daughter. And it was to happen in the most bizarre of circumstances which were to change Maidment's life and give him a renewed reason for living. In a word, revenge.

Vic West was one of Portcullis's top salesmen. His quasi-diplomatic rôle with SIS had introduced him to the top echelons of politics and the military throughout South America. He was ideally placed to offer equipment and training schemes to governments anxious to fight left-wing guerrillas and the big drug barons. But it did not stop there. West was well connected with people from so many walks of life that he was able to cash in further on the cocaine boom by also selling to the so-called drugs cartels and Communist guerrillas as well as their rival right-wing paramilitary death squads. These deals were secretly subcontracted to either Israeli or South African suppliers for a lucrative

4

cut. West had good contacts with the intelligence services of both countries.

Had this become public knowledge there would have been amazement that Oliver Maidment, former infantry colonel and junior government minister, could have been party to such arrangements – especially after his daughter's tragic death while using cocaine.

But both Maidment and West knew that if Portcullis did not supply these people, then either the French or Belgians certainly would. Moreover, only they could guarantee that much of the intelligence they gleaned in the process would be fed back to West's old colleagues at the newly developing Global Issues Department of the Secret Intelligence Service. Some of that information would be horse-traded with their American 'cousins', the CIA, or the Drug Enforcement Administration and others. Just to keep the favours square and the British profile high. When the situation was right, an arms or drugs shipment might be seized as a result.

It gave both men satisfaction for a very special reason that only a handful of people knew.

'Some lunch?' The barman's shadow fell across the papers on the table. 'Before the rush starts?'

Maidment looked at his watch, surprised to see it was nearly one. And still West hadn't shown.

With concern beginning to grow, the colonel ordered an *arepa* maize pancake stuffed with squid, and a can of Polar beer. But when the meal came he found he had no appetite for it. Glancing along the beach, he again noticed the multicoloured parasol. The sun had arced across the sky since the early morning and shade no longer covered the body of the man who basked so contentedly, face down on the towel. Even from that distance Maidment could see how pink his skin was. The music still blared, but no one seemed to mind.

Day trippers from Caracas now filled the beach and splashed in the shimmering sea. Queues were forming at the bar; Vic would have appreciated the long-legged office girls making the most of the weekend. All honey-skinned with sleek black hair.

Not topless though, like you'd see in Europe; Catholic modesty demanded the wearing of bikinis, no matter that the thin thongs cutting up between their buttocks left little to the imagination.

Yes, Vic West would like that. But still he hadn't showed.

Must be a reason, must be. He just hoped it was nothing serious like a road crash, an all-too-frequent occurrence in this country. Or something more sinister . . . but West of all people could look after himself.

Then Maidment saw the telephone on the bar. Why hadn't he noticed it before? As local calls were free he just had to dial the number of La Floresta hotel where West usually stayed in town. A strident tone reverberated in his ear. Unobtainable. Bloody Venezuelan communications! Always changing the numbers and not telling anyone, including the subscribers themselves. It was a nightmare.

What should he do? Drive back to La Floresta and risk passing his friend coming the other way? Then another thought occurred. Unusually, West hadn't used the twenty-four hour clock. Was it just possible he'd meant them to meet at eight o'clock in the evening – *after* things got quiet, not *before*, and he'd just misunderstood? Not impossible and it would certainly explain his non-appearance.

Feeling more reassured, Maidment decided he needed some exercise to take his mind off things. After locking his attaché case in the trunk of his hired car, he left a message with the barman for West to await his return.

Then he began to stroll along the beach drag. The wind was gusting in off the sea now taking the edge off the sun's fierce heat. It was pleasant for walking and Maidment found himself relaxing, thinking back over the years during which he and Vic West had shared the secret.

In fact he walked farther than he had intended and when he returned along the water-line the beach had started to empty. The sky was clouding over and his elongated shadow had lost its sharpness. There was now a chill edge to the breeze.

His legs were beginning to ache and he was thankful to glimpse the yellow, blue and red flag, wind-ragged and snapping on the pole by the bamboo bar. Almost certainly West would be there by now. Unconsciously his pace quickened.

It was then that the sudden darting movement up ahead caught his eye. Momentarily he thought it was a scavenging dog before he glimpsed the torn short trousers and brown legs of the urchin boy as he scampered away from the multicoloured parasol.

He realised instantly what had happened. The young thief had stolen something from the sunbathing man while he slept.

'STOP!' Maidment yelled and began to run. It was an instinctive reaction; he had never believed in passing by when someone was in trouble.

But after a few paces he slowed, his feet sinking deep into the soft sand. There was no way he could catch the youngster; it was stupid even to try at his age. He turned towards the parasol. At least he could tell the man, give him a description of the boy. For all the good that would do; there were thousands of deprived kids like him surviving off their wits in the *barrio* slums of Caracas.

As he approached, Maidment became aware that the sound from the radio, which had been blasting out salsa rhythms earlier in the day, had faded to a murmur as the batteries ran down. No attempt had been made to move the parasol since the morning and the man had been lying unprotected in the harsh sun for most of the day.

The colonel shuffled to a halt and his mouth went suddenly dry as he looked down at the body. The skin on the back, with its thick mat of dark hair around the shoulders, was the colour of rare steak and bubbling with clusters of small white blisters, some not so small.

A knot of apprehension tightened in Maidment's gut. Somehow the man looked familiar. The chunky short build, the thick legs and the curling grey hair around the nape of the neck.

Even as he dropped to one knee and reached out to turn him over, he knew the man was dead.

Christ, he'd been right after all. Vic West was never late.

1

'My first case of death by sunbathing.'

The cop's eyes were hidden behind stylish Polaroid sunglasses and Maidment was irritated to find his own reflection staring back at him. As the officer chewed unconcernedly on a wad of gum, the colonel felt an overwhelming urge to punch the man in the face.

Even the barman was annoyed by the cop's insensitivity. 'The dead man was his friend,' he said pointedly.

The attendant from the Policia Technica Judicial, who was struggling to get the stretcher into the back of the morgue van, was equally unimpressed with the sick humour.

'It must have been a heart attack,' he assured Maidment. 'A massive one, too, because he wasn't even able to move. If it is a consolation, I doubt he knew much about it.'

Infarto? The colonel's Spanish was far from good and it took him a few moments to assimilate the words. Vic West died of a heart attack? It didn't seem credible. Not Vic, the tough old bugger. He'd given up smoking years before and had even cut down on his King of Scots and Coke. Last year he'd passed the company's stringent medical and could still run a mile and a half in twenty minutes.

'He was fitter than I've ever been,' Maidment murmured, half to himself.

The attendant shrugged. 'It happens.' He went to close the rear door.

'I'll follow you.'

'No,' the cop intervened ominously. 'You will come with me. As the person who discovered the body, you are held responsible.'

9

The attendant said sympathetically: 'It's why no one stops at fatal accidents in this country. Your friend's body will be held in the morgue at Catia La Mar.'

A second cop drove Maidment's hire car while he was obliged to ride in the police vehicle. He might have been angered at being treated like the prime suspect had it not been for the awful sense of sadness that deepened with every minute that passed.

By the time they reached headquarters in Caracas the full shock of the loss had finally struck him and the tears were running freely down his cheeks like those of a hurt child. He owed Vic West so much and no one would ever know. Could never know.

In fact the anticipated interrogation did not prove to be such an ordeal. The investigating *fiscal* had a heavy workload with three murders that evening and he saw an obvious heart-attack case as the quickest and simplest to clear. After a few dozen terse questions, the attorney seemed satisfied and the statement was drawn up for Maidment to sign.

It was dark when he left to drive to the city morgue. The lights were still on and he ventured inside past the unmanned door: the gleaming aluminium body lockers and inspection tables were under the harsh fluorescent lighting, incongruously clinical against the grimy chipped tiles of the walls and floor where blood ran freely into the drainage channels.

A pathologist was crudely slicing and probing at the cadaver of one of the day's murder victims, muttering his findings while an assistant scribbled them down in a notebook.

The man looked up. 'What do you want?'

'You've got the body of my friend here – Señor West.'

'The heart attack?'

'Yes.'

'So?'

'Can you confirm it *was* a heart attack?'

'That's what his label said.'

'You won't – er – examine the body?'

'Not much point.' A sigh. 'I'm very busy.'

His assistant whispered something in his ear. The pathologist

10

nodded as though suddenly resigned to the interruption. Pulling off his surgical gloves, he said: 'Okay, stitch that one up.'

He walked across to the lockers and slid one open. Unlike the charred back, the front of Vic West's naked body was bluish and waxy, quite obscene. Like some macabre theatre prop. Not a human being at all, not his friend.

'What is it?' Maidment asked.

The pathologist sniffed. 'Probably nothing. My assistant noticed it.' He lifted West's foot.

Maidment peered closer until he could distinguish the slight bruising and the patch of dry blood around the puncture mark. He cleared his throat. 'What's that?'

'A hypodermic, I should say. We don't get to see many heroin addicts in Venezuela. When we do, they are usually Americans.'

'Vic was no addict,' Maidment said angrily, despite what was staring him in the face.

The pathologist smiled uneasily. 'Well, it is true I can see no other marks.'

Maidment sensed there was something else. 'Yes?'

A shrug. 'An unusually big needle was used.'

'What does that mean?'

'A large syringe of whatever—' His voice trailed. 'If it was heroin, it could have been enough to induce an attack of the heart. That is all.'

That was all. Vic West had been murdered, that was all. Some bastards had held him down and filled him so full of heroin that his heart had burst. Then they'd callously dumped him under a parasol on the beach before the sun came up.

They knew it would be treated as a heart attack. Knew the Venezuelan police and the medics wouldn't ask questions, even if they had suspicions. There were enough murders every night on the streets of Caracas to keep them more than busy.

In fact, it had then cost Maidment four hundred dollars to persuade the forensic pathologist to conduct a private postmortem, and even then he'd had to do a lot of talking.

'*Mañana*,' the man had promised wearily. He would have the results some time the next day.

But Maidment had no real doubts, for him the only question was who had done it? Who had seen through the façade of the congenial Englishman who had friends in every city on the South American continent? His apprenticeship for the business had been the best; his work in British Intelligence had long ago taught him how to cover his tracks and his real interests. His qualifications were impeccable, his track record unblemished, until now. Somewhere along the line Vic West had made the one mistake he wasn't allowed to make in his business.

Had his killers been following him for months, even years, patiently awaiting their moment of revenge? Or was this new, something more recent? Something to do with West's urgent demand for the meeting?

'Something big.' His friend's words echoed round Maidment's head as he drove through the Caracas streets to the hotel that overlooked the Plaza Altamira.

La Floresta was a ten-storey building with a narrow frontage squeezed in between other buildings and dwarfed by neighbouring tower blocks. Although it was only ten o'clock when Maidment arrived, he found its doors already locked against the thieves who prowled the city's streets after dark.

He found himself glancing nervously over his shoulder as he waited for the reluctant night manager to answer the bell and open up.

The man showed no emotion as he was told that his guest, Señor West, had met with a fatal accident and that he had come to collect his belongings. Just: 'Who will pay the bill, señor?'

Bastard, the colonel thought, but just said simply, 'I'll settle it.'

'You'll have to sign for anything you take away,' the manager warned as he shuffled to the elevator and pressed the button. As the doors wheezed open, he asked: 'It was a car crash, I suppose?'

'Why do you say that?'

They stepped inside. 'Because that's how most people die in Caracas. That or a knifing.'

'When did you last see Señor West?'

'Must have been yesterday evening. He left with two friends.'

'Friends?'

12

A shrug. 'Well, they'd been drinking in the bar, laughing together like amigos.'

'What did these men look like?'

The night manager suddenly sensed trouble; his amnesia was instant. 'I did not see their faces,' he replied. This was a dangerous city in which to notice things.

They alighted on the eighth floor and went to West's room. It was poky and a little shabby, but clean. The air-conditioning unit rattled so noisily at the window that Maidment didn't hear the manager close the door, leaving him alone.

What he really wanted to find was his friend's briefcase, but it wasn't in the room. Had his killers taken it or was that what the boy stole from the beach?

He switched off the air conditioning, able to think more rationally in the blessed silence that followed. If Vic West had been in possession of some sensitive information that he'd committed to paper, then he may have hidden it in his room. Better that than risk taking it with him on the streets in a city notorious for its pickpockets and muggers.

Methodically Maidment stripped the covers and mattress from the bed and checked the carpet edge for any sign that it had been loosened from the gripper rail in order to hide something underneath it. Then he checked the lavatory cistern and bathroom cabinet before pulling out each drawer in the fitted furniture in case something had been taped to the back of one of them.

He drew a blank. Now the exertion of movement and his mounting frustration were making him hot as the refrigerated atmosphere was slowly replaced by the humidity of the tropical night. Removing his jacket and tie, Maidment began taking West's clothes from the wardrobe to pack them into the empty suitcase he'd found under the bed. Before folding away each suit, he emptied the pockets. An assortment of business cards, some bus tickets, sweet wrappers and a laundry receipt – and a blue boarding card.

He tilted it towards the light to read the small print. Avensa airline. From Caracas to Puerto Ayacucho. Where was that? Somewhere in the southwest of the country, he thought, but wasn't

13

sure. And the date? The sixteenth. Three days earlier. Assuming West had stopped over for the night before returning, that must have been the last place he'd visited. But for what purpose?

There were no other clues.

By the time he'd cleared the bathroom of toiletries, he was sweating freely and regretting his earlier decision to kill the air conditioning. As he heaved the suitcase towards the door, he noticed the minibar. Now that was an idea.

It opened to reveal an ice-cool six-pack of beer and a row of mixer bottles. An orange juice would hit the spot, he decided. It was when he extracted the bottle that the thin pocket diary flapped down onto the worn carpet. The papers must have adhered to the moisture on the glass.

His thirst forgotten, he opened the booklet and flicked through the pages. Well, there it was. Today's entry: *0800 hours. Meet Ollie. He's going to like this!*

There was nothing entered for the previous evening when West had seemingly left La Floresta with two 'friends'. In fact, there was nothing at all entered for yesterday or the day before. On the sixteenth, the day West had apparently flown to Puerto Ayacucho, there was more scrawled handwriting. *Hotel Tomo. 1500 hrs. Meet Palechor at Las Noches Árabes.* Arabian Nights. Then, at the bottom of the page, written in capital letters and circled, were two words: WHITE VIPER.

None of it meant anything to Maidment, but then he was tired now and aware that his mind was only functioning at half-power. It could wait until morning. He closed the door of West's room and drove back to his own hotel.

It seemed that his head had only just hit the pillow when he was awakened by the electric purr of the bedside phone. Daylight streamed in through the open window and he strained to hear the speaker's voice above the clamour of the city's rush-hour traffic.

The morgue pathologist was calling to confirm that Señor West appeared to have died from a heart attack induced by a massive overdose of drugs. But not an opiate, pure cocaine. As the amount taken was so great, the man could only conclude that it was a very deliberate act of suicide.

14

Suicide! Maidment fumed as he replaced the receiver. What an insult to his friend even to suggest such a thing. No, the colonel's worst fears were confirmed. But what to do about it? He needed advice and fast.

Moments later he had reached his decision and put a call through to the British Embassy in Chuao and asked for Simon Cadbury in the Commercial Section.

When the SIS head of station answered, the colonel said briskly: 'Oliver Maidment of Portcullis here.'

'Ah, Colonel, nice to hear from you. It must be a year since we last met—'

Maidment dumped the niceties. 'Listen, Simon, Vic West is dead. I must speak with you urgently.'

There was a sharp intake of breath at the other end of the line, but no trace of feeling as he recovered from the surprise news. 'Of course, Colonel, but not over the phone. Let's be a bit discreet. Come to the Valle Arriba at noon.'

Maidment arrived ten minutes early at the sumptuous country club and was irked when Simon Cadbury sauntered in at a quarter past. The man had Harrow, Oxbridge and Foreign Office stamped through him as clearly as lettering in a stick of rock candy: striped shirt and Cavalry tie under a mushroom-coloured tropical suit which he wore with an air of studied arrogance. At thirty-three his features were still self-consciously handsome and finely chiselled. His greeting was cool, his voice slightly distant as they took their drinks on the sun terrace which overlooked the swimming pool and the lush golf links beyond.

'Was sorry to hear about Vic. Heart attack was it?'

The SIS officer had been doing his homework, Maidment realised. 'No, he was murdered. Given a massive overdose of near pure cocaine and then dumped on the beach to make it look good.'

Cadbury must have been taken aback, but his face wore the expression of a professional poker player. 'The hospital didn't mention the cocaine.'

'They didn't know. I paid for a private postmortem.'

'That was a smart move.'

15

'Not smart, Simon. He was my friend as well as employee; I had to know.'

'Any idea who was responsible?' Cadbury asked quietly and sipped at a tall glass of vodka and lime.

Maidment shook his head. 'To be honest it could be anyone from Vic's past. But my best guess has to be that it was someone he was dealing with currently. He'd called a meeting with me for something that he said was very important, very big.' He paused. 'Only he didn't make it.'

'What was it about? Some deal?'

'Almost certainly, but I've no idea what. All I know is that he travelled down to Puerto Ayacucho on business a couple of days ago.' He told Cadbury about the boarding card and the diary entries. As the man listened in silence, his lips tightened perceptibly. 'Thing is, Simon, do you think I should fly to the place and find out what he was up to?'

Cadbury didn't answer directly. Instead he said: 'This reference to White Viper—' He allowed the words to hang between them.

Maidment shook his head. 'No idea. Sounds like some sort of posh cocktail. Why? Does it mean anything to you?'

The SIS officer glanced around to make sure no one was within earshot. 'We've picked it up on a couple of DEA briefings during the past nine months or so. Of course, our Drugs Liaison Officer at the embassy is more *au fait* than me.'

'So what is it?'

'Someone's branding a new coke supply by that name.'

'Branding?' Maidment frowned. 'Ah, you mean very pure cocaine?'

Cadbury smiled gently. 'I see you have read *The Fruit Palace* – considered essential reading for anyone interested in Colombia, just like Márquez's *One Hundred Years of Solitude*. Alas, Colonel, Charles Nicholl's search for the origins of the mythical Snow White pure coke is a bit of a fantasy and can be misleading. Although in this case there are similarities.'

'I don't understand.'

'Look, all cocaine bought at source in bulk is pretty much the

16

same purity – around ninety per cent, so branding isn't usually anything to do with quality. White Viper, Snow White, call it Heinz or Kellogg's if you like, it's no different. Branding is used to indicate a reliable supply source and to help keep track of shipments. The coke business is very fragmented. Although the media refer to the Cali cartel, the Medellín cartel, the Santa Marta – in fact they're all smaller groups that form and re-form all the time as it suits them.

'If there's a big order to meet, then the product might have to come from, say, three different laboratories. Branding assures the next buyer in the chain that it's basically the same product from the same source. Likewise when transport is shared. When you've a stash of coke being moved with someone else's, you want to be able to identify it at the other end.'

'I see.'

'Branding doesn't *usually* reach the end user. To them a snort is a snort.'

'You said usually.'

'Well, in this case there is a similarity with Nicholl's book. Branding is actually reaching street level. Maybe some *narco* kingpin got the idea from the book to use as a marketing ploy. According to our DLO here, some stuff's turned up in Colombia and in the States. Also in the UK. And it's around fifty per cent pure.'

'Is that significant?'

Cadbury gave one of his patronising little half-smiles. 'Coke traffickers normally finish with their product when it arrives at its country of destination. Then it works down the local pyramid from importer to street dealer. Overall you can reckon on three cuts to middlemen by adding impurities. At street level your ninety per cent pure snow is down to thirty per cent and everyone's done very nicely thank you.'

'So if White Viper is hitting the streets at fifty per cent?' Maidment pressed.

'It means this organisation is involved much further down the chain in the user country. That's very usual. Our DLO reckons they're cutting out one or two middlemen. That keeps the end-user price competitive for a product that really *does* pack an extra punch. It's a neat trick, introducing market forces.'

'So the White Viper brand really does mean something to the man on the street?'

Cadbury gave an abrupt little laugh. 'Yeah, it means he can blow his brains out if he's not careful or give himself an early heart attack – especially if he's a first timer or doesn't dilute it himself.'

'Dangerous stuff.'

'But good value and very desirable. Encourages the end user to do a little cutting and dealing himself. Spreading the habit. So you can imagine the trouble that's going to cause. Wide boys are going to counterfeit the White Viper logo – it's just a squiggly snake on a polythene bag – and all sorts of rival gangland mayhem is likely to result.'

'I see. Who's producing this stuff?'

'No idea, Colonel. And nor does anyone else, according to the DEA briefings. But it's resulted in a lot of feuding and blood-letting in Colombia and here in Venezuela.'

'Did Vic know something about it?' Maidment asked himself aloud. 'What the hell does it mean?'

Cadbury's eyes took on a flinty look. 'What it does mean, Colonel, is that if you go sniffing around Puerto Ayacucho, then don't waste your money buying a two-way ticket. Because you won't be coming back.'

'Pardon me?'

'If Vic had got mixed up with these White Viper people, it could very well be the reason he's dead. If they're operating out of Puerto Ayacucho and you go snooping around down there, you'll end up like him. The place has been going the same way as Arauca over the past year – a lawless area full of guerrillas and drug gangsters. Before long it'll be a no-go area to both the police and the army.'

Maidment frowned. 'What about our people?'

'Our people?'

'Okay, *your* people. Couldn't you send some of them down to investigate? After all, the service owes Vic a big debt for his work

18

over the years. He was one of your own and both of us have fed you with plenty of high-grade information since he left you. Don't you want to know why he was killed – sort out those who did it?'

Cadbury's patience was wearing thin. 'Look, Colonel, I'm kept desperately short-staffed and dead agents are no good to me. The drugs war isn't top of our list of priorities; we leave that to the Yanks. Your and Vic's legal arms supplies – great, no problem, and any collateral intelligence to hand to the DEA boys is a bonus. But if Vic was getting in deep shit with the *narcos*, I don't want to know. He had a good run over here for eight years and we both know he pushed his luck.' He looked the other man straight in the eyes. 'But it just ran out. Vic may have had a lot of friends in South America, Colonel, but whenever you make a friend here, you make an enemy of someone else.'

But Maidment was hardly listening, his mind racing on to other possibilities. 'What about the DEA, Simon? You know their people here; couldn't you persuade them to investigate on our behalf?'

Cadbury's laugh was genuine. 'I'll tell you what happened the last time the DEA went down there. Three months ago they planned for a bunch of their special agents to go down to Puerto Ayacucho and take a look around. They chartered a private plane using a genuine company cover name and likewise hired a car to meet them at the airstrip. When they arrived they were faced with a welcome party of armed heavies. Nothing fraught, all very friendly with lots of jokes. Why not, there was plenty to laugh about. They handed the special agents a tape recording. It was of one of their own damn secretaries making all the secret booking arrangements on what they thought was a secure telephone. The DEA guys did the only thing they could do – flew straight back to Caracas.'

Maidment paled slightly. 'You mean the DEA is infiltrated?'

'Infiltrated, bugged and buggered. The *narcos*' first rule is "know thine enemy". The whole of Venezuela is awash with *narco* money and riddled from top to bottom with informers and those with vested interests to protect.'

19

The colonel was exasperated. 'There must be *something* someone can do.'

'There's something *you* can do,' Cadbury replied, draining his glass. 'Go home to London. Go home before someone links you with Vic and be thankful for the millions he earned your company in eight good years.' He glanced at the gold watch on his wrist. 'I'm sorry, I've got to get back to the office.'

And that was it.

Maidment drove away from the clubhouse in a blind, seething rage. For once he was oblivious to the helter-skelter of Caracas traffic, the suicidal lane-switching at high speed and the cacophony of car horns. He had no thought of where he was heading, just knew that he couldn't face the depressing confinement of his hotel room. He needed space to breathe and time to think.

Before long he found himself on one of the *autopistas*, a concrete swathe slicing through the city and towards the coast. That would do. The beach bar that had been Vic West's favourite haunt. One last drink for old times' sake.

Old times. Some good, but some bloody awful. Like the year his daughter died. 1987. Eight years ago, yet it seemed like only yesterday that Sophie had arrived home unexpectedly and wandered into the garden of the detached house in Hillsborough, a middle-class suburban district south of Belfast that was considered 'safe' enough for a middle-ranking Northen Ireland Office minister.

Even now he could remember how young and fresh she looked in the simple summer frock, sunlight catching in her auburn hair. And that mischievous and beguiling smile of hers, those knowing looks that belied her innocence. A virgin, he'd thought then. Barely twenty-one, university behind her and her whole future ahead.

He'd been sitting on the patio with Vic West and a man who had just been introduced to him at that time simply as 'Kurt'. West was giving a final unofficial briefing before his retirement from the Secret Intelligence Service to seek his fortune in the commercial market place. Apparently several major companies had expressed interest in his South American expertise.

The man whom Maidment was later to know as Kurt Mallory was a complete stranger to him. All he had been told was that the man had for a time served in the élite Special Air Service Regiment and was now what SIS liked to call a freelancer. Not on any official payroll, he was an undercover operator who was about to investigate links between the Provisional IRA and the Basque separatist terror organisation known as ETA. The minister was assured of the freelancer's reputation and that he was well regarded in certain secretive circles in both Washington and Tel Aviv where he'd been hired by various agencies from time to time. He was a first-class fingerman, an expert at covert infiltration. West didn't then mention the man's other speciality.

Yet despite the assurances, privately Oliver Maidment hadn't been sure about the man. He certainly looked the part. With a dark complexion and wild black hair, he could easily pass for a Spaniard but the minister felt there was something unsavoury about him, even allowing for the shabby jeans and dirty T-shirt. Despite the rather striking face and penetrating blue eyes – coloured contact lenses would be used, West explained – you could just sense that Kurt Mallory could melt into the background of any seedy bar in Dublin or on the Basque coast. With those gipsy looks he could be accepted as a Latin or a Gaelic son, and apparently his Spanish was as fluent as his English which he spoke with a strangely Germanic accent.

That was when he spoke at all.

Looking back now, Maidment thought, he should have guessed what was going to happen. The moment Sophie saw Kurt Mallory on the patio and his eyes met hers, you could sense the frisson in the air between them. Almost smell the pheromones clashing amongst the scents of the garden.

Not that Mallory had given her any obvious encouragement, but then he didn't have to. The polite acknowledging smile would have been quite enough for Sophie. She had her mother's determination to get what she wanted. His daughter had always possessed a bewitching sense of devilment and during three years of freedom at university she had discovered her libido and the pleasures of blossoming womanhood. A search for her 'grand

21

passion' had begun.

Only later Maidment discovered that Sophie had managed to contact Mallory through West when the man's assignment was over. She could be very persuasive when she used her new-found womanly wiles. And Vic always had been a sucker for a pretty face. She and Mallory had been lovers for six months when he first found out about it.

He had not been pleased. At thirty-five, not only was Mallory fourteen years older than his daughter, they were obviously and completely unsuitable for each other. An attraction of opposites, if ever there was one. Of course the colonel couldn't bring himself to blame his daughter, just this unkempt stranger with his selfish desire to get his leg over some nubile innocent. That was how he saw it then. Much later he learned the truth, worked it out for himself. Mallory had seemed unattainable, so Sophie wanted him. 'My bit of rough,' she'd joked with her old university friends. 'I found him a challenge. There was something – I don't know – *dangerous* about him. And because he wasn't really interested – to begin with. Actually he's rather cute when you get to know him. And fascinating – God, he knows so *much*, he's been *everywhere*!'

And Maidment himself had got to know him when Sophie died. When her search for a grand passion and another challenge and another experiment led her to try cocaine at a West End party. It was beginner's bad luck. The purity was unusually high, and Sophie apparently suffered from a weak heart. Her death made the front page of every newspaper in the country.

Father and lover met at the funeral. It was a tense moment as Mallory, who had kept his distance from her family during the burial, came forward to offer his condolences.

Maidment's wife had dabbed at her tears and eyed him coldly. 'And *did* you love her, Mr Mallory?' she demanded sardonically.

The reply was hoarse. 'More than I should have done.'

A strange answer, Maidment had thought then, but later he began to understand.

But that was much later, after his life and career went into a plunging spiral. He had barely resigned from politics to join

Portcullis when his wife had died of grief and cancer, one feeding off the other.

His old acquaintance, Vic West, who was the company's South American salesman, had returned to London and come to see him as the office closed.

He would never forget that night. Just the two of them, sitting in the darkness at the boardroom table with a panoramic view of the empty City and the moon shining like quicksilver on the Thames. Voices hushed and mellowed by the bottle of malt they shared.

It was then that he discovered he was not alone. That many others had suffered tragedies as a result of drug abuse and that a sort of unofficial self-help group existed. It had grown up over the years, dedicated to helping parents, loved ones and friends to purge their inevitable sense of guilt, frustration and anger by doing something, anything, to bring the purveyors of narcotics to justice. Jew and Arab, black or white, rich or poor; the membership was international, across all religions and cultures. Shared grief, it seemed, could transcend all barriers, all differences.

There was a secret fund to which the wealthy made willing and generous donations. The parents of an addict on a Manchester council estate would receive a visit from a stranger – and a cheque for their son's rehab treatment. Later a job offer, organised through the secret network, would arrive out of the blue to give the struggling lad a chance. That was the way it worked.

'I've never heard of this,' Maidment confessed. 'How did you get to know about it?'

Vic West was not a soft man, but even in the dim half-light Maidment could see the moisture in his friend's eyes. 'I lost my nephew to amphetamines. Lovely boy, great nature, just a bit wild as a teenager. As you know, my marriage busted before we could have kids, so young Malc was like a son to me too.'

The colonel learned that the organisation had no name. For that matter it had no offices, no employees, no letterheads and no telephone. In effect, it did not exist. It was just an informal network that brought together the highest in the land, whose sons and daughters had been destroyed by the ravages of cocaine, with the lowliest workers whose children had overdosed on heroin or were hooked on crack or ecstasy. The organisation crossed all political divides and all social classes in a common cause. Natural justice.

'It was born in the early seventies.' Even now Maidment could recall West's quiet explanation. 'A wealthy German industrialist lost his daughter to heroin. Some greedy middleman had diluted the stuff so much that she'd been virtually injecting neat brick dust. She died of a brain haemorrhage. Poor bloke was distraught and swore vengeance on those responsible.'

'What did he do?' Maidment had asked, seeing himself in exactly the same position.

'He hired a very expensive private detective,' replied West, 'a Dutchman who, as it happened, was a former intelligence officer – very well connected – whose own son, highly-gifted apparently, had hit skid row. Had to survive as a bum boy to pay for his heroin habit. The two men became firm friends with a common interest.'

'What happened?'

'Over the years the two men became three, then four, then a dozen – some of them very powerful people. Now there's an English judge, a French police chief, a Swiss banker, an Italian motor magnate, at least two American senators – all have had families scarred or members lost to narcotics. As you might imagine, many are Freemasons.'

Maidment had been puzzled. 'What exactly does this organisation do?'

West smiled gently. 'It has the wealth to pay for extensive private investigations. The dossiers that result are then handed to the appropriate authorities to provide the evidence with which to prosecute.'

'And it works?'

'Not as often as we would like. Narcotics is big business. These people can afford to buy themselves out of trouble – bribes to police and lawyers, judges and juries. But we've had some success. Several big dealers are in prison because of the Angels' work.'

'Angels?' Maidment hadn't understood.

'Just a name. Sometimes we need to refer to ourselves as something. The Avengers, the Whisperers, the Angels – the references change with fashion.'

'Could these people help me in any way?'

West smiled. 'We already have. The search has begun to find those ultimately responsible for your daughter's death. We are using our connections with several intelligence and police forces.'

Maidment's mouth had fallen open with surprise.

Yet it was to take another seven months to identify the Italian Mafia *capo*. The collected evidence was duly presented to the state prosecutors.

One year on and nothing had happened. As on so many previous occasions, the man responsible proved to be safely beyond the reach of the law.

One day Vic West had telephoned unexpectedly and arranged a secret meeting at a quiet country pub. When Maidment arrived he was to find his friend in the company of the man who had once been his daughter's lover. Kurt Mallory.

It was then that Mallory had made an extraordinary offer. He became the organiser's first executioner. And when the *capo* died in a car bombing, the murder was attributed to a rival mafia clan.

Then Maidment was at the beach. He'd driven the entire journey from Caracas without being able to recall a single moment of it. Driving blind, seeing only past events marching in a procession before his eyes. The last face he saw was that of his own dead daughter, Sophie. She was staring at him through the windscreen. There was a look of accusation in her eyes. It was as though she were there, in the car with him. He could smell her, sense her presence. Her voice was soft but insistent in his ears.

'Well, Dad, what are you going to do about it? Vic West helped you and me. What are you going to do for him?'

He jerked on the handbrake. The heat and humidity were getting to him. He was feeling faint, needed air. Stumbling out of the car, he drew in a lungful of fresh salty air and looked towards the bamboo bar and the beach. A couple with a toddler were camped happily at the spot where Vic West had been found.

Recovering slightly, he ordered a King of Scots and a Coke from the barman, just as his old friend would have done.

No, he could not take Simon Cadbury's advice just to go home and forget about it. He owed more than that. To Sophie as well as Vic himself.

There had to be another way to find out what had happened.

And then it occurred to him. Kurt Mallory.

Since he had killed the man ultimately responsible for Sophie's death, Mallory had worked for the organisation on several other occasions. But Maidment hadn't heard of him for some two years and the only person who had known where to contact him had been Vic West. There had been something close between the two men. Perhaps Mallory was retired from the killing business, or might even be dead himself. Who would know?

Colonel Oliver Maidment swallowed hard on his drink. Mallory was a former freelancer for British Intelligence. Someone at SIS must know where he was. It was time to call in the favours.

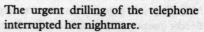

2

The urgent drilling of the telephone interrupted her nightmare.

But it was an age before she could tear herself free of it, that same bad dream ensuring she would never forget.

The noise was boring into her brain, louder and louder. Yet for long minutes she just lay there, motionless, in the twilight world between sleeping and waking. Seemingly fully conscious, yet her body gripped in paralysis, her limbs refusing to move and her silent cry for help unheeded.

'For Christ's sake answer it! It's hardly likely to be for me at this hour.'

Her husband's irritable words muttered into the pillow finally broke through to her.

Georgina Savage emerged from the bedclothes and reached for the receiver on the bedside cabinet. Blearily her eyes registered on the red digits of the radio-alarm. Three o'clock.

'Hello.'

'Georgie-girl, so sorry to trouble you at this hour.' She instantly recognised Sidney Monckton's voice, as irksomely cheery and smooth as ever. And only the deputy chief of the Secret Intelligence Service insisted on calling her by the pet name she loathed.

'Sir?' Savage untangled her legs from the sheets and placed her feet on the floor, the enormous T-shirt which she wore as a night-dress rucking around her thighs. Desperately she fought to pull her mind into focus as she reached for her cigarettes.

Monckton was saying: 'Look, something's cropped up that I'd like you to handle. I've someone with me I want you to meet. As you know, I'm due off later today and this can't really wait.' He was going to tour and inspect the new SIS arrangements in the countries of the former Soviet Union.

She drew deeply on her cigarette; it helped counter the instinctive thrill of anticipation she felt mounting in her chest. 'You want me to come in, sir? Now?'

'Would you mind awfully, Georgie?' So polite, but she knew she dare not refuse. You didn't turn down a request from Sidney Monckton and expect your career to last long enough to collect a decent pension. 'But not riverside – I'm at home.' 'Riverside' was in-slang for the new headquarters at Vauxhall Cross; she knew his address in Cheyne Walk.

'I'll be about half an hour, sir. Is that all right?'

'Most grateful, Georgie,' he replied graciously and hung up.

She replaced the receiver and fumbled in the gloom for the bedside lamp.

'For God's sake, Georgina,' her husband grumbled, pulling the sheet over his head to shut out the light. 'I've got to be up at a sparrow's fart for that meeting—'

'Sorry, Giles sweetheart, but duty calls,' she replied and reached across to kiss the tousled top of his head. He still hadn't learned to accept the odd hours that she frequently worked. He grunted, half in appreciation of her apology, half in complaint at the disruption.

Her skin still felt clammy after the cold sweat of her nightmare; she'd have to shower.

Kurt Mallory. As she crossed the carpet to the bathroom, his image seemed to materialise like a hologram before her eyes. The gaunt face, the strong nose with its slight kink at the bridge where it had been broken and healed badly, the unruly black hair. Why him? Why now? Christ, she hadn't even thought of him in nine months, and that was some kind of record. Her marriage to Giles Spalding a year ago had finally seemed to lay the ghost to rest.

She switched on the bathroom light and pulled the T-shirt off over her head. Moving towards the glass cubicle, she caught sight of the white blur of movement in the mirror. She hesitated, not sure why. Not one for vanity, she suddenly felt an inexplicable

28

urge to look at her reflection. Maybe it was the intrusion of Kurt Mallory into her thoughts; in those days she had found herself taking more time over her make-up and hair. Like a teenager going out on a Saturday night. Stupid probably. No, definitely stupid. Kurt Mallory was the last man in the world you should tart yourself up for.

Her body looked deathly pale in the unflattering light. Skin bleached white beneath the fluorescent tube, melting her contours, making her nipples seem dark and angry in comparison, emphasising the dusky thatch of hair between her legs.

Not bad, she thought. Not bad for thirty-two. The love handles on the top of her thighs had begun to swell, she'd noticed a month ago, but she'd concentrated on that in the gym and she could see the improvement. When was it that Hugh Heffner had reckoned his Playmates of the Month were past their prime? Nineteen? Well, Giles had never complained and certainly Kurt Mallory hadn't.

Even her face was relatively unlined. Just a hint of crow's-feet at the corners of her eyes and at the edges of her mouth when she drew back her lips in a smile. What was she supposed to do about that – stop laughing so much? The thought amused her and she poked out her tongue at the mirror.

Her face looked really boyish then, with the button nose and mischievous glint to her eyes. And the ears. God, those ears. A little too big, she'd always thought, and they had the habit of peeking out through the simple straight cut of her black hair. Somehow they let her down when she wanted to project a sophisticated and authoritative image. And you needed that if you wanted to hold your own against the men in the riverside power game. You didn't want to give the cliquey buggers ammunition, however trivial, when you were struggling to hold your own as Head of South American Desk. There were always half a dozen of them ready to step into your shoes.

Still, Kurt Mallory had liked her ears well enough, had seemed fascinated with them. Had done wicked things with them that had set her entire body alight. He had been good at things like that; things that Giles had not even thought about, let alone mastered. And that sometimes left her feeling a little sad. Empty.

Get out of my head, Kurt, she mouthed at the mirror.

And then she realised. The nightmare. She had forgotten about it; even as she'd taken Sidney Monckton's call, the horrific images had evaporated. All she knew was that it had been the same bad dream. And if it had been, then Mallory would have been in it. He had to be in it.

There was something else.

What was it Kurt had told her once? '*The phone calls at three in the morning – they're the ones you never forget.*'

No wonder the memory of him had flared so suddenly from the almost forgotten recesses of her mind. The nightmare interrupted by a three o'clock phone call.

She could imagine him standing behind her now, looking over her shoulder from the shadows, his features edged in light. And those eyes, fierce and the colour of gentian burning into hers.

Christ, the time? She pulled on the ridiculous plastic shower cap, ran the water and stepped inside for scarcely a minute. Then she was running back into the bedroom, trying to dry herself on the towel at the same time.

'Very comical,' Giles muttered. He was sitting on the edge of the bed in his pyjamas, observing her gloomily. 'Georgina Savage – ace of spies – if your secret service mates could see you now!'

Her wet shower cap caught him squarely on the chest and dropped into his lap. 'Go back to sleep, Giles.'

'Can't. You know what I'm like once I'm disturbed. Bloody mind starts whirring and I can't turn it off. 'Specially not with that deal in the balance.'

Big City finance. She tried to sympathise but the whole thing bored her silly. Money had never really interested her, but then she'd never needed it. Her parents – her father in the Diplomatic Corps had married his aristocratic Argentinian wife when he'd been Head of Chancery in Buenos Aires – had been comfortably off. She'd enjoyed a good public-school education followed by three years at Cambridge when she was recruited for the Secret Intelligence Service.

Of course, she told family and friends it was the Foreign Office.

Only Giles had ever quipped that she really worked for intelligence and shared his long-running joke with everyone they met. It would have been tiresome beyond belief, if she hadn't known it was true. Sometimes she wasn't sure if that was what he really thought she did.

'I'm sorry,' she said as she attempted to pull on her knickers. But her skin was still touch-damp and the material dragged uncomfortably. She cursed.

'What is it this time?' Giles asked with amused sarcasm. 'Aid for Bosnia or is it Rwanda?' She'd told him her work involved liaison with the United Nations, so perhaps that was what she truly believed.

She was only half listening. Until her legs were properly dry she'd never get her tights on. Deciding to abandon them, she extracted a cream blouse and tartan two-piece from her wardrobe. 'I won't know till I get in, Giles. They just said it's urgent.'

'You look like one of those old-time British Caledonian air hostesses,' he mused. 'Always fancy you in that outfit.'

'But not *now*, darling,' she replied lightly, slipping on the jacket and dabbing quickly with her lipstick in the dressing-table mirror.

He said: 'I'll have gone by the time you get back.'

Her shoes were on and she was moving towards the door. 'Then you'll have to fancy me tonight. Love you.'

'Aren't you going to wish me luck?' he called after her.

The door slammed, cutting off his words.

Giles Spalding glared at the empty bed. 'Shit!'

Patiently he stubbed out the cigarette end she'd left smouldering in the ashtray.

Savage left the terraced Banbury Street house in her Renault Clio and sped north towards Battersea Bridge. The roads were clear and still carried the sheen of an earlier shower. There was something about London in the dead of night that always fascinated her. A city never fully asleep, but dozing fitfully, the daily grind and bustle and chaos forgotten for a few precious hours. Too late for the nightclubbers, too early for the first day shifts. Only insomniacs awake behind their little lighted windows. And some villains, of course. It was that time of night for criminals and terrorists, the plotters and the schemers. The only others around in the wee small hours were the city's guardians, the police and the rescue services. And people like her. Like the Windmill theatre, she mused, their bizarre cabaret never closed, their routine forever changing but never ending.

She arrived at Cheyne Walk just five minutes later than she had planned, parked round the corner from Monckton's house and walked back to the short flight of entrance steps. Even before she pressed the bell on the door, which she knew would be armour-plated, Savage realised that her approach would have been detected by the TV cameras bracketed to the wall above.

After a brief exchange over the intercom, she was admitted by the armed plain-clothes detective who provided round-the-clock protection for her chief.

'Georgie-girl, so good of you to come.' Sidney Monckton stood in the drawing room, the back of his tall and somewhat gangling body warmed by the glowing coal embers in the grate. The antique furniture and Persian rug provided a perfect setting for the man in his dinner jacket and black tie. 'Again, so sorry for the late call. I'd just got back from a dinner at Grosvenor House when I found my old friend waiting for me – you know Colonel Oliver Maidment, of course?'

The man standing beside Monckton was probably in his early sixties and carried himself with a distinctly military bearing. Despite the receded crown, the aquiline features remained youthful and quite handsome, if a little thin. Tired, Savage guessed immediately. Like the expensive suit that bore the ingrained creases and slightly grubby look of a long day's travel.

She smiled. 'We've never met, but of course I know of Colonel Maidment from when he was a minister.' She extended her hand.

He shook it warmly. 'A very junior minister, I'm afraid.'

Instinctively she liked his self-effacing manner. 'And now chairman of Portcullis, I believe?'

That pleased him; perhaps he didn't realise that his company's name regularly featured in papers that crossed her desk. He said: 'Look, this is all my fault. I've just flown in from Caracas and I came straight here from the airport. Not very fair on Sidney or your good self.'

'Think nothing of it, old chap,' Monckton said cheerily. His almost permanent schoolboy grin and laughing eyes, set behind thick-lensed spectacles, were unusual in a man who wielded such influence in the corridors of power. It was a genial demeanour that could also be very misleading to those who dared to cross him. 'I'd have done the same in your position – move quick before the trail goes cold.'

Savage was perplexed. 'What trail, sir?'

The benign expression melted from Monckton's face. 'One of our former officers is dead. Victor West – I believe you've had dealings with him.'

She was taken aback. 'Er, yes, sir. He is – or he was – an "alongsider". But my dealings with him have always been second-hand. Mostly through Simon Cadbury in Caracas or via one of our other South American station heads. Usually it was inside stuff on corrupt government officials or information on drug gangs or shipments to be passed on to the Investigations Division at Customs.'

Monckton nodded, impatient at hearing what he already knew. 'Quite, Georgie. Well, I've known Vic West for a long time. Good man. Did an excellent job during the Falklands rumpus and later, linking our PIRA friends with the ETA movement in Spain. When he left us in 1987 to work for Portcullis he continued to supply us with any useful information that came his way.' He glanced at Maidment with a nod of acknowledgement. 'All, of course, with the colonel's full approval. Portcullis people have always been trustworthy "alongsiders".' He didn't add 'needed to be' if they wanted continued approval for their arms dealings from the Foreign Office and the DTI. 'Thing is, the colonel is convinced that Vic West was murdered.'

Her eyes widened. 'Do you know who did it?'

'No, but it was a professional job,' Maidment replied.

'Why?'

He related the entire story and Savage listened intently, accepting Monckton's offer of a small whisky but leaving the glass untouched as she became engrossed in the story. When Maidment finished, she said, selecting her words carefully: 'I really can understand your disappointment at Simon Cadbury's reaction – I'm sure I'd feel the same under the circumstances. But in fact he was quite correct. We really are underresourced and our interest is only in narcotics destined for the UK. And collateral information, such as Vic West often provided, is appreciated, but it's usually passed straight on to the Americans for action. If Simon thought it too dangerous, pointless, or even too expensive to send one of our agents, I really would have to support his judgement. And our Drug Liaison officers from Customs are more pen-pushers than gung-ho types.'

Maidment nodded politely, slightly impatient. 'No, no, Miss Savage, I accept all that – as a former minister, I'm all too aware of political realities. What I'm asking for is to make private contact with one of your freelancers. At least that's what I think you call them. A man by the name of Kurt Mallory.'

She stared at him and her mouth dropped open for a second before she caught herself. That name again. It was uncanny. An hour ago he'd been safely locked away in her nightmares; now he was being openly talked about. Something current. In some strange way she could sense his presence, almost imagine he had just walked into the room.

'Cat got your tongue, Georgie?' Monckton asked jovially, disguising the fact he was anxious now to get to his bed and grab some sleep before his morning flight to Moscow. 'On your Z-File, is he?'

She was aware of her cheeks colouring. 'Oh – er – yes, sir. You'd know him as Zigzagger.'

There was a flicker of interest in the smiling eyes. 'Ah, *he* is Zigzagger.'

The Z-File. Representing the final letter in the alphabet, the last resort. A coded file kept by and only encrypted by each Desk Chief personally. Jealously guarded, it had been passed down by her predecessor. For her eyes only. Reserved for the most sensitive or deniable of operations. Or the most dangerous.

Savage didn't like hearing his real name spoken openly like this and made a mental note to change his code name to Zookeeper as soon as she arrived at the office next day. But she hid her irritation. 'I am afraid Zigzagger has retired.'

'Not because of ill health?' Maidment asked, apparently with genuine concern.

No, Savage reflected, not because he'd had half a lung removed when they extracted the IRA bullet. 'No, he'd had enough, that's all.'

'But you know where to find him?' Maidment pressed.

'My last contact with Zigzagger was two years ago and he was never one to stay in the same place for long.'

Maidment looked anxious. 'But could you try? Vic West was a good friend of Mr Mallory's.'

Savage frowned, remembering something. 'And are you a friend of his too?'

The colonel hesitated, glancing down at the fingers he was interlacing with unease. 'To be honest, I didn't think it would ever be possible for us to be *friends*, Miss Savage. But I've met him. In fact got to know him quite well. He had a relationship with my late daughter, you see, and I didn't approve. But I believe he'd want to be told about Victor.'

Now she thought she understood, but she couldn't say anything in front of Monckton. 'I'll see what I can do,' she promised. 'But no guarantees.'

Maidment's shoulders dropped as he relaxed, his duty done. 'I can't tell you how much that means to me.'

Her chief then coughed politely and tapped at his wristwatch. The colonel accepted the heavy hint graciously, thanked them both, and made his departure.

Savage picked up her handbag. 'What exactly does Colonel Maidment want Zigzagger to do?'

'I'm sure you can guess.'

'Find out what happened to Vic West?'

Monckton nodded and studied the last of his whisky, swirling it slowly around the cut-glass tumbler. 'See if you can't persuade him. Don't leave it up to the colonel. I seem to remember you got on well with Zigzagger.'

Got on well, she thought. That was an understatement. Even now she felt a flush of heat in her loins. They'd got on well all right, until she nearly bloody got him killed.

Monckton was still talking quietly, almost as though to himself, and she'd almost missed his words. 'Unofficially, I'd like you to take an interest in this one. Persuade Zigzagger and go and hold his hand.'

She smiled inwardly despite her surprise at the suggestion. Kurt Mallory didn't need anyone to hold his hand. The idea was preposterous anyway. 'I don't understand, sir; this just isn't in our remit as I've just explained to Colonel Maidment.'

The ice-blue irises were hard and glittering amid the crinkled laughlines round his eyes. 'Consider yourself on attachment to Global Issues.'

The Global Issues Department, she thought. Riverside desperately trying to reinvent itself. To justify its existence and its lavish and hardly inconspicuous new art-deco headquarters on the south bank. Looking for jobs. The new and fastest-growing department at Vauxhall Cross that was considered to be the service's salvation after the Cold War thaw.

Its 'Motherhood Agenda' was concerned with the successful rebirth of the emerging democratic states of the old Warsaw Pact. Training their secret services where possible and leaving friends of Britain in high places to run them. Countering the spread of nuclear, biological and chemical weapons that the new nations, starved of foreign currency, were willing to sell to the highest bidder – bidders like Iran, Iraq, North Korea and other pariah governments.

And organised crime. In many respects that was the most immediate big threat of all and at the core of its activities, of course, the ever expanding market in narcotics. Savage understood that. Understood what so many people around the world appeared to overlook. Narcotics in themselves weren't a global threat. The high-flyer in Westminster or on Wall Street snorting his White Lady, or some HIV-riddled prostitute paying for her heroin habit, or some black kid in Moss Side stabbing a rival crack dealer – these were small personal tragedies affecting family and friends.

But the ripple went way beyond that, affected entire communities. Entire nations. There had been a meteoric rise in street crime to fund the habit of thousands, millions worldwide, leaving behind swathes of disillusioned youth to fuel violence and discontent.

The cost to every nation in terms of policing, healthcare and welfare was incalculable; the damage to the fabric of society probably irreparable.

And it went even beyond that. The dangers really *were* on a global scale. With one dollar in every four estimated to have been earned from illegal drugs, narcotics money was distorting the world's financial markets and destabilising whole national economies. To that catalogue of disaster you could add the corruption of the governments, police forces and the judiciary of many nations. Or even continents, as Savage knew too well from her own time on the South American Desk. *Narco* money could power and run entire national economies. A magnet to greedy and corrupt politicians who were all too eager to keep the world's poor firmly in their place while they themselves sucked their own countries dry.

Nevertheless, Savage had to concern herself with everyday practicalities. She asked: 'But is this business with Vic West particularly relevant to us?'

Monckton shrugged. 'If you'd asked me yesterday, I'd have said not especially. But it so happened that at Grosvenor House tonight I was seated opposite an old friend from Customs and Excise. He was telling me about a worrying new trend that's been developing over the past six months. In fact, only last week he had a meeting with all the chief constables to discuss a joint programme to combat the growing distribution of a branded cocaine which has a consistently higher purity than usual. But at normal prices. So, of course, everyone wants it. They call the stuff White Viper.'

'I see.'

'It seems someone has set up a sort of exclusive dealer network – just like car manufacturers – in London, Glasgow, Liverpool and Newcastle, using well-established gangs of villains. It's causing all sorts of mayhem with rival gangs in each region who are peddling their own stuff which now suddenly no one wants. Of course, the distribution system has to be enforced, not least to stop counterfeiting of the little packets or others in the system diluting genuine White Viper before selling it on. There've been several knee-cappings and firebombs. No point in having a branded coke unless you can assure the punters they're getting something special.'

'And you think it's connected with something Vic West discovered? The mention of White Viper might relate to the reason he was killed?'

Monckton was hesitant. 'I admit it's tenuous. Maybe it's just a catchy name that's caught on and been passed down the smuggling lines from South America. But White Viper coke has also turned up in the States as well as various European countries apparently. Not in big quantities yet, but it is starting to cause some concern. I think we can justify a look at the situation.'

Savage said: 'It's really Simon Cadbury's patch, sir. I could order him to have someone local take a look.'

'Has he got anyone of Zigzagger's calibre?'

Her smile gave it away before she admitted: 'No, sir, not to my knowledge.' It was game, set and match. 'I'll do my best to set it up myself.'

Kelly O'More was waiting for Georgina Savage at the barrier when she arrived at Shannon.

They had met some years before on the Dublin social and diplomatic circuit and become almost instant friends. There had been an immediate chemistry between them, like the reunion of two old school chums – a shared sense of irreverent humour and girlish mischief which both missed in their respective careers as 'diplomat' and lawyer, Savage as Second Secretary to the British Embassy and Kelly, the daughter of Joe O'More, a landowner and a former minister in the Irish Government. Although they hadn't met in two years, Savage had no difficulty in recognising her friend. Kelly wore the same loose hairstyle of tumbledown copper ringlets and the same easy smile. It was no surprise that the rangy body propped casually against the barrier was dressed in jodhpurs and a floppy Donegal sweater that failed to disguise her impressive figure. Horses were the great love of her life. It had been how she and Kurt Mallory had got together.

'Hi, Georgie,' she greeted, her eyes lighting up as they exchanged kisses on the cheek. 'You're looking good. Married life must suit you.'

'It does,' she laughed. 'But being single hasn't done you any harm at all, I see.'

Kelly's words were spoken in a soft Kerry brogue. 'Perhaps not, but it isn't by choice. Sure, soon only my horses will want me.' At thirty-six she was four years Savage's senior. She said: 'C'mon, the car's outside.'

As they drove the Land-Rover Discovery out of the airport and picked up the road towards Limerick city, Savage said: 'You never mentioned anything on your card at Christmas.'

One finely arched eyebrow rose as Kelly glanced at her passenger. 'About splitting with Kurt? A bit difficult that when you've nicked your best friend's fella. How d'you tell her you've been careless enough to go and lose him so soon?'

Savage chuckled at that and had to admit a certain smug sense of satisfaction. 'No one nicks Kurt – or holds on to him for long for that matter. He pretty much does what he wants.'

'Well, you did warn me.'

'So what happened?'

'Guess we just sort of drifted apart. I'd stopped living with him after the first year – when was that? – just about twelve months ago. We wanted different things. I wanted a husband and home – and kids. Hell, I'm getting a bit old for that now. The big four-o looms.'

'And Kurt?'

'Kurt just wanted to continue living in the croft with his horses and his bees. Quite happy to scratch a living with his subsistence farming and some fishing. I mean, I ask you! No electricity and no telephone.'

Savage could just imagine it and felt a pang of envy at what they'd shared. Stupid really – Kelly was far better suited to that sort of life than she. 'But great sex?'

A smile came to Kelly's lips. 'Oh sure, great sex. But you know Kurt. To him sex is like any other bodily function. Like eating, sleeping or going for a shit. However good he is, he's just as happy to go and pay a whore when he feels the need. A girl will die waiting for him to bring chocolates and flowers.' They both laughed at that. 'In the end I think it was only our love of horses that kept us together. Said he liked it when my body smelled of them. He's a bloody animal, so he is. I really had to decide between staying with Kurt or abandoning my career as a lawyer altogether. He kept saying how he'd really like to go back to Paraguay. Recapture his childhood, I suppose. Christ, why is it men can never grow up?'

'D'you think he means it?'

She nodded. 'But he hasn't got any money. I offered to pay for an air ticket, but he just gave me one of those gorgeous dark looks of his. We both knew he'd never accept money like that, especially from a woman. Sometimes I think he's a bloody misogynist.'

Kurt Mallory a woman hater! That was a laugh, Savage thought. 'He told me once that – sex apart – he treats women just like men. As equals. He likes them or not and won't pander to all the courting rigmarole in order to get to bed with someone. Can't stand all the girlie small talk.'

Kelly frowned at the road ahead. 'Then clearly I didn't pass muster.'

Her friend laughed lightly. 'You wouldn't have lasted a year with him if you hadn't.'

'I blame his mother.'

'What?'

'For trying to drown him at birth. Where was it?'

'The Landwehr Kanal in West Berlin.'

Cruel though it was, the idea touched a chord of humour in both women. As her laughter subsided, Savage said: 'Be fair, she was trying to drown herself as well – in fact she succeeded. Poor woman must have been driven mad with grief and anxiety when Kurt's father died. I mean, just think of it. She escapes East Berlin and becomes a prostitute in order to survive. Then meets this dashing British Army major and falls in love. The baby arrives and they're all set for a bright and happy life. Marriage is planned, documents being processed, and then the silly bugger goes and kills himself in an autobahn accident!'

'Yeah.' Kelly relented slightly. 'But our Kurt still wouldn't be here today if that policeman hadn't come along and persuaded her to hand the baby over. No wonder Kurt finds relationships with women difficult. I mean if you can't trust your own mother not to try and kill you—'

They were through the city now and on the road west towards Listowel and the Bay of Tralee beyond. 'Well, if that hadn't all happened and his dead father's family hadn't wanted to know him, Kurt wouldn't have been sent to that orphanage of German brothers in Paraguay. He wouldn't have been the same man and our paths would never have crossed.'

'I suppose you're right. Truth is I'm just looking for someone, anyone, to blame for it not working out. Anyone except me. Truth is, I miss the bastard.'

'Have you seen him much since?'

Kelly shook her head. 'Just a couple of times. I spend most of my time at the Dublin office and only get back to the family home near Tralee for the odd weekend. Then, of course, Dad wants to monopolise his only daughter, bless him. Lives for our games of chess, so he does. Kurt's place at Miggles Strand is another fifteen miles on and I can't phone to check that he's in.'

'But you're still talking?'

'Oh, yes. And the sex is still good.' *Still* good? So it wasn't completely over, Savage thought. Dammit, she really hadn't wanted to hear that. But Kelly hadn't noticed the stiffening of her expression and was continuing with her light-hearted banter. 'But I really am trying to give him up. Besides, I've got a new man in my life.'

'Ah!' Savage said. 'You little liar, I thought you said it was only

41

your horses who loved you now?'

'That's probably true, all the same. I don't exactly hear church bells with my new boyfriend.'

'Spill the beans,' Savage encouraged.

Kelly grinned at her. 'Want to know about my Latin lover, do you, so you can get your own back and steal him off me?'

'Latin?' Savage asked, intrigued.

'Well, Argentinian actually. Lives and works in Madrid. He's a big shot international lawyer – I met him while I was handling some work for Dad. Dead sexy name. Miguel Castaño.' She pronounced it with a dramatic Spanish flourish. 'I've always wanted a toy boy. Well, he is nine months younger than me – and years richer!'

'And *is* he as sexy as his name?'

'You'd better believe it, kid. Dusky skin, long black hair – more like a rock star than a lawyer – and the most gorgeous bum you've ever seen. In those polo breeches he's something else.'

'And?'

'And I wouldn't trust him farther than I could throw his lovely hunky body. A real eye for the girls, you see. Likes flashing his pearly white teeth at anything in a skirt.' She relaxed into her seat, changing gear smoothly and confidently as a sharp bend approached. 'Swears I'm the only woman in his life, but then he would, wouldn't he? And how would I know how many *concubinas* he keeps at his luxury villa while I'm stuck in Dublin?'

'So no future in it?'

Kelly looked wistful. 'You never know. I may be a born optimist, but I'm not holding my breath.' Then she said quite suddenly: 'Why is it you need to see Kurt, Georgie? Not withdrawal symptoms?'

Her friend shook her head. 'No, I'm well over him now, thank you.' Even as she spoke the words she wasn't sure it was strictly true. 'No, it's purely a business thing. Someone at my department's got some work for him.'

'Oh.' Kelly mouthed the word rather than said it.

'I guess it might take some persuading for him to come out of retirement.'

42

Kelly said carefully: 'Retirement from what exactly? Whenever I ask him about his past work, he's always evasive. Mutters something about a bit of this and that, then promptly changes the subject.'

Hardly surprising, Savage thought. Telling someone you used to kill people for a living is something of a conversation stopper. She said lightly: 'Occasionally he's done some investigation work for us. Mostly tracking down missing persons. Quite good at it actually.'

The Irish girl's sudden outburst of laughter was spontaneous. 'What's so funny?'

Kelly managed to contain her hysteria, fighting to get her words out through a continuing giggle. 'I – It's j-just the thought of Kurt working for the Foreign Office. I – I mean, all those toffee-nosed public-school boys with their pinstripes. And then Kurt in his dirty jeans and T-shirt, looking like a tramp.'

Savage forced a smile, sympathised with her friend's reaction. But then she knew that Kurt's work for the supposed Foreign Office was no joke. She had always considered Kelly O'More to be well versed in the ways of the world, witty and urbane. Yet, like most ordinary people, she could be disturbingly naive and trusting at times. A believer in Fairyland, as Savage and others at riverside liked to call the everyday life of the average civilian. Totally unaware that the world she thought she knew was only skin deep. Beneath it was another layer, then another. But then Kelly's ignorance equalled innocence, and really that was just as well. She had lived with Kurt Mallory for a year and still did not know that her lover did not belong to her world at all.

She said: 'It's Kurt's style – or lack of it – that makes him so good at it. He can make inquiries where no government official could. Especially in wilder parts of the world where he really fits in. South America, of course, with his Paraguayan upbringing. He can pass as Spanish, English or German.'

'You mean working undercover?'

'Not exactly.' But Savage's hesitancy rather betrayed her words. 'He has the knack of blending in. The invisible man. Insurance companies have used him to look at dodgy claims. And some international human rights charities have hired him as a trouble-shooter.'

'This job you've got for him – what is it exactly?'

A tight smile. 'I'm sorry, Kelly, I'm really not allowed to say.'

'It's not dangerous, is it?'

Perhaps, Savage wondered, her friend wasn't quite as unaware as she'd thought. 'Good God, no, of course not,' she said and her laugh at least sounded genuine.

Now Kelly made a right-hand turn onto an unmarked dirt track. Only a rotting *To the beach* sign gave any indication that this was the way to the place locals knew as Miggles Strand. The car bumped its way over the ruts and grooves for half a mile until the lane ended abruptly in a small turning circle on low cliffs overlooking the Bay of Tralee.

Kelly switched off the engine and the stillness of the place instantly cocooned them. Suddenly Savage was anxious to be away from her friend, to avoid any further questions and telling any more lies. She opened the passenger door, the April air cool after the heat inside the car. It smelled of seaweed and blue salt-water mud, reverberated with the plaintive cry of circling sea-gulls. Below her was the rough pasture strip running beside the narrow shingle beach. Rain-washed sun glinted off the surface of the bay like hammered pewter. A curlicue of woodsmoke escaped the chimney of the small fisherman's croft with its thick tar-brushed walls and slate roof. Almost without thinking she found herself seeking out the beehives. Yes, there they were, ten white-slatted boxes around a gnarled apple tree. If this were Kurt's home there would have to be bees. Bees and horses, the two legacies from his wild boyhood in Paraguay. Then she saw the black stallion and the chestnut mare that Kelly had bought him. *Creollios*, the mustangs of South America. The one gift he couldn't bring himself to refuse.

'I suppose he's home,' she thought aloud.

'He might be working on the boat,' Kelly replied, leading the way to the footpath that wound down the cliff. 'It's at the front of the cottage – you can't see it from here.'

As they neared, the hiss of the blowtorch and rasp of sandpaper reached their ears above the slapping of the waves along the shoreline.

Kelly's footsteps faltered. 'Georgie.'

'What is it?' Savage turned.

'I don't want him to get hurt.' For once the Irish girl's eyes were not smiling.

'Nor do I,' her friend replied glibly and quickly. Too quickly, she realised almost instantly.

'I mean it. That bullet in his lung, it nearly killed him.'

'He told you about that?' Mildly surprised.

A nod. 'In an unguarded moment. It was still troubling him then, so he had to say something. No details, of course. Only later I realised he must have been working with you at the time. I'm not stupid, Georgie. I've some idea of the sort of work you do.' She raised her hand quickly. 'No, don't deny or confirm it. I'd rather not have lies between friends. And I realise you're probably not allowed to tell outsiders about your work or what Kurt has done for you. Just promise me you won't ask him to do anything dangerous.'

Savage's smile was slow and reassuring. 'I promise.' But even as she spoke the words it felt like betrayal.

Then Kelly's expression softened and she grinned widely, her teeth glistening. 'Good.' She strode on, leaving Savage to follow and feeling slightly envious of how good her friend looked, long-legged in the jodhpurs and the breeze tugging at her tangled locks.

Oh, Kelly, but you *are* a fool. You really do still love him despite everything you've said.

His naked back was hunched over the upturned wooden hull, sweat glistening on the bunched sinews of his shoulder as he laboured with the sandpaper block. Dead varnish had formed a small pile by his feet.

The old man with the white beard and fisherman's sweater saw the two women first as they rounded the corner of the croft. He stopped what he was doing and turned down the blowtorch.

'You've got visitors, Kurt me boy.' The voice was coarse with age but softened by the pure Kerry accent.

'What?'

'Your lucky day, so it is.' He nodded over Mallory's shoulder towards Kelly. 'Nice to see you, Miss O'More.'

Mallory straightened his back and turned, tossing the tangle of black hair from his eyes. The smile broke quickly and easily on his lips. He leaned forward to kiss her cheek. 'My little colleen, what a nice surprise . . .' Then the words faded as he focused on the second woman.

'Hello, Kurt,' Savage said with an uneasy smile.

He nodded. 'George.'

Kelly took a backward step. 'An old friend to see you.'

It felt a ridiculously formal thing to do, but Savage offered her hand. She really didn't want him to kiss her. 'You're looking fit, Kurt.'

Fitter than when I last saw you, she thought, and her eyes unconsciously glanced at the angry knot of white scar tissue on the weather-tanned skin over his ribs.

There was a hint of a smile on Mallory's face as he wiped his palms on the thighs of his faded denims before accepting her hand. His eyes fixed on hers in the direct and penetrating gaze that she had always found a little unsettling. Was he laughing at her? Did it amuse him that she was throwing up invisible barriers, keeping her distance? His hand felt strong as it took hers, the skin warm and dry, pressing her cool flesh rather than shaking the small hand. To Savage it felt like a signal of reassurance. Perhaps even forgiveness.

'You're looking good yourself, George,' he said. That strange but familiar voice with its slightly Germanic tone. 'Marriage must agree with you.'

'Exactly what I said,' Kelly added with a grin and raised a hand in the direction of the old fisherman. 'You won't have met Matt Rooney, Kurt's right-hand man.'

As the old man politely pulled off his battered Breton cap to reveal a balding crown atop the mass of wild white hair, Mallory said: ''Couldn't manage without Mattie. What he doesn't know about fishing in these parts isn't worth knowing.'

Rooney chuckled with mirth; clearly advancing years hadn't

diminished his appreciation of a pretty girl. Unexpectedly meeting two of them at once had clearly made his day. 'Honoured I am, Miss – ?'

'Call me Georgie.'

He turned to Mallory. 'Shall I put a brew on, Kurt? And I'm thinkin' there's a dram or two left in the Bushmills. Does this call for a celebration?'

Mallory laughed. Although they all knew he hardly drank, he said: 'Why not? Is there something to celebrate?'

Savage said: 'I'm afraid there isn't really, Kurt.' But Rooney had already disappeared inside the croft to put the kettle on. 'In fact it's bad news.'

At that point Kelly sensed her friend's hesitation to say more in her presence. 'Look, you two will have lots to talk about and I promised Dad a game of chess this afternoon. What time would you like me to pick you up, Georgie?'

Mallory looked at Savage. 'You'll be going back so soon? You're welcome to stay over. There's a spare bed.'

Were her cheeks really as scarlet as they felt? Spare bed. Was he being funny? Oh, she'd be safe enough. Mallory wasn't the type to force his attentions on her. If he still fancied her, he'd just say: 'Come to bed.' Almost a command, but not quite. And they both knew she'd probably go. She said: 'That's sweet, Kurt, but I really have to get back to London. Back to work – and back to my husband.'

He smiled. 'Of course.' Knowing.

Savage looked at Kelly. 'Could you give us a couple of hours?'

'No problem.' Her friend toyed with her car key. 'By the way, Kurt, I've got a free couple of days if you're around. We could take the horses for a gallop. I'm starting to forget how to ride.'

He grinned. 'Sure. Tomorrow.'

She leaned forward and kissed him briefly. Under her breath she said: 'And *I'm* free to stop over.'

Mallory winked at her and his eyes watched the material stretched tight across her backside as she sauntered away round the corner of the croft and took the cliff path back to the Discovery.

47

'She's a great girl,' he murmured, then turned his attention back to Savage. 'What's this bad news?'

There was no way to soften the blow. 'I'm afraid Vic West is dead.'

Mallory stared at her, the warmth draining instantly from the mesmeric blue eyes, the pupils reducing to mere pinpricks.

'He was murdered, Kurt. I'm sorry.'

'Where did it happen?'

'In Venezuela. Four days ago.'

'Was he working for you?'

She shook her head. 'At least not officially. His boss came to us, asking if we could find you. Colonel Oliver Maidment from a company called Portcullis. I think you know him?'

His lips tightened perceptibly. Savage noticed because she'd been watching his reaction closely. Remembered that Mallory had once referred obliquely to someone called the colonel. Of course, there were many ex-colonels around and there was no reason why Mallory should not know more than one. It could just be coincidence, but if it wasn't, then the charming and self-effacing ex-junior minister who visited Sidney Monckton was connected. Connected to the organisation. The organisation that had no name.

Mallory's eyes narrowed. 'Yes, I know him.'

'The colonel was anxious to contact you. Said Vic West was a friend of yours and thought you'd want to do something about it. Find out who killed him.'

'Why didn't he come himself?'

'Because my people are interested to know what happened too. We're willing to support the investigation if you agree. Give you unofficial backup.'

'You?'

She looked uncomfortable. 'It could be someone else if you'd prefer. I'd understand.'

Mallory shook his head. 'You might have nearly got me killed, but you're still the best. I've met some of the other monkeys from your department.'

'So you'll do it?'

He scanned the bay, a distant look in his eyes. 'I've retired, George. This is my life now.'

Don't push it, she told herself, and waited first until she'd sat with Rooney to have the tea laced with Bushmills. Until Mallory had shown her the horses, the livestock and, of course, the bees. Until Matt Rooney had waved goodbye and wandered off to his home in the nearby village and she and Mallory had returned alone to the croft.

'You seem to have more books than ever,' she said, looking at the overstuffed shelves and cardboard boxes that filled one wall of the dim interior.

He lit a hurricane lamp and hung it on the low ceiling hook to illuminate the spartan living room with its open fireplace, table and bedstead. 'I've a lot of catching up to do and I don't read fast.'

Savage smiled at that. She remembered him telling her how his education at the Glaubehaus orphanage in Paraguay had been less than perfect for their wayward charge. And how he had run away at the age of eleven when he learned that the holy brothers of the House of Faith planned to return to Europe. That had been back in 1961 when the South American continent was even wilder than it was today. Then young Kurt, already an accomplished horseman and looking older than his years, had found no shortage of unscrupulous cattle ranchers willing to employ him as a gaucho for a handful of pesos a month.

Reading and literature had no place in the violence and cruelty of frontier life where Kurt Mallory learned the art of street fighting and to take his pleasure with town prostitutes once a month. She could imagine how the *putas* might have fought over the chance to mother their under-age client.

It was only when, at the age of sixteen, he worked his passage on a boat to England that he realised the job he wanted was not on offer to a semi-literate teenager. He didn't even get past his first interview with the sergeant at the army recruiting office. There seemed no chance that he could ever follow his dead father's chosen profession in the British Army.

As he boarded another ship bound for Africa with the idea of joining the mercenaries in the Congo, he had vowed to teach himself to read and write. Nine years later, having also fought in Biafra and Angola, he had accomplished his aim. Mallory may still have read with immense difficulty, but he had read more than almost anyone Savage had ever known. Dog-eared second-hand copies of the classics and every major work of literature lined his shelves, and she knew he had struggled through every word of every one.

Then she noticed the ancient Imperial manual on the table and the pile of paper with its uneven lines of type. 'Your memoirs?'

He sat on the edge of the torn settee. 'Memories not memoirs. Wanted to get something of my childhood on paper. Life in Paraguay, you know, the people I met, the stories I'd heard.'

'Can I read some?' She squinted. 'It needs adjusting – and a new ribbon.'

A shake of the head. 'You wouldn't like it. My spelling's crap.'

'I'd still like to. A few pages.'

'If you want.' He looked at her steadily for a moment, maybe guessing her motive. 'Have you got a cigarette?'

She had hoped he might be flattered at her interest, but he gave no sign as he took a cigarette from the offered pack. Still trying to cut it out, she thought. 'I'll return your notes.'

That clearly didn't bother him; he knew she would anyway. 'What's the time?'

He didn't have a watch, she noticed. 'Four.'

'Kelly will be here soon.'

'Kurt?'

He looked back in her direction.

It had to be now or never. 'You were close to Vic West, weren't you?'

'He was my friend.'

And you've never had many friends, have you? she thought.

Mallory added slowly: 'I've only ever met a handful of people I could trust. Vic was one of them.'

'Did he work for the organisation, Kurt?'

The still air of the croft seemed to freeze instantly. When he spoke, Mallory's voice was almost a whisper. 'What do you mean?'

'You told me about it once, do you remember? About the organisation, the network, whatever you call it. Did Vic West work for them too?'

She could see in his eyes that he wished he'd never confided in her. 'Yes. Sometimes.'

'I thought so.' So Oliver Maidment was with them too. That meant this was organisation business.

'Why?'

'I think Vic was working for them when he was killed.'

Mallory studied her expression closely. 'Then you'd better tell me exactly what happened.'

Savage sighed inwardly. Now she had him.

3

Kurt Mallory was not pleased.

He was uncomfortable in the new business suit and the restricting collar and tie and doubtful about his cover as a travel agency representative. And thoroughly disapproving that Georgina Savage was sitting next to him on the internal Avensa flight down to Puerto Ayacucho.

He had wanted to set about the investigation into Vic West's death in his usual way. Like *el vago pequeño*, he always said. A little tramp. Drifting into town with the tumbleweed, scruffy and unnoticed. It was pretty much how he dressed and lived anyway; he was comfortable like that. Being just another worthless piece of flotsam adrift on the South American continent. Just another loser. No one ever paid attention to losers and that was the way he liked it. Safer when it came to ferreting around, asking the odd casual question and knowing the right answer when he heard it.

But Savage had been adamant. 'The last time we worked together you nearly got killed. I'm not prepared to risk that happening again.'

'It's more likely to if we travel together.'

'I don't think so. We both know what they call the border area between Venezuela and Colombia – the last frontier. There are only two legitimate businesses there, the Pepsi factory and a small tourist interest. If we're not obviously connected with those we'll immediately raise suspicions.'

'Okay, but even if you are right, I'd prefer to go alone. If you're not there you can't get hurt.'

'Very chivalrous, Kurt. But what the hell do you know about tourism? I'm always using that cover, know it inside out. If you

52

go alone and someone tumbles you, I'd still be none the wiser about what happened to Vic West.'

Charming, he'd thought, and grinned at her.

Savage had balls and he liked that in a woman. Intelligence and humour too. You didn't have to endure small talk about fashion and recipes when she was around. No problem discussing philosophy or history or the ways of the world.

In fact he couldn't have imagined more agreeable company on the previous day's long haul from England to Paris and on to Caracas. No matter that she had manipulated him, or at least thought she had.

Let her think it. To him it was of supreme unimportance. What mattered was that some scrote of a *narco* had killed his friend and thought he was going to get away with it. Because the *narcos* usually did. They ruled their empires by fear and intimidation, threatening family and friends. It was a brave man who stood witness, who dared open his mouth.

But Vic was organisation and Vic had been his friend. And he had precious few of them. He owed Vic. Many a time Vic had watched his back. Their mutual trust was absolute, had to be. Then Vic had got him started as a freelancer, introduced him to the organisation. He owed Vic West and it was a debt of honour.

When the aircraft had begun its descent to Venezuela, he had glanced down at Savage, dozing with her head against his shoulder.

Why hadn't it lasted between them, he had wondered? Two years ago, around the time that he'd got shot. She'd been keen enough then, on fire for him. Breaking every rule in the goddamn book. Controller screwing around with agent and loving every minute of it. Her sexuality unleashed for the first time, if he was to believe what she told him. And he had no reason to doubt her.

Yet she had drifted out of his life, just like all the others. And he had never been one to beg a woman to stay.

They had rekindled some of the old warmth between them on the transatlantic flight. Laughed a lot and brought each other up to date. His life working his plot of land on the Irish coast and she awkward with a new life of domesticity with her husband, resisting his insistence that she should give up work and have a baby.

'You don't want that?' Mallory had asked.

She had looked at him curiously, the light in her eyes suddenly a little dimmer. 'Not just now, Kurt.'

But he wasn't sure she'd been telling the complete truth, even to herself.

His mood of wellbeing had changed dramatically almost as soon as they reached Caracas. He had never liked the place and he'd grown to like it even less as years went by. He could smell corruption in the air like the stench of raw sewage. Probably there'd never been a time when the government, either military dictatorship or democratically elected, hadn't had its hand in the country's till, its nose in the trough.

The early oil wealth had been creamed off by the ruling classes and squandered while the nation's other natural resources were neglected. Now the legitimate coffers were bare, the poor even poorer than ever, while those in power had found a new source of riches. *Narco* money. The country was awash with the stuff as the drug barons invested in new condominiums and legitimate businesses, washing their dirty money, content in the knowledge that their ill-gotten fortunes would be safe, provided they greased the right palms.

Mallory thought how the city resembled Bogotá fifteen years earlier at the start of its flirtation with the cocaine business. Before it had embraced the filthy trade with an all-consuming and self-destructing passion.

He'd seen it all before and here it was again. The kids dealing on every street corner and robbing anyone at knife-point who was foolish enough to venture out after dark. All to finance their habits and squalid little deals. Spivs cruising in flash imported cars. Street orphans snatched by death squads and their corpses sold to hospitals and private clinics for the organ transplant market. Judges throwing out solid cases against the *narco* kingpins through fear or favour, or probably both, while any unfortunate who stood in the way of the mighty money-and-politics machine would end up languishing for ever in the disgusting prisons, the doors of which were closed against the outside world and

Amnesty International in particular.

If ever Mallory needed reminding of why he loathed the *narco* business, then it was being in this sick city.

He and Savage had taken a taxi from the airport to their overnight hotel. There was something macabre about the journey, windows wound down in a vain attempt to cool the humid air; a feeling of unreality, of driving through the set of a science-fantasy movie. Car horns shrieking and wailing beneath the awesome tower blocks; vehicles racing all out and foot down, endlessly switching lanes without warning. Overtaking, overtaking, switching and overtaking, pushing, pushing, pushing. Bald tyres screeching on the oily, sweating surface of the *autopistas* that ran to and fro across the city like festering sores. Tarmac melted in the sun and reset in solid ruts, the fabric crumbling. Ample evidence of the corrupt officials who had been bribed by get-rich-quick construction companies. The roadside wrecks and endless shrines to those who had died were a lasting tribute to the shame that the city fathers did not feel.

'Christ, this place depresses me,' Savage had said, looking at the hillside *barrio* slums. The tumbledown and makeshift dwellings were stuck like glue to the impossibly steep sides, for all the world like bizarre Christmas trees with their trillion lights twinkling in the distant darkness.

Mallory followed her gaze. 'It's why we do it.'

She had turned to face him. 'What do you mean?'

'Me. Vic West and others. It's why we do what we do.'

'The organisation?'

'It's not just for the spoiled brats of the filthy rich. It's for the slum kids who get sucked into it. Here and all over the world. Users, dealers, they're all victims. *Narco* power corrupts absolutely and once it takes hold you can't ever shake it free. It consumes entire nations. And if it isn't stopped, it'll take over the world.'

Even as he had told her, he knew he was preaching to the converted. No one was better placed than Georgina Savage to know that *narco* money had already eaten up Bolivia, Peru and Colombia. It had eaten the guts out of his beloved Paraguay, had half-digested Venezuela and Brazil. Already the inner cities of the United States, Britain and most of Europe were well gnawed and Italy swallowed whole. And now it was racing through the newly independent nations of the former Soviet Union like a cancer.

With *narco* money making up a quarter of the investment funds slushing around the world, he wondered how long it would be before the financial markets just couldn't get along without those massive, ever-growing profits.

Suddenly the pitch of the engines changed and Mallory's mind was jolted back to the present. The deck of the Avensa Line aircraft canted, the descent beginning and marking the end of their short internal flight from Caracas.

Through the window, Mallory could see the wide curve of the Orinoco river glinting between the banks of tropical jungle. Then the dusty clearings and the outskirts of Puerto Ayacucho. He'd visited the place a couple of times in the past, although not recently. He also had a friend who possibly still lived there. But he had mentioned neither fact to Savage; he liked to hold something in reserve.

As Brother Hermann of his old Glaubehaus orphanage had once advised, sometimes it was better not to let the right hand know what the left was doing. But Brother Hermann had his own reasons for saying that. Nevertheless, the philosophy had kept Mallory alive so far.

Even from the air he could see the place had expanded since he'd last been there, its arid streets and low concrete houses steadily pushing back the surrounding jungle.

The river port on the border with Colombia had been founded in the 1920s – along with Samariapo, some sixty kilometres upriver – when the two settlements were linked by road in order to avoid the unnavigable rapids between them. But with the passing of the oil boom and the increasing use of road transport, both places declined.

Now Ayacucho had become a Pepsi town, the soft drinks factory really its only reason for continuing existence. Some entrepreneur had bought land because it was cheap, then he built the plant, originally for Coca-Cola. The factory needed people, the people needed housing, shops and roads, which in turn needed municipal services, hotels and petrol stations. And so modern Ayacucho reinvented itself, a floating satellite of self-sufficiency that could only be reached by air or by three-hundred kilometres of jungle dirt road from the nearest town of any size.

Its very remoteness, Mallory realised, made it territory in which *narcotraficantes* and left-wing guerrillas would feel perfectly at home.

The undercarriage wheels hit the concrete strip with a thud and even before the aircraft had come to a halt, the passengers were scrambling from their seats. Most were casually dressed Venezuelans, some more scruffy than others. There were some men in business suits and a few shabby and nervous-looking Indians, probably returning from their once-a-year trip to visit distant relatives.

The cloying jungle air wrapped itself around them the moment they began to descend the steps. There was one other Avensa short-haul jet on the apron and rows of private Cessnas, Pipers, Beechcraft and others. Although some were no doubt used for legitimate purposes, it didn't take a genius to work out that most would be used for the business of the local *narcos*.

By the time Mallory and Savage reached the entrance of the single-storey terminal something of a scrum had developed within its confines. There was much handshaking and enthusiastic Latin embracing. People milled around and suitcases cluttered every available space. Travelling light with just handgrips, Mallory and Savage pushed their way swiftly towards the exit.

Outside, Mallory had just seen the bright orange Landcruiser of their cover contact, with the legend *ORINOCO ODYSSEY – Turismo de aventura!* stencilled on the door, when the armed policeman stepped into his path.

'*Señor*,' the man said abruptly, and motioned towards a camping table erected by the door. '*Alli, por favor.*'

Mallory shrugged and turned towards the snappily dressed police lieutenant who sat with a passenger list spread out in front of him. Clean-shaven and probably in his early thirties, he looked up with the impassive arrogance of so many South American law enforcers. His dark eyes were emotionless black marbles in a sallow, pock-marked face. His cap was on the table, bright badge to the fore, his short-sleeved blue shirt ironed with razor pleats. There was a fat black automatic strapped to his hip.

Two grim-faced men in plain denim stood watchfully behind him as he spoke. '*Cómo se llama usted, señor?*'

'Harold Pike,' Mallory answered, giving the name on the passport supplied by Savage's department.

The lieutenant consulted his list, found the name. '*Su pasaporte, por favor.*'

'Why do you want to see that?' Mallory asked in fluent Spanish, as he extracted the document from his inside jacket pocket. 'This is an internal flight.'

Cold dead eyes regarded him closely. For Christ's sake just do it, Savage thought; she'd forgotten just how obtuse Mallory could be in the face of zealous bureaucracy.

'It's not your business to question,' the lieutenant said at last, 'but it is just a routine check. We don't want any trouble in this town.' He glanced at the EC passport. 'British, eh? Your accent is *gaucho ché.*'

'I grew up in Paraguay.'

Thick eyebrows raised a fraction. 'You travel alone?'

'With my boss.'

Savage took a step forward. 'Is there a problem, Harry?'

The policeman appraised the good-looking woman in the sensible beige-linen travel suit, his eyes betraying his appreciation. 'Your passport, miss.'

'Mrs,' she corrected, handing it over. 'Mrs Hayes.'

'And your business here?'

'We're travel agents. We've come to assess the tourist potential here in Amazonas.'

The policeman's impassive mask was back in place. 'You have a letter of accreditation? Some evidence of your purpose?'

She smiled briefly and fished in her handbag. Mallory had been impressed with the letters with which they'd both been furnished. From Armitage Prince, the big name corporate and exotic destination specialists whose reputation ranked alongside Hogg

Robinson and Cox and King.

Mallory doubted the company meant anything to this backwater cop, yet still the man jotted down the telephone number from the letterhead. As he did so, Savage shot her friend an anxious sideways look.

The passports were returned. 'Where are you staying in Puerto Ayacucho?'

'The Orinoco Odyssey, at their camp.'

'For how long?'

'Two or three days, I'm not sure.'

Now the lieutenant was filling in two small forms that had been printed locally on an ancient Roneo. He stamped them and signed each with a flourish. 'Keep these and your passports with you at all times. I have allowed you three days. If you need an extension, come and see me at the police station. It will be no problem – we welcome tourists here.'

She smiled a sugary smile. 'I'm impressed with your security. I was told in Caracas you had problems down here.'

The officer stared at her blankly. 'Who told you?'

'People in Caracas. People in the travel business.'

He digested this for a moment. 'There is no problem here. Maybe a year ago, some bandits and guerrillas cross from Colombia, but not now.'

'That's why you have these measures?' Another approving smile.

'Yes.'

'Security is important to us if we are to bring clients here, you understand? I have to report to my directors on these matters. If we could talk about it some time, it would help.'

Although he shrugged with indifference, Mallory could see in the lacklustre eyes that the man was flattered. 'Sure, if you wish. Phone the number on the registration note. Ask for Lieutenant Ferreira. Now, Mrs Hayes, if you will excuse me.'

A queue was beginning to form behind them as Mallory and Savage left for the open exit doors.

'You'll get nothing out of him,' he said in a hoarse whisper.

Savage grinned. 'Maybe not, but why make an enemy when

you can make a friend.'

'He'll never make a friend. He's with the *narcos*.'

'You think so?'

'Since when do the police have authority to issue local visas? Because that's what they've just done.'

'I suppose you're right.'

'And those two thugs standing behind him. Big muscles bulging in their armpits. They weren't police.'

'You can't be sure.'

He half-smiled. 'I just hope those telephone numbers at Armitage Prince will check out.'

'They will, Kurt, they will.'

A man in T-shirt and jeans was leaning against the side of the orange Landcruiser. He looked up as they approached and grinned.

'Señora Hayes?' He had a pleasant thirty-something face with a heavy moustache and tinted gold spectacles.

She shook the offered hand. 'You must be Alonso.'

'Alonso Legarda at your service.' His English was educated East Coast American.

'This is Harry. Harry Pike.'

'Hi, Harry. Great to meet you both and an honour to be doing business with A and P.' He swung their two grips effortlessly onto the rear seat. 'Thought I'd drop you at your *cabaña* – there's just time for you to unpack and get settled in before lunch. Then we can go visit the market – local Indian crafts and stuff, then maybe take a jungle walk.'

'Sounds good to me,' Savage said.

It was a bare ten-minute drive to the resort camp on the edge of town. Set in a couple of acres of wired-off private land, it comprised a low adobi construction with a tin roof forming three sides of a courtyard square where Alonso Legarda parked in the shade of a mango tree. Their adjacent cabin rooms were large, cool and spartan, polished tile flooring and limewash on the walls. The food served in the diner was similarly basic: overcooked ham omelette and chips. At least they washed it down with a glass of decent Chilean white.

'We have to cater for all nationalities and all tastes,' Legarda explained as he wolfed down his own meal with relish. 'So we keep the food simple.'

Savage left most of hers untouched. 'That's good. Better than upset stomachs for our clients.'

Legarda said: 'The jungle walk's just an hour and it's only secondary – been cut down and now regrowing. But it'll give them a flavour. Snakes, wild bees, you know. Then tomorrow we'll do a little fishing, visit the National Park on the Colombian side of the Orinoco. Most guests come for about three days. We've more than enough to occupy them.' His meal demolished, he pushed his plate away. 'Anything special you'd like to see?'

'What about night life?' Savage asked.

Legarda pushed his spectacles up onto the bridge of his nose with his forefinger. A typically evasive gesture, Mallory noted. 'None to speak of, we prefer our clients to stay here. I bring in some beer and ice. Most people like to play cards and chat.'

'Our clients may like to sample some local colour,' Savage insisted.

'Only a few seedy bars, I'm afraid. Some of the hotel bars are better.'

'It's not dangerous in town?'

'Not really.' Again the finger on the bridge of his glasses.

'Then let's visit a few tonight. I'd like you to come with us.'

'Sure, I'll tell the wife I'll be late.' Grudging.

'You can introduce us to the owners and the bar staff.' Savage smiled her appreciation. 'By the way, is there a bar called Las Noches Árabes or something similar?'

'Not that I've heard of, but then I don't drink much. Not with a five o'clock start here every day.' He was angling for a sympathetic smile and received one. 'Anything else?'

'Is there a telephone I can use? I'd like to call the police station.'

Lieutenant Ferreira was feeling generous and co-operative after his long lunch and agreed to a meeting with the representatives from Armitage Prince at six o'clock that evening.

After making her call, Savage and Mallory were driven around the town by Legarda. They visited the sullen local Indians selling their wares at the open-air craft market opposite the Museo Etnológico and dutifully admired the town's ornate church before heading out of town. They took the east-bound road to the patch of sanitised secondary rain forest Legarda considered safe and suitable for the sensibilities of European and American tourists.

On the way, Mallory had his suspicions confirmed. They were being followed. He'd glimpsed the battered dark blue Toyota pick-up twice around the town; now it was trailing some hundred metres behind them.

He leaned forward from the rear seat to speak in Legarda's ear. 'Do tourists always attract so much attention here, amigo?'

'Pardon me?'

'We've picked up a tail – we're being followed. Who is it? Police? *Bandidos*?'

Savage turned in her seat beside their driver, a look of apprehension on her face.

Legarda glanced in his mirror. 'I think you're mistaken, señor. Just locals going to work in the forest or maybe to work on the road to Autan Uran.'

Almost as though the driver of the pick-up had heard their conversation, he put his foot down. The vehicle gained on them rapidly, a storm of road dust spiralling in its wake. Now glancing rapidly and nervously in his mirror, Legarda eased off the accelerator. Clearly he didn't want to give the mistaken impression he was trying to outrun them.

The thumping racket of the pick-up's engine began to fill the interior of the Landcruiser as it crept up behind them, then pulled out. Slowly it edged alongside so that both vehicles filled the entire width of the road. The driver was in no hurry to overtake. His eyes behind the sunglasses remained looking dead ahead, one hand on the wheel, the other resting on the window and flicking ash from the cigarette butt between his fingers.

He suddenly appeared to notice them and turned his head, his face only feet from Legarda's. White teeth gleamed in a sneer beneath the dark glasses, then he was gone as the pick-up surged past.

Two men in denims and baseball caps were standing in the back, leaning against the cab roof and staring hard at the occupants of the Landcruiser. They made no attempt to conceal the Colt Commando assault rifles they carried.

Then the dust cloud smothered them and Legarda was obliged to brake, slowing until the air cleared again.

Mallory's voice was low. 'I think you'd better tell us, Alonso.'

Their driver shrugged, playing it down. 'Local boys, that's all, think they're big shots.'

'*Las drogas*?'

'Si.' Reluctant. 'But they don't give any trouble. They're just interested because you're new in town. Just want you to know they're keeping an eye on you. Want to be sure you're doing what you say you're doing here. Not from the DEA.'

'Are *they* the reason we're the only guests at your camp?'

Legarda gave a reluctant smile. 'Maybe. Word gets around and it puts the tourists off, but we have no problem. Honest. Don't let it worry you – just wait till you spend tomorrow on the Orinoco.' Then suddenly he sounded angry and frustrated. 'You'll see those *bajerós* are an insignificant nuisance compared with the wild beauty of my Amazonas!'

Lieutenant José Ferreira lay back expansively in the chair, his hands behind his head. Across the desk Georgina Savage was irritated to find her eyes drawn to the dark patches at his armpits.

'This *is* a wild place,' the policeman was saying. In the privacy of his office, he seemed more forthcoming than earlier at the airport in the presence of the two civilians in denims. 'It is an unguarded border with Colombia and very remote. Attracts undesirable types.'

Mallory watched carefully but said little, leaving most of the talking to Savage. After all it had been her idea; he would have kept well clear of the police station. 'You mean drug traffickers?'

'Yes, but of course. They want to traffic their goods up to the seaports of the Caribbean – that is common knowledge. But the guerrillas give us more trouble. Even last week they seize a wealthy local woman and demand a ransom payment. However, give us a little time and we will bring the rogues to justice.'

Savage gave a tight sympathetic smile. 'Of course. But that doesn't sound too safe for tourists. They won't want to be kidnapped.'

Ferreira chuckled as if appreciating a good joke and lit himself a cigarette.

'We take very great care of tourists, as I'm sure you understand. Indeed, if the kidnapped lady had only the foresight of taking out a little insurance . . .'

'Insurance?' Savage queried.

Mallory said: 'I think the lieutenant means insurance with the police department. If she'd paid, she'd have had protection against such accidents.'

The policeman smiled, uncertain as to whether he detected a note of sarcasm. 'Mr Pike clearly understands the way these things work. We are very understaffed here with much to attend to. And we are underresourced by headquarters in Caracas – they tend to ignore their country cousins so far away. We have only one police car and that is off the road for repairs. To go about our business we have to use the stolen cars from our compound while they await return to their proper owners.' His face took on an expression of sad regret. 'So if we receive a little financial encouragement – say, from your tourist company – we have more resources to ensure their security.'

'How much?' Savage asked directly.

Ferreira feigned embarrassment. 'Oh, at your discretion, but we could discuss it over drinks. We are humble, honest policemen fighting a lonely battle against traffickers and guerrillas. We are not greedy people.'

'Of course not,' Savage replied in an understanding voice. 'I shall recommend such insurance in the report to my bosses. Discreetly, of course.' She glanced at her wristwatch; Legarda should be waiting outside for them now in the Landcruiser, ready for a tour of Puerto Ayacucho's seedy fleshpots. 'Thank you so much for your time, Lieutenant. Just one thing before I go. I understand an old family friend is staying here in town. I was told he arrived about ten days ago and I'd love to look him up. I suppose you wouldn't know where I could find him?'

Mallory stared at her, just catching his jaw before it fell open in disbelief.

'What is the name?' Ferreira asked.

'Victor West – an Englishman.'

The policeman showed only mild interest. 'And what is his business?'

'I really don't know. Some sort of salesman, I think. That's what he used to do, travelling in engine parts or something. But I haven't seen him in years. If you've any way of knowing where he might be staying—?'

Ferreira's pride would not allow him to admit that he did not know about everything on his patch. 'That should not be a problem. There will, I regret, be a small information fee.'

Of course there would, Savage thought. 'Twenty US dollars?'

'Shall we say thirty – as a rush job? When I have the information, I'll send someone round to your camp.'

The money was exchanged and they shook hands. After he had shown them out of his office, Ferreira returned to his desk and opened the locked top drawer. He dumped the pile of Roneoed airport entry-forms in front of him and flicked quickly through them. Back ten days, fifteen days, twenty, thirty. No mention of an Englishman called Victor West.

Three numbers were missing from the sequence. Three names which had aroused the interests of the *narco* boys. Perhaps Victor West was one of them? He really should keep a note of the names he handed over, but then he'd always hated paperwork. It was the reason he'd been posted to this godforsaken hole in the first place.

That evening he would ask the *narcotraficantes* at their scheduled meeting. If they had been interested in Victor West, then they would certainly be interested in anyone asking after him. And that could be worth another hundred dollars.

He had to admit that his bank balance had been totting up nicely during the past year or so since their arrival.

'I can't believe you did that,' Mallory said as they crossed the police station car park.

Savage was unrepentant. 'Our cover's good, Kurt, so let's use it. When we got back from that jungle walk, there was a message waiting at the camp. Someone had phoned the Armitage Prince number in London. So I knew we'd been checked out.'

'You didn't tell me.'

She drew to a halt. 'Would it have made any difference?'

'You know it wouldn't. Going to corrupt policemen isn't my style.'

'We haven't got time for your style, Kurt. This place stinks and I want to be out of here as soon as possible. I know you think I'm being naive, but who better than the local cops to come up with the answers in a one-horse town like this?'

'Then why did you ask me to come?'

'Because I was told to.' She immediately regretted her words. 'No, that's not the only reason, you know that. Colonel Maidment realised you were the best man for the job. So did my boss, and so did I. It was me who was told to come with you.'

Mallory's eyes narrowed. 'Then let me do things my way before you drop us both in it. *Narcos* don't piss about. You're not playing a game with polite Russian spies here.'

She had the good grace to blush. 'You're angry, I'm sorry. I guess it was foolhardy.' Then she added defensively: 'But you haven't suggested anything yet.'

'I'm waiting for tonight.'

'What?'

'When the camp's closed up and those yobbos in the pick-up have gone home to bed.'

Savage glanced across to the Landcruiser where Legarda waited patiently at the wheel. Parked beyond him was the now familiar blue Toyota pick-up.

'I see.'

She felt the first wet spots on her face and looked up. It was starting to rain.

*

The evening was a disaster.

Alonso Legarda had proved a very inadequate guide to the town's bars. Although many people knew him, he was clearly more at home fishing on the Orinoco or wandering the riverside forests in search of wildlife than knocking back Polar beers with the local low life.

At least Savage had promised to ask no more embarrassing questions, leaving that to Mallory when he sensed that their immediate company and the moment were right.

Their first call was at the Tomo hotel. While they were having drinks Mallory went to the reception desk to inquire about West's stay. The reluctant manager consulted his registration book and confirmed the one-night stopover, but could offer no more information.

It quickly became obvious that beneath their friendly and care-free manner the inhabitants of Puerto Ayacucho lived in an uneasy atmosphere of fear. While some openly admitted there was a problem with *narcos* in the area when the subject cropped up in casual conversation, no one was going to discuss it with two strangers from England. If Mallory lingered on the topic for more than a few moments, the man to whom he was talking would inevitably make his excuses and move away.

The question of the whereabouts of Vic West was no longer raised.

'That was a complete waste of time,' Savage commented back at her *cabaña*.

Mallory shook his head. 'It just proves the hold the *narcos* have over this place. I've seen it before, you can smell it. After a few drinks people usually let something slip, but not here.'

'And you still intend to go out tonight?'

He nodded. 'It's probably the only chance we've got.'

'And you won't tell me who you're going to see?'

'Need to know.' He tapped the side of his nose. 'Your rules, George. If your police lieutenant friend decides to arrest you tonight, you'll have nothing to tell him.'

'Nice one, Kurt.' But she had to smile.

*

Back in his own *cabaña*, Kurt left the light on while he washed the gel out of his hair and let it hang free. Then he stripped off his smart casual clothes and pulled on a pair of torn jeans, scruffy T-shirt and his favourite worn canvas jacket. Feeling much more comfortable now, he slipped on some old trainers and picked up his Mobil Oil baseball cap before switching off the light. He then waited ten minutes before he slipped out of the bathroom window and into the grounds. He swiftly located the camp's guard. Armed only with a fairly useless .22 sporting rifle, the man was laughing and drinking beer with the camp's gardener near the locked gates.

After a ten-minute search Mallory found a tree beside the seven-foot steel security fence. One stout branch offered a convenient bridge over the barbed-wire top. He swung over and dropped down on the outside. Then he made his way through the wild scrub towards the main dirt road. On the way he passed a rusting and abandoned oil drum; he made a mental note of its location before continuing. If the Toyota pick-up was parked anywhere near the gates he wasn't able to see it. That didn't concern him; there were plenty of shadows to cover his half-mile walk into town.

Only a couple of battered cars had passed him by the time he reached the first of the low brick houses. A few bars were still open but the steady drizzle was keeping pedestrians off the streets.

It was some years since he'd last visited Mario Dubois and he could not recollect his friend's address. The dark streets of the town were disorientating and he saw no building that he especially recognised. He was on the verge of giving up, when he saw the turning. It was much like many others, yet somehow more familiar. He splashed through the puddles on the sandy track, trying to recall which of the tiny two-bedroomed villa bungalows he wanted. They were all very similar, set closely side by side and finished in white stucco with fancy wrought-iron security grills over the open windows. Most were fronted by small yards filled with terracotta plant pots.

Then, in one of the courtyards, he recognised Mario's beloved and battered old Norton motorcycle. He took a step inside. There was a gate set in the high garden wall on his left; the villa wall on his right led beneath a vine-covered pergola to the front door. An automatic porch light snapped on but there appeared to be no other signs of life from within. Well, it was gone midnight.

He pressed the bell and waited. Nothing. Total silence but for the patter of rain on foliage and the relentless chirruping of cicadas. His spirits sank as he rang again.

The noise of the bell must have disguised the creak of the iron garden gate behind him and the padding bare feet made no sound.

He was only aware of the man when he felt the cold muzzle of the revolver against the back of his neck and heard the click of the hammer. 'One more step, and you are meat for the Orinoco alligators.'

Instinctively Mallory raised his hands.

'Now turn, real slow.'

Mario Dubois's big frame of muscle turning to fat was hairy and naked, except for red silk boxer shorts and a shark's-tooth necklace at his throat.

'*Cómo estas ud, hermano*?' Mallory said with a grin.

Heavy eyebrows lowered over the brown spaniel eyes. 'You? Is it you?'

'Who else would look you up this time of night, you old scoundrel?'

Big white teeth broke through the heavy drooping moustache; the porch light, catching the gold filling, gave him a piratical look. He scratched at the wild black hair on his head with his free hand. 'What the hell are you doing here, Kurt?'

Mallory indicated the revolver. 'Do you mind putting that thing away. You never could shoot straight.'

His friend gave a mountainous laugh. 'That's when I'm sober – you should see me after a beer or two.' He lowered the gun. 'Come in around the back.'

'Are you expecting trouble?' Mallory asked, following through the gate before Mario secured it. Across the small unkempt garden was a raised terrace; it was just large enough to accommodate the wooden table and four chairs.

'No, just my brother-in-law,' Mario replied, switching on the exterior light. Immediately moths began battering against it. 'When I see you, I think it is one of the *narco* boys. Take a seat, *mi compañero*.'

'Not still dabbling, are you?'

Mario sniffed heavily. 'Not any more. It's got too dangerous around here. I just store some stuff for Julio, my brother-in-law. He's still young and crazy enough to think it's all great fun. And he needs the bolivars. Besides, I've got responsibilities now.'

As though on cue, the sound of a baby's burbling came from the dark interior beyond the open French windows. A pretty, plump woman emerged in a nightdress with the child cradled in her arms. 'What is happening, Mario? I heard the doorbell and heard a strange voice – it is not Julio.'

'No, it is an old friend of mine. His name is— '

'Harry,' Mallory cut in quickly. 'Harry Pike.'

Mario blinked for a second, but was fast on the uptake. 'Si, my friend Harry Pike from England.' He turned to Mallory. 'My wife Luz. Luz Elastic, I joke behind her back. What a girl! Pretty, eh, and very, very sexy?'

The woman smiled shyly and offered her hand.

'*Encantado*,' Mallory said, then turned back to his friend. 'I never thought you'd get married.'

Mario lowered his voice conspiratorially. 'Well, we're not quite married. More my *novia*, you understand. But it is all the same. You have to stand by a woman who bears you such a fine son. I think I am making love for fun, but Luz takes it very seriously! Isn't he handsome, just like his father?'

Mallory grinned to see the pride on his friend's face. 'Sure he is. Give him a sombrero and a moustache and I couldn't tell you apart.'

'He means he's an ugly little bastard!' Mario laughed and explained to the woman. 'Be a good girl and fetch the whisky bottle – er, Harry and I have a reunion to celebrate.'

Obediently Luz returned inside with the baby. 'You like a *basuko*?'

Mallory relaxed in the chair beneath the canvas awning. 'It's been a while. Just about a hanging offence back home.'

His friend quickly fetched a tobacco tin from indoors and extracted a couple of hand-rolled cocaine joints. 'And while it is, amigo, there will always be *narcotraficantes*, no?'

Mallory accepted the light and inhaled long and slow. The smoke had a sickly sweet woody smell to it. Rarely found outside South America, it was a halfway by-product between coca leaf and refined cocaine. He felt the warmth spread through his body and a flush of perspiration to his cheeks. This wasn't the ice-sharp, hyper edginess of the Wall Street snorters, but a mellow comforter that made him feel at one with the soft scented night.

When Luz had delivered the whisky and two tumblers and returned to bed, Mario asked: 'You are still with the organisation?'

'On and off. In fact it's why I'm here.'

Mario gave a smug smile of satisfaction. 'How did I guess, you old hypocrite.'

'Hypocrite?'

'You sit there smoking my best *basuko* – it is not golden Virginian— So what brings you here?'

His friend's work for the organisation had only ever been with Mallory; he did it for a favour and for the money. And because he liked the danger of it.

'One of our people has been killed up on the coast. We think he came to this town just before the *narcotraficantes* killed him.'

Mario lay back in his chair and exhaled a long stream of smoke which was sucked out beyond the veil of thin rain. 'That I can believe. Visit Puerto Ayacucho and die.'

'That's Naples.'

'It's this place too, amigo. Don't you notice the difference from when you are last here? Not so many happy faces. Not so many honest businessmen. They take their wives and their pretty daughters away to somewhere safe. The *narcos* run this place now.'

'Tell me about it.'

The big man shrugged. 'There are several gangs operating in

the region. Some Venezuelan, some Colombian.'

'Big outfits?'

'Sure, some are. Others are just locals like Julio who scratch a living from the odd half-kilo. But the Vipers are the worst.'

Mallory's reactions weren't yet blunted by the *basuko*. 'Vipers?'

'That's the name we give them. I don't know why – you'd have to ask Julio that. But it seems to fit. Vicious *bajerós* – a mix of Venezuelan, but mostly Colombian – they are happy to kill anyone who stands in their way or who asks too many questions. Five people die this year – two, I know, for not handing over a percentage of their own private deals. Town tax, the Vipers call it. The corpses were dragged out of the Orinoco by fishermen. Half-eaten by piranhas.' He picked up his whisky and downed it in one. 'So you see why I gave it up. These guys aren't live-and-let-live types like the other gangs. For a while I guide some tourists, but we don't see many now. So I shift a few emeralds across the river. Safer than *la coca*.'

Mallory stubbed out the joint; any more and he wouldn't be able to think clearly. 'How long have the Vipers been here?'

'I don't know. First noticed them about a year ago. First thing they did was stitch up the local police. You know how it works. Take the silver or the lead. They approach one guy who refuses to co-operate, so they blow away his wife and the old granny. They had no problem after that; the cops simply take the money and do what they're told. Used the police to establish their own security network. Monitor comings and goings at the airport and mount *retenes* – you know, roadblocks – so they control everything. Their thugs drive around town doing what they want. If they want booze they help themselves, or some woman walking on the sidewalk— As soon as I get the bolivars together, I'm out of here.' He paused. 'So what about this friend of yours?'

'A guy called Vic West.'

'A gringo?'

'English, not that you'd necessarily know. Quite swarthy and spoke fluent South American Spanish.'

'West – is that the name he used?'

'I can't be sure of that, but normally he played it straight. He was well known and respected as an arms salesman. Had a reputation for delivering and no double-crosses. So anyone could deal with him without fear or favour, so to speak.'

Mario stared at him. 'An arms dealer here in Ayacucho? That's a lethal combination. Was he talking to the Vipers?'

'No idea, but I've a suspicion he knew about them.'

'And when was he here?'

'Ten days ago, for an overnight stay. Apparently he met someone at a place called Las Noches Árabes. Is that a bar or a restaurant?'

The Martinique-born Venezuelan sucked on his teeth. 'Not that I know, but then I don't hit the town like I used to . . .' His words were interrupted by the rumble of a vehicle engine; it sounded in need of tuning and a new exhaust system.

'Your brother-in-law?' Mallory asked.

Mario nodded. 'Maybe he can answer some of your questions, amigo.' And he rose to his feet to open the garden gate. Mallory noticed he took the revolver with him, just in case.

Julio was young and flushed with excitement. Early twenties, Mallory assessed, with Latin good looks and neatly cut hair with a quiff that flopped over his forehead. He wore a dazzling short-sleeved Hawaiian shirt, faded denim trousers, sneakers and a lot of gold.

As Mario took the brown package wrapped in polythene from him, the young man was gabbling: 'Those bastards, they've upped their cut from twenty to twenty-five per cent! And I know why, the Gringo was in town. He and his friends were there. They think they run the place. I ask you! It's nothing to do with them. It's my deal and my money, I set it up and they take a whole quarter. Fuck their town tax. Just sit there and examine *my* property and calmly tell me that the rate has to go up to cover overheads. They don't *have* any fuckin' overheads – they don't pay for anything!'

'Calm down,' Mario warned. 'You'll give yourself a heart attack.'

The man laughed nervously. 'You'd have a heart attack if you'd seen what they did to some copper who upset them tonight. The Gringo did it himself. Chopped off the little finger of his left hand with a machete. Just like that. On the table in front of everyone—' His voice trailed as he suddenly saw Mallory seated in the shadows. '*Dios mío!*'

Mario guessed what his brother-in-law was thinking. 'It's okay, Julio, he's not one of them. This is a good friend of mine. Meet Harry Pike.'

Julio looked uncertain and slightly embarrassed. He wiped the sweat from his right hand on his jeans before stepping tentatively forward to shake Mallory's hand. '*Mucho gusto, señor.*'

'Pleased to meet you, Julio. And don't worry about me, I'm not interested in your secrets. Mario and I go back a long way.'

The young man frowned. 'Señor Pike? That is a gringo name. From America? But you speak like an Argentinian.'

Mario chuckled. 'He's an Englander, but was brought up in Paraguay. Now I'll put this stuff away somewhere safe while you help yourself to a drink. You look like you need one.'

While Julio helped himself to a treble whisky and to the *basuko* tin, Mario took the cocaine package a few metres into the garden before lifting one of the flagstones in the path. He dropped the package into a plastic cake box hidden underneath.

He returned from his task and explained to his brother-in-law the purpose of Mallory's visit, but without mentioning any names.

'Well I can tell you one thing,' Julio said in hesitant English, 'you will not find Las Noches Árabes here, because it is in Colombia. In Casuarito, just across the river.'

Mario grinned at learning the answer to the puzzle. 'Ah!'

'It's a whorehouse. Used to be a seedy place with no fancy name. Then six months ago someone new takes over and they bring these tarts from Bogotá. Real nice *chicitas*, but expensive. Wow! Now only the Vipers really use the place.'

'What do you know about this Viper gang?' Mallory asked.

Julio glanced nervously at his brother-in-law who indicated it was safe for him to talk. 'What does anyone know? Just that they shift White Viper – very pure shit. You know several outfits use some sort of brand. Like on cattle ranches. Well these guys use a snake symbol – like a double S with head and forked tongue. One local gang here thought they'd get smart. Copied the logo onto their own packaging, thought they'd get a better price. A big mistake. They got chopped with machetes – like real slow – then the Vipers blew away the entire family and burnt down five houses. Wiped out uncles, aunts, nephews. And the police did fuck all.'

Mallory grimaced, but then he'd heard it all before. 'This sounds like a Colombian gang.'

Julio sucked greedily on his *basuko*, still trying to slow his adrenalin. 'Si, most of the guys are Colombian, but . . .' he hesitated, unsure how much to say. But the *basuko* was taking effect, lowering his guard, 'there is this Englishman. Well, two or three, but one in particular. I don't know his name. In front of us, the *narcos* just call him *El Gringo* – what else?' The nervous laugh became more like a giggle. 'Comes in every now and again. You know, to inspect things and whip some ass. They are there tonight. Say, maybe your friend comes here to sell guns to the Vipers? And then the DEA cowboys blew him away? What was his name?'

Mallory considered Julio's flight of fantasy. Absently he said: 'Vic West. Victor West.'

The brother-in-law's eyes widened. '*Diablos*!'

'What is it?' Mario demanded.

Julio shook his head in disbelief. 'That's why they took off the cop's finger tonight. The Vipers say this man West was a spy, that he was snooping around here some days back. Now apparently there are two smart gringos in town, from England, asking about the *same* man! Señor West. They say they are in the travel business, but the Vipers think maybe they are DLOs.'

'What's that?' Mario asked.

'British Customs. Drugs l-liais-on officers,' Julio replied, stumbling over the unfamiliar word. 'These gringos go to the police station and ask questions. But the cop was lax and didn't tell the Vipers straight away. That's why they taught him a lesson.'

Mallory felt his blood turn to liquid ice in his veins. 'Do you know what happened to Señor West?'

A shrug. 'There is a rumour they follow him some place and

kill him. Someone says it was *El Gringo* himself.' Another shrug. 'But I don't know.'

'Did they say what they were going to do about these new arrivals, these travel people?'

Julio laughed his girlish giggle again and drew his finger across his throat. 'They will raid the *cabaña* at first light. The gringos will sing like canaries.'

'Then we'd better get out quick,' Mallory decided aloud, pushing back his chair to stand up.

The brother-in-law's mouth fell open. 'You? *Dios mío*! I had no idea.'

'I think the *basuko* addles your brain,' Mario chided. Then he turned to Mallory. 'Sit down a moment. You have to think about this. Like a good guard dog, the Vipers let you into their house, but it is not so easy to escape. You will not get through the airport and there are checks on all the roads.' He thought for a moment. 'Are you armed?'

Mallory shook his head.

'Then forget it, mi amigo.'

A thought occurred. 'Perhaps we could cross the river to Casuarito. Get out through Colombia.'

'I don't think so,' Julio replied. 'The first ferry doesn't cross until six and security is tight. You'll need papers and the Vipers will be watching.'

'And Casuarito don't go no place,' Mario added. 'A dead end. Not even an unpaved road to connect with the rest of Colombia.'

'What about the Orinoco?' Mallory asked. 'North or south.'

Mario nodded thoughtfully. 'Julio has a *voladora* – a speedboat down by the ferry. But we'll have to tow it on the road first. You probably don't realise, amigo, but the Orinoco is blocked by rapids immediately upriver – and downstream to the north there are even more.' He scratched at his moustache. 'So we could risk towing the boat a few kilometres down the road, beyond the first rapids to the south, then go by river as far as Samariapo – that's maybe forty-five kilometres from here. It's as far as we can go. Then you'll have to hire a boat the other side of the rapids there – if you can. There is an airstrip down at San Fernando de

Atabapo. If you've cash dollars, perhaps you can bribe a pilot to fly you out of the area.'

'I think the Vipers sometimes use that airstrip,' Julio warned.

'Do I have any choice?' Mallory asked.

'You are out on a limb here,' Mario confirmed, 'and it is quite easy for the Vipers to cut off the branch.'

Mallory said: 'First I have to go back to the *cabaña* and get George out before that dawn raid.'

'Ah,' Mario exclaimed. 'He is the other gringo?'

'She. Georgina.'

Mario raised his eyes to heaven and crossed himself. A female being interrogated by the Vipers didn't bear thinking about. He turned to Julio. 'Drive down to the ferry, hitch up your boat and bring it back here. Meantime, I'll go with – er, Harry – and pick up this woman on the Norton. It'll be a squeeze, but – let me get some clothes on.'

A few minutes later he returned in a short-sleeved check shirt and the inevitable worn jeans. Mallory and Julio waited impatiently.

'Let's go,' Mario said and led the way out to the Norton. He swung astride the old machine and kicked it into life as Mallory climbed onto the pillion. 'See you back here in about forty minutes, Julio.'

Exhaust crackled, shattering the stillness of the night.

Julio stared after them. What *was* he thinking of, allowing Mario to talk him into this? It was madness, running up against the Vipers. Risking his life and his small, hard-earned fortune. And all for the sake of this gringo stranger. His brother-in-law must be out of his mind. Hadn't he just told them what happened to the cop? And that was just because he'd been sloppy.

He stared down at his hands; they were sweaty and trembling.

His decision was made then and there. He returned quickly through the garden gate and into the bungalow villa. The telephone was on a Brazilian mahogany sideboard. Picking up the receiver, he dialled the number he knew by heart.

There was a pounding of trepidation in his chest as it was answered by the man he knew only as Carlos. 'It is Julio Melo here. There is something you should know. I am at my sister's house and one of the gringos you are looking for has just left with my brother-in-law. They are going to collect the woman gringo from the camp now – Yes, yes – and they are coming back here. Then they are planning to leave by boat.'

At the other end of the line, Carlos rubbed his eyes and tried to shake his head clear of the booze. 'You've done well, Julio,' he said, his voice coarse from too much tobacco. 'This will be remembered. You stay where you are and I'll send someone round. Give me your address.'

A few seconds later he hung up and scratched at the string vest where it chafed beneath his scrawny armpit. He wondered whether to rouse *El Gringo*, the man he knew only as Señor Guy. But the Englishman would throw a fit if he saw this lot. Around the room, where an hour ago the party had been in full swing, his fellow *narcos* resembled corpses. The *aguardiente* hooch and *basuko* had taken its toll, so that it looked like a machine-gun massacre, the bodies lying where they had fallen, some on the chairs and settee, curled on the laps of sleeping, drunken whores, or crashed out on the floor.

Carlos kicked the snoring, open-mouthed man by his foot. 'José! Get the fuck on your feet!' Suddenly anger overtook him. Look at them, these drunken bastards. The dreaded Vipers of Puerto Ayacucho! What a shambles! 'GET UP – ALL OF YOU!' he bellowed.

Slowly they stirred like the living dead. 'José, go and wake Señor Guy. Be polite if you know what's good for you. You others, form into four groups. One go to the airport, another reinforce the roadblocks and the third get down to the camp and get those gringos before they do a runner! If you have trouble from the camp security guard, just shoot him. The rest of you come with me.'

'Where to?' someone asked.

'The home of Mario Dubois.'

4

The Norton screamed through the deserted township and out along the road to the Orinoco Odyssey *cabaña*. Before they reached it Mallory prodded Mario's shoulder, indicating for him to pull over.

Thankfully the burbling of the shot-through exhaust died away and the tropical night noises swelled up to fill the vacuum.

'Leave it tucked away here,' Mallory said. 'Some of those yobbos could still be watching the gates. There's another way in.'

Mario wheeled his machine behind a thicket, kicked down the stand, and followed his friend.

'I was thinking,' Mallory said. 'How long will that river journey take? I can't believe these Viper people don't have their own speedboats.'

'Forget it, Kurt. We're not going by river.'

'What?'

'For the very reason you said. They've got boats and helicopters – and they'll have that airstrip at San Fernando covered, no problem.'

'But you told Julio . . .'

'Never let your right hand know what the left is doing,' Mario said with a chuckle. 'That's what you always used to tell me. Well, Julio was very jumpy tonight and I thought – hell, just to be safe.'

'Then where are we going?'

'Across the river to Casuarito. I have my own canoe.'

'But it's a dead end. You said so yourself.'

He tapped the side of his nose. 'A dead end for vehicles. But the emerald smuggler's mule doesn't need roads. About seventy-five kilometres overland. Two or three days of jungle tracks. You can manage that? You used to boast what a horseman you were.'

Mallory grinned. 'Horses, Mario, not bloody donkeys!'

When they reached the rusted oil drum he had noted earlier, he dragged it across to the overhanging tree. Climbing onto the top of the drum, he jumped up to grab the branch. He worked his way along, hand over hand, then swung his feet up and over the fence, finally turning round to crouch in the fork of the tree.

Mario's pale face stared up at him from the shadows. 'Mi amigo, I am not a fucking monkey. I'll wait here.'

Mallory dropped down into the compound and made his way swiftly through the grounds to the cabin block. The camp was silent; no sign of life. He reached Savage's door and knocked briskly.

A sound of movement came from within, a cough and the rustle of a mosquito net. Then a voice, hoarse with sleep. 'Harry, is that you?'

'Yes, open up.'

She released the lock and stepped aside to admit him. 'How did it go?'

'The good part is that I've got confirmation of who killed Vic. It was the White Viper connection – they're the gang who run this town. And that's what the locals call them, the Vipers. The bad news is that Lieutenant Ferreira and the rest of the cops here are on the payroll. They've now heard that we've been asking after Vic and are planning to ask us a few questions of their own.'

She stood there in her baggy T-shirt that was within an inch of decency and lit a cigarette. Her hand, he noticed, had developed a slight tremor. It was the only sign that she might be more nervous than she was letting on. 'I'm impressed. How the hell did you find all this out?'

'An old friend who's going to help us get out of here. No luggage, I'm afraid. So just throw some clothes on and grab your toothbrush, and let's go.'

Savage stared at him. 'Are you kidding?'

'Those *narcos* are killers, George, and they're planning to come here at first light. It won't be your nice police lieutenant asking the questions – they've already taken off one of his fingers because he didn't tell them about us quickly enough.'

The blood drained from her face. 'Christ.' She stubbed out the cigarette. 'What happens next?'

'We cross the river to Colombia.' He didn't go into details. 'As soon as you're ready, get out through the bathroom window. I'll be waiting.'

With that he left and returned to his own cabin next door. He tipped out his travel grip on the bed, found his passport and documents and an old sweater, then snapped it shut.

It was then that he heard the noise, so loud and abrupt that he turned instinctively towards the window. The speed at which the pick-up had driven at the compound gates had taken them clean off their hinges. Now the beams of the headlights were filling the camp yard. Someone was shouting excitedly. He thought he recognised it as the voice of the security guard. The cry of protest was followed by the angry stammer of an automatic weapon. Then a stunning silence. It lasted only seconds before the engine of the pick-up revved and the vehicle began advancing again.

Mallory didn't bother looking. It was all too obvious that the *narcos* had brought forward their plan of action. He made straight for the bathroom, clambered onto the windowsill and dropped down. Scarcely had he hit the ground than Savage landed by his side, now dressed in jeans and shirt, carrying a jacket.

Beyond the cabin block the sound of running feet could be heard. Commands were being yelled in Spanish, curses and expletives. Even in the darkness Mallory could see the wide glistening whites of the girl's eyes, could smell the fear on her.

'This way,' he whispered and, taking her hand, led her into the darkness.

He moved with the agility and stealth of a leopard as she stumbled blindly behind him. It occurred to her that this was a perfect example of why he was a front-line operator and she was a back-room controller. He was in his element, avoiding danger by a whisker, riding on the adrenalin wave, creeping away like a shadow. Playing small boys' games in a cruel man's world. Confident that their pursuers would lose vital minutes in confusion, wasting their aggression on each other, as they failed to find their quarry. No different now than when he had played night-time hide-and-seek with the other kids in the Paraguayan orphanage.

By the time they reached the tree she was breathing heavily, the humid air suffocating and the tension and exertion causing her to sweat until the material of her shirt was like a second skin. Mallory gave her a leg-up so she could sit astride the branch and edge herself along and over the fence before dropping down into Mario's waiting arms.

He laughed, enjoying himself. 'I have never known such treasure to drop out of the night sky!'

She scowled at him and mumbled her thanks, not sure she should have done after his lingering embrace.

'Put her down,' Mallory chided as he joined them. 'You don't know where she's been.'

Then he was on the move again, working his way back through the maze of shrubbery to where the motorcycle was hidden. Still the road was deserted, the noise of the revving pick-up just a distant burble. Savage climbed astride the pillion behind Mario, with Mallory pressed up hard against her back. It was strange, she thought as the Norton bumped its way onto the road, being so close to him again. Undignified, squashed and unable to see over Mario's broad shoulders, she was aware of Mallory's body heat burning between her buttocks. Aware, too, that the closeness of him and the excitement of their escape was as exhilarating as it was frightening.

It was no more than a fifteen-minute ride to the deserted port area where a low-walled promenade gave onto a beach of sandy shale and patches of reed grass. When the noise of the Norton's engine died, they were enveloped by the stillness. Apart from the distant honking of baby alligators, the indolent slap of the water along the bank was the only sound.

Mario covered his motorcycle with an old tarpaulin, then led the way down across the beach. Even in the darkness they could distinguish the inky outline of the regular ferryboat, its blunt bows nudging the shore. Beyond, across the river, a few lights still burned in the houses of Casuarito.

'That's strange,' Mario muttered. 'Julio's speedboat is still here. He should have collected it by now.'

He continued down to the water's edge where his old Indian dugout had been pulled clear.

Savage was disconcerted. It was long and very narrow, scarcely more than twelve inches across, with thin lengths of straight, stripped timber nailed to the hull to form the gunwales and seats. By the time they were all aboard she guessed they'd be barely a couple of inches clear of the surface.

She had no inclination to show her fear, but Mario must have read it in her eyes. 'Piranhas have a special liking for ladies' backsides, señora,' he chuckled. 'But not gringo ladies – they don't taste so good.'

Mallory helped launch the tiny craft and held it steady while she balanced precariously on her minuscule seat, the hull rocking as it was swung into the flow. Shutting her eyes, she prayed it wouldn't tip as the two men slid aboard and drew up their legs into the shallow hull. When she opened them again, they were paddling in long, slow strokes, propelling the canoe with the ease and speed of a racing eight.

She could have sworn she held her breath for the entire ten-minute crossing and had never been more pleased to set foot again on dry ground. 'What happens now?' she asked.

Mallory had begun following Mario up the steep rocky embankment to the first houses of the settlement. 'Two or three days by mule to the nearest road.'

'I hope that's just your idea of a joke.'

He smiled. 'Life really can be a bitch, can't it?'

Strains of a lazy salsa rhythm eddied on a velvet breeze through the dirt main street from one of the few bars still open. Casuarito was noticeably different from Puerto Ayacucho; this village had an unmistakable frontier feel to it, the buildings more makeshift with wooden sidewalks and roofs of corrugated tin. In the dimly lit interior of one they saw a group of Colombians playing canasta and drinking, two of them wearing straw stetsons. A mongrel dog skulked across their path and disappeared into an alleyway.

Mario stopped and pointed up ahead. An enormous woman with bright peroxide-blonde hair and wearing a voluminous shift of chiffon material was talking to a man on the sidewalk as she began bolting the doors of her establishment. 'That, amigo, is Las Noches Árabes.'

Mallory turned to Savage. 'Give me ten minutes to see what I can find out.'

She looked uncertain. 'Do you think that's wise?'

He shrugged. 'Probably not. But nothing ventured and all that. You go with Mario. If I don't join you in half an hour, go on without me.'

His friend said: 'I will wake up the man who owns the mules. He is an old friend and knows how to keep his mouth shut. We'll wait for you on the edge of town, just beyond the last house.'

'I really don't think you should, Kurt,' Savage said. But she could already see that Mallory's mind was made up.

He said: 'Vic was my friend, remember. You're not the only one who wants to know what happened. Now, go on ahead before the woman closes up and we lose our chance.'

While Savage reluctantly walked on with Mario, Mallory hung back in the shadows for a couple of minutes before sauntering across the road and onto the sidewalk.

He approached as the man said his farewell and walked off into the night.

'Are you closing up?' Mallory asked.

Her bulging thyroid eyes were set like gobstoppers in the plump round face; they were accentuated by bright blue eye shadow and thickly drawn liner. She squinted to get a better view of him as he stepped into the light from the window. After regarding him for a moment, she removed the cheroot from her small cupid's bow of a mouth. 'We only close when the last customer goes home, señor. You want a girl?'

Her tone was neutral, not quite wary and not quite welcoming, Mallory thought, noting how her scarlet lipstick had bled into the tiny pucker lines around her mouth. 'I want a drink.' He grinned. 'And maybe a girl.'

She understood; he didn't want to commit himself until he'd

seen the goods. 'Come in,' she invited, tossing away the butt of her *pucho*.

'Business quiet?' he asked conversationally as he followed her inside.

It was dimly lit with pools of light cast from red-shaded wall lamps. All he could see in the gloom were a few plum-velour chairs and a lot of gilt-painted woodwork. Someone's idea of a romantic environment in fact just looked cheap and tacky. The place smelled of *basuko*, hash and cheap scent. 'We've seen better nights,' the woman admitted as she moved behind the small bar. More plum velour and gilt. 'What d'you want?'

'A cold beer.'

The false lashes flickered. 'Last of the big spenders, eh?' He sensed she was amused; maybe she liked the look of him. Taking a can of Polar from the refrigerator, she placed it on the bar. 'Some of my girls are still here. We like money up front and no violence. If you've any hardwear, leave it behind the bar and collect it on your way out.'

With his eyes adjusting to the gloom he could now see the three *putas* seated in an alcove. Not bad, he thought, youngish and pretty and bored, one filing her nails, another flicking through a dog-eared fashion magazine, the third day-dreaming while she smoked and sipped at a strangely coloured cocktail. Each wore the usual hooker's uniform in these parts: uplift brassière beneath a blouse knotted below the bust and neon Spandex pants in garish colours which squeezed up a thin roll of fat around the bare midriff.

He replied absently in answer to the woman's question: 'I don't carry.'

She chuckled mirthlessly. 'Then you haven't been here long. Everyone carries. Are you looking for work?'

'No, and I'm not looking for trouble. I'm just looking for a friend who's gone missing.'

Her eyes narrowed shrewdly. 'That could *be* trouble around here. Does your friend have a name?'

'Vic West. A gringo. He had a meeting in this joint ten days ago.'

She hid it well, but Mallory detected the interest in her eyes as she said: 'I'm afraid the name means nothing to me.' She hesitated, curiosity getting the better of her. 'But are you *really* a friend of this gringo?' She was clearly sceptical.

'We work for the same company. It's my job to find out what's become of him. If there's been an accident, the insurance company will need the details – and the widow and his kids will need the payout.'

'Forgive me, but you do not look like a businessman.' The words died on her lips. 'But then maybe you know your job.'

He nodded slowly as though to confirm her thoughts. 'Is there somewhere we could talk in private, Doña—?'

'Doña Lacera,' she replied, now watching him very closely as though trying to decide how much she could trust this stranger. 'Fanny Lacera to our customers.'

Mallory grinned at that. 'A name with a fine tradition in your business.'

She laughed aloud, a light and not unpleasant sound for a woman of her size. 'Follow me,' she said, shifting her buttocks from the stool behind the bar and brushing aside a curtain of wooden beads. It was dark and cool in the office, the air churned by an electric desk fan. As he entered after her, she asked casually: 'And what company do you work for?'

'Portcullis. My name's Harry Pike.'

For a long moment she studied his face in silence before she reached for a pack of cheroots on the desktop and plucked out one of its contents with chipped lilac nails. 'You obviously know your way around, Señor Pike, but I would advise you not to ask questions here about this friend of yours. If he is missing, it is because someone didn't like him or what he was doing.'

'So you do remember him?'

She shook her head. 'All you men look the same to me and my girls.' With a puckered little smile she added: 'But they might remember a prick more than a guy's face.'

Mallory took a roll of dollar bills from the pocket of his canvas jacket and tossed it on the desk. A hundred, perhaps a hundred and fifty. 'Will that help your memory?'

Fanny Lacera looked at it. 'Is that all my life is worth?' She lit her cheroot.

Mallory had seen the ornamental bolas hanging on the wall. Without saying anything, he reached for the weighted thongs that were thrown at the legs of cattle by gaucho cowboys to bring the animals down. He flexed and stretched the fibre strip between his fists just inches in front of her face.

He saw the fear in her eyes then, as she realised what he was about to do. She swallowed hard, her fleshy white chins quivering, her gaze fixing his as her hand slowly reached towards the small tit of the panic-button just below the desktop.

The speed of his movement was like that of a mountain cat, swinging between her huge body and the desk, brushing away her fingers and sweeping around behind her, drawing the bolas thong tight around her throat.

A gurgle escaped her mouth as the fibre disappeared into the folds of soft flesh and her hands instinctively came up to release the pressure. A thin string of dribble escaped her lips. The cheroot dropped from her fingers.

Mallory hissed in her ear. 'Silver or lead, lady, which is it to be? You know the rules.'

She forced her hands away from her throat, opening her palms in a gesture of surrender, and Mallory relaxed his grip. Taking her by the shoulders, he turned her round and sat her firmly in the chair.

'Right, now talk,' he demanded.

Fanny Lacera glared at him and rubbed the red weal around her neck. 'Your friend was in here – I suppose about ten days ago. He had a meeting with a girl and hired one of my rooms for a couple of hours.'

'Which *puta* was it?'

'Not one of *my* girls, Señor Pike. She was not a whore, but she dressed like one. It was all a cover. You know, in case anyone was watching.'

'Who was she?'

Her fingers were still massaging her neck. 'You really are from Portcullis?'

'I promise you.'

She now appeared resigned to her fate. 'The woman calls herself Palechor. Maria Palechor.'

'Colombian?'

'From Cali.'

'Do you know how I can get in touch with her?'

Fanny Lacera considered for a moment, then reached for the drawer of her desk, careful to keep her hands well clear of the panic-button. She produced a small wad of business cards held with an elastic band and flicked through them. 'It might be genuine.'

Mallory took the card. 'A lawyer?'

'That's what it says.' She looked up at him and he saw that there were tears in her eyes. 'I just hope you really are from Portcullis. If not I will be killed for giving you this.'

'By the Viper gang?'

She looked at him strangely. 'No, they'd kill me anyway if they knew I was talking to a friend of Señor West. I mean by Maria Palechor's friends in Cali if you are *not* what you say you are.'

He gave a half-smile of reassurance. 'Well, I am. And I'm sorry about the rough stuff.'

Fanny Lacera looked as though she appreciated the apology. 'You have lodgings here in Casuarito?'

He pocketed the card. 'For tonight. In the morning I'll get the ferry and catch the first plane out of your life.'

And he could tell by the look in her eyes that his departure couldn't come a moment too soon.

The early morning sun finally cleared the garden wall of Mario Dubois's bungalow villa and lit the tiny patio where his brother-in-law Julio Mela sat nervously smoking yet another *basuko* cigarette.

He glanced sideways at the man he knew only as Carlos. The local leader of the Vipers was a thin man with hunched shoulders who habitually wore a string vest beneath his open-fronted shirt. His gaunt face with its straggly moustache was a picture of grim concentration as he leaned against the wooden upright of the awning, cleaning his fingernails with the point of a switchblade knife. Two other gang members sat sprawled on patio chairs, bored.

They both turned their heads at the sound of the pick-up as it drove into the street at speed and pulled up outside.

Carlos snapped closed his switchblade and pocketed it, looking up as José and the others entered. Among them was *El Gringo*, the tall Englishman whom the Vipers addressed as Señor Guy. None of them looked pleased.

'There's no sign of them,' José reported solemnly. 'We've checked the airport and all the roadblocks. They've vanished into thin air.'

'Hiding up,' Carlos decided, then directed his expressionless gaze at Julio Mela. 'You are playing a dangerous game.'

Julio stubbed out his *basuko* with trembling fingers, burning them in the process. 'Honest to God, I don't know what's happened. Mario told me to meet him here – why should I lie to you?'

The lids of the leader's eyes hooded as though he were tired, even half-asleep. Julio knew that expression all too well and was anticipating the words when they came. 'You would lie to me because he is your brother-in-law. You contact me to throw us off the scent – to send us looking in the wrong direction.'

'No, no!' Julio protested. 'Honest! I would never do such a thing.'

Carlos appeared not to hear the protest. 'So you have a simple choice. Tell me where Mario Dubois and the gringos are, either the hard way or the easy way.'

The young man was visibly shaking now, his eyes wide with dread of what was to come. 'Believe me, please! I would *never* lie to you! I do not know where Mario is, I swear by the Sacred Virgin!'

The leader glanced across at *El Gringo* for confirmation. Julio could not see the expression of the man's angular features because of the shadow cast by the wide brim of his stetson hat. He found that unnerving; even more so when the Englishman gave a slow nod of agreement. Carlos turned to José.

'Get Dubois's woman and child out here,' he ordered in a low voice.

Julio heard the words and sprang to his feet as José disappeared inside. 'No, no! Look, I have coke! The parcel that I paid your tax on last night. You can have it, all of it! LOOK! Look, see!' Then he was on his hands and knees, crawling along the garden path to seek the flagstone under which he kept his treasure. Splitting his nails in his eagerness to lift the heavy weight, he then held the package of cocaine aloft. 'See, see, it is all yours. Take it!'

At that moment José reappeared at the French windows. Luz was by his side, her hair tousled and her sleep-filled eyes squinting against the morning light as she held the baby in her arms. 'Julio! Please tell me what is happening? Where is Mario?'

'Exactly what we want to know,' Carlos said.

Julio was still on his knees, offering up his precious package. Now tears were trickling down his face. 'I DON'T KNOW!' he screamed.

El Gringo caught Carlos's eye and inclined his head just a fraction. Then the Englishman turned away, real slow, and walked a couple of paces. Julio watched him, wondering where he was going. Noticed the figure nine tattooed three times on the knuckles of his right hand. Was surprised when the man suddenly stopped and turned back. Was shocked when he saw the pocket-sized black Ingram that had apparently materialised from nowhere.

The violent noise made him jump and the package of cocaine fell from his hands as the sound shattered the tranquillity of the garden. His mouth dropped open as he saw the half-magazine emptying into his sister's chest and belly, the force of fire tearing the baby from her arms. Blood and gobs of flesh filled the air instantly in a fine mist like sea spume.

'NNOOOO!' The cry was wrenched from his throat, high-pitched and involuntary. It merged with the stammer of gunfire to reverberate around the garden walls, echoing back and forth in mockery of his pleading. At last the hideous noise ebbed away to a stunning and absolute silence. Even the birds had stopped singing.

Julio was transfixed, cemented to the flagstone path in terror and disbelief. He was paralysed, numbed, tears welling in his eyes and dripping down his cheeks onto his little cocaine package.

Carlos's voice was hardly raised above a whisper. His words sounded almost sympathetic. 'Now, will you tell me?'

'I don't know.' His mouth said slowly, but nothing was audible.

José smiled, seeing the joke. 'I think he means it.'

'Shit,' Carlos said, then turned to *El Gringo*. 'What shall I do with him?'

'Whatever you like,' the Englishman replied. 'We've wasted enough time here. C'mon the rest of you, we've got to find those people.'

The gang members followed him out into the street, leaving Carlos behind.

Moments later they heard a single shot.

In some eighteen hours' time the piranhas of the Orinoco would be enjoying yet another midnight feast.

Maria Palechor hardly seemed to be driving at all. She relaxed in the plush leather seat with one hand languidly on the wheel and the other on the arm rest, allowing the automatic Mercedes coupé to do all the work.

Sitting beside the lawyer, hidden behind the dark-tinted windows, Mallory was trying to regulate his breathing, to quell his rising anxiety and thudding heartbeat. The unfamiliar restraint of a tie didn't help. Silk or not, it felt suffocating. He was thankful for the ice-cool air conditioning; it dried the perspiration beneath his expensive jacket as they drove through the streets of Cali to their appointment with the *capo*.

'I wasn't sure about you at first,' Maria Palechor confessed. 'I had our associate law firm in London check you out with Colonel Maidment at Portcullis. It seems he's known you for a long time, Señor Pike.'

She had striking good looks, he thought. Dark eyes and high cheekbones, her long wavy hair dyed to a deep chestnut brown. And he found her tanned legs distracting, the tight skirt of her

91

charcoal business suit rising high across her thighs as her foot tickled the accelerator in an absent sort of way.

He said: '*I've* known Señor West even longer.'

Her smile was easy, her teeth very white and her English perfect. 'So I understand. It is only because Señor West is such a good and trusted friend of Señor Jaramillo that he agrees to meet with you.'

'I'm most grateful,' Mallory murmured. There was no point in saying more. He had already asked Maria why she had met West at Las Noches Árabes bordello in Casuarito and what they had discussed. With practised charm she had replied that it would be Señor Jaramillo and only he who could decide how much should be told.

Mallory lay back against the headrest and tried his best to relax.

Ruiz Edilberto Maya Jaramillo was known amongst his intimates as Ruiz Jaramillo, unusually adopting his mother's family name rather than his father's. According to Savage's intelligence sources, Ruiz had hated his father, Jorge Maya, who had been one of Colombia's earliest drugs barons. Bar gossip said old man Maya had been a drunkard and a wife-beater before he had been mysteriously shot to death by unknown gunmen.

It didn't take a tremendous leap of the imagination to assume that the killers were acting on the orders of the man's son, Ruiz Jaramillo. Nicknamed *El Matador*, after his reputation as a man of courage, ruthlessness and honour among his fellow *narcotraficantes*.

Neither the DEA nor other intelligence agencies were quite sure where or how he fitted into the so-called Cali drugs cartel – only that, somehow, he did. Jaramillo was distantly related by marriage to the Orjuela Caballero family who were cousins of the Rodriguez Orejuela family, recognised as the major players in the Cali organisation, along with the Santacruz family.

Jaramillo was distant enough to be able to claim no connection with the drugs business, yet for all anyone knew, he could in fact have been near the very top. And that was what the DEA, SIS and the Investigations Division of HM Customs and Excise in

London all suspected.

Mallory had learned all this since the horrendous three-day mule trek from Casuarito two weeks earlier. He and Georgina Savage had been led expertly by Mario along the steaming jungle trails of the man's emerald-smuggling route until they were able to hitch a lift by truck on the rough Puerto Carreño road. It was then to take another two days' travelling before they finally reached the capital Bogotá and made contact with the British Embassy there.

They now knew that Vic West had arranged a meeting in Casuarito with a lawyer called Maria Palechor. It took just two phone calls to establish that the high-powered company she worked for was often hired by suspected members of the Cali organisation.

Georgina Savage had then persuaded Mallory to go along with her plan to make direct contact with Palechor, claiming to work for Portcullis. There was nothing to be lost, Savage believed; he would either meet a brick wall or have the chance to renew whatever deal Vic West might have been developing.

In London, Colonel Maidment had readily agreed to the deception and falsified the existence on paper of Mr Harry Pike in readiness for the inevitable investigation by the Cali organisation. All was in place when Mallory telephoned Señora Palechor. Her reaction was guarded, but not unfriendly. An appointment was quickly made for a meeting at her office. She listened as he told her of his search for a colleague who had gone missing after having met her in Casuarito, a fact that, incidentally, she neither confirmed nor denied. Finally she asked him to book into Cali's luxurious Intercontinental hotel on Avenida Colombia by the riverside and wait to be contacted.

That had been five days earlier. Her call had come unexpectedly that morning, just as he'd finished breakfast. She arranged to pick him up by car at noon.

Now, as the car glided through the leafy city garden suburb, with its magnificent villas hiding behind high walls, Mallory realised that two motorcyclists had fallen into line behind them.

Maria Palechor noticed his uneasiness. 'It's quite all right,

Señor Pike, they are working for my client. They have been keeping watch since I left my office to ensure we are not followed. Please rest assured.'

Only then Mallory realised that he had become as tense as a coiled spring. Colombia was one of the most dangerous and unpredictable countries in the world, and to get yourself mixed up with the *narcotraficantes* was to put your head in a lion's mouth. The actions of rival *narcos*, police, army, the DEA or any number of covert organisations could so easily put you in the wrong place at the wrong time. And most were renowned for shooting first and asking questions later.

So it was with considerable relief that he realised they were turning off to a large hillside villa which looked down on the city's surrounding sugar-cane fields. As they neared the perimeter wall of strawberry pink stucco topped with terracotta roof tiles, the electronic security gates slid open to admit them. Clearly the armed guard had viewed their approach from a closed-circuit television screen in his concrete pillbox and had checked the registration number of the lawyer's car before pressing the button.

The ease of their entry was altogether uncanny; too slick and too smooth, it added to the air of deadly efficiency and hidden menace for which the Cali organisation was renowned. Their self-confidence was in itself chilling when Mallory reminded himself that every major law enforcement agency in the Western world was ranged against them. Yet they had no doubt that they were the ones in control.

Gravel crackled beneath the tyres as the Mercedes came to a standstill beside the marble-columned portico. He stepped out of the car and barely had a chance to take in the sweep of architectural splendour, the balustraded balconies and candy-coloured sun canopies, before a young woman emerged from the villa.

'This is Señor Pike,' Maria Palechor announced, removing her sunglasses.

The young woman, dressed in a floral summer frock, smiled broadly and gave an unconscious toss of her dark hair. 'My father very much looks forward to meeting you, señor,' she said in excellent English and offered a delicate hand in greeting. No more than nineteen, Mallory guessed. 'Would you both care to come this way?'

They were swallowed up by the delicious cool of the interior, Maria's high heels cracking on the black marble floor, the sound echoing through the spacious rooms on either side of an enormous hallway. Huge and sombre Renaissance oils hung in heavy gilt frames and classic bronze statues and antique Spanish furniture decorated the rooms they passed. The place resembled a museum rather than a home, Mallory decided. He was just wondering how many priceless masterpieces were secreted within the villa's walls when they stepped outside again into the glare of the midday sun.

'Papa, Señora Palechor and Señor Pike to see you!' the girl called out.

Mallory squinted against the bright refraction on the surface of the swimming pool as the big man propelled himself forward with powerful butterfly strokes. Large hands grasped the marble edge and, with one massive effort, the great muscular shoulders shot him clear of the water. The arms locked at the elbows to lift the body upright while the *capo* lifted one leg to gain a foothold on the side. As the torrent of drips fell from the mass of curly black hair on his back and shoulders, Mallory was momentarily reminded of an enormous walrus.

But Ruiz Jaramillo had overestimated his strength. For a second he balanced precariously on the edge, with just insufficient muscle power to lift his second knee clear and roll onto the terrace. The swarthy plump face, with its round rubber swimming goggles and large sodden moustache, looked beseechingly at Mallory. He began to waver, his right hand reaching out for help.

Instinctively Mallory reacted to save the man from toppling backwards. Then, as their fingertips almost touched, he hesitated. For a moment his eyes locked with the blank blue lenses staring back at him and he was filled with an overwhelming urge to let the man fall. To humiliate him in front of his daughter and his lawyer and the two bulky bodyguards who sat at nearby tables.

'*Por favor, señor?*' There was no demand and no pleading in

95

Jaramillo's husky voice.

Mallory relented, and grasped the hand.

The Colombian hauled himself clear and stood bent for a moment with his palms clasped to his knees as he regained his breath. When he straightened his back, Mallory saw that he was not quite as large as the impression he created. In fact, Jaramillo stood a couple of inches below Mallory's own six foot, although his chunky build and wide shoulders added to his stature. There was no doubt real muscle lay beneath the veneer of fat that hung over the waist of his gaudy swimming shorts.

He ripped off his goggles and grinned. 'Fifty lengths,' he announced proudly in English.

His daughter looked dubious. 'You do too much, Papa.'

Jaramillo's laugh was like a lion's roar. 'Nonsense! One length for each year, that's my motto for eternal youth.' He ran a hand through his sparse curly hair, shaking off the surplus water, and looked directly at Mallory. 'You should try it, Señor Pike. It is Señor Pike, isn't it? Like the fish. You look exactly like your photograph.' What photograph, Mallory wondered? He hadn't been aware of one being taken since his arrival in Cali, but then that was only to be expected. Before he could reply, Jaramillo was padding across the terrace, accepting the towel that Maria Palechor held out for him. 'When I am sixty, I will be doing sixty lengths.' He kissed the lawyer on the cheek before draping the towel over his shoulders. 'And eighty lengths when I am eighty,' he continued. 'It is what my doctor recommends.'

A half-smile played at Mallory's lips. 'Had you considered,' he asked slowly, 'that perhaps someone is paying your doctor to kill you?'

There was a momentary hardening of the moist brown eyes and an almost imperceptible tightening of the lips. Then suddenly the moment of tension was past, displaced by a deep, chuckling laugh. 'Very funny, amigo! I like your sense of humour – as black as my own. Only I think you make the same mistake that many people make, both abroad and here in Colombia.'

'And what is that?'

Jaramillo didn't answer the question immediately. Instead he beckoned to the lawyer. 'Come and join us for a drink, Maria.'

He led the way to a table that was out of earshot of his body-guards. Drink bottles and glasses were set out in the shade of a parasol. 'Your usual *Ron Blanco?*'

She laughed and raised her hand. 'It's much too early, Ruiz, just a pineapple juice for me.'

He poured it from one of a selection of glass jugs. 'And Señor Pike?'

Mallory drank rarely and little; he knew the dangers of alcohol in his game. 'Just a beer.'

'You see, Señor Pike, you joke that there may be someone who would like to see me dead,' he said conversationally as he handed Mallory a chilled can of Poker and poured a white rum and Chilean wine for himself. 'That is because you believe all the newspaper tittle-tattle that I am some *narco* big shot, a kingpin. No, I am not offended – I can expect nothing else when these malicious rumours are so widespread. But it is *not* something that Señor West believes. That is one reason why we get on so well.' Jaramillo flopped into one of the padded patio chairs and invited his guests to do the same. 'Because I am wealthy and live in this city, everyone assumes I am a drugs baron. It is not true. But, remember, I grow up in this city. I go to school with boys who have since become big *traficantes*, I know their families – some are even related to me. To live in this city is to live amongst such people and so one gets labelled.'

Mallory took a swig from the can. 'But you are not one of them?'

A shake of the head, the wet hair fast drying into pepper-and-salt ringlets. 'Certainly not. But some of these people are my friends.'

Maria Palechor interrupted. 'Señor Jaramillo's family wealth derives from generations of farming in the Cauca valley. Cotton, tobacco and coffee. In recent years he has expanded into light engineering, into hotels and the car franchise business. All fully legitimate.'

The *capo* raised his hands. 'But then ask yourself *who* stays at my hotels and *who* buys my cars. As this is a poor country, many of them are obviously people who make their money from *las drogas*. And so the DEA gringos kid themselves I am one of them. Sure, it is drug money, but how can I help that?'

Mallory resisted a sardonic smile. Such a plea of innocence could well be true, but he didn't believe it for a moment. No doubt Vic West too went along with the charade. 'I gather the two of you might have had a deal going?'

'Your company – what is it, Portcullis? – was not informed?'

'We have found nothing in writing since he went missing, but then Vic was very discreet. You have done business before?'

Jaramillo nodded. 'Several times in the past five years. But you must know this.'

'Such information would never reach board level. At least not officially, and *never* in writing. Señor West would have named a third party, an intermediary, so that neither you nor our company would be embarrassed by direct association. As you've said, people like the DEA are quick to jump to conclusions.'

The Colombian nodded his understanding. 'And now you'd like to complete the deal that he and I discussed?'

'Of course, if it's possible, and profitable. Ours is a very competitive business. You were talking arms presumably?'

Jaramillo hesitated. To admit that was not going to sit easily with his declaration of innocence a couple of moments earlier. 'How well do you understand South American politics, especially here in Colombia?'

'Try me.'

'All right, amigo. You probably know that since the cocaine trade began to be big business in the seventies, there have been what the press like to call two rival cartels based on families in Medellín and here in Cali. Of course the word cartel is a fiction. It is a question of separate families working both by themselves and sometimes together on export projects when it suited them. It is convenient for journalists to lump them together like a single mafioso.' He waved aside his own pedantic point as irrelevant. 'As the world knows, Pablo Escobar became the best known of the Medellín *narcos* – a common *campesino* like the rest of that organisation. A thug who got ideas above his station. Money and power went to his head. He began murdering politicians and judges in an attempt to take control of the country. During his campaign of terror he succeeded in focusing unwanted world attention on our country and its problems. And, of course, the coca business in particular.

'That was not something which my friends here in this city appreciated. It is common for us to be called 'the gentlemen of Cali'. However much some may disapprove of the cocaine trade, you must accept that the Cali families believe in quiet commercial enterprise, law and order. They have friends in the government, the judiciary and the police. And my friends did not hesitate to help bring about Pablo Escobar's downfall.'

'As you will know,' Maria Palechor added, 'Escobar was arrested after a massive police hunt and negotiated a luxury prison for himself. Finally he decided to escape and died during a shoot-out with police.'

Jaramillo picked up the story again. 'During that period the Medellín organisation went into meltdown. With its leader out of circulation the families feuded and fragmented. My friends here in Cali were able to step in and fill the vacuum. Peace and stability returned to my country.'

Mallory tried to guess what was coming next, tried to place where the pure White Viper brand of cocaine fitted into the picture. 'But not for long?'

The Colombian leaned back in his chair, clutching his drink in his lap, and stared across the patio. His daughter had changed into a bikini and was poised at the pool side. She dived, creating a sharp explosion of water. 'My friends began to notice things about a year ago. Suddenly there seemed to be a lot of very pure cocaine on the streets. No one knew where it came from, or who was behind it. The stuff was called White Viper – the packets were always stamped with a little snake symbol. It affected the domestic market here first. The street dealers wanted it and so did the users, because it was good stuff. They could dilute it and sell a little on as it was the same price as regular coca.'

Mallory observed drily: 'People always like a bargain.'

Jaramillo's eyes glittered momentarily with disapproval. 'But my friends did not appreciate it, Señor Pike. It upset the status quo. Sales of their regular product dropped and a bit of trouble started.'

'Meaning?'

Maria explained. 'Some dealers started counterfeiting the White Viper logo – not difficult, it's pretty crude. They'd try to pass off their own low-grade stuff. There were some double-crosses and shoot-outs. It attracted the attention of the police and the DEA.'

'That irritated my friends,' Jaramillo said, 'but did not worry them unduly. Coca is used only at home to supplement wages. You know, pay a man in pesos and a little angel dust, you understand? But then some of the big buyers in Miami and Madrid started to pull out of deals, some of them very big. Said they'd found alternative suppliers.'

'The White Viper people?' Mallory guessed.

Jaramillo sniffed heavily. As he became engrossed, he lapsed into Spanish. 'They ran a tight ship, security wise. No one wanted to talk. These people soon let it be known what happened to anyone who blabbed too much. They would not shrink from killing not just a man who talked, but also his wife or other members of his family. It was Escobar's old style. But you cannot keep such a large operation secret. My friends investigated and began to trace the source. The heart of their operation is deep in the Páramo de Carcasi in the foothills of the Andes. It is a wild and remote region in the northeast of our country, not far from the border with Venezuela. A land of wild rivers and rugged mountains.'

Cuchillas was the actual word Jaramillo used. The Spanish for 'blades' that so chillingly caught the unforgiving nature of such places. Even as the Colombian spoke, Mallory detected the note of awe in his voice.

The Englishman said: 'If you have located their operation, I cannot believe you haven't done something about it.' Despite Jaramillo's depiction of his Cali friends as the gentlemen of the cocaine trade, Mallory was fully aware that they were just as capable of violence and mayhem as their old rivals from

Medellín, especially the younger generation of *traquetos*. They just didn't shout about it, that was all.

'There is a problem, señor,' Maria Palechor interrupted demurely as though discussing some inaccuracy in a recipe. 'That countryside is held by left-wing *guerrilleros* of the ELN. The *Ejército de Liberación Nacional*. Traditionally these revolutionaries have been at least part-allies with the Medellín organisation. Even the police and army venture there at their peril. To destroy this base, the Cali organisation would need to field an army of their own with armoured cars and aircraft if they were to succeed—'

'That is, if conventional means were used,' Jaramillo interjected.

'Is this what you were talking to Señor West about?' Mallory asked.

The Colombian nodded. 'Victor West knew about such things. Covert operations with specialists. You know, commando types who could infiltrate this White Viper operation and discover all about it. Its supply lines, its methods of operation, its key figures and, of course, its ultimate customers. And then, of course, destroy it.'

Maria Palechor's eyes were wide with interest. 'This is something your Portcullis company could achieve for us?'

Mallory considered for a moment. 'Officially, Portcullis wouldn't touch such an operation. But it will know people who would.'

Jaramillo said: 'We have had British, Israeli and South African experts hired through Señor West before – to train our people in bodyguarding, sabotage and many other special techniques. They have always proved reliable, if expensive.'

'The best always is,' Mallory replied. 'But I must have more of an idea who we would be up against. How much do you know about these White Viper people?'

'We fear they are a faction of the old Medellín organisation,' Maria Palechor replied. 'It is an area with a long history of association with Escobar and his family. Geographically it is parallel with the city and far closer than we are here in the south. My company has investigated and finds that Medellín families own considerable land and properties in the region. In particular there are old emerald mines in the *cuchillas* owned by companies once associated with Pablo Escobar and other kingpins. We believe it is one of these which is their headquarters.'

'There is one more thing you should know,' Jaramillo said. 'Something that intrigued Victor West as much as it intrigued me. The place is guarded by English gringos. Amazing, is it not? Why should that be? I cannot think. The thugs of Medellín only trust their own and I don't know why they should have need of such people.'

Mallory stared at him. Was this a wind-up? In Venezuela Julio had mentioned the presence of a mysterious Englishman, but this was different. It almost suggested a British gang operating in Colombia. Surely unthinkable? But no, Jaramillo appeared to be in deadly earnest.

'That is why I met with Señor West in Casuarito,' Maria Palechor offered suddenly. 'We could not take him into the *cuchillas* – that would have been impossible. But this gang, which they call the Vipers, also have a strong presence in Casuarito and across the river in Puerto Ayacucho. He wanted to see these people for himself, to gauge what he would be up against. You met with Doña Fanny Lacera at Las Noches Árabes – she works for us. A spy, if you like. The families here in Cali set up the bordello as a way of collecting information on these people. Fanny thought it would be safe enough for Señor West to go there.'

But she was wrong, Mallory thought angrily. Terribly fucking wrong.

'And in the meantime,' Maria Palechor was saying, 'you continue your search for our dear friend Señor West?'

Mallory smiled grimly. 'I'm afraid so.'

She returned his smile. 'Then perhaps I can help you. He was murdered in Venezuela nearly three weeks ago. It is very strange you do not know this. A breakdown in communications perhaps? You see, his body was flown back to Britain in a private aircraft owned by Portcullis. In fact Colonel Maidment himself made the arrangements.'

Christ, Mallory thought, and felt the trickle of fear like ice water running down his spine.

Ruiz Jaramillo began chuckling at the expression on the Englishman's face. 'If we are to do business together, Señor Pike, then I suggest we are a little more honest with each other in future. Do not take us for fools and do not underestimate us.'

Mallory's smile was half-hearted; there was really nothing he could say.

'Although it is impossible for us to confirm, our best information is that Señor West was followed by the Vipers when he left Puerto Ayacucho. Something must have aroused suspicions. Maybe someone recognised him – he knew many people. And they kill him – just to be sure. It happens all the time.' He paused and gave a tight, sympathetic smile. 'And do you think you know exactly what Señor West would have had in mind to help my friends here in Cali?'

'I've no doubt.'

And he didn't. Vic West had made immediate arrangements to see Oliver Maidment and Portcullis's chairman and chief executive had flown to South America on the first available flight.

His old friend would have known this was going to be a top-secret and totally deniable operation. A job for the organisation that had no name.

And Vic West would have known that there was only one person qualified for such a dangerous assignment. Kurt Mallory.

5

Mario Dubois was a broken man when they met at the back-street café in Bogotá. 'They butchered my Luz and my son. Blasted them away – just like that! Can you believe it?' His shaggy head shook from side to side, still scarcely able to absorb the news he had heard when making a phone call to a friend in Puerto Ayacucho. The unconfirmed rumours slushing around the town's bars – that the murders had been carried out by *El Gringo* himself, the man with the three nines tattoo – and that there was now a price on Mario's head too. He should not return.

Mallory had never seen his friend cry, would not have believed that anything could have reduced the tough and amiable rogue to such a state of despair.

No words, he knew, would console the man. Yet something had to be said. 'They'll pay the price, amigo, I promise you that. They are the same people who killed Vic West.'

The big Martinican sniffed heavily and rubbed his forearm roughly across his moustache. His composure had returned, but the dark saucer eyes were still moist. 'If you are going after them, Kurt, then count me in. That is the only promise I want from you.'

Their eyes had locked across the table strewn with empty *tinto* coffee cups. 'I promise.'

That conversation had haunted Mallory throughout the seven days since his return to the croft in western Ireland. Try as he might, he couldn't shake the picture of his friend from his mind, the inconsolable sobbing. A big man with an even bigger heart, broken, his hopes for a simple and happy future shattered in a vicious blood bath. An act that had no other purpose than revenge and intimidation. Well, two could play at that game.

The weather had improved with the onset of early summer and Mallory had taken out the lobster boat with old Mattie. The beauty of the cold green sea and the hard physical work had distracted him for a time. But he knew it would not be long before the call came and, until it did, he knew his spirit would be restless.

Word had spread that he was home and on the third day Kelly O'More had called to see him. Every day since, they had taken the horses out together, galloping hard along the rugged shoreline.

Today had been particularly enjoyable, but she had detected his continuing preoccupation.

'What is it, Kurt?' she asked as they were unsaddling the horses and rubbing them down. 'What happened while you were away?'

He turned to look at her, the riding boots and snug fit of the jodhpurs emphasising her height and the baggy sweater failing to conceal her slim, athletic build. The wind had tousled her long copper hair into a nightmare tangle of curls and had made her mascara run.

'An old friend of mine was murdered.'

Her green eyes were bright with concern. 'Where? In South America? Why?'

Mallory shrugged. 'For knowing too much, for knowing the wrong people. That would be reason enough.'

'So who did it?'

'Villains. A bad lot.'

Kelly knew him well enough to know that he wouldn't talk about it. Even if he wanted to. Certainly no details. 'Christ, Kurt, do you have to get involved with those sorts of people?' Her head shook with disapproval. 'And Georgie promised me she wouldn't ask you to do anything dangerous.'

'She wasn't to know the risks. Neither did I really, until we arrived there. We were trying to find out who killed my friend and why.'

Now she understood. 'So your friend was murdered *before* you went out?'

'That's what George came to tell me that time. That and to ask my help.'

'And did you find out?'

He nodded. 'But at a terrible price.'

She sensed that there was more to come, that there was another deeper reason for his black mood. 'Tell me about it.' She touched his arm, tentatively. 'If it would help.'

Her face was only inches from his as he looked into her eyes. He thought, not for the first time, how beautiful they were and wondered why he was allowing her to slip away through his fingers? Just like all the others. He knew what she wanted, what she needed. Knew what he had to say and do to keep her, yet somehow he couldn't bring himself to say and do those things. Was it that he was incapable of showing his emotions, or just that he didn't have any? Maybe it was partly South American machismo, a legacy from his childhood. Or some primeval need for personal freedom that he was afraid to put at risk. Was it that he didn't trust commitment, couldn't believe in it? Or was it a mistrust of all women, of even this exquisite and intelligent creature looking at him with misty green eyes, offering to share his pain. Eager for him to open his soul to her, however black it might turn out to be.

The intensity of her expression touched him. Perhaps she was right, he needed to tell someone what had happened. He said: 'I looked up another old friend over there and asked for his help. It was a mistake. As an indirect result his girlfriend and his son got killed. Murdered. Shot by gunmen.'

'God, Kurt, that's awful.'

'I shouldn't have involved him.'

She was close now, her hand on his shoulder. 'Surely you weren't to know. Don't blame yourself, it wasn't you who pulled the trigger.'

He sighed. 'But that's not how it feels.'

She understood what he meant and was touched by his intimate admission. People who didn't know him would probably swear that only ice water ran through Mallory's veins. Maybe, perversely, that was what had first attracted her to him. Yet it was

106

those rare insights into his humanity, those glimpses of what lay beneath that steely veneer that had really drawn her closer over the years.

Her voice was hoarse as she said: 'Would you like me to stay over tonight? I could make the fish stew – your favourite.'

He was warmed by her smile. 'And what about *El torro rabioso*?'

She screwed up her face in an expression of mock anger, amused that Mallory always referred to her new lawyer boyfriend from Madrid as 'the raging bull'. 'Miguel doesn't arrive until tomorrow. So you'd best make the most of me while you can – before he whisks me away to marry him.'

'You mean he's asked you?'

'No, but I'm working on it.'

And her laugh set the tone for the evening which followed. Much joking and banter and music as she strummed Irish folk ballads and rebel songs on the old Spanish guitar he kept on the wall, but had never himself learned to play. They were cocooned in a quiet and private world, lit only by the smouldering turf fire with dancing shadows on the bare croft walls and the air sweet with peat smoke, while outside a storm blew up unexpectedly, fierce winds and rain sweeping in from the Atlantic and rattling at the small windows set in the thick stone walls.

They made love at midnight, or thereabouts. On the old sheepskin rug by the hearth. It was lingering, unhurried. They had nothing to prove to each other, no carnal secrets and no anxieties. Any lust seemed tempered by an unspoken desire to prolong the sensual pleasure of it all. Although she loathed to dwell on it, it occurred to her that perhaps a lifetime of stolen pleasure with whores and hookers around the world had taught him quite a lot.

That night he seemed unusually gentle and caring. She felt a shiver of pleasure to think that there was really no earthly reason why the rest of her life couldn't be like this. Languishing in his arms. Could be, she thought dreamily, if only the man were someone other than Kurt Mallory.

Then she was asleep, cradled against his shoulder as he lay motionless, staring at the dark ceiling beams. For an hour or two she had transported him, taken the burden from him and lifted his spirits. But now she was asleep and sure enough the demons were crowding in again out of the shadows. The faces of those he had killed taking shape in the flickering flame of the fire. And those who had wanted to kill him, all laughing and taunting him. Somehow the devil never seemed to give up the souls of his own.

Quietly he slid away from her, covered her long and glistening body with a rough blanket and threw more turfs on the fire. Then he pulled on his jeans and sat by the hearth, his naked upper body warmed by the glow. He broke his own rules and poured another slug of Bushmills into the tumbler and lit a cigarette. Still he couldn't quite break the habit. Silly really, when you only had one lung.

The wind gusted suddenly, shaking the bolts of the door. For a fraction of a second his idling brain thought someone was there. It was always a possibility. And just for a moment his warm and safe sanctuary was threatened, the illusion shattered and the spell broken.

At his feet Kelly stirred and turned languidly, the firelight shining on the copper strands of her hair. It could all have been so different. If only she knew the half of it, she might even understand. This tranquillity would not last, it never did.

But this was somehow a special night. One he would often remember and think about in the weeks to come. Somehow he knew it, even then.

The storm had cleared by dawn and Kelly left early for her father's home. She wanted to be in good time to meet her 'raging bull' when he flew into Shannon airport later that morning. Mallory thought she looked a little uneasy as she prepared to leave. A sense of guilt, he wondered, that somehow she was betraying him, yet knowing that was hardly fair? Perhaps she was afraid he would think she was behaving like a whore?

He smiled as he considered that. She should realise he would not hold that against her. The thought that tonight she would be in bed with Miguel Castaño, the playboy lawyer from Madrid, did not fill Mallory with jealous anger. Years of experience had long ago led him to believe firmly that mankind was more akin to the animal kingdom than most would wish to admit. Men driven to hunt and sow their seed, women seeking protection to bring up their young. Was it really conceited of him to believe that a night with the Spaniard would not match any of the times he and Kelly had spent together?

'Perhaps we can go riding again next week,' she suggested as she left.

'With or without the horses?'

'Cheeky.' She looked more relaxed at that. 'Shall I come round on Tuesday?'

It was agreed and she began climbing up the path to where her car was parked, passing Matt Rooney on his way down.

He and Mallory then set about preparing the boat for a day's fishing.

That was before the postman arrived. A postcard from London. It was signed Sally XXX. It had been over two years since he'd heard from Sally. Sally was Oliver Maidment. Three kisses meant urgent.

Quickly he read the contents and translated the meaning:

> *Dear Kurt, I have to go away unexpectedly on a business trip. It may take some months, but at least I'll be with old friends. They'll look after all my needs. I'd better start brushing up on my American Spanish.*

He replaced the card in his pocket and turned to the old fisherman. 'Something has cropped up, Mattie.'

'I see.' The old fisherman didn't try to hide the disappointment in his voice. Before Mallory had moved into the croft, Rooney didn't have a real friend in the world. He had outlived his old fishing mates and his dear wife and had been kindly treated by the villagers in that patronising way that younger generations have. That changed when Mallory arrived; he had a genuine interest in the fisherman's tales and his local knowledge. The strange Englishman with his equally strange accent had become like the son he'd once had before the sea had taken the lad from him.

But Rooney knew better than to ask the whys and the where-fores. Mallory, he'd learned, was a very private man; if he wanted the fisherman to know something, he'd tell him in his own good time.

'Can you look after the horses and the livestock for me?'

Rooney made light of it. 'Sure, Kurt, you know 'tis no prob-lem. 'Cept them bleddy waspies o' yours.'

Mallory laughed; the old fisherman couldn't abide bees. 'They'll look after themselves till I return, don't worry.' He peeled a wad of notes from his tattered leather wallet. 'That'll cover any feedstuff you may need to buy and I've an arrangement with the vet if anything serious happens.'

There was nothing else for him to worry about. Rooney knew two teenage girls in the village who were more than willing to exercise the two horses. All Mallory had to do was throw a few things into his old khaki rucksack. He travelled incredibly light: a spongebag, a spare pair of old jeans, a thick woollen seaman's sweater with leather elbows, two T-shirts and a change of socks. He'd never worn underwear since being a kid in Paraguay, so the only other things he took were the clothes he stood up in.

Taking his old canvas jacket from the hook behind the door, he set off up the cliff path without a backward glance. Although the A-reg Escort estate was battered and rusty, he maintained the mechanics regularly and it started at the first turn of the key.

Thirty minutes later he drove between the moss-covered gate pillars of the O'More family home. He had always liked the place, ever since Kelly had brought him there for the first time. Previous generations had been wealthy with numerous domestic staff to maintain the house and gardens. But now the lawns were only kept down by a tethered goat and the flowerbeds had become a tangled battlefield between advancing weeds and the original plantings.

He parked on the forecourt and rang the bell push beside the paint-peeled double door. There was no reply, but he could hear voices and laughter from the rear garden, so he sauntered round to the arched opening in the side wall. As he pushed open the wrought-iron gate, he could see the three of them seated at a wooden table on the terrace. Kelly and her father, Joe O'More, white-haired and smiling with those legendary green Irish eyes that his daughter had inherited. He was tanned and trim for a man in his seventies, looking comfortable in V-necked sweater, tweed tie and old cords as he enjoyed the sunshine. His wine glass was raised to their guest. *El torro rabioso.*

In fact, it was the Spanish lawyer who noticed Mallory first. The dark eyes were alert in the handsome face as he turned in his chair, the teeth white and faultless in an easy-going grin.

'Ah, Kurt!' the old man called, as he saw the Englishman approach. 'Nice surprise, come on and join us for a drink.'

Despite her smile, Kelly looked a little embarrassed. 'Hello, Kurt. This is my friend from Madrid. Miguel Castaño. Miguel, this is Kurt.'

The lawyer rose swiftly to his feet and offered his hand. A tall man he looked younger than his thirty-five years with a generous mane of black hair which he wore fashionably long so that it curled at the neck of his sweater. An Aran sweater, Mallory noted, with cavalry twill slacks and polished brogues. In all, a fairly passable imitation of Irish gentry. He obviously had his feet under the table already, quite at home. 'I've just been hearing about you, Kurt. Gather you are quite a horseman – Kelly was telling me you have two fine *creollios* at your place.'

Mallory nodded. 'But I'm afraid I don't play polo.'

Kelly frowned, detecting the edge of sarcasm in his voice and praying he wouldn't pass one of his instant judgements on the 'filthy rich' as he was so fond of calling them.

At least Castaño did not appear to notice. 'That is a shame. I'm sure you'd be very good at it. Perhaps the three of us could go for a ride together some time while I'm here?'

'I don't think so,' Mallory replied flatly and turned to Kelly. 'I've just called to say I've got to go away for a while, so I'm afraid next Tuesday's off.'

He saw the disappointment in the girl's eyes, and then the look of concern. 'You're not going back . . . ?'

'No, to Europe. Paris.' It was the first place that came into his head.

'Business?' Joe O'More asked. There was just the hint of mockery in the old man's eyes. Mallory knew Kelly's father enjoyed his company, although he considered him to be little more than a beachcomber. But then the man could hardly be blamed for that.

'Sure, business.'

'And what sort of business are you in, Kurt?' Castaño asked casually. 'Maybe I have contacts in Paris who could be of help to you?'

'I doubt it. I'm just doing a little translation work.'

Kelly added quickly: 'Kurt speaks fluent Spanish and German.'

Joe O'More said: 'Still, time for a glass before you go?'

Mallory shook his head. 'Afraid not. I have a plane to catch. I'm sorry.'

As he turned to go, Castaño called out '*Hasta luego!*' But if he was expecting a response, he was disappointed.

Kelly caught up with Mallory at the gate. 'Kurt,' she whispered hoarsely, 'are you telling the truth about Paris?'

He looked into her eyes. 'Of course.'

'And whatever you're *really* doing, it's not dangerous?'

'I promise.'

'How long will you be gone?'

'A few weeks, maybe months, I'm not sure.'

She was looking at him closely as though trying to read what was behind his eyes. 'Well, anyway, take care.'

Then he kissed her quickly on the lips before she could pull back; he was certain that Castaño was watching them. 'Go to your raging bull before he gets jealous.'

'Bastard,' she mouthed but she was smiling as she said it.

She returned thoughtfully to the table where her father and Castaño were laughing together. 'What's the joke?'

O'More tried to constrain his mirth. 'Miguel was just commenting on Kurt's renowned lack of dress sense.'

The lawyer showed his teeth. 'I just said that whoever your friend is doing these translations for, they are not paying him enough.'

O'More began chuckling again and sipped at his wine. Kelly smiled politely.

Why the hell had he behaved like that?

Mallory could have kicked himself. *El torro rabioso* had been charming and well-mannered enough. Was it just because the man was so obviously wealthy? Not really. Mallory had always rejected the trappings of luxury himself, felt uncomfortable with them. To him they were almost obscene. But he'd never condemned those who didn't share his view. He recognised he was one of a very small minority who got more out of life when it was basic and without pretensions.

Or was it because the man was a lawyer? The one human species he despised above all others for feeding off other people's misery. Hardly, he thought. Kelly was a lawyer and she was one of the kindest and most considerate creatures he'd ever known.

Then it only left jealousy, despite what he told himself.

But, by the time he'd reached Shannon, he had put all such thoughts from his mind. He parked the car and bought a ticket to Heathrow, checking in almost immediately. Arriving in the early afternoon he took the courtesy bus to the Long Stay Car Park.

As always, the postcard from Sally had contained a series of letters and numbers written in the margin. He reversed them to give the row and parking slot of the vehicle and its registration number. A blue Mondeo with the ignition key hidden in the exhaust pipe.

He entered and flipped open the glove-box. There was the envelope. A hundred in used notes for incidental expenses and a sheet of paper with an address and time.

After burning the note and dropping the remains out of the window, he set off towards London. He had plenty of time and practised his fieldcraft repeatedly on the journey, doubling back on himself numerous times until he was certain that no one had followed.

The precautions might have seemed overelaborate, but he knew from bitter experience that you overlooked them at your peril. The organisation operated beyond the law. Not only were the powerful drug barons and mafiosos their enemies, but they could expect no quarter from the police either – anywhere in the world.

It was eight o'clock when he parked the car near Stamford Bridge football ground in Chelsea before walking back to the King's Road. Twice more he took precautions to ensure that nobody could have successfully shadowed him, then headed south again down Beaufort Street to Pier House.

A boy and dolphin were captured in bronze, swimming for all time through the air in the gardens outside the riverside apartment block. Mallory approached the glass doors and spoke on the intercom. Oliver Maidment's voice answered and then the doorlock buzzed, allowing Mallory in. The silent elevator jetted him to the top floor; the door of the suite was opened by the colonel himself.

'Hello, Kurt.' The handshake was brisk, no-nonsense. 'Good of you to come so promptly.' He led the way through a hallway of plain pastel walls decorated with signed watercolour prints of the Thames. 'Officially this place is privately owned by a director of one of our lesser known subsidiaries. Useful if we need to put up some VIP who it wouldn't do for us to be associated with. You wouldn't believe some of the famous – or should I say infamous – people who have stayed here.'

The living room had the sumptuous but impersonal feel of a five-star hotel lounge: charcoal leather settees and smoked glass coffee table set before an artificial coal fire, a dove grey shag-pile on the floor and a glittering night view of the river through the panoramic windows.

'Take a pew. Drink?'

Mallory dumped his rucksack by one of the settees and sat down. 'A mug of tea would go down well. No sugar.'

'Tea?' Maidment was bemused. 'Ah, of course. Not a great drinker, I recall. Splendid, that's no problem.' He hesitated, clearly finding it difficult to choose the right words, to steer the best path. Mallory sensed that he still wasn't liked by the colonel despite what had passed since Sophie's death. Still not forgiven for defiling his daughter, defiling her memory. Found guilty for not resisting the natural animal urges given to all men. Guilty of accepting love from a woman for the first time in his life. Or so he had thought at the time. If he and Maidment had become closer after he'd executed those ultimately responsible for Sophie's death, then the past three years since they had last met had put the distance back between them.

'What is it?' Mallory asked, then smiled. 'Teabags and hot water, it's not difficult.'

'What?' An awkward laugh. 'Oh, no, not that. I was just thinking— Look, Kurt, I'd like first to thank you for what you did in Venezuela, finding out about Vic West. Especially as it was rather hijacked by SIS. Sorry about that, but when they took an interest, there wasn't much I could do. I needed them to find you.'

'It worked out.'

'And going to see Ruiz Jaramillo in Cali, I was grateful you did that. It explained a lot. But it could have been dangerous – could have turned out very differently. Your report was very interesting.' He smiled. 'Even if the spelling was atrocious. And you really must let me get you a new typewriter.'

Mallory cut through the small talk. 'You've called me here for a reason. On organisation business. That's why I'm here.'

The colonel poured himself a brandy from the cabinet. 'Are you still willing to help us? Come out of retirement?'

He'd thought about it a lot. He wasn't getting any younger and had pushed his luck too far too many times. 'For this, yes. For Vic West and for Mario.'

Maidment frowned. 'Mario?'

'You don't know him. A friend of mine in Venezuela. He's helped us out before as a favour to me.'

Recognition dawned. 'Oh, the man who got you out of Puerto Ayacucho, whose wife and child were murdered? God, Kurt, these bastards never change, do they?'

'What d'you want me to do?'

'Your report says Jaramillo is willing to pay my company to have this new gang – some Medellín faction called White Viper, or whatever – infiltrated, investigated and ultimately destroyed.'

Mallory nodded. 'One million US, plus all expenses.'

Their eyes met, Maidment's gaze intense. 'You know there is only one person who would stand the remotest chance of pulling this off?'

'Of course. And it was originally Vic West's suggestion. That's what he sold to Jaramillo. And Vic would have known I was the obvious choice.'

The colonel lifted one eyebrow. 'The *only* choice, Kurt.'

'So how do you want to play it?'

'I suggest you move into this apartment and use it as your base to set up the operation. You've got everything you need here. There's a small office with a telephone with scrambler and fax, a word processor . . .'

'Are you fucking winding me up?' Mallory snapped. 'I read with the speed of an eight-year-old and you've just told me I can't spell—'

Maidment raised a hand. 'Keep calm, Kurt, for God's sake. You can't do an operation like this all by yourself. There'll be others working with you to deal with all that sort of thing.'

'You're joking, aren't you? Since when have I been any sort of corporate executive? It's not the way I do things.'

Maidment's eyes narrowed. 'It's the way we'll *have* to do things this time. It's bigger than anything we've ever handled. We can't do it by ourselves.'

Mallory heard it then. The sudden raised murmur of conversation and the laughter as someone made a joke. He was on his feet, moving towards the dining-room door that stood slightly ajar.

The colonel's voice was behind him, anxious. 'We were just finishing supper when you arrived.'

Mallory pushed the door open to reveal a long mahogany table, bright with white china and silverware. Abruptly the talking stopped and the two faces turned towards him.

Georgina Savage looked stunning. A simple cutaway black number, her shoulders glistening beneath the chandelier, her face flushed with alcohol and laughter at the joke she'd just been told. 'Hello, Kurt, lovely to see you.' She inclined her head towards the man who sat opposite. 'You won't have met Dale.'

The man dumped his napkin on the table and rose to his feet. In the flash of anger that pulsed through him, Mallory hardly registered what he saw. Just an impression of a broad-shouldered

116

man, middle-aged or maybe younger, with fairish skin that had been coarsened by too many years in the sun. And the eyes. Flinty grey eyes that had seen too many deaths. A professional.

Savage said: 'Dale Forster is attached to the DEA.'

The rest of her words were lost as Mallory withdrew, shutting the door and rounding on Maidment. 'What the hell is this?' In his anger his Germanic accent became suddenly and heavily noticeable. 'I understood this was a job for the organisation. So why is George here and some monkey from the DEA?'

'I was about to explain, Kurt.' For a moment the colonel seemed lost. 'This thing is too big for the organisation alone. Think about it. Even if you manage to infiltrate and find out what we need to know, we'll then have the problem of closing the whole White Viper operation down. That means we'll have to act simultaneously in – I don't know – at least three countries. And we'll be up against big muscle and firepower. We just don't have those sorts of resources.'

Mallory shook his head, stared at the floor.

'The colonel's right.'

It was Savage who spoke; she was standing in the doorway with the American behind her.

There was a smile on Dale Forster's face; it could have been sympathetic or patronising, it was impossible to tell. 'Say, can we just sit and talk this through before we all get our wires crossed and someone blows a fuse.'

Mallory hesitated. Maidment said, 'I'll put that tea on.' And left for the kitchen.

'Let me explain,' Savage said as they sat around in the leather chairs. 'As the colonel has just said, the operation that Vic West proposed to Jaramillo in Cali is just too big for a company like Portcullis to handle. Besides, my department knows all about it and we have a vested interest now.'

'Because of these Brits working with the White Viper gang?' Mallory guessed.

'Exactly. And because we now know about it, it becomes our *responsibility* to follow it up to the best of our ability. It's not something that can be shirked.'

117

Mallory noticed that no mention had been made of the organisation; he doubted the American had been told about its existence and Savage was being discreet. 'What if the colonel and Portcullis refuse to co-operate with you? If he goes it alone?'

Savage looked pained. 'Try to cut out riverside? C'mon, Kurt, how far do you think any of you would get?' Then she smiled. 'Look, I understand any reticence you feel about an operation with our people after that last time in Spain, God knows. My chief understands too. That's why you'd have a free hand at operational level for the infiltration. Your plan and your choice of men on the ground.'

Mallory looked at her long and hard before inclining his head towards the American. 'And your friend? Is this a private party or can the whole bloody world join in? Do you seriously believe that I'd go in against a cartel with the DEA involved?'

She knew straight away what he meant. The Drugs Enforcement Administration was in too deep, its operators in the business too long. At any time their cover could be compromised or the identity of their informants known to the cartels. It was something he would never know until it was too late. And that meant DEA members and their informers could, in theory at least, be got at by criminals who could afford to pay whatever it took.

Every intelligence officer the world over knew the truth of the old espionage maxim that everyone had a price. Usually money, but sometimes prestige, status or power. Or all three. And if that failed, blackmail, intimidation or the threat of violence to friends and loved ones would always work. Most DEA agents were on the level, Savage knew, but there was always the risk of a rotten apple. Some inevitably became corrupted by the dirty business in which they worked. Worse still, others were just plain incompetent with access to too much dangerous information.

'Force of habit,' Savage said in an apologetic tone. 'Dale here isn't *actually* with the DEA, Kurt. It's just what we put about for convenience.' She glanced at the American. 'Perhaps he should tell you himself.'

Forster didn't like that one bit. Those hard grey eyes said it.

118

'Do you think that's wise?' he asked in a low voice.

Mallory answered for her. 'It is, if you want me in the team.'

Forster considered and realised that without Kurt Mallory there wasn't a team. 'As you know,' he said slowly, 'the DEA has always been in the forefront of the fight against drugs. But since the late eighties, *all* US intelligence and military agencies have been ordered by Washington to co-operate with their expertise. I'm *actually* with the Defense Intelligence Agency.'

That took Mallory by surprise. 'Not the CIA?'

Savage intervened. 'Not for this one, Kurt. Langley is too ham-strung by red tape nowadays to be effective. You know, reporting to Congressional committees and all that. And they've lost a lot of their hands-on field officers – it's all satellite and electronic intelligence now. That's why the Defense Intelligence Agency formed its own dirty tricks unit, Intelligence Support Activity. Its true rôle and function is pretty much unknown on Capitol Hill. Dale here's with Activity.'

The American winced visibly at Savage's 'dirty tricks' description. He said quickly: 'If we follow this one through, Kurt, we'll be sleeping with the enemy. Acting on behalf of one drug cartel against another. And they'll be picking up the tab. That ain't going to look too good if it gets out.'

'No die-hard Republican is goin' to be seen to approve, let alone the woolly-headed Democrats we've got trying to run the show at the present time.' He glanced at Savage. 'So, in fact, I'm not even on Activity's payroll. I'm just a no-good, two-bit ex-DIA rogue agent turned mercenary operating out of neutral territory. I have a front company in Liberia, as it happens. My expenses are met from an untraceable DIA black fund . . .'

Mallory raised his hand. 'That's enough, I get the picture. You've already told me more than I need to know. When some-one's putting your balls through the mincer, you tend to get a good memory. So, okay, you're DEA. And I hope Dale Forster isn't your real name.'

There was a faint smile on the American's lips. What do you think, it said.

'We were rather obliged to involve the States in this,' Savage

119

explained. 'South America is their backyard and this one is too big for us to go poaching. Besides, we'll no doubt be thankful for US intelligence on the ground. Dale can get access to DEA computer data without any questions being asked and, as you know, they're in control out there. The anti-drugs police and DAS – the Colombian secret police – pretty much dance to their tune. So the DEA will have complete computer listings of all foreign nationals who've entered or left the country in the past year. That'll be useful when it comes to identifying members of this White Viper outfit.'

Mallory nodded his understanding; despite his reservations about any government involvement – let alone two – it made sense. 'But we do it *my* way, right? My methods and my team.'

Forster's smile was an icy veneer. 'It's all yours.'

At that moment Maidment re-entered from the kitchen with a tray of tea and coffee. 'Do I hear we have agreement?'

Mallory said: 'If I can have Mario Dubois and Goldie as hard backup.'

Savage raised an eyebrow. 'Mario? Is he up to it? I mean, he's had no professional training.'

'He doesn't need to, he's a natural. And I owe him.'

Forster's face was expressionless. 'It's your back he'll be watching.'

'And Goldie?' Mallory pressed, looking directly at Maidment as the colonel handed him a mug of tea. 'You're in touch?'

'You'll have him, Kurt. Provided he's not away on assignment. Last I heard he was freelancing for Mossad again.'

'Ask him anyway,' Mallory said. Goldstein wouldn't let him down; would drop anything he could to come along. 'And field controller?'

Savage was putting cream in her coffee. 'It has to be someone from outside Colombia. We were thinking of Simon Cadbury from our station in Caracas.'

We, he noted, not I. It was not her idea. 'Is he any good? I've never met him.'

Maidment cleared his throat. 'I have.'

Mallory looked up. 'And?'

120

'My guess is he's never faced a dangerous situation in his life and never been under fire – unless it's ducking paper darts from his superiors, no doubt telling him to get off his arse.' He pronounced the last word in that very proper English way that expressed utter contempt. 'The only back he'd ever watch is his own.'

'He's very experienced,' Savage said defensively. 'He's the correct choice.'

Mallory looked at her. 'But it's my team, George, and my choice is you.'

She shook her head. 'That's not possible.'

He grinned. 'Better the devil you know.'

'I'm Head of Desk now, Kurt.'

'Too grand to get your hands dirty?'

'It's not protocol. It's against the rules and my chief would never allow it.'

'Have you got a cigarette?'

'What?' That threw her. Of course, Mallory was always trying to give it up. Never buying a pack, but trying to buy the odd one off a barman or waiter, which never went down well. As though the whole world was like South America.

As she fished in her handbag, Mallory said: 'From what I understand, this mission is breaking every rule in the book. So we may as well start as we intend to continue.' He accepted the cigarette and her light. 'Tell your boss I have you as field controller or it's off.'

Dale Forster looked at the man opposite him, then glanced at Savage before saying: 'And me, Kurt, am I *acceptable* to you as operation commander? Or do you have your own ideas about that too?'

Mallory ran his eyes quickly over the man, perhaps seeing him properly for the first time. Not as young as he'd first thought. Maybe early forties like himself, with an ingrained tan disguising the lines and the grey hairs amid the fair not noticeable at first glance. But the eyes still gave him away, the eyes he'd noticed at once. The colour of slate and just as hard. Shrewd and appraising, a man used to making snap evaluations.

121

Military background, Mallory guessed, the trim haircut and the gleam on his shoes confirming it. West Point, Fort Bragg and Pentagon. The creases in the suit were knife-edge, but the material Washington grey and the tie unmemorable. A man used to melting into his surroundings when it suited, but not a man to mess with.

'If you're acceptable to George,' Mallory said slowly, 'then you're okay by me. It doesn't matter, because *she's* my cutout.'

Savage almost smiled as she felt a flutter of pride at his faith in her, understanding exactly what he meant. Mallory trusted her to watch his back. His team's back.

To emphasise the point, he added: 'And if you fuck up, she'll have your balls.'

The American didn't like that, but had the good sense to hide it. Nevertheless the atmosphere, the tension, was unmistakable, each man drawing his line in the sand, testing the other.

Like two rutting stags, Savage thought as she moved the conversation on: 'The colonel will allow this apartment to be used as the base. First off, I suggest we contact Jaramillo to arrange a full briefing and sort out the contractual side. Maybe get his lawyer – the Palechor woman – to come over here to act as go-between. I'll keep out of it, at least until my chief agrees to give clearance. Palechor can meet Dale as former DEA gone rogue – they'll understand that and it'll appeal to Jaramillo's sense of humour. Getting one of his old adversaries to dance to his tune. And, of course, Kurt as Harry Pike of Portcullis.'

It was agreed and shortly after the meeting concluded. From now on Dale Forster would live in at the apartment while he organised the setup of the operation. Mallory was offered the same facilities, but declined. He'd use the place as an office when necessary, but preferred to take a room in a cheap tourist hotel where he'd have the privacy to live his life as he liked it – down at heel and working hours that suited him. He sensed it wouldn't be a good idea living in close proximity to the American for any length of time. And besides, he wanted Forster to know as little about him as he knew about Forster. Keep everything boxed and separate, that was always safest.

Mallory paused and faced Savage at the front door, his ruck-sack over his shoulder and carrying a plastic bag containing a new Harry Pike suit and a mobile phone, both of which she had provided. 'I'm only doing this for Vic,' he said, 'and for Mario. Not for your department.'

And for yourself, she thought. 'I know, Kurt. I'll come round to the apartment daily. See how things are progressing.'

She wondered if he might kiss her, if only on the cheek. Just to confirm the bond they once had. But he didn't.

Oliver Maidment left shortly after.

'That Kurt's a strange guy,' Forster said as she returned to the living room.

'He takes some getting used to,' she admitted.

'Hope we're not making a mistake. We've got quite a few Hispanics – even some Colombians – who could fulfil his rôle. Experienced people I can trust.'

Suddenly she felt weary and slumped onto the settee. 'Not Colombians, Dale, they'd be too vulnerable ever to be relied on. Family and friends at risk. We've been through all this. What Kurt has going for him that none of your people can possibly have is that he's British. And so are the gang. In our estimation that'll give him a head start.'

Forster wasn't totally convinced; his eyes said it. 'And when it comes to the conclusion, you think he'll be up to it—?' He let the words hang.

Savage lit a cigarette. 'Kurt killed for the first time, as far as I know, when he was twenty-two years old. Do you really want a complete body count? I personally know of ten others, two of those when he served for a short time in the SAS. Others were jobs associated with us.'

'Then let's hope he's not just a psychopathic killer. I've met his sort before.'

That angered her. 'Christ, Dale, some people just *can't* be satisfied. You ask me if he can handle wet jobs and I tell you it's no problem. I didn't say he enjoyed it.'

Forster's expression stiffened. 'Are you sure?'

'What?' Perplexed.

'Mallory's worked for some of our agencies in the past. Point Four, undercover policing of US aid in Latin America and some stuff for the CIA. Nothing heavy but I've read some confidential profiles. Some suggest a personality disorder – the experts reckon he might actually enjoy killing.'

Savage's eyes narrowed. 'Did you ever kill for your people?'

The American's mouth twitched fractionally, confirming, but not wanting to say so in words. Old habits.

'And just who do you think Kurt has killed for our people?' Savage asked. 'Innocent women and children?'

It was Forster's turn to be irked. 'Of course not.'

'Hazard a guess, go on.'

'Terrorists, maybe. Or some political tyrant or corrupt official you couldn't get at any other way. Some big-shot gangsters perhaps. I know the types, the untouchables. Guess I can imagine the likely scenarios.'

She smiled. 'Absolutely right. And in those circumstances yes, I expect Kurt did enjoy it. If I had the guts, I might even quite like to do it myself.' Her eyes narrowed again, lynx-like. 'Your people really don't know Kurt very well, do they?'

Forster stared back at her, unblinking, for what felt like several seconds; it was as though he could read something in her eyes. 'But you seem to.' His voice was low. 'So tell me.'

She pulled a small, tight smile. Where did you start to tell about a man like Kurt Mallory, she thought? And where did you stop? His story could fill several volumes, and that was just the parts of it she had come to know.

Quickly she recounted the double tragedy following his birth which had left him orphaned in Germany at six weeks old. His dead father's family in England were ashamed that their son should have been planning to marry a prostitute refugee from East Germany and horrified that the couple had produced what the newspapers in those flower-power days liked to call 'a love child'.

Mallory's grandfather had flown out to Berlin, where he found the baby boy in the care of an orphanage run by the Glaubehaus, a small radical sect.

At least the old man had squared it with the necessary authorities that the child had British citizenship, aware that his dead son would have wanted that. But Mallory's grandfather was also painfully aware that neither his own wife nor the rest of the family wanted the love child brought back to England. The scandal and, frankly, inconvenience would have been too much.

Then he had stumbled on the perfect solution. The Glaubehaus suggested that baby Kurt might be raised in their commune in Paraguay. There he would be loved and cared for in a God-fearing atmosphere with a real family in one of the commune villages.

Mallory's grandfather signed the necessary documents and agreed an annual fee to be paid until the boy's eighteenth birthday. The family skeleton would be safely locked away with an entire ocean to separate them.

'So the boy made good in Paraguay,' Forster observed, pouring two glasses of whisky.

'I don't know about good. Kurt was a bit of a wild child and the Glaubehaus were a strict sect, so he had a pretty hard time of it. The family had their own kids and he didn't fit in. He rebelled against his foster parents after they told him about his true circumstances. Finally he ran away in 1961 when he was just eleven. For five years he survived as a gaucho on the cattle ranches.'

'I find that hard to believe.'

'As I said, Dale, your people don't know him. Apparently he was tall for his age and the ranchers in the remoter regions weren't exactly paid-up members of Save The Children.'

She recounted his trip to England and his rejection by the British Army on account of his illiteracy before setting out to serve as a mercenary in a string of bloody bush wars in Africa.

'And this first killing of his?' Forster pressed. 'When he was twenty-two, you said.'

'I don't know the exact details. He was bumming around South America after one of his African contracts finished. He was staying with this family on a cattle ranch in Mexico. They were being given a lot of grief by a local thug and his gang. You know, a sort of protection racket. When the family wouldn't pay, cattle would die mysteriously, the water supply was poisoned then a barn burned down. Well, one day, Kurt went into town, found out where the thug was staying and slit his throat while he was asleep. The trouble was over.'

A low whistle escaped Forster's lips. 'So our Mr Mallory is some sort of hero.'

Her smile was involuntary. 'That's not what everyone would say. But if Kurt has pathological tendencies, it's not about killing, it's about intimidation and injustice. If he can do something about it – in his way – he will.'

Was that a smirk on the American's lips, she wondered? A patronising glint of humour in those fathomless eyes like ice-water pools? Well, sod you, Dale Forster.

'So, Georgie, when did Mallory first come to the notice of your people? Before we used him, I believe?'

She nodded. 'He returned from Africa in '76, at the age of twenty-five, I think, and reapplied to join the British Army. As he'd by now taught himself to read and write reasonably well, he was accepted and joined the Light Infantry as a ranker. Three years later he passed selection for the Special Air Service Regiment. They unearthed the talent he'd developed in the African bush wars for infiltration and covert operations, and by 1980 he was seconded to 14 Intelligence Company – they looked after many deniable ops in Northern Ireland. I guess that was when SIS, my people, started to take an interest.'

'And the Falklands?' Forster prompted.

'That's when we really came together,' she confirmed. 'He was deployed to Argentina doing what he does best, playing *el vago pequeño*.'

'Pardon me?'

'The little tramp – our in-joke, like Chaplin. He was in there solo with one of our Buenos Aires agents acting as go-between and cutout. He had no backup and no escape route. But no one suspected this drunken Paraguayan bum drifting around villages near key air bases. Several highly successful missions were mounted by the SAS following his intelligence reports. Indirectly you could say he was responsible for neutralising most of the

Exocet missile threat to the Royal Navy.'

'But he must have left the army almost immediately afterwards because some US agencies were using him in late '83?'

'Yes. He hadn't been well suited to regular army life and he was really too much of a loner for the SAS. Self-reliance is all very well, but you have to be a team player. And Kurt speaks his mind. Upset one or two senior officers. Besides, his stint in Argentina had given him renewed interest in South America. So he left the army and went freelance. We gave him a few jobs and passed his name on to your people and the Israelis. Good freelancers are a rare and precious commodity, as you know.' She paused to sip at the whisky. 'But basically Kurt just worked when he needed to – mostly to pay for his travels and cover his exes. He did the odd investigation job for insurance companies – claims from South America are a big headache for them – and he liked to help out for causes he believed in, like the active international human-rights charities.'

Forster raised an eyebrow. 'That wasn't on my file.'

'They've sent him out to negotiate the release of political prisoners in various South American countries. Mostly it was a question of paying backhanders to judges. Kurt was virtually a hundred per cent successful. The charities wouldn't have known, of course, but I expect he used the familiar South American choice – the silver or the lead.'

'And the last time you used him was about two years ago, right?'

'Yes, to investigate renewed links between the IRA and the Basque separatists in northeast Spain. That's when he was wounded and retired from the business.'

The American smiled, as though reassured by what she was telling him. She relaxed a little then, wondering why she'd felt it so important to protect Mallory from the American's probing cynicism? It was then that Forster's next words caught her off guard. 'And the organisation? Does he still work for them?'

'I'm sorry?' She almost choked on the whisky.

'C'mon now, Georgie, if we're going to work together, we can't have secrets. Does he still work for the organisation, the network?'

She floundered. 'I told you, he hasn't worked for us in two years.'

'Not *your* goddamn secret service.' He was losing patience. 'That secret anti-drugs network that's somehow tied up with the Freemasons.'

'I've no idea what you're talking about.' Was he just fishing? she wondered, deciding quickly that attack was the best form of defence. 'But I'd like to know, Dale. Please tell me about it.'

There was a brief glitter in those eyes. Was it a flicker of irritation – or admiration that she'd parried so quickly? His easy grin said it was of no importance. Maybe only a test. 'Just a rumour our boys picked up. Guess you guys would know if there was anything in it.'

She smiled demurely. 'If I hear anything, Dale, you'll be the first to know.'

6

Mallory didn't sleep well that night.

Lying on the hard mattress in a seedy Fulham hotel, he found that his mind was a confused jumble of thoughts. He really didn't want to be here, doing all this. It was a life he'd left behind. So why had he agreed? Was it really the chance to avenge Vic West, or the brutal murder of Mario's woman and their young child?

Or was it something else entirely? He didn't need the money and had nothing to prove to himself. Surely he'd avenged Sophie Maidment's death by now? He'd killed the man responsible. And a dozen other bastards like him since. Yet there always seemed to be more where they came from.

He stood and paced the room and stared at his own face in the chipped mirror above the sink, his face hard in the glare of the fluorescent tube. The face of a convict, the mug shot of a killer. Face-on and profile. Only the number missing.

Was that who he really was, a cheap killer who murdered for the pure enjoyment of it? A predatory beast who killed for pleasure rather than to survive? Was the taste of revenge really that sweet, even on behalf of others?

Over his shoulder he saw the face of Brother Hermann. Just for a split second; then it vanished.

He watched his reflected face mouth the words. 'Oh yes, the most satisfying sensation in all the world.'

And now he was about to put his life on the line, just to taste it once again.

He returned to the bed and sat on the edge. But this time it was different. Strictly speaking, it wasn't for the organisation. However much he trusted Savage, he knew that she was just like

129

him. Ultimately a pawn in someone else's game. And once the intelligence services were involved you could never be certain what the real game was.

The schemers at riverside could be good friends. But only while it suited them. When it came to protecting their own backsides, they'd shaft their best friends in the blink of an eye. That would include Savage and him. Especially him. He was on the outside, looking in. Expendable.

Was that why he was feeling so uneasy, why he couldn't sleep? To make matters worse, this was more than a deniable operation, it was downright illegal. On the payroll of one narcotics cartel to destroy another. What would the sniffing newshounds of the tabloids and the TV documentaries make of that? Heads could roll in high places – only, of course, they never would. That was when the knives really came out, searching for the scapegoats.

And then there was the involvement of the Americans. Necessary, he understood that, but unwelcome because it doubled the number of fat cats. Doubled the number of backsides to be protected. Doubled the danger.

Insurance, Mallory decided, that was what was needed. It was the last thought in his mind when he finally drifted into a fitful sleep in the early hours of the morning.

He awoke before eight with a plan of action already forming in his mind. After phoning down for a pot of tea, he washed and shaved before dressing in the Harry Pike suit. He downed three cups of tea before leaving and catching a tube train to the City in search of a copy of the day's *Lloyd's List*. Eventually he tracked down the specialist publication at WH Smith in Liverpool Street station.

On returning to his hotel, he ordered more tea and settled down to pore over his purchase. It provided a daily snapshot by port of the world's shipping – arrivals of merchantmen, their cargoes, destinations and anticipated departure dates, as well as reports of damage and losses at sea.

At various times in his life it had been Mallory's bible for working his passage round the world. Today he wanted a busy, cosmopolitan port that handled rusting tramps from all over the globe rather than a supermodern container facility. His finger ran down the listings until he reached Cork. Southeast Ireland. Ideal, he decided. It would add weight to his story while providing an additional hurdle for anyone trying to investigate it. Irish officials tended to be easy-going, a little lax. And, strictly speaking, it was a foreign land.

He scanned the column of ships in port, pausing when he reached the *Bombay Star*. An ageing tramp with a mixed cargo, and a long time gone from her home port. It was due to leave Cork the next day. Perfect.

At noon he walked back to the Thames-side apartment. Forster opened the door. He had his shirtsleeves rolled and tie askew and held a maple syrup waffle in one hand. 'Hi, Kurt,' he said amiably as he chewed. 'Just having a working lunch. Fancy some?'

Mallory declined. 'I just want to make some calls.'

'Sure thing.' The unspoken antagonism of the previous evening had evaporated. Forster was a pro. He led the way to a small room that served as an office; the computer was already up and running, the screen full of figures. He pointed to the telephone. 'Help yourself. Who you planning to call?'

'Jaramillo's lawyer in Cali.'

Forster glanced at his watch. 'Eight o'clock there.'

'They'll be in,' Mallory assured him, and dialled the number. Within seconds, he found himself talking to Maria Palechor. 'Harry Pike here from Portcullis. I'm afraid my company cannot help you as requested, but we can put you in touch with someone who can.'

'And what company would that be?'

'Confidential at this stage, I'm afraid. They'll want to speak person to person as soon as possible.'

'My client may not like that. He is not keen on travel.' She didn't say to a country where he didn't have protected status.

'Not your client, you, Señora Palechor. How soon can you travel to England?'

A pause as she consulted her diary. 'Er – I could come in four days, arriving Friday.'

'Our contacts will need to know the fullest details.'

'Of course.' Her tone was slightly indignant. 'And I'm sure my client will be very pleased to hear this news.'

He gave her the telephone number of the apartment. 'Call when you have your flight details. Our car will collect you from Heathrow.'

Next he tried the number he had for Mario Dubois who had returned to his home country of Martinique. It took several attempts to get through, when a slurred, sleepy voice answered.

'Boozing again?' Mallory chided lightly.

A throaty chuckle, but without humour. 'Just to kill the pain of a broken heart, amigo. Comprendes?'

'Si, comprendo.' What the hell *did* you do with yourself after your woman and child had been murdered? 'That job we talked about has come up. I need you over here. Give me the number of your bank and I'll cable you money for the fare and expenses.' That would cheer him up, Mallory knew. Take his mind off things.

When he hung up, he turned to Forster who'd been tapping away at his computer keyboard. 'I have to go away for a few days.'

The American swivelled around in his chair. 'Away? You're on the team now. You're supposed to be here, helping with the planning.'

Fuck you, Mallory thought. But he said: 'You won't need me until Jaramillo's lawyer gives us the briefing. This has all happened so quickly – I've some personal matters to attend to.'

'How long will it take?'

'I'll be back before she arrives.'

Forster smiled without humour. 'Guess I don't have much option. Just remember that I'm running this show.'

Mallory raised an eyebrow in gentle mockery. 'Does that mean you hold the purse strings?'

'Sure.'

'Then I need an advance.'

'How much?'

'A thousand pounds. Cash.'

Mallory noticed the skin loosen around Forster's mouth, read the contempt in his eyes. Thinking what a paltry sum and how easy this scruffy tramp was to please, bearing in mind this whole operation would cost hundreds of thousands to mount.

Nevertheless, Mallory had his thousand before the bank closed that afternoon. Saying farewell to the disgruntled American, he visited a Milletts store to purchase a pair of jeans, two shirts, a sweater and a cheap denim jacket.

The next morning, dressed in his new casual but smart wardrobe, he drove north out of London. He picked up the M1 motorway for a while before turning off to connect with the A41 to Aylesbury. The town had been chosen for no other reason than that it was quiet and respectable; without a vast urban under-class, engaged on widespread social security fraud, he gauged his story was more likely to be believed. On arrival, he began his search for a room to rent. He found what he wanted in a quiet back street. The uninterested landlady pointed to the payphone in the hallway – no incoming calls – and showed him the bedroom – no women visitors. It had yellowing net curtains, a sink and two-ring gas cooker. She listened impatiently as he explained his name was Jim Tate, a seaman, who had just returned home and was looking for a land-based job for a while. And no, she didn't know of anything suitable going. Her eyes only showed any indication of life when he paid her two months' rent in advance.

During the afternoon he telephoned Cork docks to confirm that the *Bombay Star* had sailed. In the evening he visited half a dozen pubs, having a meat pie and chips at the first of them. By ten o'clock he had selected the one he wanted. Its smoky public bar was filled with lager-drinking youths playing pool. Nearly all were wearing tight jeans and cutaway T-shirts to impress their microskirted and vacuous girlfriends who sat around gossiping and eating prawn-flavoured crisps. A few Sharons and Traceys here, he mused.

Settling down in a corner with a half of bitter, he observed the scene, working out which boy was with which girl. He decided that the most arrogant and loutish pool player was someone called Den. Acne-faced and unshaven, he looked to be in his

133

early twenties and about thirteen stone, muscle running to fat with a lip of beer gut over the belt of his jeans.

His girlfriend was Jeannie, tall and skinny, hard-faced and hard-smoking. She was sitting at the table next to Mallory's and looking bored as she waited for her boyfriend to finish his game and pay her some attention.

'Gotta light?' Mallory asked. And when she obliged, he said: 'That's a nice ring you've got. Engagement, is it?'

It was as simple as that. Mallory had always been mildly amused at how women could blabber for hours about their jewellery. Diamonds and sapphires, birthstones, the number of carats. Within five minutes they were deeply engrossed in banal conversation, Jeannie delighted to find someone interested in her collection of rings, interested in her. Her face softened and she began to laugh at Mallory's quips and jokes, a piercing laugh like a bleating sheep that caused heads to turn.

But, despite appearances, Mallory had only been half-listening to what she said, as he kept one eye on Den as he leaned over the table with his cue.

Jeannie laughed once too often. Now everyone knew she was being chatted up by a middle-aged chancer. A stranger in their midst. Something had to be done and Den wasn't about to lose face in front of his friends.

A shadow was cast across Jeannie's table. 'What's your game, mate?'

Mallory looked up, and smiled. 'Do you have a problem, sunshine?'

Suddenly the room went quiet. Movement stopped and all eyes were on them. Den's mouth formed into a snarl. 'It's you who's got the problem.' Then he realised Mallory had spoken with a strange accent. 'What are you? German? A fuckin' Kraut.'

'Leave it out, Den,' Jeannie pleaded. 'We're just talking.'

The man turned on her. 'I know exactly what you're fuckin' doin', girl.' His attention returned to Mallory. 'Right, Kraut, you're outa here. OUT!'

Mallory shrugged resignedly. 'Okay, okay, I know when I'm beat.' He stood up and offered his hand. 'No hard feelings.'

Den knew he'd won; a smug grin of triumph spread across his face, aware that his friends were witnessing his victory. It was all too easy. Instinctively his hand came forward to shake Mallory's, and then he hesitated. Perhaps something in the other man's eyes told him it was not a good idea.

But he was too late. Mallory sprang like a panther, snatching Den's arm with both hands, twisting it over until the elbow joint was levered against his own left forearm and his right hand had hold of the young man's little finger. The snap of the bone was heard above the gasps of surprise from the audience – until Den's wailing scream filled the public bar.

Mallory shifted stance, addressing the gang of youths over Den's bent-double shoulders. 'Your mate has just broken a finger. If you don't want me to break his elbow, I suggest you leave this pub. All of you. NOW!'

There was a mumble of consternation from the group, hesitation and a shuffling of feet.

'P-please!' Den gasped. 'Do what the bloke says!'

Slowly, grudgingly the gang shuffled towards the door, picking up jackets from chairbacks, pints of lager hastily drained. Little acts of defiance. Faces turned as they filed past Mallory and his hapless victim.

One toothy youth with lank hair wagged a finger. 'We'll fuckin' get you for this!'

Mallory ignored him. Now the bar was clear apart from a couple of middle-aged regulars and an apprehensive Jeannie. He released his grip on Den's arm. 'I suggest you get him to hospital.'

For a moment the girl's eyes met his and held them with a questioning look. Then they were both gone.

The remaining half-hour before time passed predictably enough. Catcalls and obscenities were yelled from outside as the two regulars bought Mallory a drink and congratulated him on standing up for himself. Den was a lout and a trouble-maker, most of his gang little better. The taciturn landlord was less enthusiastic at having his customers turfed out, but as a mere relief manager wasn't interested in making an issue of it.

Five minutes before closing time, Mallory went to the pay-phone on the wall, dialled 999 and asked for police. He gave the name of the pub. 'You'd better get a car down here fast. There's a big fight outside and it looks nasty.'

He returned to the bar, finished his drink and left.

Outside, Den's gang of friends was waiting, as he knew they would be. They were gathered in the shadows, drunk and menacing. He waited for them to come to him, then went for their temporary leader – the leather-jacketed youth who had threatened him – and his sidekick. Both were floored, writhing in agony on the car-park tarmac, before the weight of numbers overwhelmed him. He felled three more before he went down under the hail of flying fists and kicking boots, and tasted blood in his mouth.

Now he played for time, on his back with his legs up to defend himself, swivelling around against anyone trying to break into the circle. Then he heard the wail of the police siren and the screech of brakes, followed by shouts and the sound of running feet as the gang dispersed, taking their wounded with them.

'You all right, sir?' the constable asked, helping Mallory to his feet. 'You've got a nasty black eye there.'

'I'm okay,' he replied, trying to regain his breath. 'Sore kidneys, but no bones broken – oh, Christ!'

'What is it, sir?'

'The bastards have taken my case. Everything's in it. Passport, papers, bloody everything!'

They were very sympathetic at the station. Paper cups of tea kept coming as they took down his statement. How he, Jim Tate, was a merchant seaman who had disembarked from the *Bombay Star* in Cork the previous day after nine years at sea. He'd come to Aylesbury, a town he'd heard was quiet and pleasant, to find a land-based job and settle down, only to get beaten up by a bunch of thugs and have his document case stolen. No, he couldn't remember his passport number, his National Insurance number. Sorry.

The desk sergeant promised to do his best to find the culprits and retrieve the case, but he didn't sound hopeful.

Mallory returned to his digs at two thirty in the morning and slept soundly until nine the following day.

Feeling sore and bruised, he made his way to the local Job Centre and explained his situation to the plump and bored female clerk.

'If you're looking for work, Mr Tate, you'll need a P45 form. Do you have your National Insurance number?'

'No, that's what I've just explained. *All* my papers were stolen.'

'And you can't remember it?'

'Sorry.'

'I need the number before I can issue a P45. Do you have a passport or some form of ID?'

'Sorry, they took the lot.'

'That's a problem. I mean, I can't just issue you with a new number without verification. And without a number you're a non-person.'

'You mean I don't exist?'

She missed the mockery in his voice. 'Perhaps I can trace you on the computer. When did you last work in the UK?'

'About nine years ago.' He looked sheepish. 'Casual labour, I'm afraid. Cash in hand. On building sites and farms up in Humberside.'

'Did you have a doctor?'

'Never seen one.'

'Dentist?'

A shake of the head. 'Not for years. I've got good teeth, but I must admit I ought . . .'

'Oh, dear.' She stared at him. 'Let's start at the beginning. Where were you born?'

'Liverpool, I think. 1951.'

'Think?'

'I was an orphan. I was fostered by a local couple, but the wife died when I was five and I was sent to Paraguay to the Glaubehaus sect. My foster parents were members. Have you heard of it?'

She shook her head.

'A religious order from Germany. They brought me up at an

137

orphanage in Paraguay. I lived in South America until I came back to England in '81 when I was thirty. I worked for four years in Humberside before going to sea.'

Her eyes had glazed over and he sensed her groaning inwardly at the prospect of hours searching through computer records with little hope of success. 'At least that explains your accent.'

'The brothers speak mostly German.'

A tight smile. 'That's good. We have to be careful not to issue numbers to illegal immigrants.'

'Of course not. I understand. Why don't you telephone the local police station? Sergeant Bilton can vouch for my story and the port authority at Cork in Ireland will confirm I left the *Bombay Star* the day before yesterday.'

They wouldn't be able to, of course, but they would at least confirm that the ship had left. His story was as watertight as it needed to be.

'Do you have a contact address?'

'Yes, I'm renting digs.'

'Well, that's something. You must have a permanent address.'

'I really do need to work. And to see a dentist.'

'Of course.' She noted down his address. 'Come back to see us in two days.'

Mallory left the office with a spring in his step and a grin on his face. He doubted the lazy cow would even bother to speak to Sergeant Bilton or put a call through to Cork. It was so much easier to issue a new number.

And that meant Mallory would have his new secret identity.

On the following Friday, Maria Palechor renewed her acquaintance with Harry Pike of Portcullis.

They met at the luxurious apartment overlooking the Thames where she was introduced to a smart, bright female executive called Georgina Hayes.

Hayes worked for a small anonymous security firm to which Portcullis regularly subcontracted jobs it could not handle because of its high public profile. An American was also at the meeting; Dale Forster had been chosen by Hayes to head up the

138

operation. Palechor knew his type: a gung-ho soldier of fortune who'd probably served in 'Nam, Cambodia and Laos, then Nicaragua and El Salvador. Possibly ex-CIA, bitter at being shed as surplus to requirements. Rough, tough and unlikely to ask questions provided the money was right.

After the first meeting a Portcullis chauffeur had driven her to the Park Lane hotel. From the foyer she used a public phone to call a firm of City solicitors who acted for her in the UK. They were expecting her call; all they needed was the address where the meetings were taking place.

Within minutes the private investigator was driving towards Pier House, a camera with telephoto lens lying beside him on the front passenger seat.

Just over a month later, a solitary figure entered the morning chaos that was Bogotá bus station. He wore soiled jeans and a canvas jacket and carried a small battered rucksack over one shoulder. It was difficult to be certain of his age or nationality. His hair was long and greasy, his face tanned but unwashed, with several days' growth of beard.

No one paid him a second glance. He was just another bum, another penniless drifter. Another one of the hundreds of thousands who floated around South America in the endless search for a fast buck, forever in the vain hope of making a fortune.

His dog-eared British passport said he was Kurt Hulse. Each page was stamped to overflowing with entry and exit visas going back over five years. There were ones for virtually every country in the continent. His last entry stamp to Colombia was a month old, which meant there were two months left to run.

In fact, the passport had only been in his possession since the previous night. It had been delivered to him personally in downtown Bogotá at the Hotel Presidente by a messenger from the British Embassy. The SIS Head of Station had organised an ingeniously authentic-looking forgery.

As far as Georgina Savage and Dale Forster were concerned, Mallory had made his way to Bogotá via Paris and Caracas travelling under his Harry Pike identity provided by the secret service. But he had changed the name of the ticket-holder at the last minute to his own new identity, that of James 'Jim' Tate. A month earlier, the Job Centre at Aylesbury had issued him with a new National Insurance number and P45 which he was able to use as his basis for a passport application, bank account and American Express membership.

He had entered Colombia as Jim Tate and intended, eventually, to leave that way too. If ever someone was looking for Kurt Mallory, Harry Pike or Kurt Hulse, they would have a long wait.

It was nine o'clock and the terminal was filled with passengers waiting for buses to take them to all points of the compass. The routes fed out from the capital like spokes of a wheel, not just along made-up roads to other big cities, but also probing fearlessly down miles of rutted unpaved mud tracks to the wilderness beyond. Here, as in all of South America, the buses were the lifeline of the impoverished population. They ranged from brightly painted, geriatric *corrientes*, which offered long and often dangerous rides at knock-down prices, to ageing pullmans and supermodern luxury coaches with air conditioning and showing interminable Kung Fu action movies dubbed into Spanish. You paid your money and made your choice.

Mallory picked his way through the bodies camped patiently on the concrete concourse, past Indians with their pathetic cardboard boxes of belongings, *campesino* village women with their grubby children and trussed live chickens and down-at-heel businessmen in their worn suits and soiled shirts. Armed police sauntered by, a deterrent to the street urchins who waited for easy pickings, as he scanned the tour boards above the ticket kiosks of the bus companies: *Expresso Bolivariano*, *Flota Magdalena*, *Coopertrán*.

He reached the ticket desk beneath the Santa Maria destination board. 'How much one way?'

'Five thousand.'

Mallory peeled off the dirty peso notes from a thin roll. 'How long is the journey?'

'Nine hours. It leaves at half past.'

Of course, it was no surprise to Mallory when the journey ran to an exhausting eleven hours, and it didn't bother him. It was a pullman coach that had seen better years, but it was comfortable enough with reclining chairs and a toilet, even if it failed to flush. He even welcomed the time to adjust mentally to his new environment and to consider the events of the past four weeks.

The arrival of Maria Palechor from Cali in London had seen the start of planning in earnest. She had brought with her detailed maps of the remote Páramo de Carcasi region, some hundred and seventy miles northwest of Bogotá by road. With map-reading expertise acquired during his years in the SAS, Mallory had the ability to read contour lines as easily as three-dimensional photographs. And even the clinical interpretation of the cartographers had left him in no doubt about the wild and unforgiving nature of the terrain – rocky Andean foothills scarred and gouged by racing rainwater streams and waterfalls plunging thousands of feet into precipitous canyons to form whitewater rivers that swept away towards the Amazon basin hundreds of miles away. Roads were nonexistent, only seasonal mud tracks linking the few settlements worthy of a name. In short, it was the last place on God's earth that anyone would choose to live. Those who did would mostly be indigenous Indians, eking a living from grazing or crops, or guerrillas of the left-wing *Ejército de Liberación Nacional*, known more simply as the ELN.

According to Maria Palechor, the region was very much in their control, from which it could be assumed that the White Viper gang was paying a cut to allow them to operate in such a suitably remote and inhospitable area.

She had said: 'I recall we explained that our intelligence indicates that the gang could be operating from one of the many old emerald mines in the district. But we don't know which. I have checked with the land registry and have found that most are owned by Medellín families who may have been connected with Pablo Escobar's mafia. Several have applied for and been granted operational licences in the past two years.'

She had then drawn a circle on the map. 'Most are in this region, close to the Servita river.'

The area was some thirty miles from the nearest settlement of

Adoración by mountain track, which was itself a farther twenty miles beyond the regional town of Santa Maria. And most people regarded Santa Maria as the end of the world; it was where the bus terminated. To all intents and purposes the target area might as well have been in outer space.

'We had been hoping for more detailed intelligence,' Maria admitted.

'But?' Forster pressed.

'Our informant has disappeared and I'm afraid we fear the worst.'

It had been a timely reminder, if one were needed, of the operational risks involved.

With the financial arrangements agreed and in place, the lawyer had returned to Cali to report to Ruiz Jaramillo.

Meanwhile Mario Dubois had arrived from Martinique, closely followed by Bertram 'Goldie' Goldstein, who had just completed a freelance operation in Athens for Mossad. With their arrival the sombre mood of the planners was uplifted immediately, starting with an impromptu drinks party at the apartment.

Dale Forster's evident disapproval of such high spirits had been swiftly overcome as the two men greeted Mallory like a long-lost brother and Mario produced a bottle of Ron Viejo de Caldas dark rum from his suitcase. His carefree bonhomie and roguish good humour were infectious, while Goldie, whose shy manner, slight build, spectacles and wild hair bore more than a passing resemblance to the comic actor Woody Allen, regaled them with a torrent of anti-Semitic jokes.

Mallory had noticed Savage watching them and guessed that she was feeling somehow apart from the happy reunion. These laughing men were blood brothers. Whatever the bond between them, it was not one she could share. She was, like Forster, an outsider. These men had come to know each other through the organisation, each doing what he did for his own personal reasons, whatever they might be. These men were the organisation's executive arm, its secret killing machine.

Mallory wondered if she felt any sense of shame that she and the American were using them, asking them to do what no human being should ever ask of another.

At one point he'd seen her glance at Forster and the man smiled back at her, feeling easier now, realising he had a team and how it might all work out.

The following day, after Mario and Goldie had spent a wild night in London's West End, they had made a start on the planning thrashes, nursing hangovers with black coffee and aspirin. The Israeli had suggested that to provide Mallory with hard backup and to gain access to the area, they should pose as a wildlife film crew. Savage had liked the idea and within twenty-four hours they were in business as independent producers, the company registered and stationery printed. The first letters requesting permission to film in the area were sent to the cultural attaché at the British Embassy in Bogotá. With them were instructions to the SIS Head of Station to get everything rubber-stamped by the appropriate authorities using any means possible. That, in Colombia, would no doubt require bribery, corruption and even discreet threats of blackmail on occasions. Meanwhile arrangements were made through the BBC Wildlife Unit in Bristol for the two men to attend a crash course that would enable them to pass themselves off convincingly. Special communications equipment was hastily adapted to be secreted within the filming and sound equipment.

Savage and Forster would operate through one of the many United Nations development agencies, evaluating needs in deprived areas. That in itself would guarantee the opening of doors via the local authorities – and, for that matter, indigenous guerrillas – anxious for aid funding. Forster made light of any problems; clearly US intelligence agencies had used such 'authentic' cover many times before.

While Savage would carry communications equipment to keep in touch with the wildlife film crew, Forster himself would arrange for the international co-ordination needed when, hopefully, the entire White Viper operation was closed down at a stroke. Already they'd seen the benefits of the American's involvement. He had arranged for an Intelligence Support Activity agent on the ground to overfly the emerald mine area to take high-resolution photographs. As a result they were ninety-five per cent certain they had identified the exact location of the base and its layout: laboratory, radio shack, bunkhouses, watch-towers and defences.

In addition, Forster had persuaded allies in Washington to access the DEA computer in Bogotá for all British nationals who had entered Colombia legally in the previous two years and those who had subsequently departed. That left a balance of over three hundred. Somewhere in that list would be the thirty-odd men running White Viper.

Now Mallory felt more relaxed, leaning back in his seat as the pullman left the grey concrete towers of Bogotá far in the distance and sped through the rolling green countryside. It reminded him a little of the Welsh valleys, except for the Spanish styling of the haciendas and the accumulations of roadside garbage.

There was a lunch stop at the town of Tunja, after which Mallory found he had a fellow passenger seated next to him. He was a small middle-aged man with bright raisin eyes, the grey whiskers on his weathered face not quite dense enough to make a beard. From his scruffy denim dungarees and battered straw stetson, Mallory guessed he was a farmer. The man confirmed this as the pullman began the next leg of its journey.

Introducing himself as Victor Tafur, he offered a bag of boiled sweets. 'It's the first time I've been to Tunja in fifteen years. It's changed a lot.'

'You're travelling all the way to Santa Maria?'

'Yes. My daughter meets me to drive me back to our small-holding.'

'Whereabouts is it?'

'Just a place they call Cruz de Oro.'

'It's a village?'

The man chuckled. 'Hardly that, my friend. There is a mission chapel and a few farms like mine and a scattering of houses. Mostly Indians live in this area. Hardly even a settlement. Our nearest real village is Adoración and that is just one street.'

Mallory recognised the name; clearly the farmer did not live far from the emerald mine encampment that the Vipers used. 'What

144

brings you to Tunja?'

'I was looking for a lawyer – I am trying to sell my land.'

'It's a long way to come. Isn't there a lawyer in Adoración? And there must be several in a big town like Santa Maria.'

Tafur shook his head sadly. 'But no one I can trust, I am afraid. Maybe eighteen months ago, or even a year, but not now.'

'Why, what's the problem?'

Suddenly Victor Tafur looked wary. 'Ah, well, things have changed in the region. There is much influential money slushing around. And lawyers can be bought just like policemen and judges.'

Mallory was genuinely puzzled. 'What's that got to do with you selling your land?'

Tafur shrugged and stroked thoughtfully at the wisps of his beard. 'Let us just say that I want to choose who I sell my land to.'

Then Mallory had an idea of what lay behind the farmer's problems. There had to be a connection. He asked discreetly: 'How else have things changed in your district?'

Tafur's eyes squinted against the light as he stared at his fellow passenger, wondering if he'd already said too much to a total stranger. 'It is still the same beautiful place of my childhood. My father's home and his before him. The life is hard for little reward, but we survive. We do not ask for much. Only now it is not a place where I would want my children's children to grow up.'

'The guerrillas?' Mallory asked.

A hint of a smile crossed the farmer's face. 'Well, their presence does not help, but many are the sons of my neighbours and they give us no trouble. But then it is better that I do not talk of this.' His change of tack was quite deliberate. 'So why do you travel to Santa Maria, my friend? You have relatives there? But I think your accent is not from these parts?'

'I was brought up in Paraguay, but actually I'm English.'

Tafur's mouth dropped. 'A gringo? By the Holy Virgin, I cannot believe that!'

They laughed a lot at that and Tafur explained that he'd spent

145

time in America during his twenties when he went to agricultural college. Now his English was rusty, he said, but immediately began to put it into practice.

'It is *many* years since I was in England,' Mallory said. 'I'm going to Santa Maria to find a job – I like to bum around and just pay my way.'

'There are not many jobs in Santa Maria.'

'I'd heard some emerald mines had reopened. I know something about that.' In fact, until a month earlier Mallory had known virtually nothing about such work; Savage had organised a crash course on the subject for him.

'That may be true,' Tafur replied evasively, 'but I doubt they'll offer work to strangers.'

'What about your farm, señor? I'm good with horses and livestock.'

The farmer laughed. 'I cannot even pay myself, Señor Hulse, much as I would like a good helper around the place.'

'I'd work for one meal a day and somewhere to sleep.'

Tafur regarded him for a moment, instinctively taking a liking to this foreigner with his strange accent. 'We will see. At least you must come and visit us, meet my wife and our daughters. If you still have no work, maybe we can talk about it.'

Mallory gave a nod of appreciation. 'And tell me, did you find a suitable lawyer in Tunja?'

'I am afraid not. Their fees would be more than my farm is worth. So I am afraid I will be there for many more years to come.'

The pullman had now begun its steady climb up into the Andean foothills. Paved road gave way to a narrow track of rutted red earth that clung tenaciously to the precipitous contours of a vast river canyon. Far below, through a veil of mist that floated like a false ceiling, the mighty Chicamocha seethed and foamed along its course, silvery green until it burst in a white fury over the rocky crags of the rapids, ever fed by the streams running off the brown and rock-mottled hills, eroding deep fissures until the peaks resembled the damaged knuckles of a prize fighter who had fought once too often.

Despite the twists and turns and gaping chasm, where earlier landslides had eaten into the track, the driver saw no need for caution. His foot seemed glued to the accelerator. *Campesinos* driving their beat-up cars were contemptuously overtaken, regardless of looming hairpin bends. He would hoot at struggling *chiva* buses, with their rattling wooden bodywork and belching exhausts, to pull over and let him pass.

Mallory wondered just what it was about the macho Latin psyche that transformed a man the moment he sat behind a steering wheel. Could the pullman driver really be that oblivious to the countless little trackside shrines in memory of those who had gone before, diced with death and lost? Was the man throwing down a gauntlet to fate, challenging it to do its worst? Life in this godforsaken place was cruel and cheap, always on the edge. So why not push it a little closer, a little harder? You were going to die soon enough anyway. *Viva la muerte!* Long live death and let's fuck the angels!

Twilight settled in and with it came the rain, drumming on the roof and running in torrents across the mountain track. The tyres of the pullman spun and slid and squelched in a morass of ochre mud while, ahead, the single working headlamp picked out the trackside shrines in its sweep. More plaster Madonnas, wooden crosses and faded colour photographs. The driver's teenage assistant, or *ayudante*, opened the front concertina door and hung out on the step to give a commentary and warning of the next looming hazard. And the pullman thundered on.

Villages were few and far between now, just occasional clusters of adobi houses beside the road, perched precariously on the canyon edge. Far out in the distant misty void, lights began twinkling like stars as Indians lit candles in their remote homestead shacks. Somehow those isolated signals of humanity served to emphasise the aching emptiness of the bleak landscape. Then the night closed in completely, absorbing them in swathes of white vapour as the pullman climbed into the cloud base.

By the time they stopped in the narrow, single main street of Colonia San Miguelita, where the houses, shops and bars opened straight onto the rain-sluiced and broken tarmac, the coach was

147

two hours behind schedule. The driver had parked outside a café where he planned to have his supper and some beers. Mallory was relieved that the man was at least taking a break. After some relaxation and with a hot meal inside him, there was a better chance that he'd continue the manic journey without hurtling the pullman and all its hapless passengers into some unseen abyss.

'I could do with stretching my legs,' Victor Tafur said. 'Do you fancy a drink, amigo?'

Mallory followed him through the squeeze of children who had gathered by the pullman's exit to quiz the passengers about everything and anything. Who were they, where were they going, where had they come from, where did they live, what did they do? The pullman's stopover was the highlight of their day. Inside, candles threw macabre shadows around the walls and reduced the café's customers to sinister, half-lit ghosts.

'Power lines down?' Tafur asked as the barman served two anis-flavoured *aguardientes*.

'Yes, all over the area as far as Santa Maria.'

The farmer lifted his glass. 'Welcome, mi amigo, to the land that God – and everyone else – forgot.'

It was to be almost another three hours before the pullman finally rolled into the Santa Maria bus station a few minutes before midnight. Rain sheeted from a thunderous sky, setting the lacquered puddles dancing as the passengers stepped wearily down to the ruptured concrete concourse.

In the couple of seconds that it took Mallory to say farewell to Victor Tafur, he was soaked and his hair flattened. Steam began rising from his clothes as he shouldered his rucksack. With no lights on anywhere, he fumbled like a blind man along an alleyway towards one of the streets that led to the town plaza. Thankfully, like most South American towns, it was built to a grid pattern and it was relatively easy to find one's way about without getting lost.

His boots splashed through an inch of water as the concreted street became a fast-flowing stream, carrying the deluge away to the lower slopes. Tripping over the broken and uneven sidewalks, he felt his way past the walls of shuttered houses and shops.

Then, suddenly, he was outside the entrance of an hotel, its sign illuminated by a thoughtfully placed Gaz lamp. El Imperial. At eleven dollars a night, it was the nearest Santa Maria had to a luxury hotel. Above him, in one of those unlit windows, he knew Georgina Savage would be sleeping. Unless she had lain awake, worrying about him. Thinking about him. Wanting him, even. He felt a sudden stirring of warmth beneath his sodden jeans.

He put the thought firmly from his mind and walked on. Barely fifty metres and he reached the plaza, the presence of its trees only discernible by the rustling of their leaves beneath the remorseless patter of rain. Even the huge edifice of the cathedral which dominated the centre had melted completely into the inky gloom.

Two small hotels, Tafur had informed him, cheap and not so cheerful, both on the square. He stumbled into the first, barely able to read its signboard – La Concordia – in the darkness. Cracked hallway tiles led to an unmanned reception desk and a collection of sagging sofas. The hotel had been built around this central lobby area; several levels of balconies and rows of bedroom doors faced in on all sides. High above was a fanlight on which the rain rattled like gravel; a rapid drip of water plinked loudly into an old copper spittoon positioned for the purpose. After he'd rung the bell several times, a fat *mestico* woman waddled in from a room behind the desk. Rubbing the sleep from her eyes, she was clearly unamused at being disturbed. Yes, she had a room available – three dollars a night and a shared lavatory on the landing. He followed as she shuffled up the creaking wooden stairs by torchlight and along the balcony of the first floor. The lock on the door was missing, he noticed, as she pushed it open to reveal the bare, unpainted cell. An army of cockroaches vanished at the sudden influx of light as she played the beam over the bed with its moth-eaten cover, a cracked porcelain washbasin and a wooden chair.

'Okay?' she asked, lighting the candle that stood in a saucer on the seat of the chair.

'Home from home,' he murmured.

But either she didn't hear or didn't care, and left him to it without a further word.

He unpacked his old sleeping bag and rolled it out on top of the bed. He never travelled without it; it was his protection against other people's fleas, other people's lice. Within seconds of climbing in, fully clothed, he had fallen into a deep and dreamless sleep.

It had begun.

7

Georgina Savage was already awake as the first pearly radiance of dawn seeped into the eastern sky. In fact she had slept badly, disturbed by the relentless Andean rain and wondering about Mallory. Presumably he'd survived the treacherous journey from Bogotá, but was he on schedule and now in town?

The previous day had gone well for her and Dale Forster. Their journey had been made forty-eight hours earlier, travelling in a white Chrysler Cherokee which the American had arranged to be liveried with blue United Nations transfer symbols. This affectation would not have been the normal practice of that institution, but Forster wanted their presence to be high-profile and above suspicion. He saw the advantages in everyone being aware that the UN was in town and for the purpose of their research to be public knowledge.

Yesterday had begun with a meeting with the town's Administrator, who had greeted them warmly and had coffee and biscuits brought by his secretary. A small ferret-faced man, he had been anxious to find out how much aid money might be lavished on his area, and Savage guessed by the particular line of his questions, how easy it would be to syphon off a percentage of it for himself.

Forster had obviously been here before. He made it sound as though the money was almost a foregone conclusion if the Administrator co-operated with them fully and put up a good case to satisfy the UN commissioners.

'Of course, much will depend on our having access to the surrounding area,' he had explained. 'We have to be free to visit the outlying villages where money on irrigation and healthcare programmes might be spent.'

The Administrator had been relaxed and expansive. 'That is no problem. We can arrange for a police or army escort for you – the guerrillas, you understand.'

Forster had nodded. 'I understand, but nothing can really be achieved without the co-operation of those people. We really can't have ourselves or other UN workers later being seen as targets by the guerrillas. It's my understanding that many of them are drawn from the local population. They must be made to realise that the results of our mission will be of benefit to their own villages and families.' He paused for effect. 'Do you think that a meeting could be arranged between us and the local guerrilla leadership?'

The man had sucked on his teeth. 'Ah, now that might prove difficult. Our only contact with them is usually over the sights of a rifle.'

Lying bastard, both Forster and Savage had thought. In a remote region like this, there had to be give and take. A little honest horse-trading. Otherwise the guerrillas could overrun the town, just as the army could mount a sweep-and-destroy operation over the surrounding hills. Far safer for the status quo to be maintained by mutual standoff. Live and let live. In South America there was a certain natural order about things and there was little doubt that here, too, the warring parties found a way to compromise whenever it suited them.

'Anyway, give it some thought,' Forster had concluded as he rose to shake hands. If it suited the Administrator, he would probably find a way.

Savage recalled the prolonged meeting as she showered and dressed in beige safari culottes and a coffee-coloured blouse. Throwing open the window, she peered down into the rough concrete-paved street. It was bustling already with colourful and rattling *chiva* buses, ancient American limos, and Japanese pickups, all plying their trade. The sunlit sidewalks were filled with shabbily dressed townsfolk and *campesinos* who'd come in for a morning's shopping; ragged denims and straw sombreros were much in evidence. After the blackout and pitiless downpour of the previous night, she found herself sharing the people's obvious sense of recharged vitality in the rain-freshened air and the gathering warmth of the sun. It showed in the friendly waves and the happily gossiping women on the street corners.

She hadn't quite known what to expect to find in Santa Maria. Fully aware of the dangers that awaited them, she had anticipated that the town would somehow be dark and dangerous, with menace lurking in every shadow. Certainly the bright and pretty, if run-down, adobi buildings and the cheerful inhabitants lingering in the leafy main plaza had all come as a surprise – and not a little relief.

'Are you up?'

She turned to find Dale Forster standing at her door. 'Sure, but next time would you mind knocking? I could have been taking a shower.'

He grinned, unperturbed. 'Just my luck you weren't, rosebud. Anyway the door was open – not a clever idea anywhere south of Mexico.'

Savage felt a rush of irritation. 'Is it my hearing or did I miss the apology? And the door was open because the lock is bust. Just like the sink plug is missing.'

There was an unmistakable look of mockery in those smiling eyes. 'You've operated in South America before, so you ought to know Rule Number One. Always pack a door-jamb device and a universal basin plug.'

'Thanks for that, Dale,' she retorted, nevertheless aware that he had a point; overlooking such basic essentials made her feel rather foolish. 'Now would you like to tell me what plans you have for the day?'

'Let's talk about it over breakfast, rosebud.'

'Fine,' she replied with a tight smile, 'just as long as you stop calling me that.'

He feigned surprise at her complaint. 'A sweet English rose, that's all.'

'Get stuffed, Dale.'

He'd changed, she thought, as they crossed the road to the courtyard cantina that had an arrangement with the hotel to

153

supply breakfast for its guests. From almost the moment they'd set foot in Colombia, the American had become a different man. Back in London his behaviour had reminded Savage of some corporate executive, tense and tight-lipped with a distinct lack of humour, shrewd and utterly focused as he assembled the team and planned the operational details. Now he seemed more relaxed, perhaps happier being in the field, at the sharp end. But if that sense of freedom was going to result in his trying to lord it over her and lapse into patronising sexism, then she intended Forster would be in for a rude awakening.

'Maybe today we should enlist the help of the town priest,' the American said. It didn't surprise her that he'd gone native and ordered potato soup for his breakfast.

'Never a bad idea in South America,' she replied. Priests were always a fount of knowledge in rural areas. And not to be outdone she ordered a *santafereño*, bread and cheese that was eaten after dunking it in the accompanying drink of hot chocolate.

That caused Forster's eyebrows to rise, she noted with amusement, but he didn't comment, simply saying: 'The priest can get us the informal introductions to those who really count – doctors, teachers, local businessmen. Maybe we can get the priest's help to set up a public meeting to spread the word that the UN being here is good news.'

Savage smiled. 'Ever thought, Dale, that maybe you're in the wrong job?'

It was just then that she noticed him. A nondescript individual in torn jeans, a canvas jacket and baseball cap had sauntered into the cantina. He was unshaven with long greasy hair and his shoulders hunched as he sat down alone at a table. She heard him ask the waitress in colloquial Spanish what was the cheapest meal they had, then ordered vegetable soup and bread.

Only then did she realise with a small thrill of satisfaction that Forster hadn't recognised him.

The single-engined Piper bucked and tossed on the afternoon thermals and Peter Stafford found himself peering through the scratched perspex windows at the fragile, trembling wings. With a kind of detached and morbid curiosity, he wondered when they were going to snap off.

You can't allow yourself to believe you're really here, he told himself. Not letting some macho police pilot practise his aerobatics while you sit cramped up in this little eggshell with four other passengers and their luggage. Not trusting your life to this frail craft being thrown around the sky at the whim of the crosswinds. Not flying low between the bleak canyon sides of the Chicamocha river that carved its way through these forbidding mountains. Really believe where you are and you'll throw up or shit yourself. And not necessarily in that order.

How many times in his life had he been driving a car when he'd had a breakdown? Nine, ten times? And here he was in an aircraft with a similar engine which was probably badly maintained like most things mechanical on this continent. Even if the pilot was a bloody genius, there was nowhere to land in an emergency. Everywhere just rocky peaks and precipitous slopes or else raging rivers.

Before he'd left he'd promised himself two things, as any sane and rational man might. That he wouldn't fly in anything that didn't have at least two engines and that he'd never fly in the afternoons when the Andean thermals were at their most unpredictable. And here he was, doing both. Why?

Well, he knew the answer to that one. You don't reply to some mysterious ad in *Soldier of Fortune* magazine, get short-listed for some no-questions-asked mission to Colombia and be interviewed by two bruisers whose muscle weight Arnold Schwarzenegger would have envied, get paid a small fortune in used dollar bills, only to complain that you didn't like flying in small aircraft. These people, whoever they were, weren't paying for wimps.

Warrant Officer First Class in the British Paras. That's what had appealed to them. Up through the ranks of the red-bereted headbangers, working boy made good with the social niceties of the officer class learned quickly as a necessary extra for the mess. They liked that, just as they had no problem with the fact that he'd been dishonourably discharged from Her Majesty's Armed

155

Forces. Pete Stafford had tried to evade his interviewers' questions, but the men were faultless in their technique. Hard man, soft man.

'If we find out you've been lying to us later,' Beavis, apparently a one-time corporal in the Prince of Wales's Own, had promised, 'we'll break your fuckin' legs off and feed 'em to the condors.'

'You can tell us the truth,' said the other, a former Marine whom he knew only as Dan. 'After all, we aren't exactly looking for sodding social workers.'

And when Stafford had finally admitted his discharge had followed him being caught in flagrante delicto with the battalion commander's wife, Beavis and Dan seemed highly amused. Instantly it had been deemed worthy of another round of drinks from the bar of the Las Vegas hotel. However, that first application, some twelve months earlier, had not proved successful, although they told him he'd at least made their shortlist. So he had returned to Britain, jobless and penniless. And he was still in that unhappy state, struggling on a computer retraining course, when he'd received the surprise telephone call a week earlier.

'We need a replacement,' Beavis told him without much preamble. 'If you're still interested, we'll cable you the money for an economy ticket to the States. As far as family and friends are concerned, that's where you'll be for the next year, working on oil exploration in the desert and not reachable by phone. We'll give you a post office box number in Miami. All uniform and kit provided. The pay's a thousand dollars a week and a ten thousand annual bonus after the first year.' He added ominously: 'Which you *will* collect.' It was obviously not a job you were expected to quit.

So here he was. Overnight flight to Miami, changing airlines to Bogotá via Caracas and a regular internal flight to Bucaramanga, the capital of the up-country state of Santander. Then it was to be a scheduled Aerataca flight by twin-engined Otter through the Andes to the remote strip at Santa Maria. Only it wasn't to be, because it had been cancelled. Guerrillas had phoned a warning to say they'd mined the landing area. This happened regularly, the bored desk attendant informed him. Usually they were

156

hoaxes, but not always, and the airline wasn't prepared to take the risk.

Infuriated at a day's delay, Stafford had found himself commiserating with two fellow would-be travellers. Introducing themselves as Goldie and Mario, they explained that they were a natural history film unit under contract to the BBC. Apparently they planned to make Santa Maria their base while they recorded the life – and no doubt sex lives, Stafford thought with a smirk – of the animal kingdom.

'I don't want to spend another night at that hotel,' Goldie, the Jewish cameraman, said. 'Security's piss poor and there are no locks on the doors. Someone tried to break in last night, and there's us with fuck knows how many thousand pounds worth of kit. Our luck can't hold, some thieving little snot will get his hands on something.'

'Maybe there's some other private commercial flight going,' the man's partner, Mario, suggested. He was a big, mustachioed man from Martinique.

The desk attendant smiled. 'Why don't you speak to someone in the police office? They fly out regularly to Santa Maria. If they'll take you, we'll refund them your fare.'

It was another of those commonplace South American arrangements. Not exactly illegal, but it was hardly ethical for police pilots to combine operational flights with a little private enterprise and to pocket the profits. Nevertheless it resolved the problem for Stafford and the natural history unit because the police Piper was due to fly in an army colonel to investigate the guerrilla threat. That had left room for three more passengers plus the film equipment.

The little aircraft dropped suddenly in an airpocket, a sickening sensation like the fall and abrupt arrest of a lift in a shaft.

'God, I'm going to be sick,' muttered the cameraman. He was wedged tightly between Stafford and Mario the sound-man.

'Not over my recording gear, thank you!'

The pilot overheard and laughed. 'If anyone throws up in my airplane, he walks the rest of the way.' He brought the nose of the Piper round, tilting the wings so they could see the awesome range of *cuchillas*. Bare, desolate and inhospitable. 'There, can you see? Up ahead is Santa Maria.'

Light reflected on the sprawling mass of adobi buildings spread across a plateau atop the canyon wall at two thousand metres above sea level. Even from that distance Stafford could make out the symmetrical grid of streets around the bright greenery of the central plaza where the tiered frontage of the cathedral glistened like sugar icing in the westering sun.

What a bloody stupid place to have a town, Stafford mused. Before the days of air travel, it could only have been reached by miles of tortuous mountain track. And why had they thought it necessary to build not just a humble chapel, or even a modest church, but a sodding great cathedral? In his mind's eye he could just visualise the hundreds of mule carts lugging building materials up the mountainside.

Mario might have been reading his thoughts. '*Es magnifico, eh, amigo?*'

Stafford nodded. 'But why here, in this place?'

The man smiled. 'I see you do not understand South America. In such a place it is important that God's presence be seen. To create such a wonder is not just a feat of human endeavour, it is an act of faith.'

As the pilot levelled out, Stafford could now see the grass strip on the outskirts of the town. It was cut like a shelf into the mountainside, sloping slightly to slow incoming flights and to add speed to those aircraft taking off straight out over the river canyon.

He found his knuckles tensing as the strip grew rapidly to fill the cockpit windscreen, aware that if the pilot was just a few feet too low they'd fly smack into the rock beneath the shelf – an instant fireball. Then they were down, wheels hitting hard and the plane bouncing skyward. Stafford held his breath. From the corner of his eye he saw Mario cross himself. Down again, then up like a rubber ball, each jump less energetic than the last, until they were running smoothly over the cropped grass and the tail finally came down.

'Fuck me,' the cameraman muttered, 'who taught this arsehole how to fly?'

But the pilot had not heard, instead transforming instantly into a Grand Prix driver, spinning his Piper round with abandon and racing towards the perimeter fence.

Relief only swept through Stafford once the whine of the engine finally died and the hatch doors sprang open.

As their luggage and the film crew's equipment were unloaded from the rear compartment, Goldie lit himself a cigarette. 'Would you like to share a taxi into town?'

Stafford shook his head and scanned the motley collection of parked vehicles beyond the perimeter gate. 'No thanks, I think I'm being met.'

'Ah, I see. Anyway, Pete, I've been rude. Didn't ask what an Englishman's doing in this wild west town?'

For a moment Stafford almost forgot his cover story. 'Er, I'm a mining engineer.'

Mario nodded, grinning widely. 'Emeralds, eh?'

Surprise registered on the Englishman's face. 'How did you know?'

'There are plenty around here, it's well known. I used to be in that game myself.'

Stafford lowered his voice. 'Well, keep it to yourselves. I don't think my bosses want it spread around.'

Mario agreed. 'This region is full of *bandidos*, *guerrilleros* and undesirable types who'd steal the coins from their dead grandmother's eyes.'

Just then Pete Stafford noticed Beavis. He was standing next to a brown Range Rover by the gate. 'That's my lift. Say, perhaps we can drop you off somewhere?'

Goldie grinned. 'Sure, that would be good. We're staying at the Imperial. They say it's the only hotel worthy of the name.'

Brian Beavis watched impassively as their recruit approached carrying a canvas kitbag over one shoulder and an aluminium photographer's case in his other hand. Pete Stafford was talking to the two men by his side, a raw-boned Latino with a drooping moustache and a straw trilby and a skinny Jew with thick-rimmed spectacles who reminded Beavis of some comedy actor whose name escaped him.

'Who the fuck is Stafford talking to?' Dan Crabtree asked from the driver's window. 'They're loaded with bloody film equipment, and he's carrying some of their stuff. Isn't that a bloody BBC sticker on it? Jesus, all we need's a fuckin' *Panorama* team!'

Beavis grunted. He was a big man; he'd tortured his mother when he'd been born at twelve pounds thirty-six years earlier and hadn't looked back since. Now the shaven bullet head and short neck sat appropriately on a combined fat-and-muscle weight of sixteen stone. He looked every bit the experienced mercenary he was, right down to the frosty blue eyes set deep in a weathered square face. A nose that had been broken in two places completed the picture. 'Don't worry, Dan, I'll mark the bastard's card.'

'Hi, Mr Beavis,' Stafford called in greeting. 'Sorry, if you've been hanging around. You heard the flight was cancelled?'

'I heard.'

'I met these two guys on the flight. They're making a wildlife documentary. I wondered if we might drop them off at their hotel?'

Beavis's eyes did not blink and he did not speak for several seconds. Stafford started to feel uncomfortable, realising he'd said the wrong thing.

Goldie shuffled his feet. 'Look, no problem if it's out of your way. It's a bit of an imposition.'

Beavis glanced at Crabtree, who shrugged. 'Chuck your stuff in the back.' No point in drawing attention by being unneighbourly, he decided.

Five minutes later both cameraman and sound-man stood outside the hotel, surrounded by their equipment, as the Range Rover sped away. They said nothing, but looked at each other for a moment and shared a knowing grin.

'Listen, Stafford,' Beavis said darkly as Crabtree negotiated the plaza and took the country road towards the village of Adoración, 'don't you ever pull a stunt like that again. While you work for us, you keep yourself to yourself, savvy? Don't talk to strangers about *anything*. The boss has strict rules about that and breaking them is punishable by having your balls crushed in a nutcracker. Just the presence of gringos round here gets tongues wagging and wagging tongues start speculating, and we don't encourage speculation.'

Pete Stafford sat on the rear bench seat and offered an apology. 'I just didn't think. It won't happen again.'

'Too right,' Crabtree retorted. He was a similar build to Beavis but five years younger and physically fitter. His cropped hair was dark and he had a bayonet scar that showed white against the tanned skin of his right cheek. 'And you certainly don't talk to anyone from the media.'

'They were hardly media. They're a freelance production company working for the BBC natural history unit . . .'

'And you'd be none the wiser if they were fuckin' *World In Action*,' Beavis cut in. 'You'll soon learn that in Colombia nothing is what it seems.'

Stafford was starting to realise that fast. And no doubt that included the outfit Beavis and Crabtree worked for. If this emerald mine was kosher, they'd hardly object to him talking to a wildlife film team. Either the mine itself was operating illegally or its production of precious stones was being smuggled abroad. Still, he could live with that if the money was good enough.

Crabtree was saying: 'Not that you'll get much chance to talk to strangers. The camp's thirty bone-shakin' klicks from the nearest settlement. A boil on the arse end of the world. You stay in camp until we decide we can trust you to keep your trap shut and stay relatively sober. Then you might be allowed out for some R and R on a Saturday night once a month. The local whores aren't worth a shag unless you put a bin bag over their heads.' He chuckled at his own description. 'Still, we never promised you life here would be easy. And we've a good stock of bin bags.'

The roughly paved streets of Santa Maria had given way to a rutted laterite track that followed a switchback course down the steep brown slopes of the canyon towards the wide river valley beyond. They overtook a chugging *chiva*, packed with dirty-looking *campesinos*, splashing puddle water on the gaily painted bus side as they passed.

'How many guys in the team?' Stafford inquired.

'Thirty now we're back up to full strength,' Beavis answered. 'There's usually around twenty at the camp at any one time. The

161

rest will be out on errands or riding shotgun for a consignment delivery.'

So that's it, Stafford decided. A hired gun to protect emerald couriers. Oh well, it was better than sitting in a classroom unable to make head nor tail of a computer program. 'What exactly am I expected to do?'

Crabtree laughed harshly, expertly lighting a cigarette single-handed as he swerved to miss a looming pothole. 'Anything and everything, matey. You told us you'd be happy doin' whatever and not asking questions. That's why you're here.'

Beavis added: 'You said at your interview that you were good at motor mechanics, but not qualified. Well, our ex-REME grease monkey has just lost his number two, so we thought you could fill in. Plenty of work to do with roads like these and spares are difficult if not impossible to get hold of. You need a PhD in Creative Engineering to work here, so you won't be getting much free time.

'But you'll still be expected to take your turn on guard duties – the area's swarming with gun-happy ELN guerrillas and the *campesinos* round here will nick your Y-fronts if you drop 'em for a crap. Then there's the police and army. They're based back in Santa Maria and don't venture out much for fear of the ELN. But that doesn't mean they're *not* capable of mounting a raid – and if they do, we have to be ready to stand fast and give them a bloody nose.'

'We certainly can't trust our Colombian partners farther than we can throw them,' Crabtree added, negotiating the ruts beside a dizzying drop into the valley. 'Bunch of gung-ho wankers until the shit hits the fan, then the chances are you wouldn't see them for dust.'

'Partners?' Stafford queried.

'Yeah, you don't operate in Colombia without the local mafia's say-so. Officially their boys run camp security, but whenever there's one of them, there needs to be two of us. More trouble than they're worth, but we have to live with it. Pedro the Peasant takes care of our local policing needs.'

'What do you mean?'

'Pedro's the Colombians' head honcho,' Crabtree explained, 'all bandoleers and machetes. It's his job to police the local population. Not everyone approves of us being here or wants to co-operate. Pedro makes sure they keep their complaints to themselves and assists us when necessary – or if not, his boys slap their legs or sometimes silence them for good.'

Stafford swallowed hard.

Beavis noticed. 'I hope you're going to have the stomach for life here, Pete. South America can make Northern Ireland or Bosnia seem like Disneyland.'

'I can hack it.'

'I do hope so. We weren't sure about you before, that's why you weren't on our first selection. Much as we approved of you bonking your CO's wife, there are more inspiring reasons for being discharged from the army.'

Oh dear, sweet Maud – you gorgeous dyed-blonde, forty-something nymphomaniac – why ever did you tempt me? He sighed. 'You mean criminal?'

Beavis smiled gently. 'Let's say reasons that showed a healthy disregard for law and order, because out here that's exactly what you'll need.'

Stafford felt increasingly out of his depth and hid it with a sudden surge of irritation. 'I told you, I can hack it.'

'Harry will make sure you can,' Crabtree intervened with a smirk, 'believe me.'

'Harry?'

'Harry Morgan, our boss. One of your own, Pete, an ex-Para. Eats people like you for breakfast!'

Both men laughed at their shared private joke.

'Oh, shit!'

Crabtree hit the brakes as they rounded the blind bend and the Range Rover slithered to a reluctant halt in the churned red mud. Some fifty metres ahead a log had been placed across the road where half a dozen scruffy individuals had gathered, all armed with a mixed collection of weapons. One stood to the fore: a young, slim man with a toothbrush moustache on his upper lip and an absurdly wide white sombrero with a pointed top.

Stafford gulped. 'Who are they?'

'Local *guerrilleros*,' Beavis replied tetchily. 'And that's the Cisco Kid – their leader.'

Stafford had only ever seen a brief clip of the 1950s TV Western series for kids, but he instantly saw the resemblance to the dapper cowboy hero.

'I'll reverse up,' Crabtree decided, looking back over his shoulder as he changed gear.

'No!' Beavis countermanded. He reached under his seat and produced two Ingram 9mm sub-machine guns. 'If we back down now, they'll think they've got us running scared. Bad psychology.'

'If you're sure, Brian.' Crabtree clearly wasn't.

Beavis handed one of the weapons over the back seat to Stafford. 'Poke that out your window. But keep it down, not pointed at anyone. Just let 'em know we're ready. If the balloon goes up, take out as many as you can, starting with Cisco.' He watched for a couple of seconds as Stafford released the mag, checked the breech, and reloaded. Good, he thought, the boy doesn't panic in a crisis. Beavis liked a man with a cool head. He said: 'Drive on, Dan. Nice 'n' steady.'

The huge tyres spun for a grip, the four-wheel drive finally biting, and the vehicle lurched clear of the criss-crossed furrows.

Five guerrillas were still spread in line behind their leader, weapons held at port. Calm and confident, not yet threatening. In the rear, Stafford lowered his window and let the Ingram rest casually along the sill as he scanned the sparse undergrowth and rock clusters for signs of a stop group behind them. None. This wasn't so bad, he thought. Fucking amateurs.

Crabtree eased on the brakes and leaned out of his window, aware that the guerrilla leader could see the second Ingram at rest in Beavis's lap. 'Hi, Cisco, how you doing?'

The brown baby-face with its dark eyes peered in. He was ridiculously pretty with pouting full lips and long, dark lashes. 'Señor Dan.'

'Yeah, yeah,' the mercenary confirmed, 'and this is Señor Brian, who you know, and a new guy in the back who you don't. Señor Pete. He's a Para. Don't mix with him if you know what's

164

good for you – he's one mean hombre.'

Cisco inclined his head towards Stafford in acknowledgement, his eyes fixed on the Ingram.

'So what's the problem?' Crabtree asked. 'Collectin' road tax again? Now you know we don't pay your road tax, so be a good *chico* and shift that log.'

A flicker of irritation showed in the guerrilla's eyes. '*Quisiero ver El Señor Harry. Prontó por favor.*'

'What's he say?' Beavis asked.

'Dunno. Something about Harry.'

Stafford gave a polite cough, 'Er, I think he says he wants to see Señor Harry as soon as possible.'

'Speak the lingo, do you?' Beavis asked, his surprise edged with sarcasm.

'Just schoolboy stuff. It's a bit rusty.'

'Ask him why he wants to see Harry.'

Stafford obliged. 'He says it's a private matter between the two of them.'

Beavis's cheeks coloured. 'Cheeky spick. Okay, say we'll pass the message on – *if* he opens this fuckin' track and let's us get on with our business!'

This time Stafford stumbled over his words, but Cisco followed the general drift. Grudgingly he backed off and ordered his men to drag the log to one side.

'He'll be wanting to renegotiate his slice of the action,' Crabtree decided, gunning up the big V6 engine. 'Harry pays Cisco and his merry men an amount each month to keep them off our backs. Not exactly protection money, because we could easily give them a bloody nose. But it's worth it just to avoid the hassle. Trouble is, the slimebags are always wanting more.'

'We also promised them some decent arms,' Beavis added, 'and a spot of training. But Harry's stalling on that. Maybe that's Cisco's beef?'

Stafford glanced over his shoulder. The *chiva* they had passed earlier was now halted by the log which was back across the road. *Campesinos* were spilling out of the vehicle at gunpoint. 'How do the locals take to being turned over by the guerrillas?'

165

Beavis laughed. 'With resignation – a lot are probably related anyway. Most of them have got fuck all, so there's nothing to rob. Anyone who's got anything of value – say, a few dollars – will keep it in his socks or stuffed down his underpants. But young Cisco's got wise to that. He's started making them all strip off. Last month they kept all the passengers' clothes on the Tunja–Santa Maria road. They had to drive into town bollock naked. Quite a hoot really. Guess the ELN's uniform allowance hadn't arrived.'

His pitiless chuckle faded as he shared Crabtree's concentration on the pot-holed track. The decline had steepened dramatically, the trail narrower, the bends sharper and the drops ever more breathtaking. It didn't invite small talk between passengers and certainly no one had a mind to distract the driver's attention.

Forty minutes saw them at the bottom of the canyon. There the track straightened out somewhat, following a gentle descent into the river valley itself. This was subsistence farm land, the thin soil offering coarse grazing for a handful of scrawny cattle and sheep. Only a few crops were attempted, mostly withered fields of maize or beans. Outside the occasional adobi dwellings were tethered goats or scavenging pigs and chickens. By one roadside hut Stafford saw an Indian squatting and staring vacantly at the horizon. He wore a trilby over long, straggling hair which fell onto the shoulders of his woollen *ruana* poncho and he was smoking a long bamboo pipe.

Marijuana, Stafford wondered, and felt he understood the need for creature solace in such a starkly beautiful but terribly lonely place.

Having encountered no other vehicles – just two men on mules loaded with produce for market – they eventually reached Adoración. The village was hardly worthy of a name. Two rows of traditional, white-painted drystone buildings with thatched roofs rose straight out of the ground on either side of the muddy street. As the Range Rover splashed along it, Beavis pointed out the general store and the El Bar, both of more recent clapboard construction. They were set back from the main drag and resembled a Wild West filmset. It was the only place that showed any sign of life; mules were tied at a hitching rail and a battered 4x4 was parked outside while a local farmer loaded up his monthly provisions.

'For the next year, this'll be the centre of your universe,' Beavis said. 'A visit to the *voliche* or the whorehouse will seem like going to the West End to take in supper and the latest Lloyd Webber.'

'Sounds great,' Stafford muttered. Christ, what had he let himself in for?

Beyond the town, they crossed the rickety wooden bridge. The wild waters of the Servita foamed and crashed around the rotting timber piles and Stafford found himself holding his breath until they'd cleared the thirty-metre span.

It was on then for another twenty cratered kilometres. The land of boulders, scrubland and occasional clusters of wind-blown trees was becoming ever more desolate as they began climbing in the lee of the east canyon wall.

The sudden appearance of the chapel when they rounded a bend took Stafford quite by surprise. It looked down on the road from a rocky promontory: a long, low building of ancient lime-washed stone and terracotta roof tiles topped with an ornately carved three-bell housing above the front gable.

'They call this place the Cruz de Oro,' Crabtree said, 'after the first gold crucifix that was made for the church from gold panned by early prospectors in the Servita.'

Below the chapel was a minor crossroad and three near-derelict huts which looked to be inhabited by Indians. Alongside them was a bar; its bamboo shutter was down and the rusting, paint-peeled tables and chairs looked singularly uninviting.

'Our local,' Beavis said, 'when the owner is sober enough to open up.'

The gradient was increasing rapidly, the track winding up between enormous boulders and stands of eucalyptus. After another few kilometres, Crabtree suddenly swung left onto a narrow sidetrack that could so easily have been missed by anyone not familiar with the route. It plunged down a wooded spur of land and across a wide running stream before recommencing the climb.

167

Screened by trees, the camp itself was constructed on a gently sloping plateau with the canyon side rising quite steeply behind it. Stafford caught sight of a watchtower and someone with binoculars before it was hidden from view by the high steel-mesh fence of the compound. Tall gates swung open on their approach to reveal a gathering of unsavoury looking *campesinos*. Tattily dressed in sandals, straw stetsons and sombreros, most wore bandoleers of ammunition over their shoulders and carried an assortment of small arms and rifles.

The men stared morosely as the Range Rover passed through the sandbag emplacements on either side of the gate. Crabtree braked outside a low, primitive construction of breeze blocks and corrugated tin which formed one side of the open compound square.

'Home sweet home,' Beavis said, climbing out. 'This is the bunkhouse.'

He led Stafford through improvised double doors of marine plywood which the new arrival guessed were only ever closed against wind and rain. There was no glass in the windows, just torn mosquito nets stapled to the wooden frames. Rows of camp beds ran left and right, the men's kit parked in neat piles between each one.

'No lockers,' Beavis said, 'but the men have their own ways of dealing with anyone caught thieving. So resist the temptation if you want my advice.'

Above his head, a line of electric cable threaded through the timber rafters, half a dozen bare bulbs providing night-time light from a generator. A few of the beds were occupied: one or two men slept; the others, dressed in vests and boxer shorts, were reading or listening to Walkmans. Some looked up, nodding their acknowledgement in an uninterested sort of way. They passed a communal trestle table loaded with dog-eared paperbacks and a pile of hard porn magazines.   •

Once Stafford had dumped his kitbag on his allocated cot, Beavis led him back out and across the compound, pointing out the various tumbledown buildings as they walked. There was a second bunkhouse, constructed out of timber; probably built to house the original emerald miners, it looked to be in imminent danger of collapse. However it still served as billet for Pedro Goméz and the Colombian mafia's hard men. A second breeze-block building housed the cookhouse and mess with a small lounge filled with unmatching and dilapidated armchairs and a makeshift bar. A small timber cabin provided the admin office and quarters for Harry Morgan and his number two, a man called Thripp. It also included a spare bunk for any of the organisation's visiting hierarchy.

Stafford noticed a second, inner compound, its steel fence topped with razor wire and a solitary block-built structure on the inside. An armed guard stood by the gate – not a Colombian, a gringo.

Beavis offered no explanation before they arrived at the workshop. It was an open-fronted framework of eucalyptus to which corrugated tin had been nailed to form walls and a sloping roof. Stafford could hear the hiss and sizzle of an oxyacetylene torch as they approached. The man who was working in overalls under the jacked-up Korean Rocsta jeep slid out on his back-trolley and climbed to his feet.

'Doug, meet your new oil rag,' Beavis called out. 'This is Pete Stafford – Doug Tallboys, our resident mechanic magician.'

True to his name, Tallboys was a couple of inches over six feet, the dirty overalls hanging loosely on his thin body. In his late thirties, his thinning ginger hair was wild and uncombed, the face unsmiling with humourless pale blue eyes that appeared to be devoid of lashes.

He wiped his hands on a cloth before greeting the recruit without enthusiasm. 'So you're the new boy, eh?' The accent was Scottish Borders, Stafford thought.

'For my sins, Doug.'

A flicker of bleak amusement showed for a second in the eyes. 'More than you know, son, more than you know.'

Beavis said: 'Take Pete under your wing, Doug, and show him the ropes. As I told you, he's not a professional mechanic, but restoring MGs is his hobby, so he ought to be a bit better than useless.'

169

'Glad of *any* help I can get around here. These macho soldier boys are fucking hopeless with anything mechanical that doesn't kill people.'

'See you later then,' Beavis said, 'Dan and I have got some work to catch up on.'

As the burly former soldiers strode off together, Stafford glanced around at the workbench and array of tools. 'How many vehicles do you have to service?'

'Well, there's the Range Rover you arrived in,' Tallboys replied. 'We've two of them – the staff cars, I call them. Harry Morgan and his number two have first call, then Beavis and Crabtree. That's our officer corps, so to speak. Then the rest of the shower run round in five of these open-topped Rocstas. Well, only four now, as we've had to cannibalise one for spares. Not bad bits of kit.' He nodded towards the Colombian bunkhouse. 'But those bastards cause me the real headaches. Turn up in any clapped-out old vehicle they've won at cards or nicked off the local *campesinos* and expect me to keep them running. Sometimes off-roaders, sometimes trucks. So I hope you can improvise?'

Stafford grinned; there was something about the other man he liked. 'I'll learn.'

Tallboys tossed his rag into a corner. 'I've been working since first light – time for a break. I'll show you the mess.'

'Do you always eat this late?' It was almost three in the afternoon.

'Aye, as a matter of fact I do.' They began walking. 'The rest have usually finished by now.'

Stafford sensed it, and the words were out before he'd thought twice: 'You don't get on with the others?'

The Scotsman glanced at him. 'Let's say I like to keep my own counsel. And you, Pete, have you done much of this kind of work before? Freelance mercenary stuff?'

A shake of the head. 'No, first time. Straight off the dole queue.'

'And before that?'

'Three Para.'

Again that hint of a grim smile. 'I might have known.'

'What d'you mean?'

'Most of them here are ex-Paras or Marines – at least they claim to have been, at one time or another.'

'You don't believe them?'

Tallboys shook his head. 'I didn't say that. It's just that most of them are the sort you'd cross the road to avoid, if you get my drift. Question them closely and they tend to clam up.' He stopped walking and looked directly at Stafford for a moment as though considering how much he dared say. 'Look, you're new to all this, so let me put you in the picture before you put your foot in it. Probably everyone in this outfit has served in the British Army or the Royal Marines at some time – and been kicked out for one reason or another. They're the dross. Psychopaths, nutters and Walter Mittys. Head cases, the lot of them. They're not even proper mercenaries – I know, because I've worked in Angola and South Africa. But nowadays there's not much call except for Bosnia and these guys aren't in the running to get themselves seriously shot at.'

Stafford didn't completely follow what the Scotsman was trying to say. 'Does it really matter, Doug? I mean, all they're doing is guarding a bloody emerald mine.'

At that point Tallboys almost exploded with a burst of laughter. 'Oh, Jesus, Pete, you really did come up on the down train, didn't you? Emeralds my arse. That's all a cover – and a pretty transparent one at that. These guys are in the dirtiest business of all. C'mon, this *is* Colombia. You, my son, are now up to your neck in the cocaine business. Just like me. And there's no way out.'

Tallboys began walking again and Stafford found himself trotting to keep up. 'Are you serious – about the cocaine?'

'I wouldn't joke about something like that. Personally, I don't find it funny, but it's too late now. I was conned into this by Beavis, just like you. I wasn't their normal type of recruit either. It's just that they were desperate for an experienced mechanic and I fell for the line they shot me.'

They had reached the mess hall now, the trestle tables and benches deserted. At the far end a fat, middle-aged Colombian woman tended cooking pots on an open range. 'Two *cuchocos*, Martha, and two coffees,' Tallboys called out, sitting astride one

171

of the benches and turning back to Stafford. 'Listen, son, you'll have to make your own decision how you handle this situation. But if I were you, I'd choose my friends carefully. Fortunately for you you're allocated as my assistant. I'll find enough work to keep you busy – that's certainly no problem here. With any luck you'll be spared other duties and won't have to get blood on your hands. At least I carry some clout here, if only because I know one end of a spanner from the other.' He glanced towards the kitchen area to ensure Martha was out of earshot. 'Nevertheless, you ought to know who in particular to avoid.'

Stafford was still stunned by the revelation, shocked that he could have been so stupid. 'Beavis and Crabtree seemed okay.'

'Aye, but they're still hard cases. They'll do what's necessary, no questions asked. Anyway, they're hardly ever here, always organising recruitment or supplies or sorting out problems in Bogotá or wherever. Like Harry Morgan himself, they're too busy with admin to get involved with the fine detail. They'll give orders and expect things to get done – they don't give a shit how. That falls to Harry's second-in-command, Guy Thripp. Says he's ex-SAS, but who knows? He's a right cunt. Don't get on the wrong side of him or his mate Billy Susan.'

'Who's he?'

'Billy Susan's the gaffer, or foreman if you like, of the rest of the men. If Thripp is God, then Susan sits at his right hand. You might not like what you see here, but don't complain to anyone. Especially those two. That's what happened to your predecessor, Hal. A young ex-REME – great lad.'

Stafford felt the air suddenly turn chill. He remembered Beavis telling him with scarcely concealed menace that he'd collect his annual bonus and now Tallboys was saying there was no way out once they were in. It seemed almost stupid to ask, but he had to. 'My predecessor, he didn't leave?'

Tallboys hunched over the table and played his fingers over the clogged cellar of damp salt. 'Oh, Hal left all right. In a box with a bullet in the back of his head.' Beyond the compound fence the distant savage mountains were blurred with mist. 'He's buried out there somewhere in the *cuchillas*.'

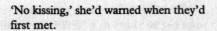

8

'No kissing,' she'd warned when they'd first met.

Like whores the world over, there was one thing that she kept sacred. Mallory always found it sadly amusing how street girls would happily give blow jobs and offer their arses if the price was right, yet forbid the simple touching of lips. The one small, hopeless dream that had to be kept alive, flickering like a candle in the wind, to make life bearable. One small gesture, one token of where the line had to be drawn. Affirmation that one day her prince would arrive and with it her salvation.

Lucila was no different.

She sighed languidly as he gently unshafted himself from her body and rolled over to the edge of the bed, placing his feet on the floor. It was quite dark now, the room lit only by the feeble street lights of Santa Maria. Outside he could hear salsa music throbbing from the bar next door and the voices of the Saturday night revellers.

Saturday night. He'd been in town five days and five nights; on three of those he had spent time in bed with Lucila.

'Could I buy a cigarette?' he asked.

She giggled, her head propped up on one elbow as she regarded the muscled contours of his back, fascinated by the whorl of scar tissue around the old exit wound. 'Such a strong man and still you cannot give it up?' she teased, speaking in hesitant English.

He turned to look back at her. A pretty mulatto face with dark moist eyes and a pout that she thought made her look like Marilyn Monroe. Around twenty-eight, he guessed. Wild and

173

frizzled hair, black but with a few early strands of grey. 'I need something to calm me down after all that excitement.'

She indicated the packet on the chair which was hung with her discarded clothes. Bright turquoise Lycra pants, gold lamé top and a frilly brassière that was running to holes. He removed two cigarettes, gave her one, and lit them.

'You are a strange man, Señor Kurt,' she said, inhaling deeply.

'Really?'

'I have many customers over many years, since I am fourteen years old and have to help feed my mother, my brothers and sisters. But I think I never meet anyone like you.'

He grinned 'How d'you mean?'

She gave a shy smile, the colour of her cheeks deepening with embarrassment. 'My customers pay and then do what they want. No one thinks about me – I know, why should they? But you do. For most of the hour we spend together you are making love to me, not the other way round. You care that I should feel good too. I have never known this.'

'When the woman feels good, it makes a man feel even better,' he said. It wasn't just a ploy, he meant it. Yet his approach had always worked particularly well with whores over the years. They always appreciated the smallest kindness. Just to be treated like ordinary human beings for a few precious moments could mean the world to them. Gave them back their dignity. And he had lost count of how many times one simple gesture had been rewarded during his investigative assignments by being taken into their confidence and sharing secrets. Cynics might laugh at the old cliché of whores with hearts of gold. But there was always some truth in old adages and he'd rarely met a whore who didn't respond to being treated with respect.

'Then I am very lucky to meet you. Even my boyfriend does not treat me like you do.'

Hardly surprising, Mallory thought; her so-called boyfriend was a pimp. But he said: 'I'm the lucky one, Lucila.'

She stared thoughtfully at her cigarette and blew gently on the tip until it glowed. 'And I think that all Englishmen are not like you.'

He raised an eyebrow; he'd been right all along. 'You don't know any Englishmen. You said so.'

'I am sorry.' Her eyes were wide and earnest, anxious that he should not think ill of her. 'I did not tell you the truth. I was frightened – well, I still am but now I feel I can trust you. When you asked me that first night, I think maybe you are from the police. That is when I still think you are Colombian.'

'You're afraid of the police?'

She shook her head. 'No, I am afraid of the gringos if they think I tell the police that they are bad people.'

'And are they bad people?'

A shrug of those naked, slender shoulders. 'I do not know. They are rough with me, but so are many customers. It is just that they tell me and the other girls not to talk about them to anyone. They pay extra that we keep quiet. And say they will do bad things to us if we do not. But one thing I wonder is how you hear about these people?'

Mallory made light of it. 'Someone I met in a bar in Bogotá. I mentioned I used to work in mines and was looking for a job. He said he'd heard that some emerald mines were being reopened up here. He thought it was an English company.'

She reached out and touched his arm. 'These are not nice people, Señor Kurt. I do not think you should be involved.'

'I need the money,' he grinned, 'to pay for your charms for a start. A man must eat and have a roof over his head. Now please tell me, how well do you know these Englishmen?'

She bit her lower lip. 'This will be private between us?'

'I swear to you.'

'Well, I have had just two men go with me.' She felt ashamed to admit to him it was both of them at the same time; it was what they wanted and why they paid extra pesos.

'Do you know their names?'

'Just – I think – Señor Guy and Señor Billy. These are English names? They come sometimes on a Saturday. I think they are in town to collect supplies.'

'Do they speak Spanish?'

Lucila shook her head. 'The tall, thin one called Guy, he

speaks a little, but not very good. He has a tattoo on the back of his right fist. Three figure nines in a row. I say this to the priest in confession and he says maybe it is the other way. Three sixes.'

Mallory murmured: 'The sign of the devil.'

She giggled sheepishly. 'I think that is true. He can be very cruel. The other one is nicer – well, he is rough but at least he does not *smile* when he hurts me. He speaks no Spanish, just the fuck word. His face has a mouth that is like a girl's and long eye-lashes, although he is short and quite ugly, I think. But he can be funny after he has a good fucking. There is a tattoo – it makes me laugh. The man called Guy tell me that once Señor Billy is drunk with his friends in some place – Hong Kong, I think. He falls asleep and cannot be woken. So his friends have this idea – when he wakes up he finds there is a big red rising sun tattooed on his backside.'

He shared her humour, but added: 'You don't have to let them hurt you, Lucila, remember that. Tell them no violence or else no fucking.'

She looked touched by his concern. 'I do not think they would like me to talk to them that way. And like you, Señor Kurt, I need the money.' Then a thought occurred to her. 'There have been other Englishmen from the mine, but they did not go with me. The girls tell me that one man has a tattoo of a wolf – here.' She tapped her right forearm. 'And the other a heart and roses on his shoulder. These men look the same, they are twins. But they do not come for many months now, maybe because there was big trouble one night. There is a row over money and my friend Monica is badly beaten. Then another customer tries to help but these gringos drag him outside. It is a cold, wet night and they all disappear. The customer is never seen again. There are rumours that he is murdered, but no one knows.'

Mallory frowned. 'What about the police?'

Lucila gave him a quizzical look. 'What about them? They come and ask a few questions, see if they can get a shag for free, and then they go. No one cares about our customer, he was just a *campesino* from somewhere up in the *cuchillas*.' Then she added brightly: 'But maybe he is still alive. Maybe he is living in

Adoración and I see him when I go there.'

The name of the village struck home. 'Adoración? You're going there?'

Suddenly she looked sad. 'Yes, to work. I will miss you, nice Englishman. There is a club and some good girls there, and I have been asked to go. My boyfriend says there is a new owner and that there is good business.'

'But surely, business can't be good there?' But even as he spoke the words he guessed the answer.

'It is the gringos from the mine. They go there, do not come here so much no more.'

He was about to reply, to try and persuade her not to go, when there was a knock on the door.

'Come,' Lucila called in Spanish.

As the door swung open, Mallory glimpsed the scarlet Lycra pants and bare midriff in the light from the hallway. It was Monica.

For a moment she stared fully at Mallory before removing the little pearl cigarette holder from her mouth as she half-smiled. 'Now I see what you like so much about Señor Kurt.'

'Monica!' Lucila protested. 'Don't say such things to my customers.'

The older woman laughed. 'I have not yet met a man who does not like being flattered in that department, my girl!'

'What do you want?' Lucila demanded, concerned that her friend was poaching.

'The gringos are downstairs. They ask for you again. I wonder what special treats you give them that make them so eager.'

'I think it is because I speak a little English,' Lucila replied frostily.

Her friend just smiled again and quietly closed the door, leaving them to get dressed.

'Can you do me a favour, Lucila?' Mallory asked. 'Tell those men I was asking about the reopened emerald mine, that I want to get a job. Say you told me nothing. It might even earn you a few extra pesos.'

She knotted the front of her bolero. 'That could be dangerous

177

for you.'

He shook his head. 'I doubt it. Please, for me?'

'If you are sure.' She reached up then and kissed him briefly on the lips. 'But take care. If you get a job, then maybe I see you in Adoración.'

Mallory made his way into the narrow passage where light from downstairs could be seen through the tiny gaps between the floorboards. He took the wooden steps down to the lounge where *putas* sprawled in lewd and extravagant poses to catch the punters' eyes. There was an archway in the wall that led to the adjoining bar where he ordered a can of Poker beer before taking an alcove seat.

There was no mistaking Guy Thripp or Billy Susan. They stood together, the long and the short of it, elbows behind them on the counter as they faced into the bar to admire the girls passing by with plump backsides encased in colourful shrink-wrap leggings which successfully held in a multitude of sins. Thripp's thumbs were thrust into his belt and Mallory could just discern the 999 tattoo on his right hand. Although both men had dressed down in dirty jeans and Thripp even wore a straw stetson like he thought he was some kind of Western hero, they were just too new and unfaded for them to be anything but gringos. Their skin colour, their mannerisms and demeanour set them instantly apart.

Just then Lucila flounced happily into the bar, waved and beckoned the two men. Throwing back their heads in unison, they drained their drinks and disappeared through the archway after her.

This could be a dangerous gamble, Mallory realised; these men would be capable of doing anything to some no-hope stranger if they thought he knew too much. At least he'd contrived to meet them in a public place to preserve an element of safety. And, anyway, he had to start somewhere.

He had just finished his beer half an hour later when Lucila reappeared at the archway and pointed him out to Thripp and Susan. For a moment they questioned her, probably doubting that he was anything other than just another *campesino*, before

178

they strode purposefully towards him. In one deft and synchronised movement, they separated as they reached the table, each taking a chair on either side of him and pressing in close.

'Señor,' Thripp said in a low, angry rasp, 'I understand you have been asking after us?' His face, which was long and angular with high cheekbones, was dominated by a long drooping moustache and deep-set eyes. 'You speak English, yeah?'

Mallory hardly needed to feign a look of apprehension and a nervous laugh. 'I ought to, amigo, I *am* English.'

Billy Susan wore a suspicious frown which did nothing for the pretty mouth and eyes in an otherwise squashed and ugly face which had the skin texture of lumpy porridge. 'Not with that fucking accent you're not. What are you? German? Austrian? Maybe Polish?'

Mallory gave his usual abbreviated explanation: an orphan brought up by German brothers in Paraguay. 'So, if you're with the Englishmen operating the emerald mine, then – yes, I've been asking after you. I've been bumming around South America for a year and my money's run out. I need a job and I used to work in mines.'

'Where?' Susan demanded.

'Kimberley – I was an overseer in the diamond mines.'

Thripp's eyes narrowed. 'Who told you about the mine here?'

'Some guy in a bar in Bogotá. He came from these parts. Said I might find a job going.'

'What bar?'

'I don't know, just a bar. Up in the Chapinero district.'

'And this guy's name?' Susan pressed.

Mallory was beginning to feel uncomfortable with both men so close, the smell of their breath in his nostrils. 'Gerardo, I think. Hell, it was no big deal. He just mentioned it in passing and I thought why not? It was worth a bus trip. There were no other jobs on offer and I'm pretty desperate.'

Thripp grunted. 'Well, there's no jobs on offer here either, so you've had a wasted trip.'

'I speak fluent Spanish and I probably know South America better than England. I can turn my hand to most things – apart from my mining experience. I'd do anything.'

The tall man pulled a smile that was half a sneer. 'Unfortunately you appear to have a physical defect. You seem to be deaf. I said there is no vacancy. And we don't go around employing any old hobo who just drifts into town.'

Mallory shrugged. 'It was worth a try. If you hear of anything—?'

The two men were already on their feet. 'Sure,' Billy Susan said, 'we'll let you know.'

Mallory awoke the next morning in a cold sweat.

As he opened his eyes and reorientated himself, recognising the poky hotel bedroom with its crumbling plaster ceiling, the confused dream melted away. All he retained was a picture of Guy Thripp's face. In close-up, staring at him.

Only then Mallory wondered if he'd met the man before?

Something about him had seemed familiar, but he wasn't sure what. Many unrelated people have physical similarities, mouths and eyes in particular. It is as though they could be linked by the same genetic strain, the threads running back into the branches of a long-lost family tree.

After all, the existence of facial similarities was the basis of police Identikit systems. So maybe Guy Thripp just reminded him of someone else he'd once known. It still left Mallory with a distinct feeling of unease.

By the time he'd hauled himself out of his sleeping bag, he'd made a decision. There was nothing more to be gained by staying in Santa Maria. He'd made contact with two gang members, which was a start. They were probably near the top of the organisational structure, he deduced, because Lucila reckoned they were the only ones who regularly visited the town to collect supplies. In other words, while the rest of the gang might frequent the distant village of Adoración, these two were trusted to keep a low profile. Also the way in which they had turned down his request for work without any inclination to refer to higher authority suggested they were well up in the gang's pecking order.

Unfortunately Mallory's first ploy hadn't worked out; he'd have been exceptionally lucky if it had. But at least they knew he

180

was around and why. Now he had to get closer to the camp to improve his chances of crossing paths again. He wanted to make his second move at the earliest opportunity, although as yet he had no idea what that might be.

After rinsing his face and torso at the basin, he dressed, selecting a dull red kerchief which he tied loosely around his neck. Then he left the hotel and crossed to the Café Cosmopolita beside the cathedral on the central plaza. He ordered chicken broth and drank coffee until five to eight. Picking up someone's abandoned newspaper, he walked to the nearest bench beneath the trees at the plaza's edge, lit a cigarette and began a relaxing read.

The signal that a meeting was requested was simplicity itself. If either Mallory or one of the other two teams wanted a meeting, they would sit on that bench at eight and display an item of red. Mallory's kerchief, Savage's red leather handbag or Mario's red shirt. A chance encounter would then be contrived in the town *cementerio* at noon.

Just a few moments later Georgina Savage and Dale Forster walked by, engaged in animated conversation with a Colombian who was well dressed in a suit and therefore almost certainly a member of the municipal authority. Clearly the UN cover was working well. None of the three appeared to notice Mallory as they made their way towards the Cosmopolita for their breakfast meeting.

At ten to twelve Mallory headed for the outskirts of town, past the pungent vegetable and cattle markets to the long flight of steps that led up to the *cementerio*. Horizontal concrete body-lockers formed walls six feet high, each small square door accepting a deceased's remains before being sealed, leaving a little shelf to form a shrine. Some held a vase of flowers, some were closed with little gates of wrought iron or glass; those of poorer families carried a cheap print of Christ or tacky religious trinkets made of plastic. These sad and bizarrely decorated walls created a number of criss-crossing corridors beneath a rain-threatening sky.

A mother and daughter were kneeling together, engrossed as they arranged a fresh spray of flowers for the recently departed man of the house. Mallory moved along to the next corridor where an elderly *campesino* stood alone, staring at a shrine. He crossed himself, his cheeks wet with tears. No one else. Mallory moved on.

Savage was standing in the last of the corridors, taking a photograph.

'You don't think people will mind?' she asked as Mallory approached.

'Not if you're discreet. Tourists will be tourists.' He looked around, checking they couldn't be seen or overheard. 'How are things going with you and Dale?'

'Fine. The UN cover is a dream. People can't do enough for us, hoping there'll be a big investment programme. We've had meetings with all the major dignitaries, civil servants, the priest, teachers. As usual, of course, we're getting more from the informal chats over drinks. We're building up a pretty thorough picture of the realpolitik of the region around Santa Maria.'

'Such as?'

'Well, this really is Medellín cartel country with ties going back centuries, hence the emerald mines and a lot of other land owned by many families. They've obviously got involved with the cocaine cartel in more recent years. No particular history of drugs in the area though, until our Viper friends moved in. Pablo Escobar used to have plenty of supporters locally and it seems quite a few businesses here were set up using *narco* funds. Everything that Jaramillo and Maria Palechor said stands up – it would be very difficult for the Cali cartel to get a look-in around here.'

'What about the *guerrilleros*?'

'Mostly ELN revolutionaries making the most of the remote nature of the *cuchillas*; they have quite a lot of support from farmers and others who think the government's neglected them. Quite a few locals, mostly youngsters, have joined up as part-timers. In the old days the guerrillas were well connected with Escobar, even business partners. They'd actually grow coca for him in the Amazonas. He'd also paid them to provide protected areas for *narco* operations and prevent interference from the police or army. And, of course, when he was alive Escobar shared the guerrillas' aim of bringing down the government. You could say they needed each other.'

'Any trouble from the ELN around here?'

'Apparently there was when the Soviet Union collapsed and funding dried up – and when the Medellín cartel first went into meltdown after Escobar's death.'

Mallory understood. '*Guerrilleros* need money like everyone else.'

'But it's been quiet for some eighteen months. They make their presence felt, but not sufficiently to make the army venture out of their barracks.'

'Eighteen months,' Mallory repeated. 'Since about the time the Vipers got established.'

'That's what Dale and I thought,' Savage agreed. 'The Vipers couldn't operate without the guerrillas' co-operation. So palms get greased, the region has no violence, God's in his heaven and all is well with the world.'

'What about the army and police?'

'Well, the army's main priority is fighting the guerrillas, so if things are quiet, there's no incentive for them to go looking for trouble and getting themselves shot.'

'And the police?'

Savage shrugged. 'I can't be sure. As you know, generally in this country they're pretty dedicated to breaking the cartels. The DEA has a strong influence. Nevertheless, there has to be a rotten streak – I mean, we know operational intelligence leaks like a sieve. I've met the local police chief – a fat, complacent bastard called Alberto Gonzalez. He assures us there are no *narco* activities in the area. Perhaps he really believes it.'

Mallory shook his head. 'Don't be naive, George. This is South America. If Gonzalez has told you he knows nothing, then he's lying.'

She was irritated by his certainty. 'How can you be sure? Anyway, just because he's economical with the truth to a couple of UN representatives doesn't mean he's in cahoots with the Vipers. That's what you're implying.'

Mallory was losing patience: 'Listen, just wise up, will you? I learned something in the local whorehouse—'

A look of dismay came over her face. 'Oh, Christ, Kurt, not again—' She bit her tongue in mid-sentence, angry at herself for letting it show she still cared, could still be jealous of some two-bit hooker.

'You know the way I operate,' Mallory snapped back. 'In this sort of place, it's one of the best ways to find out what's really going on.'

'But some pox-ridden *puta*, Kurt?' She was exasperated.

'*Las nennas*,' Mallory corrected calmly. 'Like dames or chicks. It's more polite than *puta*. Don't forget the girls carry more respect here than back home. People understand that sometimes it's the only way they can make a living, bring up kids. There's no welfare here.'

Anger flashed in her eyes. 'Don't come that old "some of my best friends are tarts with hearts" routine again, Kurt.'

He ignored her outburst; there were some things she and others would never be able to understand. 'Some members of the Viper gang got involved in a brawl at the whorehouse. It's fairly certain a punter was murdered by them. The local police barely went through the motions of an investigation. It was a sham, a whitewash.'

'You can't know that,' she challenged. 'I know South America too, Kurt. This *is* my patch. The police aren't exactly the most efficient in the world.'

Mallory smiled faintly; there was so much she had yet to learn. 'Efficient, no. They probably wouldn't catch anyone. But they love their power and their swanky uniforms. In a backwater like this, there'd be a big commotion, a big police presence. Lots of interrogations, interviews. They love all that stuff. But strangely they virtually ignored this case.'

She raised an eyebrow. 'You mean a pay-off?'

'Smells like it. Just work on the assumption the police *are* involved and you won't go far wrong. Meanwhile, I've made contact with two of the Viper gang.'

'God, Kurt, that's wonderful.'

He couldn't resist a jibe. 'One of the benefits of working the whorehouses. Anyway, it wasn't that wonderful. I asked for a job and got turned down. But at least they know me now, and my presence shouldn't raise any suspicions.'

'Have you got names?'

'Just first names – if they're genuine. Guy and Billy. Both in their mid-thirties.'

Savage thought for a moment. 'Guy's a fairly unusual name. I'll have Dale run them through the DEA computer.'

He wondered whether to mention that there was something familiar about the tall man called Guy, something that unnerved him. But he decided he was being paranoid. 'It's time I got closer to the emerald mine. Maybe travel to Adoración for a start. We could use the film crew cover plan. What progress are Mario and Goldie making?'

She smiled. 'More than Dale and I are with contacting the local guerrillas. Mario's found a schoolteacher who has some former pupils who've joined the ELN. I think they're close to sorting something out.'

That was good news. 'Right, then let's arrange a chance encounter tonight. There's a busy bar called El Loro Verde – the Green Parrot, on Calle 7. I'll be there at nine. Tell them to sit next to me and start discussing how they need a hired help to travel with them, cart their gear and do some general running around.'

Savage nodded. 'Consider it done, Kurt. And good luck to the three of you.'

Two days later Mallory was helping to load up Mario and Goldie's hired Diahatsu Fourtrak with cameras and recording equipment.

The chance encounter at El Loro Verde had been textbook: the two men discussing loudly the need for an assistant, asking the barman if he knew of anyone suitable, then Mallory apparently overhearing and offering his services. Goldie's amazement that he was English, despite appearances. Much celebration and drinks all round. By the next morning everyone in town would know that the wildlife film crew from England had hired the stranger

185

who was desperate to find work.

'So when's the meeting with the *guerrilleros*?' Mallory asked while Mario was steering cautiously down the canyon switchback towards the Servita river.

'Maybe tonight, maybe *mañana*,' his friend replied. 'We're just to find rooms and someone will contact us.'

'Very cloak and dagger,' Goldie observed. 'Guess they want to be sure there are no police spooks around.'

'And what's the name of this farmer you met on the bus?'

'Tafur. Victor Tafur,' Mallory replied. 'His smallholding is in the region of Cruz de Oro.'

'And you're sure he'll put us up?' Goldie asked.

'I can't be certain, but he's amenable and broke. I'm sure the sight of a few dollar bills will persuade him. The point is, the location could be perfect for us. It can't be more than five miles from the mining camp.'

'Sounds ideal. So let's hope your friend can be persuaded.'

It was almost dark by the time they'd completed the seemingly endless, bone-rattling journey across the valley. The lights of Adoración winked fitfully through the grey mist of twilight as they approached. Doleful *campesinos* watched with mild interest from their doorways as the Fourtrak splashed down the main street and children ran in its wake, eager to see who these new arrivals were. The distribution of candy bars and a few inquiries led them to a cheap flophouse with two rooms spare. Mario and Goldie took one, Mallory the poky understairs cubbyhole that was barely large enough to squeeze in the camp bed and single wardrobe.

They found a cafeteria and settled down to a meal of *chevito-hasado*, grilled goat meat served with yucca and *platano*, and a bottle of vinegary Colombian wine. Goldie's request for a decent vintage from Chile or the Argentine met with an expression of blank indifference from the overweight owner. The place was half full, the tables taken by several families and one large group of farm workers enjoying a boisterous game of cards. It was Goldie who first noticed the two gringos talking quietly over coffee in one corner. Only the occasional word of English was audible. They were shabbily dressed and might have passed unnoticed had the new arrivals not been on the lookout.

Mallory and Mario allowed themselves a discreet glance and nodded their agreement; almost certainly they were Viper members in town for a meal.

It was then that they heard the four-wheel drive pull up outside. Moments later the door opened brusquely and the local *comisario* strutted in. There was no mistaking who he was; Mallory had seen the type too many times in the remoter areas of South America. Ostensibly a mere policeman, in reality a *comisario* would often be the only official representative of government and as such wielded immense local power. But rather than enforce the law of the land, many were a law unto themselves. Policeman, tax collector, judge and jury and, as often as not, executioner, if they could get away with it. Others, of course, brought the only welcome semblance of civilisation and justice to otherwise lawless lands; dedicated men who were ill paid for a dangerous and thankless task.

Any doubt as to which category this man belonged was instantly resolved by the ostentatious pair of chrome-plated six-shooters of which General Patton would have been proud. They rode at his hips, ivory butts forward, in a tooled leather holster rig. He wore an army camouflage cap with a peak and a matching combat jacket over his blue policeman's uniform; the trousers were tucked into knee-length brown boots.

Mid-forties, Mallory guessed, given the grey hairs in the heavy moustache. Or perhaps he was younger, the sun and the drink and too many doses of the clap having taken their toll. He stood for a moment, legs astride, surveying the room. A respectful two paces behind him, three henchmen wearing odd items of police uniform scowled at the customers and faced down anyone who dared stare a moment too long.

With sycophantic little gestures, the patron scurried forward to show the *comisario*'s party to a window table. There the policeman dumped himself into the chair at the head of the table and demanded a huge *churrasco* steak for himself, leaving his deputies to agonise over what they could afford.

Mallory watched with interest, noticing how suddenly the *voliche* began to empty. Even the two members of the Viper gang finished their meal, acknowledged the policeman with brief nods, and left.

Goldie ordered more wine. He was relaxed and jovial, sharing jokes with Mario. Playing his own rôle as the outsider, Mallory remained quiet and withdrawn. But he knew both his friends from the organisation were looking forward to the inevitable encounter with the *comisario*. They all shared a loathing of the abuse of power and the insidious intimidation that went with it. They were eager to establish exactly what sort of man the *comisario* was, to find the measure of a potential enemy.

'Ask for your bill,' Mallory whispered in Goldie's ear. His Jewish friend nodded, agreeing that it would prompt a reaction from the policeman in the now deserted room.

Sure enough, as the three of them paid and rose to leave, a voice like a bullhorn nailed them to the spot. 'I do not believe you have introduced yourselves, señors!' it boomed in Spanish.

Goldie turned, that practised simpleton's smile on his face. It was the same smile Mallory had seen the moment before the little Israeli had killed someone. 'Ah, to whom do I owe the pleasure?' He blinked at the *comisario* through the thick lenses of his spectacles.

'Chief of Police, Major Oscar Pulgarin.' The man had demolished his huge steak in record time and was still chewing, shreds of the meat entangled in his moustache. 'It is necessary for strangers in town to make themselves known to me.'

Goldie raised his hands in a gesture of supplication. 'Oi vey! Forgive me, officer, I am unaware of the local customs in this place.'

The *comisario* sucked thoughtfully at some meat that had caught between his teeth and glanced at his deputies who watched expectantly. He smiled, sensing some sport. His smile was one of those warm, generous smiles that fooled you unless you watched the eyes. 'Then perhaps you should make it your business to ask.'

Goldie gave a convincing look of utter bewilderment. 'I am

sure you are right, *officer.*'

'Unannounced strangers have been known to be arrested and thrown into jail. Not here, of course, but other places. These are troubled times and policemen must be on their guard. Guerrillas, *narcos,* bandits— There are so many undesirable types nowadays.'

Goldie reached into his inside pocket for his document wallet. 'Does that include natural history film-makers?'

That took Pulgarin by surprise; he sat upright in his chair and leaned forward with his elbows on the table. This was not something he had been expecting. He studied the documents in silence.

'A letter of introduction from the director of the Animal Eye Production Company,' Goldie began evenly. 'A letter of accreditation from the British Broadcasting Corporation and the Commercial Section of the British Embassy in Bogotá. Then authorisation from your own Department of the Interior. And a letter of permission from your immediate superior in Santa Maria, Lieutenant Colonel Gonzalez . . .'

Mario glanced sideways at Mallory and winked.

Pulgarin grunted and looked up, blood colouring his cheeks. 'I will keep these for the time being. You understand that I shall have to radio Colonel Gonzalez to confirm all this.'

'I'm sure that isn't necessary,' Goldie replied.

'Oh, but it is. So that I can issue you with a local permit, for which a modest fee will be required.'

'Fee?'

'To cover the cost of administration. And of course, you will be requiring a police escort.'

Mallory groaned inwardly.

Goldie said: 'Filming wildlife is a specialist business, *Comisario.* Hours of patient waiting, lying still in a hide in uncomfortable conditions – hardly suitable work for one of your esteemed officers.'

Pulgarin was unmoved, dollar signs in his eyes. 'You will need to be escorted. It will cost, of course, but the life in these parts is wilder than you might imagine.' He drew a notebook from inside his jacket. 'Now, where are you staying in Adoración?'

Goldie told him. 'But tomorrow or the day after we hope to base ourselves at a ranch near Cruz de Oro.'

'That is useful. My police post is in that area. You can come there to collect your permit – *if* I receive the necessary authority, of course. Now what is the farmer's name?'

'Señor Tafur.'

The *comisario* looked up. 'That is not well advised. The man is a trouble-maker.'

'We have nowhere else.'

A shrug. 'It is up to you. Now, please, may I see your passports?'

'Bastard,' Mario said with feeling as the door of the *voliche* swung closed behind them.

'It's only to be expected,' Mallory replied. 'Besides, he doesn't know we have a complete duplicate set of all the documents.'

Goldie chuckled. 'It's good to pull one over on scrotes like him. What d'you suggest we do, Kurt?'

'Forget about him,' Mallory said. 'He's only after greasing his palm. We'll just avoid him as best we can. Let him come looking for us – if he can be bothered.'

They were approaching the boarding house. The lights were off and there was no moon, just inky shadows everywhere.

Mallory sensed it first. That tell-tale ripple of the small hairs at the base of his neck. Then he smelt it. The faintest tang of unfamiliar body odour.

The voice came from behind them, talking over the metallic click of a cocking handle. 'Don't move, gentlemen,' in Spanish. 'Just stand still and no one will be hurt.'

As the three of them raised their arms, Mallory had a torch shone in his face. Invisible hands came from behind, roughly checking his jacket and denims for weaponry.

More torches came on, criss-crossing beams illuminating the muddy forecourt. There were dark figures, the unmistakable outline of rifles. One of the men turned and began walking towards the alleyway that ran beside the boarding house.

'Follow him,' someone ordered.

Mallory stumbled after Goldie and Mario, an armed stranger bringing up the rear. They walked for some time through the wasteland behind the primitive houses, disturbing chickens and tethered goats. At last they reached a timber shack where candle-glow flickered from behind the hessian curtain.

'Inside,' said the voice again.

The door opened onto a small living room, just large enough to take the iron bedstead, table and chairs and a small kitchen area. It smelled of mildew and tobacco smoke.

There were three men, Mallory could see now. Two were older men, unshaven and wearing battered straw stetsons, bandoleers of ammunition showing beneath their woollen ponchos. The third was young, slim and more smartly dressed in olive drab fatigues under a fringed buckskin jacket.

He removed his wide-brimmed sombrero with its pointed crown and waved it in the direction of the table. 'Please be seated, señors,' he said in Spanish. 'I am sorry if we startled you, but we have to be cautious.'

'And you are?' Goldie demanded, feigning indignation.

'They call me the Wolf.'

'*El Lobo*,' Mario echoed. 'The local guerrilla leader?'

The younger man smiled. 'We would prefer to describe ourselves as the people's socialist revolutionaries. And, I understand, you have requested a special meeting with me to discuss your business here.'

Goldie nodded. 'I spoke with a teacher at the school in Santa Maria. He said he would try to make contact with you. To guarantee us safe passage.'

The man tugged a pack of cheroots from his shirt pocket and lit one. 'And so he did. Here you are, safe and unharmed. You are here to film wildlife for the famous BBC?'

'Indeed we are.'

'I love these programmes when I am a boy. But, of course, there are not many television sets in this part and anyway reception is bad. I like the one on polar bears. Did you make that?'

'Sure,' Mario lied obligingly.

191

'Then I have many questions to ask you.'

Goldie said: 'Of course, but later, once we are settled in. The thing is, we understand this region is in your control, so we want to be sure there will be no trouble.'

El Lobo smiled again. 'I was once the pupil of the teacher to whom you spoke. He is a good man and I have promised him you will come to no harm from us.' He hesitated. 'But, of course, the BBC is very famous, very rich, and we are just a humble peasants' army. A donation to our cause will persuade my followers not to take matters into their own hands. Robbery and kidnap is not unknown. These people have no homes, no livelihood. They need money for shelter and food.'

Mario saw no point in hedging. 'A thousand dollars?'

The response was instant. 'I had more in mind, three thousand.'

'Two,' Mario snapped back.

El Lobo smiled again. 'When both parties are unhappy with a deal, it is a sure sign it is fair. So we are agreed.' He reached towards the table and picked up the dusty bottle of *aguardiente*. 'A drink to celebrate, I think. Now tell me, what do you hope to film in our beautiful country?'

The mood became quite convivial. Weapons were laid aside, the guerrillas sprawled around drinking and smoking, while Goldie explained their intentions. How they hoped to capture Andean wild cats on film as the main subject but, as nature never performed to order, they would cover anything that moved.

It was then quite bizarre as these veteran guerrillas began relating anecdotal tales of their own adventures with wild cats, snakes and even dogs, each story taller than the last.

Finally *El Lobo* said: 'It is reported to me that you have spoken to Comisario Pulgarin.'

'You are well informed,' Mallory observed.

'We need to be. And I should warn you that Comisario Pulgarin is a very dangerous man. He will find a way of taking money from you for one reason or another. He invents his own laws and his own fines and sends his thugs to collect. Be warned.'

Not so very different from yourself then, Mallory thought. But he just said: 'Thanks for the advice.'

'And you, señor,' *El Lobo* said, regarding the Englishman's torn and dirty clothes, 'you are a film-maker too?'

'Just casual labour. I needed a job.'

El Lobo regarded him for a long moment. Something in the young man's eyes suggested that he was not sure he believed him.

'This must be Cruz de Oro,' Goldie decided, lifting his foot from the accelerator. 'There's the chapel.'

The Fourtrak had slowed to a halt in the rocky gulch that formed a bend in the road. Amid the tumble of grey boulders ahead of them, the white adobi walls of the building dazzled in the early morning sunshine. Stars of light reflected off the brass of its three bells, so bright that it hurt the eyes.

'Thank God for that,' Mario said. 'I thought we'd never get here.' The track had become steadily worse since leaving Adoración, crossing the Servita river and striking out into the wilderness beyond. They'd blown one tyre in a rocky pothole and had no other spare.

As Goldie moved forward again, trying to negotiate a route through the impossible ruts, Mallory glanced again at the hand-drawn map. 'Just past the outcrop and the chapel, there should be a left-hand turn.'

They entered the shadow of the ravine, the wheels spinning in the quagmire left by the recent rains. To the right they saw the single-storey bar with its tables and chairs and a few weathered dwellings. On the left, a stony track led up the slope beside the outcrop.

'Here it is,' Goldie announced and swung the wheel. The Fourtrak tore itself free of the mud and strengthened its grip on the dry shale, gathering speed as it climbed. As the trail passed the chapel, they could see that it had been constructed on a small plateau of sandy earth. Its position offered a commanding view of the countryside, sloping away to the far distant river. The track began to bend round a long, wooded spur of land before plunging down towards the valley floor. The soil here was friable and lifeless. It had dried quickly and now a dust cloud followed them through the scrubby landscape.

There was no fence to mark the perimeter of the ranch, just an archway over the track formed by three eucalyptus poles. A yellowing cow skull had been nailed to the crossbeam and on one of the side supports a rough, hand-painted sign said simply TAFUR. Half a dozen scrawny bullocks were spread out in the empty distance, patiently foraging for a few withered clumps of grass. High in the cobalt sky a vulture circled. No building was in sight.

Goldie grunted, 'Almost makes the Negev Desert seem lush.'

'Godforsaken hole,' Mario agreed.

Mallory said nothing. Perversely he liked the place. He remembered how Victor Tafur had told him about its harsh beauty and how his family had loved it for generations despite the struggle to scratch a living. No matter where you lived in the world, he thought, home is always home. Besides, in some ways, it reminded him of the Paraguay of his childhood.

Then the view disappeared, the track twisting unexpectedly to the right and down a short, sharp slope to a rocky, tree-topped cutting. Momentarily the growing warmth of the sun was replaced by the cool air of the dappled shade. As his eyes adjusted to the sudden gloom, Goldie almost missed the sharp bend that veered to the left.

'Shit!'

He hit the brakes, spinning the wheel. The Fourtrak responded slowly, the rear end fishtailing before the tyres bit and the vehicle straightened up. Then they were out in the open again, the sunlight brilliant.

It was at that moment Goldie saw the black stallion in his path. The magnificent beast was rearing, its flanks and haunches glistening like silk as its hooves pawed the air. Simultaneously Goldie noticed the girl on its back, riding without a saddle. He was distracted by the white summer dress she wore, rucked high over her tanned thighs.

In the back Mallory was jolted again as the Fourtrak swerved. He cursed and peered forward to see what the problem was. The sight of the girl whipped at his senses. Her hair was long and as glossy black as the horse she rode. She was fresh-faced, with a flawless dusky skin that suggested she was barely out of her teens. He had a fleeting impression of white teeth, her full lips drawn back in a snarl as she struggled to restrain her mount.

Mario gawped. 'God, what a vision!'

The horse settled, dust swirling around its hooves, just inches in front of the Fourtrak as it finally grated to a halt. It was only then that they saw the shotgun. Held in the girl's right hand, it rested across the base of the stallion's mane and pointed straight at the windscreen.

Her eyes were wide, dark and angry. 'This is private property!' she shouted in Spanish. 'Turn round and get out of here!'

Goldie wound down his window. 'We have come to visit Señor Tafur.'

She gave a sneer of derision. 'I am aware of *that*! And I shoot you if you do not turn round this instant!'

Goldie was nervous. He never trusted women to act rationally, especially when they were riled. Especially when one of them had a gun pointing at him. 'We are friends of Señor Tafur.'

The smile transformed her face, but it didn't quite reach her eyes. 'From England, of course?'

That threw Goldie. He spoke perfect Latin Spanish, so why should she think that. 'I have come here from England, yes.'

'Then I think I will shoot you now.'

Mallory had become aware that from her elevated position on the horse the girl could only see Goldie and Mario in the front seats. If she lost her temper, she could take out his two friends with a single blast before Goldie could either reverse or turn. Quickly and as quietly as he could he opened the rear door just sufficiently to allow him to drop silently to the ground.

Goldie was pleading to be believed. 'Honestly, we are friends of Señor Tafur.'

'I know my father's friends. And you are not any of them.'

'Please don't point that thing at us. We mean no harm. Can't we talk?'

Now Mallory was under the Fourtrak, wriggling forward beneath the high chassis. Just feet in front of him he could see the shuffling hooves of the stallion.

'You threaten to kill my father. To destroy our farm and cattle. We are sick of your tricks. Your lies! It is my turn to have the gun, and now you are not so brave, I think. So get out with your hands in the air.'

'I'll turn round like you said,' Goldie offered, reaching for the gear lever.

She raised the shotgun a fraction. 'OUT!'

Mario glanced at his friend and shrugged. They had no real option. The doors opened and they stepped down to the ground.

'Throw away your weapons.'

Mario spoke for the first time. 'We are unarmed, little one.'

'I don't believe you.'

He grinned. 'You are welcome to search me. It will be a pleasure to be searched by the prettiest girl in Colombia.'

The smooth skin of her forehead fractured in a frown; somehow these did not sound like the men she knew. 'I will only search your body when you are *dead*, señor! Now drop your pants and remove your shoes and start walking – back to your camp. Come on, quickly!'

Mallory sprang from beneath the engine of the Fourtrak. The girl was startled by the sudden movement and tried to switch her aim. But the horse reared, its eyes wide and wild, and the shotgun blasted into the vehicle windscreen, glass shattering in all directions. Then Mallory's hands grasped the barrel, wrenched it from her.

The girl's foot came out to kick him away as she grabbed for the reins to make her escape. Mallory fell back, his face bruised. But in those few moments of distraction Mario had sprinted around the far side of the stallion, behind the girl's turned back. In one swift and powerful manoeuvre he managed to get his arms around her waist. She yelled and the horse bolted. Although she attempted to hold onto the animal with her knees it was hopeless and she crashed backwards into Mario's embrace sending them both sprawling to the ground.

Mario laughed as she struggled. 'Señorita, you are so forward, and we haven't even been introduced.'

196

Her flailing fist caught him in the eye. With a yelp he released his grip. She sprang to her feet, backing away, cornered, her hair tumbling over her face.

Mallory broke open the shotgun, ejected the remaining cartridge, and threw the weapon aside. 'You see, we don't come here to harm you or anyone.'

She looked puzzled and frightened, but her stance remained defiant. 'But you are the English? From the mine?'

'We are from England, but we have nothing to do with any mine.' He smiled to reassure her. 'My name is Kurt Hulse. I met your father on the bus from Tunja. He invited me to visit. I am working for these men, helping out. They are wildlife film-makers.'

She was bemused, shaking her head in disbelief. 'I think you come to cause trouble, to ruin the best day of my life.'

'What is your name, pretty one?' Mario asked, still nursing his eye.

'Juanita.'

'Your papa would be proud of you. For one so pretty you pack a heavy punch.' He grinned and she blushed, beginning to realise these strangers really did offer no threat.

Mallory said: 'Would you take us to your father?'

Still she looked uncertain. He stepped forward to retrieve the shotgun then handed it back to her with the cartridge separate. 'I'm sorry about the rough stuff. We really thought you were going to shoot.'

She looked sheepish. 'I was.'

Mario looked understanding. 'Just trying to find the courage, eh?' He was beguiled by another of her shy smiles. 'So you will take us?'

Juanita gestured to her stallion, now calmed and grazing several hundred metres away. 'I must catch my horse first. It will not be easy, he is a bad boy.'

'You go with these two,' Mallory said. 'I'll bring your horse.'

She frowned. 'He will not go with strangers.'

Mallory laughed. 'He'll come with me, I promise you.'

9

Harry Morgan looked up from his paper-strewn desk as Guy Thripp entered. 'Not another fuckin' interruption.'

'Sorry, boss. Thought you'd want to know. The Cisco Kid's turned up with a couple of Panchos.'

'Can't you handle it? I've enough on my plate trying to work out how we're going to get this production stepped up.'

'I can,' Thripp replied, 'but we've been fobbing him off for weeks. Then he buttonholed Crabtree and Beavis the other day, remember?'

He remembered. And Thripp was right, it was best to keep the Cisco Kid and his bloody revolutionaries on board, keep them sweet. He had enough headaches keeping the production lines going and organising the convoy runs. And it wasn't just the product; absolutely everything from food to bog paper had to come in by convoy along hundreds of miles of unmade road. The last thing he needed was Cisco disrupting them in a fit of pique.

Morgan leaned back thoughtfully in his chair, balancing it on the back legs. He was tall and broad-shouldered, smartly turned out given the primitive living conditions. His olive fatigue trousers and bush shirt might be faded after countless boil washes at the camp laundry, but they were clean and knife-edge ironed. It was part of the Para culture: always be smarter, fitter, quicker and tougher than the next man. No excuses. That culture had stayed with him, even after they had kicked him out. Personal hygiene and appearance remained his first priorities each morning, even if his shower was just a holed bucket of cold water and he had only a blunt blade to drag across the skin of his square and weather-hardened face. Standards were everything, which was why he kept his hair, nowadays more salt than pepper, brushed thoroughly until it stood upright like iron filings under a magnet. Lice or fleas didn't stand a chance.

And it certainly didn't hurt to set an example, especially with the ragtag bunch he had working under him. At length, he said: 'I'm sure you're right, Guy. Show him in, but alone. Keep his goons outside.'

Thripp tipped the brim of his stetson and turned to the door.

'What's he call himself?' Morgan asked. 'The Fox or something?'

The other man grinned. '*El Lobo*. The Wolf.'

'Fuckin' ridiculous.'

A few moments later, Thripp returned with the young *guerrillero* leader. His denims and a buckskin jacket with fringes would have done Davy Crockett proud, his enormous white sombrero was clutched in his hands.

Harry Morgan gave the smile he reserved for VIPs. 'Nice to see you – look, sorry, can't keep calling you *El Lobo*.'

The toothbrush moustache inverted as the man showed a smile of even white teeth. In Spanish he said: 'Your men call me Cisco. A cowboy hero on TV, they say. Fights for good and justice. That is fine.'

The Englishman grimaced and turned to Thripp. 'What's he say, Guy?'

'Call me Cisco.'

Morgan grinned. '*Hablo Español* – er – *poco*, – er?'

'*Muy poco*,' Thripp added helpfully; his vocabulary was marginally larger than that of his boss.

'Sure, speak very small – er, I mean, little Spanish. Can we try English?'

El Lobo was obliging. 'I try. Me speak small too.'

'Christ.' Morgan shook his head in frustration. And wondered for the umpteenth time why the hell Beavis and Crabtree hadn't managed to find anyone on their team who could speak the lingo. He'd high hopes when the new recruit Pete Stafford showed up, but he turned out to be pretty awful too. 'How can we help you,

Cisco?'

'You promise training, si? Remember?'

'Sure, I remember.' A steady and sincere smile.

'But, there is no training.'

'Ah, well—'

'Where is training?'

'It comes. Soon. Er – *Pronto*. Training come *pronto*. We very busy.' Now he was talking pidgin. 'Much work. Much to do. We start soon.'

God, Morgan thought, why had it ever been promised? Training and arms. A bad idea, but *El Lobo* was right, it was all part of the deal.

'You promise me.' The young man's eyes were bright and intense.

'My word, Cisco. You have my word.' Another smile and an extended hand.

With a handshake his word was accepted. 'Señor Harry, in return I tell you things. We are team, yes? Work together.'

'Sure we do. Buddies.'

'I tell you there are three men come from Santa Maria. Make film.' He did the Charades game hand motion for a camera. 'Shoot wildlife. BBC.'

Morgan couldn't resist a smile. 'I know.'

El Lobo was surprised. 'You know?'

Thripp added helpfully: 'Our people met them in Santa Maria and the *comisario* tells us they have now come to Cruz de Oro. He will keep an eye on them.'

'You do not mind?'

Morgan said: 'I mind, but if they're genuine it's better not to draw attention to ourselves. Not rock the boat.'

'Please, they are on the river?'

'No, no.' Oh, for God's sake, he thought in near desperation. 'No, Cisco, I do not mind.'

'We will leave them, too.'

'Fine.'

'And the UN?'

'What?'

'United Nations. They come, maybe. Want see me, get – er – safe passage. Two peoples.'

The two Englishmen exchanged glances of concern. Thripp muttered: 'This place is getting like Piccadilly Circus.'

'The UN is to come here?' Morgan asked. 'To Cruz de Oro?'

'I do not know. Santa Maria, Servita valley, maybe Adoración, maybe Cruz de Oro.'

'I don't like it,' Thripp said.

El Lobo may not have exactly understood the words, but he understood the intonation. 'We *want* these two peoples here. UN survey is good for the people, for the *campesinos*. You understand? Much money comes.'

Morgan considered for a moment. 'I don't think we're in the business of harassing the UN. For the same reason we'll not interfere with any wildlife film crew. We don't want to attract the attention of the outside world.' He didn't add that he would use Comisario Pulgarin to do that; the man was a wizard at producing bureaucracy to order on his patch. It should prove deterrent enough. 'Comprendes, Cisco?'

Morgan's elaborate sign language appeared to have got through. 'Si, comprendo.'

They parted on good terms. Courteously Morgan and Thripp showed him to the door and stood outside to watch him and his escort leave the compound.

'Cisco's a pain in the backside,' Thripp muttered.

'At least he didn't ask for a bigger cut,' Morgan replied. 'That's what I was expecting.'

'Give him time.'

'At least he's keeping the police and the army out of the area.'

'What about this film crew?'

'Our local sheriff's been briefed. With any luck they'll get pissed off with Pulgarin and move on. Anyway, as long as they keep their cameras pointed well away from us . . .'

'And the UN?'

'Did you know about them?'

Thripp nodded. 'Only that there's a couple in Santa Maria. Researching for some sort of project fund. I doubt they'd even venture this far. If they did, it would only be for a day or two.'

'Then just make sure the local population are warned to keep their mouths shut.'

'Don't worry, Pedro will see to that, no problem.'

Harry Morgan stepped back into the shack and turned. 'In the meantime we'd better show willing with Cisco. Can we get a couple of bods to do some training with them?'

'I guess so. What d'you have in mind, boss?'

Suddenly Morgan felt weary. 'Fuck me, Guy, can't you think of something? A bit of target practice, a bit of fire-and-man-oeuvre. Anything! Just keep the bloody Cisco Kid off my back.'

Thripp smarted, but bit his lip. 'Whatever you say, boss.'

But Morgan noted the tone of insolence in the reply, and it added to his growing irritation. 'And what are you doing about that farmer?'

'Victor Tafur. I thought I'd let him simmer a while.'

'Without that airstrip, we can't meet the new production targets,' Morgan reminded testily. 'So never mind about simmer. Turn on some heat. Let's see the bastard boil!'

He slammed shut the door of the shack, inches in front of Thripp's nose.

Goldie and Mario could smell the tension in the dry air as they drove with Juanita into the fenced yard of the Tafur family's hacienda.

It was a humble, single-storey affair of white-painted adobe with arched windows and doorways and a roof of thatched reed.

As the Fourtrak pulled up outside and the dust settled, Victor Tafur came out to meet them. Not exactly in greeting; he looked apprehensive and carried a pitchfork with the points foremost.

There was a look of relief in the farmer's wary, darting eyes as Juanita quickly allayed his obvious anxiety, explaining that these strangers were friends of the man called Kurt, the man he had recently met on the Bogotá bus.

Only then did Tafur lower his pitchfork, smile broadly and invite them in. The place was gloomy and smelled of woodsmoke from the open cooking fire. Above it hung a row of hams, glistening with fat that dripped and spat into the embers.

His wife, a timid-looking woman who wore her grey hair in a bun, stood by the giant hewn-timber table that filled most of the room. She gave a bobbing little curtsy as she was introduced. Clinging shyly at her side was Juanita's ten-year-old sister, every inch a tomboy in faded dungarees. She shrank back as Mario ruffled her hair and chuckled.

Tafur turned to his eldest daughter who was lingering at the door. 'You say Kurt is bringing your horse?' He sounded sceptical.

'I think this is him now,' Juanita replied, watching the dust trail advance.

Victor and his wife joined their daughter. 'He must be a fine horseman to have mastered that one so quickly,' the farmer observed as Mallory dismounted and tied the reins to the hitching post.

'Victor!' he called, catching sight of the farmer. 'It is good to see you.'

'And you, my friend.' They shook hands. 'I see you have met my eldest daughter. This is my wife and our youngest daughter, Nancy. Come, Maria, coffee for our guests.'

'You're too kind,' Mallory replied.

As they gathered round the table, Tafur said: 'I understand you are working for these gentlemen?'

'Yes, a natural history film unit.'

'So they have just explained. How wonderful! And it is good you find a job with them, because I really do not have money to hire you, however good you may be with horses!'

Mallory shared the farmer's good humour. 'In fact, Victor, I was hoping we could pay *you*. These people need a base while they film and Adoración is much too far away. I wondered about your farm?'

Tafur looked uncertain. 'I am afraid our home is very small, as you can see.' He thought for a moment. 'Ah, but there is our barn. It is dry and there is straw for bedding. Not much, but . . .'

'It sounds perfect.'

'Maria can provide a breakfast and supper.'

'Even better.'

Tafur laughed. 'Then I may even be able to pay *you* for a little help around the place after all! Especially as Juanita is stealing my ranch hand.'

'Papa!' the girl protested. 'I am marrying him, not stealing him.'

'I have hardly seen him for weeks while he builds your new home.' He turned to Mallory. 'You have chosen a wonderful time to call. In just two days it is Juanita's wedding. It will be quite a party.'

Goldie said: 'I hope you will not be greeting the bridegroom with a shotgun!'

The farmer looked shame-faced. 'Ah, yes, I am sorry about that. Juanita at first thinks you are from the emerald mine.'

'She said something about Englishmen,' Mallory confirmed.

Tafur sighed, weary. 'Yes, I am afraid these people give us much trouble.'

'Is that why you are trying to sell your land?' Mallory coaxed, remembering their conversation on the pullman.

He nodded. 'Our land stretches up to the canyon. There is an area of several hectares that is very flat. The English want to build a landing strip for aircraft.'

'Is it good land?'

'No, but I will not sell to such people.'

Goldie said: 'But they are just miners?'

Tafur shook his head sadly. 'That's what they say—'

'But what?' Mallory pressed.

'Maybe I should not say this. But, by the Mother of Jesus, everybody around here knows. They are *narcos*. I will not sell to such people. Why should I?'

'Can you afford to be choosy?'

The farmer stared at him. 'Yes, my friend, because I do not want to sell at all. Look, I am Colombian and so I do not view the drugs business in the same way that the Americans do. But that is their problem, not ours. If they want this stuff, why shouldn't poor peasant farmers grow it or help to provide it? When the Americans stop wanting, Colombians will have no one to produce it for and the problem ends, no?'

Mallory nodded; he was well aware of the South American perception of the problem.

Tafur continued: 'But these English, they are something else! They are evil people without souls. This whole region is intimidated by them and their gang. They are only here a few months when five farmers are murdered in front of their families in five separate settlements. The English say that these men have been spreading lies and rumours about the mine. That they deal in drugs not emeralds and that their deaths are a lesson to us all.'

'It is true,' Juanita added. 'It was horrible. But it was worse because those men were innocent of such things. They just talk amongst themselves like everybody does; they do not cause trouble.'

Mallory's eyes met Goldie's; both men recognised the pattern. It was little different from the intimidation employed in authoritarian states or from the IRA's methods of policing its own ghettos in Northern Ireland. Traditionally Colombian *narcos* just did it a bit more ruthlessly.

'Then everyone is frightened,' Tafur continued. 'There is a silence of fear. But it gets worse. The English have a big operation. They need building materials, fuel, equipment, chemicals for their laboratory and much food and canned drink. An army of trucks is needed to keep them supplied. So they say to one peasant, you bring this, or take that in your truck. We do not care what else you are planning to do. Do this for us now! We pay you what we think. And the people are too scared to say no. If they do, maybe they are beaten up or worse. Or maybe their house is burned down.'

'Have you had trouble, Victor?' Mallory asked.

'Everybody has. Last year I had a farm hand run down and killed by a car at night when he refuses to drive supplies to Santa Maria. Nothing can be proved, but we know who was responsible. And then they say they want to buy my land. The money was not bad, but I do not want to sell. There is a big row and many threats. Then our stream is poisoned with chemicals. Juanita is threatened when she goes shopping to Adoración. That is why I try to find a private buyer. I *want* to go now, but I will not give in to these people.'

'Good for you,' Goldie murmured.

'What about the police?' Mario asked.

Tafur gave him a strange look. 'What about them? Comisario Pulgarin is the last person you go to for help, believe me.'

They believed him.

At eleven o'clock the next morning, Mario was adjusting the tripod of the camera, having selected a powerful close-up lens. He tilted it down and tightened the locking bolt to hold it in position.

It was ideal weather for filming – high, bright cloud that cast minimal shadow. Even high up on the rocky spur of the canyon wall there was little breeze and he paused for a moment to look out over the valley. The Tafurs' hacienda was just discernible, looking like a pretty plastic model on a railway layout. Way beyond, a deep dark scar of greenery marked the course of the Servita.

Mario turned back to his work, erecting the reflectors and adjusting them to even out and lighten up what shadow there was.

Twenty metres away, Goldie was seated in the back of the Fourtrak. He had the false front of the sound recorder flipped down and was adjusting the dials of the radio set behind it.

Still nothing. A mere crackle of faint static around Mallory's frequency. Insufficient power and mountain atmospherics. He wasn't really surprised and resignedly switched off and closed up the false front.

It was fifteen minutes before Mallory appeared, jumping down over the rocky hillside with the agility of a chamois antelope.

He arrived at the spot where Mario had set up. 'What are you filming? Your feet?'

The Martinican looked pained. 'No, mi amigo, wildlife.' He jabbed his finger at a cluster of little stones. 'Beetles.'

Mallory grinned. 'What sort of beetles?'

'How the fuck should I know? A beetle's a beetle.'

'A rare Andean carpet beetle, I should think.'

Mario shrugged. 'It's not my fault.' He made a wide gesture to encompass the surrounding country. 'We've been here a whole day and I see nothing! No wild cats, no jaguars, no mountain foxes. Even the snakes are hiding.'

'What about birds?'

'If you hadn't noticed, they fly away when we go near.'

Mallory said, with a wink: 'There's more to this nature filming than one thinks.'

His friend scowled and looked beseechingly to the empty heavens. 'God, give me a fucking condor.'

Goldie approached from the Fourtrak. 'Did you pick up my signal, Kurt?'

'Not bad at all, but I gather you couldn't hear me?'

A shake of the ragged woolly hair. 'I'm not surprised. You haven't got any power with that thing. A thousand metres, bah! Where do these manufacturers get their figures from? I reckon five hundred metres on a clear day – not counting on atmospherics.'

'So we'll need the solar relay booster?'

Goldie nodded and held one out in his hand. It was a smart contraption, a radio relay transceiver disguised in waterproof plastic casing that resembled a boulder. A thin wire aerial could be run out on a spool and hidden in grass or shrubbery to pick up the weak source signal and power-boost it to a range of some five miles. Then the powerful listening device in the Fourtrak would receive and enhance it. The device was powered by a twelve-inch plug-in solar panel.

'The problem is,' Goldie reminded, 'we'll have to get this placed within five hundred metres of the emerald camp.'

Mallory smiled grimly. 'That's assuming I ever manage to get inside.'

'Faith, my friend, faith. The opportunity will come, you'll see.'

Suddenly Mario moved back from the camera and stared down the slope. 'We have visitors.'

Goldie quickly placed the relay booster on the ground, indistinguishable from other rocks, and slid it away with the side of his foot as the off-road vehicle came into view.

It was a flashy big Nissan Patrol which had been customised with bits of chrome from other vehicles, including an enormous, gleaming front fender off an American limo and an array of spotlights. Eventually it stopped a little lower down the slope.

Comisario Oscar Pulgarin, complete with camo fatigues and ivory-handled six-shooters, climbed down and adjusted his aviator Ray-bans. His companion was a fat greaseball with an enormous belly that hung over his trouser belt and he wore a large floppy sombrero. The two men began to mount the steep, boulder-strewn incline.

Not surprisingly the policeman arrived first, stood in front of the camera Mario had set up and looked out at the view. 'I see you have made a start.'

'We have our schedule,' Goldie answered flatly.

The sunglasses gave Pulgarin an inscrutable look, but at least his crooked smile suggested he was in good humour. 'It is a pity you do not bring some pretty film starlets with you, eh?'

Mario smiled back. 'Unfortunately we are stuck with wildlife.'

'So what are you filming here?'

'You're standing on them.'

Pulgarin looked down at his calf-length boots and shuffled his feet. 'Beetles?'

'Dead beetles now.'

Goldie added: 'Dead Andean rock beetles. Very rare.'

The *comisario* frowned. 'Rare? My police post is overrun with these things.'

'Then the government will probably put a preservation order on it,' Goldie replied.

Blank black lenses radiated pure vitriol for a couple of seconds, then Pulgarin's smile returned. 'Of course, you are joking with me. Yes, very amusing.'

'Unless you are an expert,' Goldie explained, 'one beetle looks very much like another. Now tell me, *Comisario*, to what do we owe the pleasure?'

At that point Pulgarin's deputy arrived, wheezing, and immediately began hand-rolling a cigarette.

The *comisario* said: 'You haven't called at my police post for

208

your passports.'

Goldie shrugged. 'Why should we? We knew they were in safe hands. Besides, you're the only person who'll want to see them.'

Pulgarin nodded to the deputy and the man dug into his pocket to produce the passports, now covered in greasy finger-marks, and handed them over. 'I will hold onto your other documents – for safe-keeping.'

'I suppose there's a fee for that?' Mallory interjected.

'But of course. Just like a bank. Security is to be valued in these lawless regions. Shall we say ten thousand pesos each? You can pay when you collect.' He removed his Ray-bans then and made a show of polishing them with his handkerchief. 'Now, I have spoken with my chief in Santa Maria by radio. He confirms it is okay for you to be here. But he warns you are not to film any-where near the emerald mine. It is just over the ridge above us.'

'Oh, really, why?' Mallory asked.

'Security, of course. The people at the mine are sensitive about that, naturally. And we don't want to have you accidentally shot by a security guard, do we?'

'Thanks for the warning.' Goldie almost sounded sincere.

'And my chief insists I provide you with an escort. This is Gilberto, he will look after you.'

Gilberto had managed to set fire to his roll-up; he inhaled deeply, then coughed and hacked before spitting on the ground. He beamed a smile of rotten teeth and offered his hand.

'Perhaps we should look after Gilberto,' Mario said under his breath.

'He is a good man,' Pulgarin said. 'For ten thousand pesos a day, he is good value.'

The money was exchanged and the *comisario* departed in his Patrol, leaving Gilberto to protect his charges.

In fact, it took Mario very little time to work out how they could handle the fat deputy. He enjoyed his food – demolishing most of the team's picnic lunch by himself, and he liked his drink – a bottle of dark rum was supplied by Goldie. And he liked to sleep after either. He enjoyed women too, and was courting an Indian widow who lived on the road to Adoración. It seemed the amiable Gilberto had every known vice, as well as a few new ones he'd invented himself.

After drinking half the rum, he shared an amusing little secret with them. Although the *comisario* had a radio in his police post, it didn't work. Hadn't done for years. So his supposed conversation with his chief in Santa Maria was quite impossible. Pulgarin really was quite a character, quite a wag in fact!

In the early afternoon, with five minutes' blurred and shaky footage of squashed beetles and a hovering vulture in the can, the unit returned to the Tafurs' hacienda.

Gilberto had left his ancient estate wagon there and was more than delighted when Goldie told him he was finished for the day. He was free to pay his *vieja* a surprise visit. It was a ploy they were to use regularly in the coming days and Gilberto was not a man to look a gift horse in the mouth. He grabbed life's little perks with both hands.

When he had gone, Maria produced a steaming pot of coffee and the three men joined Tafur, his wife and Juanita around the massive table. There was only one real topic of conversation, the forthcoming wedding.

It was half an hour before Tafur asked how the filming had gone.

Goldie shrugged. 'It's a slow business and we are new to the area. It will take some time before we locate all the various habitats.'

Tafur agreed. 'You really could do with some local knowledge.'

At that moment the conversation was interrupted by the noisy arrival of the battered farm pick-up, driven by Juanita's fiancé. A priest climbed down from the passenger seat, his cassock floured with dust from the journey.

Ricardo was a darkly handsome Colombian in his mid-twenties. It was easy to see how the lush swept-back hair, the long-lashed eyes and ready smile had charmed the farmer's daughter. He shook hands cheerfully with the strangers and introduced the priest from Cruz de Oro.

'I'd like you to meet Father León.'

The priest, too, had good-looking and swarthy features and appeared to be only a few years older than Ricardo, with just a hint of grey at the temples.

With unexpected seriousness he said: 'You do us a great honour by coming to this place to film God's creatures. As a child I collected many books on wildlife. So if I can be of any help, please let me know. Many in my congregation know the best places to go to find different animals. Indeed, you could do worse than ask Ricardo here.' For the first time the priest's solemn expression was lightened by a smile. 'If he will have the time to drag himself away from his new wife.'

Juanita's fiancé was enthusiastic. 'It will be my pleasure to guide you, of course.'

'But I must issue a word of warning,' the priest added. 'I regret this is not a safe part of the world. There are guerrillas and robbers who could cause you problems. Many would target rich foreigners for kidnap and ransom. Animals are indeed God's creatures, but sometimes I wonder about mankind.'

'Amen to that,' Tafur said with feeling.

The priest took the offered cup of coffee from Maria and sipped at it with relish. 'Indeed, it is over just such a matter that I am here.' He turned to the farmer. 'This morning I had another visit from our mutual friends. They gave dark warnings that the chapel might be burned down if I marry your daughter and Ricardo tomorrow.'

Juanita looked aghast. 'But why? What are they trying to do? What have I ever done to them?'

'Sssh, child,' Tafur said softly and placed a consoling arm around the girl's shoulders. 'We will not let them intimidate us. It is not you, but me they are angry with. It is all part of the pressure. You and Ricardo shall marry – regardless of their threats.'

Father León shifted his stance; he looked uncomfortable. 'That may not be wise, Victor. They said if it goes ahead they will be there. To add their blessing to that of God, was how they phrased it.'

Tafur's face stiffened. 'Are you telling me the ceremony cannot

211

be held, Father?'

'No, no. If you wish it, we will go ahead. It is just that I think you should seriously think about the consequences. Not for the church or for yourself, but for your daughter and her husband.'

Ricardo took Juanita's hand. 'No one will stop us, Father. It's unthinkable.'

'These are dangerous people,' the priest reminded.

'I am all too aware, Father,' Ricardo said. 'You will remember I was beaten up by them just a few months ago for refusing to co-operate.'

A thought occurred to Mallory. 'Father, this is none of my business, but it would be a shame to ruin the big day for these two young people. Juanita's father has a barn where the ceremony could be held. I know it is not a church, but you could bless the place, perhaps?'

Father León lifted an eyebrow. 'That is an interesting proposition. It is time we all stood up to these people.'

Mallory smiled. 'Leave those pigs waiting at the chapel, thinking the wedding's been called off, while all the time it goes ahead here in the privacy and safety of your home.'

Juanita's expression changed, her face radiant at the prospect. 'Señor Kurt, what a wonderful idea.'

Meanwhile Mario had been standing idly by the window, enjoying his coffee and a cigarillo. He saw the approaching dust trail on the track from Cruz de Oro.

'Excuse me, Victor, but are you expecting visitors?'

Mallory saw then the sudden look of fear in the farmer's eyes. It was palpable. You could almost smell it on him. Maybe it was the tone of Mario's voice that set alarm bells ringing. Like Mallory himself, his friend had an instinctive sense of impending trouble. A mood change in the atmosphere of a place, a certain spoken phrase that hid a real meaning, even simple body language. And body language transferred itself to the way a vehicle was driven. Essentially, most men drove in a relaxed manner; a man looking for trouble drove with aggression, powered by adrenalin. Hard, precise driving allowed a man to build up his courage and self-confidence.

The farmer said: 'I am expecting no one.' He stepped forward to join Mario by the open window. His mouth began to go dry as he saw the vehicle take form within the dust cloud. It was a Rocsta jeep. He crossed himself. In a barely audible whisper, he said: 'It's them.'

Mario and Goldie glanced towards Mallory, who gave an almost imperceptible shake of his head. Their firearms were still secreted in the Fourtrak which was parked outside. While there was still time to reach them, this was not the place to go breaking cover. They were not here to protect farmers, brides and priests. Their target was the Viper gang and an opportunity might just be presenting itself.

Suddenly Ricardo went to the wooden wall rack by the door and took down the shotgun.

'I am not sure that is wise,' Tafur said as the lad thumbed in two cartridges of bird shot.

'It is the only language they understand.'

Maria put a protective arm around little Nancy. 'We'll go to the bedroom. Victor, *please* be careful. All of you. Don't go looking for trouble.' There was an edge of despair to her voice.

They then heard the throaty roar of the Rocsta as it entered the dirt yard and skidded to a halt. Startled chickens flurried in all directions and Juanita's tethered stallion pranced nervously at the sudden commotion.

Mallory followed the others to the door, but hung back in the shadow of the archway to view the scene. The open-topped Rocsta had pulled up thirty feet from the hacienda and the driver and his front passenger were getting out. Both Latinos and both wearing the shabby unofficial 'uniform' of the *campesino*: ragged jeans, filthy torn shirts and straw stetsons. But while the driver was thin and unshaven with nervy body movements, the other was corpulent and confident. His face was fat and round, his long shaggy hair matched with a heavy Zappa moustache, and he had the air of a man who believed in his own reputation – no doubt all of it bad. He looked and felt invincible, Mallory thought. Quite capable of using the 9mm Ingram sub-machine gun which he carried casually in one hand.

Mallory became aware of the increasing tempo of his own pulse rate as the adrenalin started to flow. He would have to do something, but he didn't yet know quite what. And the prospect was scaring him shitless. He looked relaxed and cool, he knew that, leaning against the door jamb, idly studying his nails, just glancing up from under the shading peak of his old baseball cap. No one would guess the dread terror he really felt.

Keep calm, think. Take a long slow draught of air. Force yourself to control your feeling of panic, to consider the options with deadly cold logic. Assess the enemy. The big man standing a few feet in front of his vehicle smoking a cheroot, looking complacent and almost genial with a wide grin revealing yellow teeth. Armed? Look again. Yes, a hunting knife strapped to his ankle. Remember that.

The driver. A pace or two behind, subordinate, less sure of himself, but with vacant dark eyes that meant he was probably slower-witted, less able to muster rational thought, and therefore dangerous. A pistol stuffed in his waistband. Probably experienced, but definitely not professional.

Then he noticed them for the first time. Sitting relaxed in the rear seats of the Rocsta. Despite the shadows from the wide-brimmed hats, he identified them immediately as gringos. In the doorway he shifted position slightly and thumbed up the peak of his cap for an unobstructed view. The two men turned to face each other, to exchange some comment or maybe a joke. Sunlight picked up their features for a fleeting second. Then Mallory had no doubt who they were. The men from the whorehouse in Santa Maria. Guy, the tall one. A triple nine tattooed on his knuckles, confirmed by Lucila. The killer of Mario's wife and child. And the other man whom he knew only as Billy. His heart began to thud, his body trembling, feeling like the vibration of a pneumatic drill.

'What do you want, Pedro?' Ricardo shouted from the front of the gathering by the door. He held the shotgun pointed to the ground.

The fat man allowed cheroot smoke to escape through his teeth as he smiled. 'To offer our congratulations to you and your bride-to-be, of course.'

Ricardo's face remained expressionless. 'Fine, so you've done it. Now you can go.'

Another smile, and Pedro Goméz flicked his cheroot ash in the direction of the shotgun. 'You plan to go shooting birds, boy? That is all that thing is good for.' He looked at his driver and both men laughed. Then he returned his attention to Ricardo. 'We would have brought a gift, but we hear a rumour that you do not marry after all?'

Juanita clutched her fiancé's arm.

Father León spoke up. 'It is possible the marriage may be postponed.' His voice quavered slightly. 'We are thinking the couple are not ready for a lifelong commitment . . .'

The smirk widened on Pedro's face. 'I really am sorry to hear that. But then they are both so young. And Juanita is so pretty – I am sure she will have many suitors.' A chuckle. 'I might even ask her to marry *me*!'

Ricardo snapped, 'Shut your filthy mouth!' The twin barrels lifted a fraction. 'Now get out of here!'

Pedro raised his left hand. 'Okay, okay. That is not so friendly. But think of this. In just a few weeks you could be away from here. Maybe settle in a nice new hacienda and ranch in a place that grows lush green grass rather than tumbleweed. Eh? Maybe then you and your bride will see a real future for yourselves. Think about that, boy. Persuade that stubborn old future father-in-law of yours. But don't take long about it.'

Victor Tafur could stand no more. He stepped forward. 'For the last time, Pedro, I have no intention of selling.'

'Is that so?' The Colombian jerked a thumb over his shoulder in the direction of the Rocsta. 'Even when my boss, Señor Guy, suggests we add one million pesos to our offer? Let us call it a wedding present.'

Two thousand pounds sterling, Mallory thought. Around three thousand dollars. A small fortune for a peasant farmer in the Servita valley.

'I am *not* selling,' Tafur repeated.

All humour drained from Pedro's face in an instant and a pink tongue appeared to wet his lips. 'That is a shame, because these are such troubled times.' His eyes began to wander. Along the line of people gathered at the doorway, to Ricardo's battered pick-up, the hired Fourtrak and Juanita's stallion at the tethering post. 'So unpredictable. You never know when an accident might happen . . .'

It occurred so fast that no one was expecting it. Almost concealed in his huge paw of a hand, the Ingram burst into life. He didn't even bother to aim it, just fired straight from the hip. Juanita screamed. The horse uttered a strange, gurgling shriek of pain and surprise as the line of 9mm rounds studded the satin pelt of its flank. With eyes wild and wide and its mane tossing in a frenzy, the haunches collapsed under the animal's body weight.

The silence that followed was stunned. Disbelieving.

'See what I mean?' Pedro said apologetically.

The dying horse twitched and whimpered. Juanita broke from her fiancé and raced across to the stricken beast. She dropped to her knees, taking its head into her lap, stroking its cheek and gasping out words of consolation. Red foam bubbled from the horse's slack lips and spread in a livid pattern across the white cotton of her dress.

Mallory had about five seconds to assess the situation, to double-guess the turn of events. Knew Ricardo would react with fatal consequences and yet the lad was the only one with a firearm. Twenty feet to the Colombian gangster and only his secreted Chinese Poignard fighting knives to bridge the distance. Bad odds.

Then he noticed the bolas hooked to the front door for decoration, two balls of lapacho hardwood joined by a thong of guembepi fibre. He moved swiftly to remove them just as Ricardo raised the shotgun. Pedro pivoted, ready for the reprisal. Searching for the girl's fiancé, anticipating the lad's blind anger. Mario pulled Tafur back. Goldie gave a mighty heave into Ricardo's back, the shotgun detonating as the lad pitched sideways.

The rounds from the Ingram sliced through the air where Ricardo had been standing, chewing a cluster of holes in the hacienda wall. Pedro cursed and arced round on the balls of his feet, seeking his target on the ground. If he hadn't, the Colombian might have caught sight of Mallory as he twirled the bolas rapidly above his head. Concentration was everything; it was thirty years since he had last used one in Paraguay, but in an instant he was a boy again. Remembering the feel of the device, its weight, the need for a straight-armed throw to keep a good gap between the two balls during flight. Suddenly it was only yesterday when he had been a master of the technique.

Pedro heard the strange whir of displaced air as the bolas left Mallory's hand. Distracted, the Colombian's eyes flickered sideways to see the loose star of weighted thongs spinning towards him. But that was all. Then all he was aware of was the stunning impact as they struck his face, going into centrifugal rotation, wrapping around his throat with the speed and strength of a baby python. The Ingram fell instantly from his grip as he toppled backwards under the impact, his fingers desperately trying to unravel the living creature that was throttling him.

Mallory was moving in fast on the Colombian's driver. The tall thin man with the vacant eyes had been watching events earlier with smug amusement. An unaffected bystander. But all that had changed. Now his boss had been pole-axed and lay writhing on the ground and someone was coming at him. Running fast, crouched low, unarmed, but nonetheless menacing. Feverishly his hand tugged at the pistol in his waistband. It was caught on the belt buckle, resisting. He yanked it free.

The double-horn Poignard fighting knives were kept in two horizontal scabbards fixed to Mallory's trouser belt and hidden by his canvas jacket. As he closed on the panicking driver, his right hand reached behind his back, fingers locking around one haft. His eyes fixed on his target, mind totally focused.

Suddenly the driver's pistol was out, the man's arm high, his elbow bent, the barrel pointing skyward. Then the driver tried to bring it down, to level it at the stranger rushing towards him. Mallory's left arm brushed the gun aside, following up with a right-hand thrust. He was not aiming at the man's body but some point beyond it. Like a karate blow that snaps a block of concrete as though it were a candy bar, the tempered steel tip of the Poignard punched into the driver's upper abdomen, just below the ribcage, in a power-driven upward thrust. Just left of centre. Material, flesh and muscle – even bone – offered no resistance as the seven-inch blade sliced into the heart.

Mallory heard the astonished cries of those who watched. But not the driver. He was frozen, speechless, hooked and hanging on the blade. His legs had collapsed under him, his arms limp and lifeless by his side. Wide, disbelieving eyes stared at the man who was killing him, content to leave his victim like a gasping fish. Enjoying the moment.

Mallory's biceps began to tremble at the effort of holding the dead weight, but still he stood there, determined that the men in the Rocsta should remember this. Then, slowly, he lowered the blade of the Poignard and allowed the body to slither free. It twitched once, twice on the ground, then lay still.

Only then he breathed again and looked across the yard to where Pedro still lay on the ground, the skin of his face almost blue as Mario used a knife to cut away the ravelled thong from his neck. Goldie stood above them, calmly removing the magazine from the Ingram while the Tafur family and the priest watched in shocked silence.

Then the solitary slow handclap began. It was the tall Englishman Mallory knew only as Guy. At his side Billy Susan sat, unsmiling, another Ingram clearly in view.

The man called Guy levered himself over the open side of the Rocsta and dropped to the ground. Although he appeared to be unarmed, he showed no visible concern at the prospect of death or danger. He walked with languorous strides towards Mallory and the dead man.

Then he stopped, just a few feet away, and tipped up the brim of his cowboy stetson with his thumb. His eyes were dark and glittering, whether with amusement or anger it was difficult to tell.

In English, Mallory said: 'You should teach your men some manners.'

There was a pause while the other man regarded him carefully.

'I think you've already done that.' He indicated the figure of Pedro, now stumbling breathlessly to his feet. 'But he's the one you should have killed. He'll not forgive or forget.'

'And you owe the lady the price of a horse.'

Now a smile surfaced on the angular features, perhaps admiring the stranger's cheek. 'You think so, eh?'

Mallory wiped the blade of his knife on the dead driver's shirt. He guessed the Englishman was recalling just how quickly the driver had met his Maker. 'I think so.'

The man reached into his jacket pocket, very slowly, aware that Mallory was watching his every move. He drew out a roll of dollar bills and peeled off some notes. 'Two hundred. I think that's the going price for a nag.'

'Not that one. It was special, a fine *potrilliό*. Make it five.'

The Englishman's grin deepened and he plucked out another two hundred bucks. 'Don't push your luck.' He glanced across at the Tafur family, Mario and Goldie, then looked back at Mallory. 'You asked me for a job in Santa Maria. So what are you doing here?'

Mallory said: 'That's a wildlife film unit. They hired me.'

'To do what? Be a one-man army?'

'To help out, this and that.'

The man nodded. 'A bit of a waste of your talent – what was your name?'

'Kurt. Kurt Hulse.'

At that moment, Goldie stepped forward. 'Look, I don't know what's going on here, but I can do without all this violence.' His eyes blinked behind the thick lenses of his spectacles. 'I hope you won't give us any trouble if we're filming in the area?'

Guy Thripp studied the skinny Jew with his mad tangle of black hair. 'Just take the *comisario*'s advice. Don't point any camera near me or my men and keep out of our way. You'll be all right.'

Then Goldie turned on Mallory. 'And you're fired. I wanted an errand boy, not a bloody murderer. I don't need this sort of hassle.'

Thripp said: 'There's no hassle.' He waved across to Pedro

Goméz and pointed to the dead driver. 'Get this bag of shit loaded.' Then he turned back to Goldie. 'It's easy enough to dispose of a corpse out here. No worries.'

Goldie said: 'He's still fired.'

Thripp nodded slowly, a thought occurring to him. 'Well, Kurt, you've cost me one of my men. The least you can do is replace him. You said you wanted a job.'

Mallory glared at Goldie for a second, then said: 'Give me a minute while I grab my kit.'

10

'So tell me about yourself,' Thripp invited.

He was sitting in the rear with Mallory. Despite having been dumped face down in the cargo section, the corpse had started to leak and the stench was putrid. Pedro was driving, but spent more time scowling at Mallory in the mirror than watching the track. Billy Susan sat beside him in the front, repeatedly shouting at him to look where he was going.

It took most of the journey to the emerald mine camp for Mallory to recount his life story and answer Thripp's questions. Orphaned childhood in Paraguay, a spell as a mercenary in Africa, then bumming around the world. Close enough to the truth to make it sound convincing.

'So no formal military training?'

'I can handle myself.'

'I've seen that. No offence intended. It's just that . . .'

Mallory looked at him.

Thripp sniffed hard for a second and stared out at the passing countryside. 'It's just that something about you seems familiar. I used to be with 22. You know, the British SAS? Can't have been there.'

Christ! Mallory felt his heart skip two beats in succession, a spasm of fear knotting in the base of his spine. Now I know where it was, he thought, and when. Who you are, Guy Thripp, and what you were.

He was hardly listening as the man continued: 'So you know South America well and speak the lingo?'

'Sure. I'm more at home here than in England.'

Billy Susan chuckled. 'And there's me thinking you was a Kraut.'

At last they had arrived at the camp compound, the gates swinging open as they approached. When the Rocsta jolted to a standstill, Thripp ordered Pedro to get rid of the body. In time-honoured fashion it would be left for the condors to pick clean. Then, after a couple of days, Pedro's men would burn the bones until nothing remained.

Thripp turned to Mallory. 'You come with me and Billy. We'll introduce you to the boss man.'

Grabbing his rucksack, Mallory followed them to a small shack. The door opened onto a small untidy office area with two old wooden desks that came from a previous era. 'This is where I work,' Thripp announced, pointing at an ancient upright manual typewriter and a pile of paper. 'As you can see, running our – er – export operations isn't easy without mod cons. That suits to a degree, being this remote. But electricity and telephone lines don't extend beyond Adoración so we're stuck with unreliable generator power. So no phones or fax or computers. We have to radio our small office in the village and send all paperwork by messenger. Makes us pretty labour intensive. I work alongside Harry Morgan, the boss, and we share this office. Billy's the gaffer and oversees the manpower. From now on that includes you.' Susan's rosebud mouth pulled a smile that looked obscenely pretty in the pock-marked face. 'If Billy says shit, then you shit. His orders aren't orders, they're holy commandments. Goddit?'

Mallory nodded.

Thripp moved to the left and threw open the door to the adjacent quarters. It was barely large enough for the two camp beds on which a middle-aged man sat as he pulled on a pair of leather boots.

'Sorry to disturb, boss, but have you got a minute?'

Harry Morgan climbed to his feet. He was tall and heavy, all muscle, with that flattish, lived-in sort of face that had ex-Para stamped all over it. And he was smart.

'What is it, Guy?'

'We ran into that bloke I told you about. The one who asked me for a job in Santa Maria. I thought we could use him. He's a bit handy.'

Morgan stepped into the doorway and fixed his eyes on Mallory. 'Don't think we have a vacancy for a tramp. Got enough of them here already.'

Thripp said: 'He killed Pedro's driver.'

Morgan blinked and looked at his number two. 'Say again?'

'We were doing some business down at the Tafur ranch. Pedro got a bit excited. This bloke stood up to him – quite a spectacle, boss, you should have seen it. Floored Pedro with one of those bolas contraptions, then stabbed the driver before he could draw breath, let alone his gun. Thought we could use him. He speaks the lingo.'

Slowly Harry Morgan nodded; clearly he trusted Thripp. Lighting a cigarette he walked in and across to his desk. 'Okay, Guy, tell me what this is all about.'

He remained silent and thoughtful, just blowing occasional smoke rings while Thripp and Susan related events at the ranch in detail and what they knew of Mallory's background.

When they had finished, Morgan reached into the drawer of his desk and extracted a bottle of Black Label. 'Get some mugs, Billy. Maybe we've something to consider here. Join us in a drink, Kurt?'

'I don't drink.'

The boss nodded in slow appreciation. 'That's good, Kurt, very good. In a godforsaken place like this a man can get to depend on this stuff. But just make this an exception, eh?'

'A small one then.'

Billy Susan dumped one chipped glass tumbler and a number of tea-stained china mugs on the table for Morgan to distribute the whisky. 'So you're one of us, Kurt? British, but speak fluent Spanish and German. And you know how to handle Latin bums like Pedro Goméz, it seems. Now, what do you know about this operation?'

Mallory accepted one of the mugs. 'They say you've reopened one of the old emerald mines.'

'Who's they?'

'Folk in Santa Maria and Adoración. The drunk I met in Bogotá.'

A ghost of a smile played at Morgan's lips. 'But you don't believe them?'

Mallory shrugged. 'Maybe, maybe not. This is Colombia. It's famous for its emeralds as well as its coca.'

Morgan's face was a picture of innocence. 'Coca?'

'The guns, the heavies, knocking the locals around to demand loyalty – well, that could be emeralds. Sounds like the white lady to me.'

'Or White Viper,' Susan chuckled at his private joke.

'And tell me,' Morgan said, 'would you have a problem with that?'

A grin cracked Mallory's face. 'I may be one of you, Mr Morgan, but I'm more South American than British. If it earns the old *campesinos* a few bucks, I'm all for it. If I get something out of it – even better. Just what would you want me to do?'

Morgan shot Thripp a knowing glance before replying. His number two nodded shrewdly. 'You see, Kurt, we have a little problem. This operation is a partnership, see? You probably realise that.'

Mallory nodded. 'No foreigners are going to operate here without a Colombian mafia's say-so.' He hesitated. 'In fact, I'm surprised they've allowed you to have your own men on the ground at all.'

Thripp said: 'They didn't in the beginning and we got ripped off pretty bad. Individuals and local groups of villains all pointed the finger at each other. We didn't know who the hell to believe.'

'So we took the pragmatic view,' Morgan said, sipping at his whisky. 'Said if they wanted our money and expertise, we needed to get in deeper. So we upped our investment in return for our own muscle on the ground to protect that investment. They provided Pedro Goméz and his gang of hooligans and Guy here organised our team. They're supposed to work together but in truth it's more like a mutual stand-off.'

While they were in a talkative mood, Mallory decided to push

224

his luck. 'I don't understand why the Colombians should want you at all. What expertise do you have they don't already have themselves? Why let you have a slice of the action?'

Mallory quite distinctly felt the air chill as Morgan's eyes narrowed. 'Let's just say we understand some markets better than they do.'

'You mean Europe,' Mallory said, nodding as though it made absolute sense to him. He avoided eye contact as he added: 'I guess the US is becoming pretty much saturated – and anyway, the price per kilo is much higher in Europe.'

'Know a lot about it, do you?' Billy Susan said hoarsely.

Mallory shrugged. 'I know South America, what makes it tick, how it works.' Time to get off the subject, he decided. 'So how can I help?'

Thripp glanced at his boss, unsure whether he should say more. But Harry Morgan seemed satisfied. His number two said: 'Basically we don't trust Pedro's crowd. Although they've been supplied by our Colombian partners, we never know when they might decide on a little action of their own. For that matter, our partners themselves are capable of mounting – what shall we say? – a hostile takeover bid. None of our lads speaks more than a few words of the lingo. Usually "How much?" and "Take your knickers off." Harry, me and Billy, well, our vocabulary's a bit bigger, but not much. What I have in mind is to put you in with Pedro's lot. Call it a liaison rôle, but in fact it'll be to keep an eye on them and report back to us. You've got off to a good start, killing that idiot of a driver. They respect that sort of thing.'

'I've also made an enemy of Pedro.'

Billy Susan chuckled. 'Then we'll soon see if you're up to the job, won't we?'

'I'll need a firearm. Preferably a 9mm automatic.'

'No problem.'

'And I'll do things my way.'

Harry Morgan had no intention of paying this stranger the same rate as Thripp's men. He said: 'Five hundred dollars a month.'

Mallory shook his head. He didn't want to sound too eager.

'I'm not putting my life on the line for fun. This is a chance for me to sort my life out, get some cash together and start over. I'm getting too old for bumming around the world. So make it a thousand and we're talking business.'

'Seven fifty.'

'I said a thousand.'

Morgan smiled. 'Done.'

Mallory shook the offered hand. 'Just one thing. What's this vendetta with the Tafur family?'

Morgan scratched at his chin. 'It's no vendetta. We want the old bastard to sell up. There are very few places around here suitable for a landing strip and he's sitting on a prime site. Perfect. Only he won't budge. Until he does, all product and raw materials have to come and go by road to Santa Maria with all the attendant risks and costs. Once we've got our own strip, we get more profits and a lower profile – and we can quadruple our output within six months. We've offered the old sod a good price, but he just won't take it.'

'We've been too soft,' Thripp added.

Morgan shot him a disparaging look. 'Maybe, but my people and our Colombian partners would like to do it all nice and legal if possible. Quietly and no fuss. There's no halfway house though, because that'll draw attention to us – we don't want any law cases or any government or press involvement. So if Tafur won't co-operate we'll just have to put the fear of God into him.'

'I see.'

'Anything else?'

Mallory considered. 'Tell Pedro Goméz to leave me alone.'

'I will,' Guy Thripp promised, 'but you'll still have to look after yourself. You made a fool of Pedro in front of everyone. You've dented his machismo and he won't forgive you for that. Watch your back, because he'll choose his moment.'

Harry Morgan said: 'Welcome aboard.'

Mallory settled into camp life.

He was billeted in the Colombians' bunkhouse and allocated a wooden camp bed. There were around thirty men in all. Hired muscle. Most had at one time or another worked for Pablo Escobar of the now disintegrated Medellín cartel. Within a week Mallory had established that many had killed in what they affectionately called 'the good old days' before their master had been imprisoned in luxury then escaped only to meet his death at the hands of the 'armed police'. The men could be relied on to do exactly as ordered: intimidate, torture or murder, all necessary and regular activities to keep the *narco* machinery well oiled and efficient. They were so deep in the filth, they'd never be able to climb back out. Helpfully, Harry Morgan gave them liberal bonus perks of White Viper cocaine to keep them sweet.

Other Colombians worked in the laboratory, a sealed compound within the camp. These chemists had learned their trade down in the wild areas of the Chapare and Beni in Bolivia.

From the start Mallory was treated with a grudging respect. Word of how he'd killed the driver with a fighting knife that had seemingly appeared from nowhere and his ignominious defeat of Pedro Goméz had arrived before him. Generally the Colombians didn't speak to him voluntarily, but they responded politely enough to his questions. Pedro himself had protested vehemently to Harry Morgan at having this Englishman imposed on him, until it was explained that Pedro's own chief from Medellín had been consulted and had agreed to the liaison rôle. After that he avoided Mallory as best he could; thankfully, as foreman, Pedro had his own wooden hut and the two men rarely had to be in each other's company.

Gradually, as the days rolled by, Mallory became more accepted by the rank and file. He spoke their language and understood their psyche. He had a good repertoire of jokes and anecdotes that gained him a fair measure of popularity.

English-born he might be, but they would scarcely have guessed it. To Pedro's men he was, to all intents and purposes, one of them. As each day passed he was thought of less and less as an outsider.

His work was varied. With three other Colombians, he accompanied a local truck to the airstrip at Santa Maria to collect and deliver large plain packages. Invariably a sealed envelope was handed to the pilot. On one of those trips he saw Georgina Savage and Dale Forster across the street, but made no attempt to contact them. Other duties were more distasteful. An Indian who had been press-ganged into helping load and unload trucks was suspected of stealing part of the consignment, which he fervently denied. That night he was visited on the orders of Billy Susan. Half a dozen of them, led by Pedro, burst into the man's primitive house where he was eating a meagre supper of maize and bean soup with his wife and daughter. He was dragged outside while one of the gang forced a double-ended stave into the ground. Mallory knew what was coming. *El palo hablar*. The talking pole. A neat South American trick that was as old as the Conquistadores. There was nothing he could do but watch and jeer with the others as they tied the man's hands behind his back, removed his trousers and sat him on the upturned stave point. Then the men stepped back and allowed gravity and body weight to do the rest. They had their confession immediately and, satisfied, walked off into the night, leaving the impaled Indian to die.

On another night they visited a man who had been overheard gossiping about the mine and its involvement in *la coca*. He was held down and his lips sealed with an industrial staple gun.

Mallory had felt sickened but, strangely most might think, not by these acts of barbarity in themselves. If he'd ever seriously considered it, he might have accepted that his childhood and later life had brutalised him, blurred the fine line between violence that was justified and violence that was not. What angered him was the intimidation that was at the core of it all and the utter helplessness of the victims. Did it matter whether they were innocent or not? The Indian was an impoverished, half-starved *campesino* and the other man a fool with a loose tongue. But there was no plea for clemency for them, no court of appeal; no lawyers in cloaks and fancy wigs, no divine intervention.

Pedro Goméz, Billy Susan, Thripp and Harry Morgan. They were no better than each other. Mallory recognised the type. Almost without exception the gringos in Morgan's outfit were from deprived or broken homes. They'd grown up in the thuggish yob culture of the British underclass. Ill-educated and with little or no moral guidance they had faced a bleak future with a choice of menial labour, the social or crime – or all three.

As a way out, each of these men had joined the armed forces. The system had reinforced and encouraged their swank and their violent ways – Mallory noticed how many were former Paras. But before the military could remould them to include a few balancing virtues, like a little humility, almost all had left of their own accord or had been cashiered.

And that was what else Morgan's men had in common. They were all failures and they knew it and hid their lack of self-esteem and self-respect behind a wall of swaggering brutality. In this domain they were gods in a godless world. Strutting with arrogance and in the knowledge that they were safely beyond any law, any retribution.

It was to destroy people like them that Mallory had first agreed to work for the organisation. Of course, Goldie and Mario understood; it was in their blood too. And if any others of his few friends had known what he did, they would probably applaud his sense of justice. But not if they knew the methods he sometimes used.

Amongst outsiders, only Savage had ever known and, he thought, understood. Partially at least. But he realised it was something she could never accept.

But then she had never known how he'd felt as a boy in Paraguay. When Brother Hermann had been his mentor and tormentor.

However, apart from those chilling incidents, the first week passed quietly enough. Other than discovering as much as he could about the details of the gang's operation, his most urgent task was to decide how best to establish communications with Goldie and Mario. He had not dared walk into the camp with any incriminating kit that didn't fit with his cover story. And, sure enough, on the second day he found that his rucksack had been disturbed while he was out. The single hair he'd wetted and placed across the fastenings was missing and inside he could see that the contents weren't quite as he'd left them. Any item of communications equipment, however well disguised, might have been found.

229

The only concession to the decision he'd made to go in 'clean' was his private false passport under the name of Jim Tate. This he kept in a concealed pocket stitched to the inside of his baseball cap – the most likely item to be overlooked in a cursory body search. Even if it had been found, he had a perfectly reasonable explanation for it, one that fellow criminals would fully understand.

In the pre-ops planning stage in London, it had been decided that either Goldie or Mario would probably need to hide a portable radio relay booster within a few hundred metres of the camp compound. Unbeknown to him, Goldie had positioned it during his fourth night with the *narcos*. They had been filming five kilometres away the previous day and that night had pitched their two tents beside the Fourtrak. At midnight, when deputy Gilberto was in a deep alcoholic slumber, Goldie had stealthily approached the camp and put the unit in position.

The other decision which had been made during the journey to the Tafur ranch was the means of contact to be used in Adoración. That, Mallory realised, could be provided by the *puta* called Lucila who would by then be resident at the whorehouse there.

By the time Saturday arrived he was more than ready for some female company at El Tigre and a respite from the constant need to be on his guard at the camp.

He hitched a lift into the settlement at sundown in one of the Rocstas. It was driven by the camp's vehicle engineer, Doug Tallboys. His somewhat taciturn manner hid a dry humour which began to surface only after a couple of Club-Colombias at the bar.

'While you're working here for Harry Morgan, just shut your eyes and think of Scotland,' he advised. 'That's what I do.'

'That bad, eh?'

Tallboys drained another bottle. 'Well maybe it doesn't bother you. I mean, I heard how you stuck Pedro's driver the other day. Well, so what? He was just a murderin' shite anyway. But those "police patrols", as Billy Susan likes to call them – you know, keeping the locals in line. I don't have the stomach for that.'

230

Mallory wondered if the man was testing him. 'Maybe it's necessary?'

The Scotsman regarded him with frosty grey eyes. 'Yeah, in this business it probably is. Trouble is you can't complain to anyone. Not Harry, Guy or Billy or the rest. They won't tolerate it. Means they're treating us no better than the locals.'

Tallboys's companion was a wan-faced ex-Para in his late twenties. His name was Pete Stafford. 'I wish to hell I hadn't got involved.' The fear was showing in his eyes.

'Now, now,' Tallboys warned. 'Careless talk costs lives. Yours, if you're not careful.'

Mallory regarded both men carefully. 'So you didn't know what you were getting into?'

Tallboys said: 'Not until we arrived and then it was too late. They conned us into it – now we're on one-year renewable contracts.'

'I'll drink to that,' Stafford said, making a sudden and determined effort to be cheerful. 'Just over eleven months to go!'

The Scotsman looked at Mallory. 'That's what Pete's predecessor thought. Made the mistake of mouthing off to Billy Susan and now he's dead. When these guys say *renewable* yearly contracts, that's what they expect us to do. Renew. How else can they ensure no one blabs to the authorities back home?' He turned back to Stafford. 'A word of advice, sonny. If you ever plan to abandon ship, don't tell me, or Kurt or anyone. Just do it and run like the devil's after you. Because, believe me, he will be.'

Mallory said: 'Still, it's a job.'

Tallboys used the table edge to remove the cap from another bottle. 'Sure. It pays the mortgage and feeds the wife and kids. But I tell you something, Kurt. I used to be proud to be a soldier – if you allow a REME grease monkey to call himself a soldier. Northern Ireland, Germany, Hong Kong and the Falklands bash. Even met some great blokes in the mercenary side of things in Africa. Felt I was contributing *something* to make the world a better place. Helping get rid of the bad guys, I suppose. But here?' He belched lightly. 'I feel like I'm wallowing in sewage and I'm never going to get clean again. Sorry! Stupid that, just the drink

231

talking.' He lifted his glass. 'To good ol' Harry Morgan and his merry men! God bless 'em!'

'And may they rot in hell,' Pete Stafford added darkly.

Mallory waited until gone midnight before he made his way to El Tigre. By that time most members of the Viper gang had already indulged themselves or were too drunk to do more than think about womanising.

He entered the adjoining bar and glanced around. Only a few of Pedro's crew were around, talking morosely in corners, sparing him a cursory wave of acknowledgement. Passing into the bordello's reception area, he saw that the girls were sitting around gossiping, smoking and drinking cups of *tinto*. Heavy eyelids fluttered alluringly in his direction, but without much enthusiasm; it had been a busy evening. With disappointment Mallory realised that Lucila was not among them.

A hand tapped him on the shoulder. 'Señor Pike.'

His heart froze in horror the second he heard the name. Then his pulse seemed to kick-start with a thud, racing as he turned.

The short peroxide hair, the bulging eyes and scarlet cupid's bow were unmistakable. 'Fanny Lacera?'

She was smiling. 'I never forget a face.'

Mallory found himself sweating. 'But you forget names, Fanny. It's Kurt Hulse.'

Understanding flickered in her eyes. 'Of course it is. Are you looking for a particular girl?'

'Lucila.'

'Ah, sweet Lucila. From Santa Maria, but then you probably know that. She's busy at the moment. Would you like a drink while you wait? Come with me.'

He followed the enormous backside hidden by drifts of chiffon as she waddled through to her office.

She opened the drawer of her desk and produced a bottle of five-star brandy as she said: 'I hope we're not going to have a repeat of last time. My neck was sore for days after.'

'Not if you tell me what you're doing here? Why did you leave Venezuela?'

She poured shots into two balloon glasses and handed him

one. 'Expansion, señor. My backers thought I did so well at Arabian Nights that we should buy out this place.'

'Backers?' he queried, then realised what she meant. Her backer was Ruiz Edilberto Jaramillo, suspected but unproven head of a Cali family. And this was part of his intelligence operation against their mutual enemy.

'They have an eye for profit. And my clients like a familiar face, someone they can trust. I've even brought a couple of my girls from Casuarito. And tell me – er – Señor Kurt, did you ever manage to contact the lawyer lady in Cali? Maria Palechor?'

Mallory swallowed the brandy. As if she didn't *know*. 'Forget it, Doña. And remember we have never met before.'

There was an intense gleam in her eye. 'I thought as much.' At hearing footsteps on the stairs, she turned. 'Ah, here is Lucila now.'

He stepped outside the office to be confronted by the girl and, standing behind her, Guy Thripp and Billy Susan.

'Kurt!' she cried, her expression lightening the instant she recognised him. 'You come here like you promise.' Quickly she leaned forward and kissed him on the cheek.

Thripp didn't like that; it showed in his eyes. 'Watch this one, Kurt, I think she's got crabs.'

Billy Susan tittered.

'That's okay,' Mallory replied easily, slipping his arm around the girl's waist. 'I expect she got them from me.'

After a brief and silent glare, Thripp strode away with Susan at his heels.

'What is the matter with him?' Lucila asked as they climbed the stairs.

'Just jealous,' Mallory answered. But he guessed Thripp didn't like the reminder that down-and-outs like him were using the same woman.

As she opened the door to her room, she said: 'I must not forget, one of my gentlemen leaves a package for you. His name is Mario, a marvellous man who makes nature films. He says you left these things behind when you work for him. He said you told him you will come to me tonight. I am so happy to hear it! And

233

here you are!'

She peeled off the skimpy pink dress and immediately he saw the bruises. 'Those men, they did this to you?'

'Señor Guy and Señor Billy, sure. But don't worry, it is just my job. You want to make love now?'

Back in Santa Maria she'd used the expression 'Make sex'. Things were looking up. 'Best offer I've had all week.'

It was strange, he thought later as he rode in the *collectivo* that had been sent to bring the Saturday night stragglers back to the camp, how men buried their fears and their anger in a woman's body. When she was riding the wave, oblivious to everything but her own ecstasy, how she didn't feel the pain or the relentless pounding of her inner flesh. How focused you could become, not on pleasure but on ridding yourself of frustration, hatreds and even anger that had nothing to do with love or passion. Or even the woman herself.

Somehow he had felt cleansed when it was over and they'd shared a cigarette and a couple of silly jokes. It was as though she'd happily absorbed all the filth and guilt of his life within herself. Absolved him.

On his return to the camp, he took the package and a flashlight to the latrines which were situated a good distance from the nearest building. There were three cubicles like sentry boxes made from corrugated tin which were placed over deep cesspits with a eucalyptus frame to squat over. Once inside he opened up the brown-paper package. The miniature microphone and speaker were concealed in a yellow plastic biro and the aerial was provided by a coil of wire with a tiny female plug fitting that snapped onto the point of the pen. He ran the aerial wire around the roof of the latrine, then clipped a second lead onto the reverse end of the pen. He attached this to his flashlight battery. All being well, there would be sufficient power for the signal to reach the relay booster hidden a few hundred metres beyond the camp fence.

He spoke in German: 'Lancelot to Galahad, are you receiving? Lancelot to Galahad, are you receiving?'

Five more times he tried before he picked up the hiss and

crackle, a disembodied voice breaking up. Goldie Goldstein. Thank God for that, he thought. This contraption had been provided by Dale Forster. No doubt it had worked well enough in trials at some signals laboratory at Langley. But the speaker was too tiny to provide much more than an indication that someone was on the receiving end. It was virtually a one-way system. 'Lancelot to Galahad. Message follows.'

It was the following morning when Goldie forwarded his taped and encrypted signal from the disguised radio in the Fourtrak by burst transmission. The message contained details of Mallory's call the previous night and an update of his and Mario's own situation.

A hidden radio in the UN Cherokee picked it up, the tape spool switching on automatically. There were now two signals waiting on the tape; the first had come in overnight from the American Embassy in Bogotá.

On his way back to the hotel in Santa Maria following breakfast with Savage at the Cosmopolita, Dale Forster went to the parking lot to check the Cherokee. He sat in the back and drew the curtains before opening the disguised radio and running the messages back at normal speed. He wrote for several minutes in his notebook, then closed everything up and returned to the hotel.

Savage was waiting in her room; this time he knocked before entering.

'I've got those name checks off the DEA computer,' he announced. 'It doesn't do to have an unusual Christian name in this business.'

'You mean Guy showed up?'

He nodded. 'Only one Englishman called Guy on the list. Guy Thripp.'

She stared at him as though he'd used a dirty word.

'What is it, Georgie?'

'Are you winding me up?' she demanded.

Forster glanced down at his notebook. 'No. Guy Thripp.' He spelt it out. 'Do you know him?'

But she wasn't hearing him.

She was sitting in the car in San Sebastian, northeast Spain, over two years earlier. Sitting alone, knuckles white with tension, observing the meet at the little café on the plaza. The transparent earpiece and hidden throat mike her only communication with their backup. The heat in the car stifling, the sun on the white buildings dazzling all around, her heart thudding.

Seeing Mallory sauntering along with two known members of the Provisional IRA towards the café.

Three men from the Basque separatist movement ETA already there, drinking coffee. Seeming relaxed, but not. Watchful and alert. Jumpy, but hiding it well.

The work nearly done, the meeting made and the links established. Names and faces to complete the jigsaw. And the mission almost complete.

Then she saw him. A man reading a newspaper, leaning against a lamppost. But not reading. His head at that odd angle that suggested he was talking into a microphone on his lapel.

She knew who he was and her heart sank. It took just a quick glance around the plaza now to pick out the rest of his team. The street cleaner; the man under the bonnet of his car searching for a fault; the woman looking at the postcard rack. Suddenly she could identify them all, zoom in like a telephoto lens. A second ago they had all appeared so innocent. How could she have been such a fool as to have missed them?

The Spanish anti-terrorist unit was mounting an operation. Wires were crossed, their people and hers not talking, not confiding. Now something was going down and her man with it.

That's when she had called for backup. To get in and get her man out. Fast. Screaming into the mike.

But her backup was a cockup. In the wrong place and its guard down. A four-man SAS team in plain clothes, badly positioned. Stuck in traffic and unable to close.

So she'd done the only thing she could do, broke cover. Started the engine of her car, cut across the line of moving vehicles until she was alongside Mallory, then threw open the door. The IRA men startled, starting to run.

Then hell had broken loose, Spanish undercover men moving in, shots being fired and terrified pedestrians diving for shelter.

That had been when Mallory had taken a round in the lung, staggered and thrown himself into the car as she hit the gas, driving away with the door still flapping.

Guy Thripp had been the man commanding the backup.

'Georgie, are you okay?' Forster asked.

She shook herself free of the memory. 'What? Oh, yes. It's just that I know Thripp. He used to be with the SAS. Well, I met him once – no, twice, on an op that went wrong. He screwed up and they kicked him out soon afterwards, I heard.' She stared at the American. 'More to the point, Dale, he knows Kurt.'

It was Forster's turn to stare. 'Christ!' His voice low and hoarse.

Savage tried hard to think, to remember the details. 'No, wait. Thripp and his team had only just been assigned. They'd been shown a photograph of Kurt before the operation.'

'So *did* he actually meet Kurt?'

'Yes. But only when he was coughing up his lungs. Blood all over his face. In fact Thripp's first aid probably saved his life.'

'Are you saying Thripp wouldn't necessarily recognise Kurt now?'

She nodded. 'Possibly not. Thripp's team had to get out fast before the whole thing blew up into an international incident.'

Forster glanced down at his notebook. 'Well, I think we might have gotten lucky. We've had a signal from him via Goldie. He hasn't mentioned any problem, but he has given us a list of names.'

'Including Guy Thripp?'

The American nodded. 'And the man we couldn't trace. Billy Susan. If Kurt's right, they've all or mostly been professional soldiers at one time or another.'

'I'll go through our embassy here and get them to check MOD records.'

Forster added: 'Apparently they were all recruited through small ads in *Soldier of Fortune* magazine. I know a number of agencies monitor those ads to get wind of anything suspect brewing. I'll see if I can find someone who can pinpoint the ad and maybe who's behind it. Your boy's done good, Georgie.'

She allowed herself a faint smile. 'Did you doubt it, Dale?'

'Not if I listened to you.'

There was no mistaking the inference in his words. Somewhere he'd picked up the vibes, sensed how she felt about him. She found his smug perception irritating. 'Was there anything else from Kurt?'

He told her that Fanny Lacera was now running the brothel in Adoración.

'What do you make of that?' she asked.

Forster shrugged. 'I don't have a problem with it. Fanny's part of the Cali cartel's intelligence operation, a successful part. So we shouldn't be surprised that they've taken advantage of it and moved her closer in to the Viper operation. After all, according to Jaramillo, the last agent they sent to snoop around here disappeared without trace. If this woman's got good cover, he's going to use her. We would, given a similar situation.'

'But Jaramillo didn't tell us he was doing it, Dale. That worries me.'

'Why should it? Relax, babe. After all, this is *his* turf. It stands to reason Jaramillo would want his own eyes and ears in the region.'

She still wasn't happy. 'But we've agreed with him that we'll take care of it. That's what he's paying for.'

'Then maybe he wants those eyes and ears to be sure we do a proper job of it. Maybe he doesn't trust us completely. I mean he trusted Vic West in the past, but West is dead. He might not be sure that Portcullis without West is as sound as it was. He'll be aware that some people in the company have high-level links with the British Government, and that your government has links with ours. There's got to be a danger, however remote, that he's being set up for some sort of sting operation by the DEA or some intelligence agency. If I were him I'd want to keep a pretty close eye on things too.'

Savage smiled ruefully. 'Well, I guess that's not a million miles from the truth. We're getting Cali to pay for an operation we'd mount anyway.' She thought for a moment. 'We can't prevent Jaramillo being a little cautious of Portcullis, but at least we can counter that by feeding him an intelligence update.' She indicated Forster's notebook. 'And that list of names would make an impressive start. It's important we earn his trust.'

'When will you go to see him?'

'There's a flight to Bucaramanga this afternoon and I can get an inter-connecting flight to Cali. So probably some time tomorrow.'

It was a bad dream. He was standing in a brilliantly lit room. White floor, white ceiling, white walls. His hands were tied behind his back. And all around white snakes slithered. White on white. Hard to see except for their darting little forked tongues. Just a few, he thought at first. Then, squinting against the brightness, he saw that there were hundreds of them. Maybe thousands. There was no door in the room. No way out.

'*LEVANTATE, GRINGO!*'

Mallory was awake with a jolt. Pedro Goméz stood at the foot of the cot, hands on hips and his sombrero askew.

Christ, the bastard's come for me. I knew he would eventually, and I'm not ready for him. 'Get up, gringo!' Pedro repeated in Spanish.

'What d'you want?'

'You come with me this morning.'

'Why?'

'We have an important person to collect.'

'Why do you want me?'

A gold tooth glittered in the smile. '*I* do not want you, gringo. It is orders from Señor Billy. He wants you to interpret. We leave in five minutes.'

They travelled in two Rocstas to Adoración, Pedro driving the first with Mallory and Billy Susan riding passenger. Four heavies, laden with sub-machine guns, followed in the second. As they passed the chapel at Cruz de Oro the bells were ringing boisterously, calling the faithful to mass.

'You know what I hear, gringo?' Pedro asked Mallory, who was

239

in the rear. 'I hear that young bastard Ricardo marries the Tafur girl last week at the hacienda while I and my friends wait at the church. What do you think of that?'

'Doesn't bother me.'

'Perhaps it should, gringo, because I also hear it is your suggestion. You enjoy trying to make a fool of me?'

Mallory half-smiled. 'I don't have to try, Pedro. You do it all by yourself.'

Come on, you bastard, try it now, and I'll have your liver slit and on the jeep floor before you can draw breath, let alone that bloody great machete of yours.

But Pedro was cautious now, had not forgotten the speed at which his driver had died. 'Don't push your luck, gringo.'

'Listen, when I suggested that idea to Ricardo, it was before I knew we'd be working on the same side. So let's forget it, eh?'

The Colombian grunted. 'The boy still has to pay the price. It has to be understood around here that what I say goes. If people get away with disobeying our orders there will be chaos.'

Billy Susan was becoming impatient at not understanding the heated argument in Spanish. 'What's he moaning about, Kurt?'

Mallory told him.

'The man's got a point. Violence is the only language some people understand. If one little jerk is allowed to disobey us, they'll think they can do what they like. Anyway, the time's come to stop pussyfooting with the Tafurs. They've turned down a fair offer for their land and now they've cocked a snook by going ahead with the wedding. There's a principle at stake here.'

'Meaning what, Billy?'

But the Englishman just grinned and said: 'Meaning that the Tafurs will find there's a price to pay for defying us. You'll see.'

The conversation lapsed then, discouraged by the constant rocking and jolting as the road deteriorated.

When they finally crossed the Servita river bridge and entered Adoración, the big black Landcruiser was already waiting. It was surrounded by four enormous bodyguards in flapping silk suits baggy enough to conceal an arsenal of weapons. The arrival of the Medellín chief was hardly low profile.

240

Barely thirty years old, Felix Bastidas was much younger than Mallory had anticipated. He emerged from the air-conditioned cool of the Landcruiser with the practised air of a Spanish aristocrat while managing to look like a B-movie version of Al Capone. That included a white panama worn at a deliberately rakish angle, a cream cotton suit and silk tie with a gold pin. But the walking cane and white kid gloves were way over the top, Mallory thought. Only the spats were missing.

'*Mucho gusto, Señor Bastidas,*' Billy Susan said, offering his hand.

There was an arrogance in the Colombian's full chiselled lips and thick brows that didn't really go with his baby face. Bastidas removed one glove with deliberate slowness leaving Susan to wait, with his arm stretched out like a tailor's dummy. '*Encantado. Cómo le va?*'

'What's he say?' Susan hissed.

'You've got lovely eyes.'

'What?'

'He says how are things?'

'Tell him fine. Tell him welcome to Adoración. We've all been looking forward to this important meeting with our respected Colombian partners.'

Felix Bastidas transferred to the Rocsta, sitting rather disdainfully in the back with Billy Susan while Mallory took the front passenger seat beside Pedro. When the other Rocsta pulled away with the four Viper heavies on board, they followed in its wake.

Mallory noticed that Bastidas looked tired after his long drive, so he was hardly surprised when the Colombian demanded to know how long it was going to be before he could fly direct to the mine and avoid the hours of bone-shaking travel on the unpaved roads?

Very soon, Susan had assured, but then wearied of the three-way translated conversation, leaving Mallory to talk to their guest. It left him free to ask a few questions of his own. Bastidas appeared to appreciate some light and intelligent conversation and, once he'd overcome his natural aversion to the stranger's filthy clothes and body odour, he began visibly to relax.

241

Felix Bastidas, Mallory learned, was a distant cousin of the infamous Pablo Escobar. The man had been his hero while he was at university, combining business studies with an extracurricular interest in left-wing activism. He had thoroughly approved of Escobar's anarchic stance against the Colombian government and especially the Americans' meddling in his country's affairs. Likewise he applauded Escobar's flirtation with the revolutionary guerrilla movements.

'After all, Señor Hulse, I have studied revolutionary history in Latin America. We have given birth to the longest-living group of revolutionaries in the world. Since La Violencia in the forties and fifties we have fought against successive bourgeois governments. Nearly half a century – and yet, although the first, we have achieved the least!'

That was going to change, or so Bastidas had thought. Yet when he left university to play his part in the Medellín cartel and to encourage political upheaval, he was just in time to witness the meltdown of Pablo Escobar's empire.

'Those middle-class rats from Cali were swarming all over the corpse of my cousin's business even before it was dead. Pointing fingers and helping the DEA finish the job. Then picking the bones clean, grabbing the whole cocaine trade for themselves. Smug that they are safe now with their friends in the government to protect them. The Medellín has fragmented into small gangs doing the best they can to survive.'

'And you're the leader of one of them, sir?' Mallory asked politely.

'I have brought several factions together under my leadership. Mostly these gangs comprise younger men who are hungry for power and change. And I mean political change. Our revived *narco* business is already bringing in vast rewards. But as the old saying goes, money cannot bring happiness. Certainly it did not for my cousin. And look at those bastards in Cali. They have big houses, big cars, big yachts. They have so much money they don't know what to do with it. What is the point of so much money that it will take years for it all to be safely laundered. That is no incentive. Now some of them even turn down new deals –

242

they are too much trouble even to bother.'

'But you have a different plan?' Mallory prompted. It was all beginning to take shape, to make sense.

'Oh, yes, Señor Kurt. I do not intend to amass a fortune just to let the Colombian government or the Americans seize it and imprison me or hunt me down like a common dog. My success will be to avenge my cousin and finish what he began. But whereas he did not have the political vision, *I* have. I am forging close links with as many guerrilla movements as I am able, trying to bring them together. Unknown to most, I am largely the architect of the Co-ordinadora Nacional Simon Bolívar, the new pan-guerrilla front. Money from this operation will be used to fuel the movement, to buy arms and run operations to bring about a people's revolution at long, long last. Not just here, but also in Venezuela. Later, maybe Bolivia, Peru and Paraguay. Simon Bolívar's dream will yet come true.'

Mallory lapsed into deep thought. This man was dangerous. A fanatic and a dreamer, but a powerful one who was already on the road to success. What he was too blind to see was where that road led. To years of violent upheaval and innocent deaths. Even if he were eventually victorious in freeing the country of corrupt and self-interested government, the people would still be peasants in a nation financed by and almost totally reliant on the self-consuming narcotics industry. And however well-intentioned Bastidas's aims, there would always be others more interested in their own wealth, power and domination to challenge his leadership.

When they arrived back at the camp compound there was a welcoming committee awaiting Felix Bastidas. Harry Morgan and Guy Thripp shook the Colombian's hand with polite enthusiasm and showed him to his temporary quarters. The hut was spartan but had at least been thoroughly swept and cleaned.

Morgan ambled across to Mallory. 'So what do you think of our Colombian partner?'

'Interesting. Pleasant enough.'

Morgan chuckled. 'Don't let that gentlemanly act fool you. He can be a right bastard – gave us a real hard time in the beginning.

243

Screwed us rotten until we came up with a new deal that meant more to him than it did to us.'

'Meaning?'

The ex-Para tapped the side of his nose. 'Need to know, Kurt, need to know. His enemies call him the Great Pretender – pretensions to succeed where Escobar failed and restore the dignity of the Medellín families. And all that crap! Wears that fancy gear and cane when he's playing the part, but then just vanishes when it suits. There's a popular legend around that he's a master of disguise. Reckon he must be, because he wouldn't last five minutes if he was always poncing about like that. Just a word of warning, keep your back to the wall when he's around.'

'Bent?'

'As a corkscrew.' Morgan grinned. 'How'd you get on with Pedro?'

'He was behaving himself.'

'Well, don't lower your guard. The whispers are he's out to get you. Did he say anything to Bastidas I ought to know about?'

Mallory shook his head. 'No. Just let Bastidas see he didn't like having me around. But as we got on well together, it rather fell on stony ground.'

'Good. Now if you can shave and get cleaned up, you can join us for lunch. You'll find some old clothes of mine in the laundry shack. They should fit where they touch, if nothing else.'

The cookhouse had excelled themselves. Mostly the food they had served since Mallory's arrival had been a fatty broth of pork and unfresh vegetables. Under serious threat of death or mutilation, the chefs had achieved a remarkable turnaround, serving up an excellent *sobrebarriga* for the camp's exalted guest. Mallory tucked into the belly of beef, rice, plantains, red beans and yucca with relish. His enthusiasm earned glares and pointed comments from Morgan and Thripp who were anxious for him to start interpreting. Clearly Mallory hadn't been invited for his social graces.

'Señor Bastidas would like to know if you can step up the military training of the guerrillas?' he translated. This was news to him and was a part of the operation of which he had been totally unaware. 'There have been complaints from the Wolf, the local guerrilla leader.'

Perhaps the wary look on Thripp's face explained why. They hadn't been doing much training. 'Tell him we'll do our best, but our resources are limited.'

Mallory passed the words on and gave the response. 'He says he wants to launch a renewed and sustained campaign against the oil pipelines in the next few months. He wants the first units to be fully trained in the next couple of weeks. And he's asking about the first arms shipment.' He hid the interest from his voice.

'Tell Señor Bastidas he'll get his men trained quicker if he can supply us with some interpreters, as I've said before. Regarding the arms, the first consignment was shipped into Venezuela yesterday. Over the next two weeks they're being moved discreetly by road and air to Puerto Ayacucho. Delivery from there will be by mule train overland or flown to Santa Maria.'

As the Colombian listened to Mallory's words he showed increasing signs of agitation. 'Please inform Señor Morgan that is not good enough – or fast enough. This location was chosen not only because it is remote and in guerrilla-held territory, but because the river canyon provides the only cross section over the Andes for low-flying aircraft. What is the use of that if we do not have the airstrip I was promised?'

Morgan listened grimly. 'I think I got the gist of that, Kurt. And you know what the problem is. The owner of the site isn't accepting our money offer or bowing to threats.'

As Mallory passed back the message, he had already anticipated Bastidas's angry reaction. Typically South American, he saw a simple solution. 'If these people have refused our silver, then there is only one alternative. No one can be allowed to jeopardise my mission. It is too important for that. I want aeroplanes flying in the arms from Puerto Ayacucho by the end of the week. And I want to double our output of the product over the next month or six weeks. The market in Europe and the former Soviet states is wide open. Not to capitalise now is foolhardy. It leaves a vacuum that others will fill if we don't. And meanwhile my people are anxiously awaiting their freedom.'

Morgan was noticeably unmoved by Felix Bastidas's political fervour, but he politely made the right noises. It was finally agreed that the Medellín chief would return in two weeks' time. By air. Then there would be a major progress meeting with Harry Morgan's boss.

That was the first time Mallory heard mention of Stan Summers.

11

Is that Miss or Mrs Hayes?' Ruiz Edilberto Jaramillo asked as he took her hand and pressed it to his lips.

Savage said: 'Mizz.'

The Cali chief chuckled. 'Ah, very *enigmatica*. Is she or isn't she?'

'It's irrelevant, Señor Jaramillo, because I'm not available.'

'A mysterious lady who is not available. What a combination to get male pulses racing!'

Maria Palechor stood patiently waiting for her client to tire of the chase; he was always the same when introduced to a pretty woman for the first time. The shadows were lengthening across the terrace by the pool; it had been a long hot day. She busied herself pouring fruit juice into three tumblers and carried them on a tray to the table where Jaramillo and Savage sat.

'I met Señora Hayes in London,' she reminded.

'Of course,' Jaramillo said. 'Your people were recommended by Portcullis.'

Savage took the offered glass of lemon. 'We deal with their – let's say, trickier assignments. Like this one.'

'And how is it going?' The question was pitched so, so casually.

'That's why I'm here. You're paying a lot of money. I thought you should have a progress report.'

'And?'

'We've got our man in. The Vipers have taken him on.' She opened her shoulder bag and handed him a neat little plastic folder. 'That's a list of the entire membership. All the British nationals are ex-military – our experts in London will get more

247

background eventually. The list of Colombian members is less complete – many use nicknames or first names and it'll take time for our man to get all the full names without rousing suspicions.'

Jaramillo ran his eye over the typewritten sheets. 'Very good.'

'They are also co-operating with the local ELN guerrillas. I believe their leader is called *El Lobo*. The British appear to be helping with some training.'

The Colombian grunted. 'That is not so good.' He stroked his heavy moustache. 'Mr Pike has done well.'

If he'd been expecting a startled response, he was to be disappointed. 'So has Fanny Lacera,' Savage replied evenly. *Touché.* 'Your eyes and ears on the ground?'

A soft laugh. 'Ah, dear Fanny. Such a trustworthy soul.'

'I hope so, Señor Jaramillo. We're not too happy to find her on the scene. She knows Harry and that could jeopardise our operation.' Her eyes hardened. 'You should have told us.'

'Of course,' he said, but didn't sound as though he meant it. 'You must realise, however, that we need to be able to observe what's happening down there for ourselves. An insurance if you like. Don't worry, Fanny won't compromise your operation. In fact you might find it useful to have a friendly face in the area.'

Maria Palechor interrupted. 'If she can be of help to you, don't hesitate to use her.'

'I'll remember that.' Savage glanced at her wristwatch. 'There is one more thing.'

'Yes?'

'We are due for an interim payment, now that we have successfully infiltrated.'

Jaramillo glanced at Maria Palechor who nodded in confirmation.

Savage added: 'We wish to make a change and have the amount paid to our account in a different bank.'

'Why is that?' the lawyer asked. 'If it isn't an impertinence to ask.'

'Not at all. As you will be aware it is absolutely essential that Portcullis runs no risk of association with this operation and their well-placed sources advise that this particular Caribbean bank is safer and more impenetrable than any other they have known.'

As she gave Maria Palechor the details, she noticed the flicker of interest in the lawyer's eyes.

Then it was time for Savage to depart and make her way back to Santa Maria, Jaramillo providing one of his chauffeured cars to run her to the airport.

She sank back into the plush leather and lit a cigarette, feeling not a little smug. A small seed had been planted. Unknown to Mallory, Forster or any of the others. A secret she shared only with Sidney Monckton, her deputy chief at riverside. Not only the Medellín cartel, but also the Cali operation itself was firmly in their sights.

And only time would tell if the seed would grow and bear fruit.

Back at Jaramillo's villa, the *capo* was saying: 'It would seem, Maria, that all is going to plan.'

'In every respect, Ruiz, better than we'd dared hope.'

'Sometimes it pays to be audacious.' He sounded very confident. 'And the bank the lady mentioned?'

'I've heard of it. Good reports by all accounts.'

'Then perhaps we ought to take a closer look.'

'Only ever seen Stan Summers twice since I've been here,' Doug Tallboys said that night. Mallory had casually brought up the name while having a beer with the engineer and Pete Stafford in the bar at Cruz de Oro. 'Came around to see each of us. See if we had any complaints and give us a pep talk.'

'Didn't tell him what you really thought, I bet,' Stafford said.

'Only about rotten mattresses and lousy grub. Nothing more serious than that. Stan Summers was all jokey and smiles. Sort of Essex boy made good. Flash git. But underneath he was just a gangland thug. He knows what Harry Morgan and Guy Thripp are up to. That's why he hired them. I mean, after all, he is a bloody drug smuggler or distributor or something.'

But to Mallory something didn't quite add up. This had been the best day so far. He'd learned more than he even dreamed there was to know. Drugs funding for an aspiring political revolutionary to pay for arms. But that and the use of hardened professional mercenaries somehow didn't quite square with a typical villain from London's East End.

Perhaps Georgina Savage and Dale Forster between them would be able to make more sense of it, find the link in the jigsaw he felt certain was missing. They would have the resources, the necessary data. One thing was certain. Both the US and British intelligence services would be seriously alarmed by the news he now had.

Again he waited until after midnight before visiting the latrines. He rigged the communications device and spent five minutes transmitting everything he had uncovered. In two weeks' time it was likely he'd get to see Stan Summers and hopefully learn more of where the drugs were destined and, with any luck, the source of the arms supply. Then, God willing, he could leave this world behind for the last time. Again.

He smiled grimly as he dismantled the aerial. His croft in Ireland, old Mattie, his horses and his bees. They all seemed a lifetime ago. Another era. And Kelly O'More. Another story. He'd barely allowed himself to think of her since he'd landed at Bogotá. Fear of discovery and inevitable torture or death concentrated the mind, left no room for reminiscences and dreams. They blunted the edge. Even now, just the thought of Kelly warmed him, distracted him. When he returned to Ireland, he decided, it would be different. She was his last chance of salvation – the one that this time he would not allow to get away.

He edged open the door of the latrine and peered into the compound. Darkened buildings without lights, a row of trucks and four-wheel drives, a cloudy moon casting dappled shadows. The low but distinct noise of men snoring and the background mumble of a generator. An Indian's dog yapping somewhere in the hills. All clear, and the weight of fear was lifted from him.

He closed the wobbling door and sauntered back towards the bunkhouse; finding himself humming a tune. The last song he and Kelly had sung together that night at the croft.

A figure took shape in the indigo shadow between the two buildings ahead of him. He recognised the heavy body and the defiant stance.

'Your midnight ablutions go well?' a voice asked in Spanish. The beam from Mallory's torch lit the fat and gleaming face. 'We are such creatures of habit. That is always a mistake. It is how hunters hunt animals when they go to water at twilight – without fail.'

Mallory took a backward step. His free hand crept under his jacket and around his back towards the two reversed scabbards of his Chinese fighting knives.

Then they sprang. The two men had been lurking in a doorway, deliberately waiting for him to pass. Now they both had hold of his arms, twisting them up into the small of his back, struggling against his resistance. Pedro Goméz stepped forward, a huge grin of satisfaction on his face, and swung his fist. It caught Mallory off guard, smashing into his solar plexus with the power of a hammer on an anvil. The Colombian had given vent to all his suppressed anger in one tremendous blow. His victim doubled over, crippled, the air forced from his one remaining lung and the vomit splattering on the ground. The torch and the fighting knife fell from his hands. His muscles gave out and he felt the ligaments begin to tear as his arms were pushed high up behind his back.

Pedro reached down and picked up the knife. 'Ever seen a man eat his own balls, gringo? Not a pretty sight.'

Mallory tried to regain his breath, fought to ignore the pain in his arms. 'Don't be stupid, they'll know it was you. Everyone knows you want to get even.'

'There you go again. Calling me names. Well, I don't think your gringo friends will lose any sleep over you. We managed okay before you turned up.'

The Colombian ran the blade lightly over his own tongue, then tasted the blood drop it left behind. He looked approving as a small red trickle rolled down his chin.

Again Mallory tried reason. If only Pedro's two accomplices would relax their grip, if only he could kick his boot up into the Colombian's crotch without breaking his own arms in the process. 'Harry Morgan will know it's you. Him and Guy – and

251

Billy – we're all English. We stick together. Christ, you'll be sorry if you harm me!'

Mallory had almost convinced himself, but not the man in front of him. 'That may be true *if* they found a body. But you will just disappear – we have the truck waiting. You are a bum. One day you appear, the next day you are gone. That is the trouble with bums. It is expected.'

Without warning Pedro's hand shot out and grabbed Mallory's genitals through the material of his denims, squeezing hard. His other hand fumbled for the zipper. An involuntary scream escaped Mallory's lips.

'Kurt? Is that you?'

Mallory gasped as he heard the familiar voice.

'What the hell's going on?'

Pedro released his hold, the pain now surging into Mallory's groin. He ignored it and tore his arms free from the grip of his anonymous attackers. Suddenly they panicked and pushed him aside as they ran off after their leader. Mallory collapsed against the wall of the bunkhouse and slid to the ground.

'Kurt! You okay?'

He opened his eyes to find himself staring into Doug Tallboys's face. Pete Stafford stood behind him, watching the running figures as they were swallowed up into the night.

'Sure, Doug, just a bit sore.'

'Wasn't that Pedro?' Stafford asked.

'Yes. I think he wanted my balls for breakfast – literally. It was my own fault, I was expecting it some time. I just got careless.'

'Then I'm glad we came along,' Tallboys said. 'I know Billy Susan warned him not to try anything on. Said what the consequences would be. He'll be mad when I tell him what happened tomorrow.'

'Thanks for your help,' Mallory replied, climbing unsteadily to his feet, 'but do me a favour and don't mention it. I'd prefer to handle this my own way.'

Tallboys frowned. 'If you're sure?'

'I'm sure.'

*

252

Mallory returned to the bunkhouse. It was in darkness as he made his way to the cot, removed his jacket and lay on top of the mattress. He knew exactly what he was going to do. Three hours, he decided, that should be enough.

He drifted through the drowsy twilight world between sleep and wakefulness, checking his watch from time to time. When the hands reached three, he slid his legs from the bed and reached for his rucksack. What he wanted was in a small plastic bag, one of the items Goldie had sent via Lucila in Adoración. He pulled on his jacket and stuffed the bag into one of its pockets, then moved to the window beside his bed. Easing back the hinged mosquito net frame, he lifted himself over the sill and dropped to the ground.

He rolled each foot as he moved, spreading the weight gently from heel to toe. It was a stalking technique he'd learned as a boy and it guaranteed absolute silence.

The uneven snoring reached his ears before Pedro's hut emerged from the darkness. Mallory circled it once until he found an open window. Then he extracted the bag and from it two flat rectangular Old Holborn tobacco tins. The first, in which nail holes had been made around the sides, contained two stubby nightlight candles. He lit these before opening the second tin which had a perforated base and held a sachet of powder.

After spreading the yellow sulphur to a quarter-inch depth over the bottom of the tin, he placed it on top of the flickering candles before lifting the entire contraption carefully onto the sill. Already the fumes were snatching at his lungs as he gently eased the window closed. It creaked, but the rhythm of Pedro's snoring remained undisturbed.

Satisfied, he returned to the bunkhouse and waited until five before making his way to the latrines which took him past Pedro's hut again. He heard no snoring. A grey dawn mist had settled over the compound and he could see no one about. Only the cookhouse showed a light. He quickly opened the window of Pedro's hut and extracted the coil, gagging at the wafting stench of sulphur. Leaving the window wide, he continued on to the latrines where he disposed of the tins in the cesspit.

The success of his action was not confirmed until after breakfast when he was drinking *tinto* with Tallboys and Stafford.

Billy Susan entered to make the pronouncement. 'Thought you ought to know, lads. Pedro Goméz has just been found dead. Looks like a heart attack.'

There was a moment of surprised silence. No one cared much about the Colombian, but the news was nonetheless disquieting. The man had only been in his forties; it was a sobering thought.

'Keep it to yourselves, of course,' Susan continued. 'We'll get rid of the body discreetly. We don't want gossip spreading and any outside authorities taking an interest in us.'

A slow ripple of conversation resumed and some decidedly black humour accompanied by irreverent laughter.

Tallboys stared across the table at Mallory. 'Seems your guardian angel is looking after you, Kurt. Perhaps you could put in a good word for me.'

'That's incredible,' Pete Stafford said.

Billy Susan appeared at Mallory's side. 'Don't suppose you know anything about this? There was a strong rumour Goméz had it in for you, was going to sort you out last night.'

There was a flicker of a smile on Mallory's face. 'Vengeance is mine . . . saith the Lord.' He looked up. 'Sorry, Billy, my juju doesn't extend to heart attacks.'

'I said it *looked* like a heart attack.'

'So?'

'There was this strange smell.'

Stafford laughed nervously. 'Probably the bastard's socks.'

Billy Susan glared. 'Just you understand, all of you, that I won't tolerate personal feuds or vendettas. If you have problems, talk to me about them and I'll dispense any justice.' Stafford looked suitably chastened as the man turned back to Mallory. 'In view of my sad bit of news – I know you will miss that little shite – you'd better take command of Pedro's gang for the time being. We might even get some work out of them for a change. Collect as many of them as you can find, arm them with picks, saws and shovels, and get as many trucks as you need. I don't care if you beg, borrow or steal them from the locals. Just have everyone

254

ready by ten thirty.'

'What's happening?' Mallory asked.

'We're going to build ourselves an airstrip.'

The terrain ran like a natural shelf along the canyon wall. Although studded with occasional trees and a general covering of scrub, the ground itself was remarkably level despite a gentle incline running from north to south.

From his position beside the driver of the truck, Mallory could see right down through the wooded slope to the Servita valley and the Tafurs' hacienda in the far distance.

The Colombian gang had reacted grudgingly at first to his taking over from Pedro Goméz. Sullen, suspicious eyes followed him wherever he went; all would have known of their leader's failed attempt to abduct and murder Mallory the night before. And no doubt many believed the whispers that the Englishman was somehow responsible for Goméz's unexpected and premature death. Yet none could know for certain. There was no evidence, just hearsay. That suited Mallory. It earned him a reluctant respect and strengthened his authority and position in the primitive pecking order while ensuring that gang members kept their distance. After all, they would reason, they *knew* he had knifed the driver to death. So what did it matter whether he had or hadn't also killed Pedro Goméz? This strange Englishman who was so uncannily like them, was clearly capable of anything and best avoided.

Billy Susan hadn't mentioned the incident again; he had other things on his mind. Working from a sketchmap, he and Guy Thripp issued instructions for Mallory's Colombians to follow. Armed with machetes they began hacking away at the undergrowth and sawing trees flush to ground level. Several smaller shrubs were dug up with the roots intact and replanted in used chemical containers that had been transported from the cocaine laboratory. It was Morgan's smart idea apparently that these should be dragged out from the tree line and positioned on the strip when it wasn't in use, making accidental discovery from the air highly unlikely.

The work progressed steadily throughout the day, the scrubby dead wood and chopped tree trunks loaded onto an assortment of beat-up lorries for disposal or burning at another location. Over a hundred square metres had been cleared by noon when the first truck arrived with a delivery of soil to fill up holes and generally level out the surface.

Mallory stopped for a break, removing his baseball cap and wiping the sweat from his brow. The sun was high and it was a windless day.

Thripp came to his side and lit a cigarette.

'Can you spare one?' Mallory asked.

The packet was tossed in his direction. 'Keep them. And do me a favour – buy your own.' He surveyed the work gangs. 'If the rain holds off, I reckon we should make Bastidas's deadline. We should be able to get his first plane down at the weekend.'

'The arms shipment?'

'Yeah.' Thripp glanced at him. 'But just forget all that stuff you interpreted at the meeting, right?'

Mallory forced a grin. 'What meeting?'

'That's better. Anyway Bastidas was right, it's about time we stepped up the operation. We've had a lot of teething problems and I guess we've got slack.'

Mallory looked sympathetic. 'South America's a difficult place to work in. Especially for gringos.'

'Tell me about it!' Thripp snorted. 'We got ripped off and messed about a lot at the start – till we got the hang of things and started breaking a few heads. Now it's going like clockwork, so it's time to move up a gear.'

Thripp's head turned suddenly as they both heard the sound of horses being ridden hard. Afterwards Mallory would curse himself for not having foreseen what was inevitably going to happen sooner or later, although, rationally, he was forced to admit there was precious little he, Goldie or Mario could have done to prevent it. Victor Tafur, his daughter Juanita or her hot-headed new husband just wouldn't have listened. And Mallory could hardly have blamed them for that.

The two horses broke from the tree line that dropped away to

256

the valley. A magnificent chestnut mare was ridden by Ricardo; close behind was Juanita on a smaller piebald which reared skittishly as the two of them came to a thundering halt in a cloud of dust. Ricardo glanced around at the scene of devastation for several seconds before he noticed Mallory and the other Englishmen standing together. Sunlight flashed on the young man's spurs as he urged his horse into a trot. He held the reins in one hand and a shotgun in the other.

Mallory's heart sank.

Ricardo stopped thirty paces short, Juanita by his side in leather chaps and waistcoat. 'What the hell do you think you're doing?' he shouted across to Thripp in Spanish. 'This is private land – now get off this instant!'

It hardly needed Mallory's translation. 'That fuckin' upstart again,' Billy Susan muttered darkly. 'Some people never learn.'

'Let me speak to him,' Mallory offered.

Thripp nodded.

Mallory crossed the rough terrain where the scrub had been cleared. 'Hello, Ricardo, Juanita. Congratulations to you both.' He glanced at the nervous piebald. 'And how is your new horse?'

A quick smile flashed on the girl's lips. 'He has a sweet nature but is still a baby.'

But her new husband ignored the pleasantries. 'So now you are one of them, Señor Kurt.' It was an accusation, not a question.

'It's just a job. These men are very dangerous. Please forget about this and just go home.'

Ricardo shook his head in disbelief. 'Your friends Goldie and Mario say you are a good man. That is also what I thought when you stood up to these bastards at our ranch. But they are wrong. You are just as bad as these people.'

'Ricardo, please!' Juanita protested. 'Do not insult Señor Kurt.'

Mallory waved it aside. 'It's okay. I'd be angry too in your position. I'm just warning you as a friend that no good can come of this. You cannot win against these men.'

Ricardo was contemptuous. 'Because they murder and torture? Well, I refuse to be intimidated by them or by you.' He turned

257

towards Thripp and Billy Susan. 'We don't want your blood money. We are just honest farmers who only ask to be left alone. Now you try to help yourselves to our land.' He lifted his shotgun and fired into the air. Juanita struggled to rein in the agitated piebald. All work had stopped now and all eyes were on them. 'I will not tell you again! GET OFF OUR LAND!' He glared defiantly at the Colombians standing around with their machetes and spades.

Billy Susan exchanged a brief word with Thripp then detached himself from the group of gringos and strode purposefully towards the two riders.

Mallory turned to Ricardo. 'Listen to what Señor Billy has to say,' he advised quietly.

Susan stopped in front of the big chestnut and looked up from under the brim of his straw stetson. 'Listen, boy, we've had enough of you. And don't say you haven't been warned.'

The gunmetal glinted as his hand moved swiftly up from his side. Mallory stared. He wasn't seeing this, just didn't believe it would happen this way. The single sharp report was as deafening as it was shocking, the sound reverberating along the canyon side.

Juanita's piebald reared, its eyes white and startled. The chestnut shifted its stance as its rider stiffened in the saddle. Ricardo's face was waxy and staring, a frozen mask, the man already dead from the .38 dum-dum slug that had smashed through his breastbone and gouged out a fist-sized cavity where his heart had been. Slowly he toppled, sliding sideways to the ground, one boot still caught in a stirrup.

Mallory lunged at the piebald and yelled, slapping it hard across the rump. Juanita snatched at the reins as the horse bolted and the second gunshot from Billy Susan scorched past her.

'Shit!' he swore. 'Christ, Kurt, what are you playing at?'

They all watched as the piebald raced in a circle around the clearing, Juanita gradually regaining control and spurring the creature on. Colombians scattered as she charged them, screaming at them in fear and hatred, and headed back towards the tree line and the valley.

'Sorry, Billy,' Mallory said. 'I just couldn't let you kill the girl.

It was just instinctive. I didn't think.'

Susan's face was red with rage. He pushed the barrel of the .38 hard under Mallory's chin, the metal still warm. 'Don't you ever – *ever* – do anything like that again, you fuckin' Kraut. Understand?'

Thripp came over. 'Okay, Billy, give it a rest. You got the one that mattered. Let her tell her old man what happened – it'll have more effect.' He kicked the shotgun out of Ricardo's stiffened grip, knelt down and checked for a pulse. 'He's gone.'

'I'll have him dumped in the Servita,' Susan said.

'Okay.'

Mallory intervened. He wanted to stop anyone else at the ranch getting ideas about revenge. 'That's hardly hearts-and-minds. At least let them bury their dead.'

'A bit late for hearts-and-minds,' Thripp replied.

'I'll take the body back. Try and persuade them to let you get on with building the strip.'

'You hardly managed to persuade the new husband, did you?'

'No, but this might make a difference.'

'I hope so,' Thripp replied easily. 'Because I've had enough of them. I want them out of this valley – the whole bloody family. Tell them that when you deliver the corpse.'

One of the Colombians helped Mallory lift Ricardo's body into the back of a Toyota pick-up and cover it in sheeting. He then took the vehicle alone back down to the main road and turned right for Cruz de Oro.

There was no one in sight as he pulled up outside the chapel. Still no wind, he noticed, and the afternoon had become hot and dusty. High above, a hawk swooped and cawed in a powder-blue sky.

He climbed out and walked slowly across the dirt forecourt. The sun-dried timber door creaked open at his touch. It was blessedly cool in the empty nave and considerably larger than it appeared from the outside. Eucalyptus beams criss-crossed between the stone walls in support of the vaulted ceiling rafters and shafts of dusty light from the high-set windows illuminated the roughly hewn pews. A row of white plaster saints stood like

259

sentries at intervals along the right-hand wall, the left dominated by a garishly painted, life-sized carving of the Crucifixion.

Mallory crossed himself and was about to leave when the priest emerged from the small vestry door beside the altar. 'Señor Kurt – this is a surprise! In fact, although I cannot condone killing, I was hoping to thank you for at least saving young Ricardo's life the other week.'

'Your thanks are premature, Father.' There was no easy way to put this. 'I'm afraid Ricardo was murdered about an hour ago. I have his body outside.'

Father León stared in disbelief, the colour draining from his face. 'Murdered?' He let the word hang, his question echoing in the hallowed silence. 'I hardly need to ask who did this thing, do I?'

Mallory shook his head. 'I'm on my way to the ranch now. I'm sure Victor and Juanita will need all the comfort you can offer, Father.'

He nodded weakly. 'Of course. That is very thoughtful of you.'

'I'm only sorry it happened. If I could have prevented it, I would have. Ricardo pushed his luck too far. He was very courageous.'

'But foolish?' Father León searched Mallory's eyes, trying to understand the man. 'And you, Señor Kurt, you are still working for them?'

'I need the money.'

'Enough to do the devil's work?'

'We all have a cross to bear, Father. That is mine. Shall we go?'

They walked to the pick-up where the priest looked at the body, crossed himself and spoke a few words in Latin. Then they climbed aboard and headed out towards the hacienda.

'You know,' Father León said, 'I have never known hatred until recently. Oh, I've disapproved and despaired on occasions. Even loathed someone or something. But never actually *hated*. It is a loathsome feeling. Like bile in the gut, but all-consuming. It can take over your brain and your common sense, distort logic and destroy one's very soul. Since those people came to Cruz de Oro I have actually been given to blaspheming. Can you believe that? And me a priest. I have been tempted – maybe late at night, alone with my innermost thoughts – to call on the sword of the Dark Angel to destroy these people. Maybe, I think, that will be the only answer.'

Then perhaps, Mallory thought savagely, your prayers have been answered. 'God can move in mysterious ways.'

'Indeed.' But the priest had no idea what he meant. 'In the past eighteen months twelve people have disappeared, plus, if rumour is to be believed, one of the Europeans from the mine. At Confession numerous members of my flock have confided that they have assisted the gringos after acts of gross intimidation. I know some have been savagely beaten and others tortured. I wonder how long a priest can rely on prayer alone?'

Mallory didn't answer. He'd long ago given up on prayer as an answer to the injustices of the world. Sometimes only evil could ever destroy evil.

When they reached the hacienda they found Juanita's piebald tied to the hitching post; it had been ridden hard, its flanks flecked with foam. The film crew's Fourtrak was also parked outside.

Tafur met them at the door, a pitchfork in his hands.

'You won't be needing that, Victor,' Father León said. 'Señor Kurt comes as a friend. We have Ricardo's body with us.'

There were tears in the farmer's eyes. 'Some friend he turned out to be.'

'I'm sorry,' Mallory said. 'I'd have stopped it if I could.'

'Shall we bring the body in?' Father León asked.

Tafur nodded. 'I'll clear the parlour table.'

Inside the gathered figures formed a tragic tableau: Juanita weeping in her mother's arms; Goldie and Mario standing to one side, offering consolation by their very presence. Both knew that no words would help.

After the body was laid out, a clean white sheet was drawn up, hiding the savage wound, until just the head showed. Two bright coins had been placed over Ricardo's eyes.

Juanita kissed her husband goodbye then turned, sniffing back her tears. 'Thank you for bringing my Rico back to me, Señor

Kurt. I honestly think I will never see him again . . .' Emotion was threatening to choke her. 'I am sorry. Rico would not want me to cry. I must be brave. Like him.'

Mallory said: 'He was very brave. You should be very proud of him.'

Her eyes were misty. 'But where did it get him? He should have listened to you.' She swallowed hard. 'And I must thank you for saving my life. You acted so fast, striking my horse like that. It was only afterwards I realised what you had done.'

Later, as Mallory was about to leave, Mario came with him to the door. 'Which one killed Ricardo?'

'Billy Susan. A short guy with sort of girlish features. Usually goes around with the tall one called Thripp, the one who thinks he's a cowboy. Why?'

'Maybe this Billy Susan is the one with the three nines tattoo. The one who killed my Luz and my son.'

'We don't know that.' Mallory didn't want to lie to his friend, but he wasn't yet ready to tell him the man with the three nines tattoo was Guy Thripp. Mario was a good man in a crisis but he could also be impetuous. The time would come – in due course.

Mario Dubois watched his friend climb into the pick-up. Juanita joined him by the door. Her voice was low and hoarse, her eyes still moist with tears. 'He is a strange man. I like him, but there is something about him . . .'

Mario nodded. 'He is a lion amongst jackals.'

She looked at him curiously, not understanding exactly what he meant. 'You have been very kind to me since you came here. And today— I don't know, I feel you share my loss of Ricardo, yet you hardly knew him.'

He pulled a tight smile. 'I lost my wife and child to people like these.'

'Yes?'

'In Venezuela. So I think I understand your grief and your anger.'

Father León overheard. 'I am sure it would help the pain if only we could do something about it. But then, of course, Our Lord tells us to turn the other cheek.'

262

'I prefer an eye for an eye,' Mario growled.

The priest looked thoughtful. 'Perhaps it is indeed time that we stood up to these people.'

It was then that Mario remembered something about one of Mallory's signals. About an arms shipment destined for the local guerrillas. Due at the weekend.

That was a thought, but one, he decided, he would not share with Goldie. Or even with Mallory.

The single-engined Cessna Stationair made its first pass over the strip at just gone noon.

Mallory watched from the tree line with Harry Morgan and Guy Thripp as the brightly coloured six-seater banked away steeply, gaining height to sweep in a long slow turn over the Servita valley. Then it came in again, straighter and slower this time, the pilot feeling his way down, anxious about the close proximity of the canyon wall. Mallory found himself holding his breath until the fixed wheels finally kissed the shorn grass. There were just a couple of moderate bounces before the undercarriage settled and the aircraft began slowing rapidly as it ran out of strip. Then the machine was taxiing around and driving back towards the welcoming committee.

But it was to be later that evening before Mallory was introduced to the man who stepped out of the aircraft in an expensive, fawn-coloured tropical suit, striped open-necked shirt and enough gold chains and bracelets to supply a jewellery shop.

Stan Summers was almost a cliché of himself. Bad boy from Essex made good in the only ways he knew how and all of them illegal. Of medium height and stocky build he had the jaunty manner of a stand-up comedian. The thinning hair was close-shaven and the chunky face was all smiles and twinkling eyes. His jokes and quips were constant and mostly unfunny, but the gang members laughed obligingly as necessary.

When Felix Bastidas arrived in a second aircraft just before last light, Mallory was instructed to join them all for a light supper and drinks at a corner table in the camp bar.

''Eard good reports about you,' Summers said as they shook

hands. 'Guy says you can handle yourself and the Colombians have been working better since Pedro's – er – little accident. Says you've got the lazy little sods working like demons. Quite right too.' He took a heavy swig of whisky from his tumbler. 'Even Felix here thinks highly of you.'

Mallory shrugged. 'I'm doing my best, that's all.'

'Well, you can do your best again now and act as interpreter for these little business hiccups Felix and I have to sort out.' His smile suddenly became fixed and a little too sweet. 'Then you'll forget everything you hear. Don't want to do what the old pharaohs of Egypt used to do to their tomb-builders and pluck out your tongue, do we?' He chortled and Thripp and Billy Susan shared his amusement.

The discussion that followed was protracted, detailed and sometimes heated. On occasion both men showed signs of strain and dropped their polite veneer. More than once the foppish young Bastidas from Medellín gave way to only slightly veiled threats of pulling out of the partnership.

'Look,' Stan Summers explained, 'this is a new route we're opening up for you. There are bound to be problems. It's dog eat dog in Russia nowadays and Moscow is no longer a safe place. You've got to have the right contacts, to know the right mafia. We deal mostly with ex-KGB; they're best positioned, know the system inside out. But there's always some rival mafia trying to muscle in.'

Mallory translated liberally, referring to similar problems faced by the Medellín cartel from its rivals in Cali, and Bastidas smiled. 'I know the feeling all too well.'

'We're winding down the old Dutch Antilles route through the Caribbean,' Summers said. 'It's too well known now and we've had a couple of consignments intercepted at Rotterdam in the past six months. And Spain is getting more difficult too. Let's leave those routes to your chums from Cali while we take the stuff direct to St Petersburg. Everyone there can be had for a price – it makes life a lot easier. You've seen how it works and, believe me, it'll get better.'

It confirmed what Mallory had already begun to piece together from snatches of overheard conversation around the camp. Once the White Viper cocaine was processed and finished at the camp laboratory, it had, until now, been taken by road to Santa Maria and then flown out. Now the product could leave by air directly from Cruz de Oro.

Small single-engined aircraft would fly certain quantities at low level through the mountain corridor, avoiding radar, and down to Buenaventura for both the traditional US destinations and in-country consumption. But these were highly competitive markets which kept prices low and attracted animosity from the Cali factions.

By far the biggest proportion of White Viper coke would continue to be destined for Europe. It would be flown east by a motley collection of private pilots and aircraft, passing over the remote jungle valleys that made up the upper reaches of the Orinoco basin.

To avoid antagonising Venezuelan authorities, the aircraft landed at strips cut in the El Tuparro National Park. It was an ideal location, still just within Colombia's borders, but completely isolated and unreachable by road. The handful of unarmed wardens presented no problem, happy to look the other way and mind their own business. The silver or the lead policy worked as well as always. Meanwhile the cocaine was man-handled to the Tomo river where local fishing canoes took it to the confluence with the mighty Orinoco which marked the border with Venezuela.

Once landed at Puerto Ayacucho under cover of darkness, the loads were divided according to their final destinations, some by air but most by road. A variety of ingenious smuggling methods were used, consignments being delivered to warehouses and factories in out-of-the-way towns and villages. Packages were concealed in hollowed-out planks of tropical hardwood supposedly destined for the European timber markets, or in concrete fence-posts, hidden in fresh fruit like yams and coconuts or canned meat or even chocolate bars.

Stan Summers's preferred method was to conceal the coke in steel drums of toxic chemicals as a deterrent to Customs rummage crews. Until recently the goods had been shipped from the Venezuelan port of Coro to Curaçao in the Dutch Antilles. There the goods would be temporarily warehoused before onward shipping to Rotterdam. The beauty and simplicity of this route was that all goods entering from the Dutch possession in the Caribbean were legally considered by Customs officers to have originated from the European Community country itself. Blind bureaucracy from Brussels might be a nightmare for most honest businessmen; for Stan Summers it was a godsend.

Another earlier route was by sea to Galicia, the traditional smuggling area of a thousand caves and rocky inlets in northwest Spain. Through family contacts of Felix Bastidas, arrangements were made for fishermen to meet a freighter offshore in international waters and cross-deck the cargo. But in recent months the Spanish authorities had been tightening the screws; consignments of White Viper had escaped, but other smugglers had not been so lucky.

So now it was all change again. This time freighting was direct from Venezuela to St Petersburg, the Baltic Russian port of Leningrad that had now reverted to its original name. What Mallory did not know yet was where the cocaine went from there.

At least he now had the answers to two other questions that had been puzzling him. The source of the arms in this two-way traffic was Russia with its endless supply of weapons of all types. And there were plenty of greedy mafiosi eager for foreign currency and with no scruples about whom they supplied. That answered the second question: why Colombians with well-established family connections in Europe should even consider a partnership with an English gang. Stan Summers obviously had contacts that Bastidas didn't, and the Colombians' priority for guns was even higher than that for money from drug trafficking.

It was interesting, Mallory mused, that Bastidas had ditched old Medellín distribution methods for the longer, slower and more costly approach of using maritime freight as favoured by the gentlemen of Cali. In the old days Pablo Escobar had adopted gung-ho direct distribution techniques, using dozens of private aircraft or high-powered motor launches to reach the United

States. A world of high drama and bloody shoot-outs with the US Coastguard and the DEA. Inevitably such methods had contributed to the man's downfall.

'So I have your absolute assurance that the arms will be in my hands by the weekend?' Bastidas asked.

It was not a problem for Summers. 'And after that at fairly regular intervals. If you can imagine it, even as we speak there is a succession of ships strung out across the Atlantic.'

That appeared to satisfy the Colombian, but there was something else on his mind. 'You know I want to step up production? Double or even treble it in the next six months. This is necessary to pay for our other requirements.'

Mallory translated and saw the concern in Summers's eyes. 'Tell our friend I am having to consult with my masters on this one. It's not just the practicalities of supplying the cocaine, but rifles and small arms are a different ball game to what he wants. Anti-aircraft missiles and anti-tank rockets move it into the big boys' league.' The man considered for a moment. 'Tell him I'm due to have a meeting here with our mutual friend. It'll be up to him to put it to my masters.'

Bastidas clearly wasn't happy with the reply, but it was the best he was going to get. Although the conversation continued for a while longer, Mallory found himself preoccupied with what he had discovered – that the Colombian's revolutionary talk was far from empty rhetoric. Obviously he saw himself as heir apparent to Simon Bolívar with every intention of taking on the governments of Colombia, Venezuela and . . . it had all the makings of a civil war that could engulf the entire continent.

The other surprise had been Stan Summers's reference to 'his masters'. So the trail didn't stop at the Essex gangster. Fleas upon fleas upon fleas. So who was the real *narco* kingpin of this setup, he wondered?

At last Bastidas stood and shook hands with Summers before turning to Mallory. 'Thank you for your patience and hard work, señor. It is appreciated.'

When the man had gone, Summers relaxed visibly. 'Can't say I like these Latinos, Kurt. Too fond of getting everything their own way. Used to buying up everything and everyone – either that or using violence to achieve their ends.'

Learning those tricks pretty quickly yourself, Mallory thought. But he said: 'Like upping the coke production?'

Summers waved a dismissive hand: 'That's not the problem – well, actually it could be. What I meant was his demand for heavy support weapons.'

'Difficult to get hold of, I suppose.'

Summers laughed. 'Not these days, Kurt. You can buy anything you want in Moscow. It's just that if we start supplying that stuff, before we know it this place will turn into a bloody war zone. And that's not good for the coke business. Discretion, that's what we like. Still, as I told him, that's not my decision.' He poured more whisky. 'But on the production side, that's a different matter. Only trouble is our friends down in Bolivia want to sever their connections with us. Well, I'm sure they can be persuaded to continue at present levels – for a price, of course – but they're hardly likely to want to get in deeper.'

Mallory was intrigued. 'Why do your Bolivian suppliers want out?'

'Quite simple, Kurt, they want to paddle their own canoe. For years the Colombians have dominated the scene down there. The cartels in Medellín and Cali had all the markets and distribution sewn up. Bolivians were reduced to first-stage suppliers, growing the crop then stomping the leaves into paste. Bottom of the shit pile. And the Colombians knew it, liked to throw their weight around, kick ass. That's not the Bolivians' way. In recent years several of their own kingpins have emerged, setting up their own laboratories and their own export routes. Mostly out through Brazil, but some through Chile and Argentina. That way, of course, they keep all the profits for themselves and get rid of the Colombian middlemen and their heavies.'

Mallory was well aware of the antagonism between the two nationalities and the growth in Bolivia's self-contained trade, but he adopted an expression that suggested it was all a revelation to him. 'And your suppliers want to go the same way?'

Summers nodded. 'Inevitable really; I just hoped we'd have a year or two longer before it happened. The trouble is our partnership with Felix Bastidas. He insists *his* men deal with the Bolivians in case we try to muscle in. He doesn't say so, but it's pretty clear. You can imagine how the late Pedro's heavies get on with the laid-back Bolivians. Chalk and fuckin' cheese! I've sent down Brian Beavis and Dan Crabtree to try and sweet-talk the Bolies round, but apparently they're not having much luck. So my plan's to fly down the day after tomorrow and see what I can do. Thought you might come along, seeing as you appear to know the old Latino psyche. Translate with a certain gloss, so to speak.'

Mallory could hardly believe his luck; this was an opportunity he couldn't have dared hope for. But he just gave a nonchalant shrug. 'Whatever you say. But I tell you one thing, Mr Summers, and you can take it or leave it.'

'What's that?'

'The Colombians know their business. They grab the Bolivian suppliers by the balls and don't let go. That's why they're hated so much but it's also why they're so successful. You make the mistake of treating them like businessmen in Chingford and Bastidas, believe it or not, is more of a gentleman than Escobar ever was. I've no doubt he makes Pedro's men behave more reserved than is their natural inclination. If you want the Bolies to sing to your tune, I suggest less carrot and more stick. Definitely more stick.'

Summers considered that for a long moment. 'Well, come along and see what you think. Maybe I'll let you put your theory to the test.'

The prospect of going to Bolivia both excited and terrified Mallory. He was getting in deeper and deeper, which was exactly what was wanted. But the deeper he got the more dangerous it became, the risks multiplying with every day that passed. And there was no way out now without blowing his cover.

His midnight message was longer than usual that night as there was so much information to pass on. And when he returned to the bunkhouse he found it difficult to sleep. When he did eventually, he dreamed that he was drowning. The sea was the colour of blood.

He felt haggard and tired the next morning when he went for his breakfast in the cookhouse canteen.

'You heard about our turbulent priest?' Doug Tallboys asked between mouthfuls of potato soup.

'No.'

'Bastard's asking to get his balls cut off,' Derek Rutter said. Mallory had only met Rutter, a short and thoroughly unpleasant Geordie, a couple of days earlier. The man had just returned from Viper business in Venezuela with his sidekick, a pasty-faced man with cropped blond hair called Mick Pye.

'What's happened?' Mallory asked.

'Inciting the locals to mutiny,' Pye laughed. But then the man seemed to find everything amusing, particularly the misfortunes of others.

'I tell you,' Rutter warned, 'Guy Thripp and Billy Susan won't put up with it. They know they'll get it in the neck from Harry Morgan if things get out of hand – especially while the big white chief's visiting.'

Tallboys poured some coffee from the jug on the table. 'Apparently the priest told his congregation last night we were a bunch of murderers and fornicators.'

'Not far off the mark!' Mick Pye chortled.

But the Scotsman clearly wasn't pleased with being included in such a general description. 'He had that girl Juanita stand up and tell everyone how Ricardo was killed. Then Victor Tafur does his party piece and tells everyone what's going on at the strip.'

'That's totally out of order,' Derek Rutter growled. 'As I say, the priest and the farmer are asking to have their balls cut off and served to Harry Morgan on a plate.'

'I think he'd prefer to have the girl served up on a plate,' laughed Pye. 'Tasty little cow; wouldn't mind giving her one myself.'

Tallboys ignored him. 'Anyway, at the end of it all, the priest said the time had come for all good Christians to start defying us, saying he personally was going to raise the matter with the church

270

hierarchy in Bogotá.'

'I'm sure Harry'll be quaking if he gets a ticking off from the Pope,' Pye said with a grin.

Mallory put him right. 'Don't underestimate the power of the Catholic Church in this country. If they complain, the government will listen – very carefully.'

'Then I reckon we ought to do the rounds today,' Rutter decided. 'Break a few legs and light some fires. Stamp our authority and remind them what happens to people who refuse to co-operate and start blabbing amongst themselves or to anyone else. We've got nothing much else on today. I'll put it to Billy, I'm sure he'll approve.' He turned to Mallory. 'You game, Kurt?'

'Sure, but not today.' He really did not want to spend the day watching acts of violent intimidation or even torture when he was helpless to prevent it. 'I've probably got to do some interpretation. Some Spanish guy's flying in this morning.'

Rutter shook his head. 'You won't have to interpret for him. Bloody spick talks better English than I do. So what about it?'

It was then that Tallboys intervened. 'Actually I was hoping Kurt could give me a hand today. I've got three vehicles need urgent servicing and Pete's down with dysentery.'

Mallory glanced at the Scotsman and wondered if the man realised that he, too, had no taste for the Vipers' 'policing' work.

As they walked together across to the workshop, the compound gates opened to admit one of the Rocstas returning from the strip where a plane from Bucaramanga had just landed. Billy Susan was driving, Harry Morgan beside him. In the rear sat Stan Summers alongside the new arrival.

He was tall and tanned, casually but expensively dressed. Maybe late thirties, maybe younger with the hair fashionably long, curling at the collar. As the vehicle passed, the man turned to say something to Summers and Mallory saw the face.

Sweet Jesus Christ!

Quickly Mallory turned away in a cold sweat, his heart racing. He simply could not believe whom he had just seen.

The Spanish visitor was none other than *El torro rabioso*, Kelly O'More's toyboy lover from Madrid. Miguel Castaño.

12

Mallory worked on the engine service like a zombie, his mind reeling with the implications of Miguel Castaño's unexpected presence.

His immediate fear was for his own preservation. He knew the lawyer and the lawyer knew him. Somehow Castaño was aware he was here and had come to identify him. It had been an elaborate trap from the start, someone getting to him through Kelly. An old enemy with a score to settle. God only knew there were enough of them in different places around the world. And was Kelly a willing or an unwitting accomplice? Were George Savage and SIS somehow involved?

As soon as he and Doug Tallboys had reached the workshop he had made a point of rubbing grease on his face. Though that had been fairly pointless, he realised later, if Castaño had come with the idea of unmasking him.

If anyone knew he was at Cruz de Oro it would hardly need Castaño's personal presence to unearth him. After all, Kurt Hulse was the only gang member the Vipers hadn't actually recruited, the only one who had just drifted onto the scene.

Gradually Mallory's pulse rate subsided and he began to rationalise, his mind slowly clearing, although panic still fluttered in his chest. His imagination had been playing tricks, feeding on the natural paranoia of every undercover operator.

No, Miguel Castaño's presence was remarkable. A remarkable coincidence, but nothing more sinister than that. In fact, when he thought about it, such a coincidence wasn't that remarkable after all. Castaño, if he remembered rightly, was Argentinian-born but had his practice in Madrid. Naturally his clients would be

Spanish and the people they did business with would be mostly of Spanish descent – that went with the old colonial ties. Like South America. Language was the common denominator, especially in the world of narcotics. The Italian Mafia liked dealing with Italian immigrant families in America. Likewise Greeks with Greeks. Turks with Turks. They felt safer with their own, more secure. Mallory had no doubt that Castaño liked life's rich trappings and there was no richer vein to tap into than narcotics. And his company was bound to have many South American clients. So it was not so surprising that Castaño should be here.

More surprising, on reflection, was that he had ever been in Ireland. Desperately Mallory tried to recall what Kelly had told him about the man? That's right. She'd met him at her Dublin office when her law firm had been acting on her father's account. And amiable old Joe O'More ran an import-export business. Mainly foodstuffs. Old Joe?

Mallory shook his head at the thought. There you go again, he chided himself, leaping to conclusions. Joe O'More was the least likely *narco* kingpin imaginable. And Castaño would be a strange lawyer of international reputation if he didn't have more than one client in more than one country. So, he had a client who sold oranges to Dublin and another who imported quality Irish beef. Or something like that. What could be more normal? Nevertheless, as soon as possible he would warn Kelly to sever all contacts with Castaño, maybe go through Savage.

And then, possibly for the first time ever, he felt the painful and self-destructive stabs of sexual jealousy. Not that just any man had been making love to her, entwined in those long, lissom limbs and enjoying her soft laughter. But *this* man. Lawyers were bad enough, any lawyers. But lawyers who manipulated the law for the *narcotraficantes* were the scum of the earth. Probably worse than the untouchable *narco* kingpins themselves. After all, it was often they who actually made them so untouchable.

He remained in a heightened state of tension all morning, making several clumsy mistakes on routine servicing which brought a complaint from Tallboys who was usually the most forbearing of bosses.

273

'You forgot to change the oil filter, Kurt. What is it with you today? You got girlfriend problems or something? Keep your mind on the job, eh?'

Mallory had made some quip, but still could not relax until he saw Billy Susan drive Miguel Castaño back out of the camp. Only then did Mallory's fear recede sufficiently to enable him to concentrate again. Later he learned that Castaño had spent the entire night at El Tigre in Adoración, with Summers picking up the tab for Fanny Lacera's girls. He flew out from the strip the next morning.

Meanwhile, that night Mallory made another transmission, telling of the lawyer's unexpected arrival and informing his control that he himself would be travelling to Bolivia the next day with Stan Summers, Morgan and Thripp.

Again that night he found sleep elusive.

The call from Billy Susan came at dawn. Dressing hastily and throwing his few possessions into his rucksack, Mallory made his way to the cookhouse where he found Summers demolishing a full English fried breakfast in ebullient mood.

'The food here is crap, Kurt, but at least they do a decent fry-up. More bacon?' Then he confessed: 'Lookin' forward to this trip, Kurt, I really am. I like Bolivia, especially Santa Cruz. Not so much hassle down there, more *tranquilo*. Treat the coke business like it's the most natural thing in the world. Even with the DEA pokin' around and causing upsets, you don't feel you're goin' to get gunned down at any time like here.'

Mallory knew what he meant. 'Different culture, Mr Summers, but still don't relax your guard . . .' He paused, considering how to put the question. 'But I thought you were concerned that the Bolivians aren't going to play ball. Yet you seem happy enough now.'

'Oh, the Bolivians are still a worry, Kurt, but then I've been thinking about what you were saying. Less carrot and more stick. Well, maybe it should be more of both, but with the stick first. Anyway, I'm relying on you to sort them out. No, it's the other problem that had been worrying me more – beefing up the quality of armaments we're supplying to Bastidas. Our lawyer reckons it might shorten the life of our involvement here, but we'd clean up in the process. And he thinks our masters will probably go along with it. Anyway we'd be in control of the supply pipeline. I hadn't thought of it that way. If there's something we don't want to deliver, we don't. Just say it was intercepted at the warehouse in Russia or somesuch. Bastidas might not like it, might complain, but he can do fuck all about it until he finds a way to get an alternative supply. And he won't find that easy. So, always think positive, Kurt, that's what I've learned.' He finished the last of his fried bread and dabbed his mouth with a paper napkin. 'Think positive.'

A light aircraft flew them off the strip, taking just thirty minutes to reach the regional capital of Bucaramanga where they transferred to a Twin Otter for the scheduled run to Bogotá. After an hour's wait at the international airport they boarded a Lufthansa through-flight to La Paz.

Two hours later the cabin staff were distributing *maté* to counter the effect of altitude sickness on their pending arrival at the highest capital in the world, perched on the Andean Altiplano some twelve thousand feet above sea level. Mallory watched fascinated through the window as the aircraft eased down between the volcanic peaks of two cordillera ranges to the windswept and treeless plain which stretched to the horizon in every direction. Once landed, they spent a couple of hours kicking their heels and drinking coffee before the delayed connection to Santa Cruz was announced.

It was a journey of startling contrasts. Just two hours and a distance of a little over four hundred kilometres after leaving the dizzying heights of the Andes, they were in the swampy, humid lowlands of the Amazon basin. Midway they had touched down briefly at Cochabamba in the Chapare region. Apart from Peru, this and the Beni area to the north were the only places in the entire world where the climate was truly suitable to sustain a profitable crop of coca leaf. It was a fact not readily appreciated that only these fertile slopes halfway down the Andean flanks offered the unique combination of well-drained soil and humidity necessary to cultivate the notoriously fickle plant.

Mallory fully understood why the peasants in this hard and unforgiving climate had no hesitation in capitalising on the only good fortune with which God seemed to have blessed them. No other crop offered such wealth, albeit meagre by Western standards. Was it any wonder that when the Americans offered them money to burn their coca plantations they obliged, took the money and set off deeper into the jungle to replant all over again? It was no surprise to Mallory; in their position he was sure he'd have done the same himself. Nevertheless, the Western world seemed surprised when the bribes didn't work.

Moreover it was difficult to explain to a people who quite legally and historically had grown and chewed, smoked and used coca leaf in cooking since before the time of the Incas. Did it make any sense to them that the crop could only be grown in the Yunga region for home consumption while everywhere else it was burnt or sprayed by herbicide after bullying from a foreign nation state?

The short onward hop took them to Santa Cruz. Bolivia's second largest city, it had an air of tranquillity in the dusty afternoon sunlight. In the late seventies it had been a moderately thriving agricultural and cattle centre. Then, at the start of the cocaine boom, the small jungle city burgeoned into a sophisticated metropolis, expanding with lush residential avenues and palatial villas hiding discreetly behind high walls. On the streets every other car appeared to be a BMW or Merc, or luxury Mitsubishi jeep: all the tell-tale hallmarks of *narco* superwealth.

This was in stark contrast to the shabby *campesinos* of the city centre and the urban plazas, eking a living as street traders or shoe-shine boys or hiring out the hammocks they slung between roadside palms for fifty pesos' worth of afternoon snooze.

Los Tajibos was a five-star luxury hotel complex of low-level rooms and apartments that spread itself over several acres of tropical gardens and palm-edged swimming pools. White garden furniture and candy-striped sun umbrellas dotted the manicured lawns on islands linked by little Japanese water bridges. The male guests tended to be plump, tanned and content in designer swim shorts, positively jingling with gold chains, bracelets and Rolex

Oyster Perpetuals. Their womenfolk, whether wives or girl-friends, were inevitably long-limbed and honeybrown in minuscule bikinis. *El otro nombre del paraíso*, the hotel sign proudly proclaimed. The other name for paradise.

Mallory could think of another name for it. Hell on earth. Such ostentatious and wasteful luxury was anathema to him. A playground for the filthy rich in Bolivia's cocaine capital. With the white stuff making up eighty per cent of the country's exports, the place had inevitably been built, however innocently, on *narco* profits and had only one purpose: to cater for visitors who came only to trade in the stuff or to benefit from some other aspect of the city's drugs-generated wealth.

As the obsequious receptionist allocated rooms and bellboys eagerly swooped to take their luggage, Mallory thought briefly of the Tafurs on their farm, scratching a subsistence living under constant intimidation from the Vipers. Of Lucila whoring her body to keep alive. Of Mario's young family butchered in Venezuela for petty vengeance. Of the millions upon millions of *campesinos* throughout the continent who saw no benefit but only suffered under the all-pervading corruption and self-interest of politicians and businessmen. And all for what? For people like these in their carefully reserved paradise and their neighbours in the anonymous villas in the surrounding avenues.

If only the drugs wealth were shared to some extent, he considered, there might, almost, be some justice in it all. Like some fairer redistribution of international wealth. But then things never did work out like that. Mankind would never change.

Tiled terraces led to their rooms, large with triple-sized beds, minibars and space for a coffee table, sofa and chairs.

Mallory had brought with him the clean clothes Harry Morgan had supplied a few days earlier. After showering, shaving and gelling back his hair, he put them on. The transformation was considerable and now he looked the part as one of Stan Summers's henchmen.

He met his boss, Harry Morgan and Guy Thripp at the bar and joined them for drinks. Brian Beavis and Dan Crabtree had also arrived. They were clearly enjoying the change from primitive camp life, sipping fancy cocktails and happy to pose in slacks and colourful short-sleeved shirts while they eyed up every passing beauty. And there was no shortage of them.

'What's the name of the man we're meeting?' Mallory asked.

'Raúl de Quilindo,' Summers replied. He looked very much at home in this place, Mallory thought. 'At least that's who I know him as. An old Santa Cruz family – he used to be a cattle rancher until he got into the white stuff. He should be here any time.'

Mallory looked out across the restaurant floor to the open-air swimming pool, now with elaborate floral candleboats floating across the surface. The cages of exotic tropical birds had been covered over for the night but the occupants still made occasional loud squawks of protest.

Christ, he thought, for all its opulence, this place is depressing. I feel just like those birds. Caged, trapped. And I can't even complain.

The restaurant was filled with families and small groups of businessmen. It all seemed so innocent, no visible indications that anyone was in the *narco* game.

Then he saw them. Three men, swarthy and heavily built, sweeping through from the reception area, wary eyes checking the identity of each guest, seeking out familiar and unfamiliar faces, sniffing the air for the smell of a stakeout or for sight of one of the DEA agents they knew. Leisure time in the capital of coke was like that sometimes, the hunted and the off-duty hunters sharing the same watering holes, on nodding acquaintance, mutual standoff by agreement.

Mallory and the rest of Summers's group were rapidly clocked by the first of de Quilindo's men. He had on slacks and a floral shirt which he wore outside his trousers to conceal the handgun on his belt. The alert eyes moved over them; a quick count. Five. Then he scanned on, looking for any armed backup, any nasty surprises. He nodded to his two colleagues now stationed at strategic points around the bar. His signal was acknowledged. All clear. A fourth man spoke rapidly into his mobile.

A few minutes later Raúl de Quilindo appeared, his sour-faced wife and teenage son by his side amid an entourage of more heavies. The man was stocky and casually dressed: chino trousers and a cashmere sweater in canary yellow. Dark crinkled waves rippled back off the forehead of a perspiring gargoyle face complete with flat nose and disagreeable mouth. Two of his minders accelerated ahead and commandeered a cluster of tables and chairs in a quiet corner. Another minder broke away towards the bar, gesturing for Summers's group to follow. As at a sheepdog trial they found themselves manoeuvred into the charmed circle; guests at nearby tables were politely but firmly told to find somewhere else to sit.

De Quilindo was amenable enough in a taciturn sort of way, although the humour of his reluctant smile never reached his lacklustre eyes. His English was good but heavily accented. 'You haven't met my dear wife and my eldest son who will soon inherit his papa's business interests,' a raw, throaty laugh, 'and allow me to retire in peace to enjoy the fruit of my years of labour.'

The small talk continued for some time until Stan Summers could stand the chitchat no longer. 'Much as I enjoy your company, I really have no great wish to be here,' he said. 'Mr Beavis and Mr Crabtree came down to negotiate an expansion of our business arrangement and they now tell me you are not interested. And that nothing will persuade you otherwise. In fact, they say you would actually prefer to cancel our existing contract as well. Is this correct?'

The Bolivian pulled a tight smile that verged on the sympathetic. '*Verdad, señor*. It is unfortunate, but just one of those things.'

'A contract is a contract,' Mallory said suddenly in rapid Spanish, then translated for Summers's benefit.

The Englishman nodded his agreement. 'A gentleman's word is his bond.'

A shadow passed over de Quilindo's eyes. He turned to his wife and muttered something in her ear. She made her excuses and left for the powder room. Now the Bolivian returned his attention to Summers. 'Look, señor, I do not mind doing business with you, but the truth is you are not *needed*. We are setting up our own supply routes which means we can avoid co-operation with Colombians like your partners. I do not want my

279

son here to take over my business knowing that one day he may be blown up in a car because he does something they do not like.'

'My partners do not behave in this fashion, I trust?' Summers asked.

'Not as much as others, that is true. But they are still an intimidating presence.' A wan smile broke on the creased face. 'I realise it is difficult for you with Colombian partners from Medellín.'

Mallory made a suggestion. 'I think our partners could be persuaded to take more of a back seat. Leave you to deal with Brian and Dan here?'

De Quilindo considered for a moment. 'That would be an improvement and much welcomed. But it doesn't alter the fact that we don't need you.'

'We can improve on your percentage per kilo. Make it well worth your while,' Summers replied.

'Alas, señor, it is not just up to me. I admit you and I have always got on well and your plans have brought my family a welcome upturn in profits. But here it is not like in Colombia. We do not operate in what the DEA calls cartels with just one, or three or four *capos*. Here, there are many families who co-operate on one project, then on another. Alliances are made and break up as it suits everyone. So it is not me you have to convince. In particular, it is two of our main suppliers in the Chapare.'

'Could we meet them?' Mallory asked. 'Give us the chance to reason with them.'

De Quilindo shrugged. 'Sure, if they are willing to meet with you. But I warn you, I know these men well, they will just tell you to go get your coca leaf from Peru.'

Summers was furious, his face reddening, but he caught Mallory's glance which told him to play it cool. The Bolivian's wife returned and they all tramped ceremoniously into the restaurant to eat, de Quilindo's heavies standing sentry at key points around the room. But the conversation was strained, the excellent food somehow failing to appeal, although the Bolivian and his family made the most of it at Summers's expense.

'Bloody cheek,' he growled when the de Quilindos finally left and he retired to the bar to vent his anger. 'Go to Peru indeed!'

Harry Morgan said: 'We could talk to Bastidas, ask him to put out feelers.'

'It would take a year or more to get a satisfactory new operation going even if we could find suitable suppliers.'

'Maybe we can talk de Quilindo's friends round,' Crabtree suggested.

Stan Summers shook his head. 'You heard him. He's not at all hopeful.'

Mallory realised this was his opportunity to become fully accepted by Summers and the rest of the gang's hierarchy, to break down the final barrier – if only he could pull it off. He said quietly: 'I'll make sure you get the co-operation you want. And that's a promise.'

After two days of enforced luxury at Los Tajibos, sunning themselves at the poolside and eating lavish meals, they finally received the call from de Quilindo. He had spoken to the leaders of several supply gangs in the Chapari coca-growing heartland and persuaded them to attend a meeting with the Viper representatives.

They should fly back upcountry to Cochabamba the next morning when he would meet them with two four-wheel-drive vehicles for the journey into the interior. Stan Summers was pleased that they had actually achieved agreement for a meeting, but he was clearly nervous. His concern seemed to be more at the prospect of snakes, soldier ants and bird-eating spiders than the tough *hombres* of the Amazon rain forest he was due to meet.

In accordance with Mallory's plan, Felix Bastidas was telephoned in Medellín and requested to send a backup team of his Colombians. They were to go ahead and wait discreetly at the rendezvous. Bastidas also promised that one of his contacts in Bolivia would supply them with small arms.

The following morning the five members of Summers's party, including Mallory, caught an early flight to Cochabamba. They arrived in mid-morning to find de Quilindo and two of his heavies waiting with the promised vehicles. They were driven to the Hotel Portales, a smaller version of the sumptuous Los Tajibos, where they changed into more suitable casual clothes and collected the package of handguns which had been left for them. The 9mm Berettas were hidden discreetly under jackets before the men rejoined the Bolivians and their transport.

De Quilindo had assured them the journey by road into the interior would take no more than four hours. In the event the nightmare lasted over six. Soon after leaving the paved streets of the city the road north became a wide ribbon of deeply rutted laterite track. Speed was impossible as the drivers snaked to miss the worst of the potholes and avoid the superbuses and lorries similarly wandering all over the road. At times they would be engulfed in red dust clouds that completely obliterated the route. It was thicker than fog, making eyes itch and throats sore as it was sucked in through the air conditioning. At least they were spared the soaring humidity as they descended slowly from the mist-shrouded mountains into the subtropical jungles of the Amazonas.

As they entered the Chapare region there was a fixed checkpoint manned by the anti-drugs police. Ahead of them lorries were being searched for drugs consignments or for chemicals used in the coke labs. Superbuses and colourful *chivas* alike were disgorging lines of resigned *campesino* travellers. The bowler-hatted Indian women were paid particular attention by the sullen, green-uniformed officers; the multilayered silk skirts were notoriously effective for hiding money and packets of cocaine. Passengers milled around, making the most of the opportunity to stretch their legs, snatch a few drags on cigarettes or buy some dried fish or jelly beans from the child vendors.

Despite the air conditioning, Stan Summers was clearly in a sweat. De Quilindo noticed and his amusement showed. 'My people have telephoned ahead. Just wait a moment.' Another police officer emerged from the wayside office and scanned the long queue of vehicles. 'Our man, I think.'

De Quilindo opened his door and sauntered across to the policeman, indicating his unlit cigarette. They exchanged words and a lighter was produced. For a moment they huddled against the sultry breeze, long enough for a puff of blue smoke to emerge and the dollars to be passed. The Bolivian returned to the car and the officer waved them on to the head of the queue, signalling to a colleague to let them through.

As always, Mallory thought, it is the peasants who are stopped and stripped of their penny packets of coke, so often given in part-payment by the gangs who employed them to work in the stomping pits, the peasants who were forced to hand over a few precious bolivianos in bribes or go to jail. As always it was the kingpins who escaped.

De Quilindo's two-vehicle convoy pressed on.

The settlement of Villa Tunari was a mile-long strip of primitive housing, some concrete and tin, some bamboo and wattle, that ran along both sides of the laterite road. It was littered with the skeletal wrecks of abandoned vehicles that had come this far and no farther. The place boasted some open-fronted shops, a petrol station and a motel where de Quilindo's driver pulled in.

'This has got to be the fuckin' arsehole of the world,' Summers muttered as he climbed out.

The reception and covered bar area of Las Palmas was set off the main road behind a low hedge. Behind it, a path weaved between stunted palms to chalet-style bedroom blocks. It was the most popular watering hole in the area. At night the bar would fill with coca workers anxious to slake their thirsts after a day's sweaty toil in the jungle and to sample the locally caught *suribí* river fish. Only the incongruous sight of maroon rayon quilts and heart-shaped pillows in the spartan bedrooms gave a clue to its other function. A love hotel for the local *putas* and their desperately lonely clients destined to spend months away from wives and families.

By nine o'clock the bar was in boisterous full swing and Summers and his colleagues were getting quietly tanked on endless bottles of chilled lager. Even de Quilindo and his henchmen were relaxing, the language barrier breaking down. Mallory said he'd drunk too much and felt sick. He made his excuses and returned to his room. There he changed into his old clothes, ruffled his neatly combed hair and slipped out of a side entrance to the main thoroughfare. Hulking great lorries and buses were still thundering back and forth in the darkness as he slipped through the shadows to the café-bar where the taxi drivers gathered.

After a few minutes' hard bargaining he found a man willing to take him the ten miles to Puerto Rosa, a muddy riverside village off the beaten track. It comprised just a few dozen tumbledown hovels of timber and rattan weave and a rotting jetty. There was no glass at any of the windows and inside men were drinking and talking or playing cards or craps by the light of paraffin lamps. Only men, no women here.

Mallory slapped at his cheek, killing a mosquito. The moist, fetid air was thick with them, their low and pervasive buzzing audible despite the din of cicadas and croaking bullfrogs.

There was only one hotel, the Rotonda; a rattan-walled dosshouse with camp beds and rooms the size of toilet cubicles. Bastidas's ten Colombians had the run of the place and were drinking beer in the open-sided bar when he approached. He found the group's leader, a man called Jesus Ortega, and went over his plan in minute detail. The man was on Felix Bastidas's regular enforcing team in the area. Their job was to ensure that the Bolivian supply gangs delivered the promised quantities on time and to resolve any problems that might arise.

Jesus knew de Quilindo's operation and all his suppliers well. That included the two larger local supply gangs who wanted to sever their connections with the Vipers. 'Can you identify the vehicles the two top men drive?' Mallory asked.

Jesus nodded. 'Ortiz is easy. Always a Suzuki Samurai, white with a blue lightning flash on the side. The other man is called Ramirez. He's not so showy – maybe because he was once run in by the DEA Yankies. He always travels in different vehicles and always stays overnight in different places.'

'Then at the meeting tomorrow, I want you to come to me and quietly tell me which vehicle he is using.'

The Colombian grinned. He liked this stranger, liked his plan. 'No problem.'

De Quilindo had arranged for the meeting to be held in the covered open-air bar of Las Palmas motel at eleven. By that time all overnight guests would have left and it would be too early for the lunchtime crowd. They would have the place to themselves.

Stan Summers glanced at his watch. He was perspiring already as the temperature and humidity began to crank up remorselessly. Beavis and Crabtree were content to wait, sipping their coffee. Harry Morgan and Guy Thripp were calm but impatient.

Mallory leaned against a column, eyeing the road. 'Here comes the first of them.'

A battered pick-up pulled into the dusty, weed-ridden parking lot and two men climbed out. Other vehicles followed at short intervals, each local *capo* with a driver and at least one minder. Ortiz was the last to arrive in his white Suzuki Samurai with the blue lightning flash.

'They're all here,' de Quilindo told Summers.

Mallory took his cue and addressed the gathering. There were about nineteen men representing seven supply gangs, including drivers, bodyguards and hangers-on. 'This is strictly confidential, my friends, so if you'd like to send your staff to one of the rooms, beer will be supplied at our expense.' That met with the approval of the workers who followed one of de Quilindo's men towards the motel rooms. Mallory didn't mention that two local *putas* had been hired to serve the drinks and flirt outrageously to provide an effective distraction.

When only the *capos* remained, Summers rose to address them, this time with de Quilindo to translate his words. 'I want to thank you all for coming here at such short notice and for co-operating with us during the past year or so. My friend, Raúl de Quilindo tells me some of you wish to quit your association with us. Well, before reaching any decision, I would like you to listen to what we propose.' And he began to detail his plans for increased production and a hefty fifteen per cent on the offer price to the supply gangs.

While he talked, Mallory slipped away to the front of the motel where Jesus Ortega waited by the line of parked vehicles. 'That old Chevvy is the car belonging to Ramirez.'

Mallory nodded and strolled in its direction. When he reached it he dropped down by the rear and slid under on his back. He

285

took the two clear plastic throwaway cigarette lighters from his pocket and strapped them to the still warm exhaust box with a strip of insulating tape. He climbed back to his feet and walked quickly to Ortiz's Samurai where he repeated the process.

Then he returned to Jesus Ortega and handed him a package of used dollar notes. 'Right, that's a thousand dollar loyalty bonus for each driver and minder. Tell them they now work for us and take their orders from you. If there are any dissenters, shoot them.'

The Colombian smiled. 'They will be the men who work for Ortiz and Ramirez. It will be a pleasure to feed their corpses to the piranhas.'

'Is everything else in place?'

Jesus Ortega nodded. His men, armed with Ingram sub-machine guns, now had the motel surrounded and were poised to enter the chalet room where the Bolivians' staff were raising cans of beer in appreciation of an erotic and apparently impromptu dance routine.

Mallory moved back to the bar area to see how Stan Summers's appeal was going. But, as he had anticipated, it wasn't.

Ortiz, a fat Bolivian with heavy jowls and thinning black hair, was on his feet, waving a fist in the air. 'Listen, we are not interested! We have our own plans, our own way of doing business. Okay, we listen to *you*. Now *we* tell you, get out of our country.' As he turned round to see what support he had from his fellow *capos*, everybody heard the muted but unmistakable crackle of gunfire from nearby. Fear showed briefly in Ortiz's face. 'What was that? What is going on?'

Mallory stepped in front of Summers; as he did so, Morgan, Thripp, Beavis and Crabtree drew their concealed automatics. 'My best guess, Señor Ortiz, is that you've just lost your driver and bodyguard.'

The Bolivian glared, nervous, not sure whether this was some sort of joke at his expense. But then he decided not to wait to find out. 'I'm getting out of here!' He turned and began pushing aside chairs that cluttered his path to the exit.

'What the hell are you doing?' de Quilindo demanded. 'This

was not agreed!'

'Shut up,' Summers snarled, 'unless you want a second navel in your forehead!'

Meanwhile, Mallory had focused on Ramirez, a tall distinguished-looking man with silver hair. 'And you? Are you co-operating? If not, I suggest you go now. I am afraid I don't think your driver will be joining you.'

The man rose angrily to his feet, eyes blazing, but in the face of the pointing automatics he thought better of what he was about to say. Turning on his heel, he stomped out after Ortiz.

'The rest of you will now wait to hear what I have to tell you,' Mallory ordered. Then he paused as he heard the engines of the two vehicles start up outside. 'Now, you can do exactly the same and walk out. But before you do, I should warn you of a few facts of life. We've always acted fair with you and you've made a nice profit out of our arrangement. Now you stand to make even more. So we don't like it when anyone throws that back in our face – like those two.' The engine noise was now receding as each of the two angry and humiliated *capos* took out their frustration on their accelerator pedals. 'While we've been talking your drivers and bodyguards have switched allegiance to us. Those who refused have now been shot. You all face that same choice . . .'

He let the words hang for effect and the timing was even better than he'd anticipated. The heat from Ortiz's exhaust had melted the thin plastic of the throwaway lighters. As the petrol tank above it was only a quarter full, the result was a violent and shattering explosion. The shock wave shook the entire town.

Mallory smiled. 'Which one of your friends do you think that was saying adios?'

Bloodless, confused and nervous faces stared back at him, then winced as the second mini-car bomb blew. Not so loud, the tank of Ramirez's pick-up was filled with petrol, so while not fully exploding it became an instant and massive fireball. Out on the street the sleepy settlement had become suddenly alive, the inhabitants emerging from their houses and running towards the wrecked vehicles.

The coke suppliers began to shift uneasily in their seats,

exchanging glances and anxious low whispers. No one was willing to be the first to challenge these malicious gringos and their Colombian thugs. Mallory picked up snatches of conversation and caught the mood of these men. The fish was hooked. Maybe they'd been hasty. Things hadn't been so bad before, had they? And the profits had been good and demand regular. So why change now and risk bloodshed? After all, who wanted to end up like Ortiz and Ramirez? They all had wives and families to think of.

Mallory called out again. 'Señor de Quilindo's English friends want us all to get on well together from now on, especially as you all know what is at stake. We'll serve refreshments, some beer and *tapas*, and we'll talk to each of you individually to discuss any problems and how they can be overcome.' His tone was icily reasonable as he raised a glass. 'I give you a toast, my friends – to another successful year working together! And more profits than ever before from White Viper.'

Slowly, reluctantly, glasses and bottles were lifted. Conversation quickly gathered pace in the excited and elated tones of men who had just escaped what had seemed like certain execution.

Mallory's gaze shifted towards Summers and caught his eye. The Englishman winked. 'Well done, old son.'

Juanita Tafur raised the matter on the evening of the day they buried her husband.

Her mother was clearing the plates from the wooden table, the parlour dark and hazy with smoke from the open fire. Her father sat at the head, grieving but feeling obliged to utter trivial sentences about the meal, the weather and the harvest prospects which were never good. Anything to re-create some air of normality, some sanity and sense that life had to go on, that young Ricardo's death was a predestined will of God, pretending that somehow it was an unfortunate accident devoid of intention or malice. Otherwise his family would tear itself apart in its sorrow and its anger.

Father León, seated at the other end of the table, understood what his friend was going through. In recent months he had seen it all too many times when he had buried other members of his congregation or had gone with them in the ambulance to the hospital in Santa Maria. How often could he say 'Put your trust in God' or 'You must learn to turn the other cheek and to forgive' or 'It is His will' for it still to have any meaning? He had said all he could tonight. Best now for silence and for time to do the healing.

Strangely it helped that the wildlife film crew were staying there. Rather than proving intrusive at this time of private and personal anguish, the presence of the two men was a comfort. These strangers had been so kind and understanding that it revived the family's faith in humanity, the little Israeli called Goldie listening patiently as Victor Tafur repeated the same sentences over and over again, Mario talking quietly to Juanita, holding her hand and sharing with her the emotions he had felt after the death of Luz and his son. The sharing of the grief was an unburdening as they wept together and even, sometimes, managed to laugh between the tears at some amusing incident remembered. She liked this big, bluff man with his coarse ways and rough good humour.

And it had been he who had told her what she now repeated at the table, addressing herself to the priest. 'At the church, Father, you told us all that we should stand up to these people. I agree, as my Rico would have agreed, but we cannot stand with machetes and pitchforks against machine guns.'

Father León smiled awkwardly, wondering what was coming next.

'At the weekend there is a consignment of arms being flown in to the new airstrip. It is to be taken to the mining camp and I wonder if it would be a sin if some of us farmers intercepted them, took them for our own protection?'

The priest stared at this slight girl with her wide and earnest eyes. He was momentarily speechless. Goldie and Mario were seated near the fire, smoking their cigarillos and taking turns at wrestling a length of rope with the farm dog. Mario appeared not to hear the conversation, but Goldie did. He felt the chill hand of fear; this was not good news.

'Where did you hear this?' Victor Tafur asked, recovering from the shock of his daughter's suggestion.

'In Adoración,' she lied. 'I was talking to one of the *nennas* in the hardware store. She used to be at school with me. We went for a coffee together and she said one of the men from the mine mentioned it.'

The priest was troubled, not knowing how to decide between what *felt* right and what he thought he knew to be wrong. 'You would have to know the time, the route, and have friends willing to help.'

'I know the time,' Juanita replied, 'and there is only one route.'

'And there will be no shortage of people with a score to settle,' Victor Tafur thought aloud, suddenly warming to the idea of doing something – anything to make a stand.

Father León reached a decision. 'No, there should be no settling of scores. Murder is a heinous sin and other acts of revenge are little better in the eyes of God.'

'But *if* it could be done?' Juanita pressed.

'Without death or injury?'

'I think so,' she replied, remembering what Mario had told her when they had sat alone by the fire the previous night.

'It would be no sin to use those weapons to protect yourselves, I am sure of that.'

And he started with surprise when she suddenly leaned forward and kissed him on the cheek. 'Oh, thank you, Father. I knew I could count on you.'

Later when the priest had gone, Goldie went to the front door and beckoned Mario to follow. It was a tranquil night with a waning lemon moon and not a breath to stir the warm air. Somewhere out in the *cuchillas* they heard the cavernous roar of a jaguar.

'You know about this?' Goldie asked. It was more an accusation than a question.

'What?' Mario tried to play dumb, but he was a lousy actor.

'Don't mess with me. This is your idea, isn't it?'

A shrug. 'Well, maybe I let slip something to Juanita. Maybe not, I forget.'

'You lying bastard. That's why she made up that cock-and-bull story about the *puta* in Adoración. To protect you. For God's sake, Mario, what d'you think you're playing at?'

The big man tugged a cigarillo from his shirt pocket and stuck it in the corner of his mouth. 'Maybe I think it is time something was done.'

'That is not your decision to make,' Goldie snapped. 'There are lives at risk here, not least your own. And mine. And especially Kurt's. Had you thought about that?'

'Of course.' He put a flame to his cigarillo. 'I am not stupid and Kurt is a dear friend. But he will not be here, he will still be in Bolivia.'

Goldie shook his head. 'Any trouble can be dangerous for Kurt. Anything that makes them wonder where the tip-off came from.'

'Why should they assume it is Kurt? That doesn't make sense. It could as easily be the other gringos or one of the Colombians.'

'I still don't like it. Don't you think these people have suffered enough without inviting trouble?'

Mario smiled that roguish smile of his. 'And maybe they just feel a little better if they can shoot back.'

'That's not the point. It puts our mission in jeopardy – that is all that matters. That is what Kurt would say, you know that. The time for revenge will come.'

'Listen, Goldie, Kurt is a dear friend to us both. Maybe the three of us are the only ones in the world we can trust. But he is not always honest with us.'

'Meaning?'

'I think he knows which man killed my Luz and my boy, but he does not say. He is afraid I'll do something rash.'

Goldie stared back hard. 'I can see he was right.'

Mario ignored the barb. 'But we *do* know who killed Ricardo. The man called Billy Susan. It is time to settle at least one score.'

Goldie shook his head. 'I tell you, Mario, I want no part of this.'

That had been two days earlier and Mario Dubois found himself going over the conversation in his head as he lay hidden in the rocky outcrop above the road, waiting for the dawn.

Juanita was beside him, waking with a start. She glanced around, remembering where she was, and gave a little shiver.

'So typical of a woman to fall asleep,' he goaded.

She laughed lightly and huddled deeper into the warmth of her woollen poncho. 'I sleep like a cat, always with one eye open.'

'If you say so.'

A small fist struck him on the bicep before she struggled to sit up and peer over the cluster of boulders. 'It will soon be light. Is everyone ready?'

He nodded. There were some thirty *campesinos* in position, hidden beside the track. They had all volunteered, had all suffered at the hands of the Vipers one way or another. Many more had wanted to take part, but on Mario's advice only the youngest and fittest were selected. Most were armed with machetes and butchers' knives, but there were also three double-barrelled shotguns and two antique rifles that hadn't seen action since the days of La Violencia, the political unrest of the forties and fifties. Father León was unhappy about this, no doubt envisaging some massacre of revenge. He impressed on all concerned that the weapons should be used only as deterrence, to be fired only in extreme circumstances of self-defence.

'It is a clever plan of yours, Mario,' Juanita said. 'But are you sure it will work?'

He pulled the lopsided grin that she liked so much. 'No, my little one, there are no such certainties in life. Its success will depend much on the courage and determination of these people and how fast they move. Surprise is everything. But these are South Americans with hearts like lions, the sons of Simon Bolívar.'

Her white teeth glistened in the gloom. 'And daughters, Mario.' She pulled out the silver-plated revolver from beneath her poncho. 'I for one shall fight like a *tigre*!'

For one dread moment he thought she was going to shoot him and she laughed as she read it in his eyes. 'Boom! Boom! Do not worry, I will not shoot my hero.'

'Where did you get that from?'

'It is my grandfather's. From when he was an officer in the army. We keep it in the family chest. I first discovered it when I was a little girl.'

'Does Victor know you have this with you?'

The long black hair tossed free of the poncho as she shook her head. 'No. I am old enough to make my own decisions.'

'Is it safe?' He took it gently from her and checked it over.

'I am not a fool, Mario. It has been well looked after and oiled.'

Reluctantly he handed it back. He was glad she was up here with him, removed from where the action would take place. This girl had touched his heart – or more truthfully stolen it, he thought ruefully. Such fresh-faced youth, such natural sweetness and generosity, such good humour and vitality. The thought of anything happening to her was just too awful for him to contemplate.

Even now he was beginning to regret that he had ever suggested this idea. He hadn't really thought it through. Hadn't really expected Victor Tafur and the priest to take to the idea with such enthusiasm. If he'd got it wrong – and there were many things that could go wrong – these simple peasants could be decimated. He certainly had no doubt as to the capabilities of those Viper gangsters and their Colombian cohorts if they were given the chance.

What these local people really needed to be sure of success were some of the specialist weapons he and Goldie had secreted in their Fourtrak. But that was out of the question without breaking their cover. As it was, he had to tell Juanita that he'd once seen the idea in a movie to explain away expertise more appropriate to a military commander than a wildlife sound-man.

It was to be another hour before the sun was fully up and the first blush of platinum light touched the canyon wall. The ambushers tensed as the sound of vehicles drifted up from the valley, engines straining against the sharp incline that led towards the airstrip. An open-topped Rocsta jeep came first, Billy Susan beside the driver and two armed Colombians in the back. More Colombians were smoking and laughing in the battered truck that followed it, commandeered from one of the farmers who now lay in wait.

The two vehicles grumbled past, swaying drunkenly as they negotiated the ruts and potholes in the trail and leaving acrid plumes of exhaust hanging in their wake. Another sharp turn and they disappeared from view, the clatter of their engines receding until the quiet of the countryside settled in again.

Only then did the ambush party emerge with their picks and spades. Organised into teams they worked furiously to hack and clear six shallow channels at intervals across the full width of the track.

Had they had more time in which to work and had the ground been less rocky, Mario would have gone for a *matar burro* or killing donkey. A disguised trench one foot deep and one foot wide, it worked equally well against aircraft, vehicles and horses.

This was a compromise. When the channels were completed men appeared carrying lengths of timber planking. Two rows of six-inch nails had been hammered into each. One was positioned in the first channel, points uppermost, and anchored with steel pegs. Once all six were fitted, the topsoil was redistributed and a dusting of dry earth was sprinkled to hide the signs of disturbance and to disguise the protruding spikes.

The work was barely complete when they heard the distant buzz of twin aero engines. As they scurried for cover, the aircraft began its first pass of the strip, then circled before coming back on its final approach.

Twenty minutes later, the machine took off again, soaring over the track and banking hard round before setting course back towards Venezuela. It was a further half an hour before the sound of the returning vehicles reached them. Mario wriggled forward for a better view, Juanita at his side.

The Rocsta nosed around the high bend just where the trail started to plunge down the steep straight where the vehicle trap was buried. It ran for some forty metres into a cutting before kinking sharply to the left at the bottom, following the contour of the canyon spur. Close behind the jeep came the truck, now loaded down with wooden packing cases.

With a carefree spin of the wheel the driver of the Rocsta entered the steep straight, hitting maybe thirty or thirty-five miles an hour. The truck followed more slowly, negotiating the bend and cresting the start of the downhill straight.

Halfway down the Rocsta driver began to slow, ready for the sharp left-hander at the bottom. Mario winced as he sensed the man's foot stab at the brake. Then the front wheels hit the first row of embedded nails. There must have been an actual sequence, but all four tyres appeared to blow together. With a dull popping of compressed air, the vehicle lurched and toppled, dropping several inches, frayed rubber spinning like demented Catherine wheels, rims scraping on the nails. It kept on moving like an uncontrollable bobsleigh, bumping and sliding towards the bend. Recovering his senses, the driver threw the wheel hard over. But the rims were gyrating like bacon slicers, churning up the soft earth and unable to gain a grip. In panic the driver stamped on the brakes and the rims stopped fast. The combined effect was to send the vehicle skiing into a left-hand slide on the bend, but far too wide. It left the track at some fifteen miles an hour, airborne for a moment before it plummeted into the deep trackside ditch and rolled over. Someone screamed.

Coming fast behind was the truck. Its driver had no time to react. He didn't even know what had happened, probably assuming in the split second available to him that the Rocsta had struck a land mine.

He, too, jammed on the brakes, felt the spikes biting into the heavy-duty rubber. In a cloud of dust the truck swerved and careered madly over the trap. Two tyres shredded, then a third. But the fourth wheel remained intact, instead ripping out one of the nailed planks and sending it flying skyward.

Finally the entire suspension collapsed, the last wheel wrenched free and sent bouncing into the trackside undergrowth. The body pan hit the ground with a tremendous thud, throwing the Colombians around like skittles in an alley before it slewed in a wide semicircle, finally coming to rest in a whirlwind of choking ochre dust.

'Come on,' Mario urged beneath his breath, fearing that Father León, Victor Tafur and their peasant army would hesitate and miss their chance. But he needn't have worried. With a series of whooping yells and war cries they emerged from the shrubbery. Still shouting and waving machetes they swarmed towards the two wrecks, grabbed the dazed occupants and snatched away their weapons.

Under the priest's direction the *campesinos* were pushing the gang members back onto the track where the farmers waited with shotguns. The injured were dragged unceremoniously into the circle.

On the outcrop, Juanita looked down in wonder and delight. She turned to Mario, her eyes shining and threw her arms around his neck. 'This is wonderful! You are wonderful!'

Never usually one to be shy with women, this time Mario felt distinctly awkward. He wanted to seize the moment and crush her to him. But something held him back. She was so young, too young. Too pretty and too innocent. A delight. And he didn't want to blow his chances by misjudging how she felt.

When she released him, he acted as though he'd hardly noticed and moved back to the edge of the outcrop. A half-smile on his face, he surveyed the scene below. 'We have been very lucky. But your people must watch them like hawks, be sure they find any hidden weapons. I think your Ricardo would be proud of his people this day, don't you think?' There was no reply. 'Don't you think, Juanita?'

He turned his head; she was gone.

Scrambling to his feet he began following her down over the maze of strewn boulders to the track.

There Father León stood facing the group of prisoners, Victor Tafur by his side. Two *campesinos* had hold of Billy Susan and dragged him to the front. His forehead was grazed and a trickle of blood had congealed around his left eyebrow and cheek.

'These weapons are being confiscated,' the priest announced. 'They will be distributed to the local population for their protection against any further acts of intimidation. Go back and tell your boss that. We have had enough. The worm has turned. In future, fire shall be met with fire.'

Billy Susan glared. 'You're making a big mistake, priest. Half your congregation are earning a good living thanks to us. All you have to do is co-operate and mind your own business and there'll be no trouble from us.'

Father León stiffened his back. 'You're engaged in the devil's work. We don't want you here, do you understand? In fact if you do not dismantle your camp and leave the territory in the next few weeks I will take up the matter with the police chief in Santa Maria.'

The Englishman gave a snort of derisive laughter. 'That will not get you far.'

'On your payroll too?' Father León suggested. 'Then I will raise the question with the Cardinal in Bogotá.'

'You are making a big mistake,' Susan repeated.

Juanita stepped out from behind the priest. 'No, Señor Susan, it is you who are making the big mistake. In fact you made it when you murdered my husband and thought you would get away with it.' She pulled the silver-plated revolver from beneath her poncho and pointed it at his forehead. A two-handed grip, unwavering. 'This is for my Ricardo.'

'NO!' Father León shouted.

The gun blasted a single shot. A neat round hole appeared in Billy Susan's head as the impact blew him off his feet. He landed on his back, his empty eyes staring at the sky. His legs twitched once, twice. Then he lay still. No one else moved, neither *campesinos* nor gangsters; all just gaped in stunned disbelief.

In an instant Juanita recovered from her moment of madness. Her mouth opened in a scream of horror and she dropped the gun as though it had scalded her. She stared at the corpse, not believing what she had done. Then the hysteria swept over her. She began yelling and shouting, begging God and the priest for forgiveness, turning on Mario and beating her small fists against his chest. Blaming him, herself, the world, as the shock of it hit her.

Mario reached for her then and hugged her to him. 'Justice is done,' he whispered.

She was shaking uncontrollably as he led her away. He was aware of her breathless sobbing, the warmth of her tears against his cheek.

13

'Victory from the jaws of defeat,' Stan Summers declared happily on the long car drive back to Cochabamba. 'Now we're virtually in control of the whole supply network as well as distribution. You was right, Kurt, there's only one language these Latinos understand.'

Brian Beavis and Dan Crabtree had been left behind to sew up loose ends with Jesus Ortega and his Colombian enforcers. They were likely to have an easy time of it. With Ortiz and Ramirez out of the way and Raúl de Quilindo and the other suppliers suddenly becoming co-operative, Mallory was hailed as the hero of the hour.

He was reasonably satisfied himself, but for different reasons. His trip to Bolivia had provided him with invaluable information on the supply network he would not otherwise have had. Jesus Ortega knew the system backwards and during their meeting at Puerto Rosa had given him chapter and verse on the local supply gangs: names, routes and locations of many secret coca fields, stomping pits and laboratories.

Moreover he had successfully eliminated two local *narco* bosses who had so far evaded both the Bolivian authorities and the DEA. And he felt not the slightest pang of guilt or remorse for his actions. This was what he believed in. Rough justice. Reaching where legitimate law enforcement couldn't. Another small act of vengeance for the millions who suffered or even died as a result of this filthy business. A balancing of the scales of justice. On behalf of Sophie, Mario's Luz and their son and Ricardo. One to chalk up for the organisation.

When they finally returned to the luxury of the Portales hotel,

Summers and the others were keen to celebrate with a meal and a piss-up in the bar. But Mallory complained of a headache and left them to it. He had no desire to stay longer in their company. Soon it would be time to finish the job and every assassin knew the golden rule through bitter experience.

Never get to know your victim too well. For even villains and cut-throats like these were human. They had their good points and few were intrinsically evil. Most had their excuses or reasons, tales of misfortune or circumstances that led them to what they had become. No doubt every mother loved her wayward son. Every murderer, deviant or drug-dealer loved his mother, his wife and his children. And those who waited at home would never believe their sons, or husbands or fathers were capable of preying on the misery of others for a living. And probably they would not want to know.

And neither did Mallory. He didn't want to know that Stan Summers had a pretty blonde wife and three gorgeous kids who lived in a half-million-pound detached house in Chelmsford with a swimming pool and tennis court; that with his third marriage Guy Thripp had at last found happiness and they both adored their little boy who had Down's syndrome and wasn't expected to live beyond the age of twenty; that Thripp felt rejected and abused by the army he had served loyally for all his adult life, or that bossman Harry Morgan intended to spend his ill-gotten gains on private nursing care for his senile mother.

He didn't want to know these things; already he knew too much. It would make everything more difficult when the time came.

It was with these thoughts that he strolled through the linking covered walkways to his room in one of the terraced accommodation blocks. A huge floodlit statue of Christ stood on a nearby hilltop. It was an awesome spectacle, appearing to be unsupported in the night sky, the arms outstretched. Blessing the inhabitants of this city of *narcotraficantes*, Mallory wondered absently, or forgiving them their sins?

He inserted the key in the door of his room and eased it open. Then he froze.

Something wasn't right. He sensed it. The room was in darkness, silent. But something wasn't right and his pulse quickened. His hand slipped to his jacket, easing up the flap to reach the Beretta automatic he still carried. He drew the weapon and dropped to one knee.

Then he caught it, his nostrils flaring. That perfume.

'Kurt?'

'Christ, George?'

She sounded tense, nervous. 'Quick. Come in and close the door.'

He pulled it in behind him and reached for the light switch. The sudden brightness stung his eyes. She was standing by the window, wearing chino slacks and a bush shirt, the pageboy haircut dark and glistening. 'How d'you get in here?' He felt the relief ebb through him and found himself grinning. 'Sorry, stupid question.'

'I had to see you.' She indicated the Beretta. 'Would you mind not pointing that at me.'

'You shouldn't be here. Not just for my sake, for your own.'

Her smile was strained. 'You gave us a fright, just saying you were coming here, giving us barely a day's notice. It wasn't in the plan.'

'I didn't know myself, but it was too good to miss.'

She shook her head. 'But with no time to arrange backup. I couldn't pull out Mario or Goldie and send them, they're too well known now. And Dale wasn't keen to enlist the help of the local DEA.'

'Thank God for small mercies.' He gave a wry smile. 'So you came yourself? I'm flattered.'

'Don't be. I'm your control; I just couldn't leave you out on a limb. Not after last time.'

'Ah, a guilty conscience?'

'Maybe. I had to find out what was going on, whether you were heading for trouble. Guy Thripp might have recognised you and have a surprise planned. I freaked out when I realised it was him.'

'It's been no problem, he hasn't tumbled.'

'I still needed to be sure where you were.'

'Down in the Chapare.'

'I know. Our Customs DLO in La Paz has his ear to the ground and the jungle telegraph travels fast.' She saw the concern in his eyes. 'Don't worry, I was discreet.'

'I'm sure.' He removed his jacket and sat on the edge of the bed. 'Haven't got a cigarette, I suppose?'

For the first time she smiled naturally, her shoulders relaxing. 'I see nothing has changed.'

He accepted the cigarette and the light. 'Maybe not. But then maybe it has. At least I know now I was right to quit this game after last time. This has been a nightmare.'

'You look exhausted. And you've lost weight.' Concern showed in her eyes.

'Fear is the best diet.'

She attempted to lighten the mood. 'I must try it.'

'You wouldn't like it.' He grinned, pleased to see her again despite knowing her presence was unwise and against all the rules. She could just have used the phone. But then she was control and she was running him. 'We're flying back tomorrow, so all this sneaky-beaky stuff is a bit unnecessary.'

'It is necessary, Kurt. Something's happened back at Cruz de Oro. The locals have staged some sort of uprising against the Vipers. They seized that arms shipment yesterday and have warned the gang they're going to use the weapons for self-defence.'

Mallory stared at her for a moment. 'Good for them,' he said.

'But not for our operation, Kurt. This is no time for anyone to go rocking the boat. Has Stan Summers mentioned it?'

Mallory shook his head while he savoured the tobacco smoke. 'No, but if it happened yesterday he wouldn't know. We've been virtually out of contact down there and it'll be a week or two before the Vipers can establish their own communications system.'

Savage looked thoughtful. 'I can't believe he won't get a message soon. He'll probably go ballistic when he hears. I'm sorry, you wouldn't know either. They killed Billy Susan.'

Mallory was stunned. After a long pause he said: 'Then there

301

will be hell to pay.'

'That's what Dale and I think. They're bound to get paranoid over who spilled the beans about the arms shipment. Aren't you going to be a prime suspect?'

He considered for a second. 'I might have been, except now my star's in the ascendant. After my showing down here, Summers thinks the sun shines out of my backside.'

'Just as well.'

'So who did put the locals up to it?'

'Goldie contacted me. Said Mario dropped them the nod, told that Juanita girl he's hot on.'

Mallory could hardly believe it. But then, he thought, his friend hadn't been the same man since Luz and his son were butchered. Clearly his grief and his thirst for revenge had affected his judgement. 'Who knows about Mario's involvement in this? If he's blown his cover, he could be in more danger than me.'

'I realise that, Kurt. So does Dale and he's furious about it. Goldie seems to think Mario told Juanita not to implicate him and she's been playing along. But it would just take one slip-up.'

'I guess there's not much we can do about it, except hope.'

She looked at him candidly. 'There is one thing we could do. Close the operation down now. You could walk out of here with me tonight and catch the first flight to Miami. One phone call to Dale, and Goldie and Mario can be on their way to Santa Maria.'

Mallory shook his head. 'And blow the whole operation? Then Summers really would smell a rat.'

'It's not ideal. But we've got all the data you've accumulated so far, plus all the new information on their supply network here. True, there'd be no time for a co-ordinated swoop in three countries and we still know precious little about the European end—'

'So it would have been a complete waste of time,' Mallory retorted. 'The cartels are expert at this sort of thing and Summers is no fool. At the first whiff of serious trouble with the police or the DEA, they'll scatter. The laboratory might shut down, but it'll just be months before the whole thing is up and running again somewhere else. It's too big a money spinner for them to let go.' He stubbed out his cigarette in the bedside ashtray. 'And

I can't see your American friend being too happy about the idea.'

Savage pulled a tight smile. 'He isn't, especially now he knows the extent of Felix Bastidas's plans for destabilising the major drug-supplying states. But then Dale's not got much say in the matter if you decide to pull out. Your safety must come first, and Mario's and Goldie's.'

'It's nice to know you care.'

'I do care, Kurt. I think you know that.' Her face was very close to his, her eyes dark and moist. 'I always have.'

Slowly, very slowly, his mouth descended on hers. As his arms encircled her, he felt her stiffen momentarily. Then she melted a little, giving in, and her lips and teeth began working against his own, her tongue gently prising its way in. The kiss lingered for a full minute, maybe longer, before she drew back. Her voice was hoarse. 'Christ, Kurt, I miss you.'

'I thought it was over. What about your husband?'

She smiled nervously, embarrassed as she fumbled in her handbag for a cigarette. He noticed her hands were trembling as she lit up. 'Do you want me to admit it? That it's been a mistake? Wouldn't that make you feel better?'

'No,' he said truthfully. 'I hoped you might be happy.'

She exhaled a long coil of smoke. 'I should be, Kurt, I really should. But Giles is not you and you're a pretty hard act to follow.'

'Forget about me, George, I'm no good for you. We decided once it was over. Let's leave it that way.'

'Trouble is, Kurt, I can't live with you and I can't live without you.'

It was his turn to smile. 'Give your husband an even break, George, and yourself.'

'That sounds pretty much like a rejection.' She sniffed heavily, trying to regain some composure. 'I'm sorry, it's been a tense few weeks. My nerves are playing up. God knows what it must have been like for you.'

'Not good, George, I admit that. But I still don't want to pull out – not if it means Summers and Harry Morgan and the others are going to get away. How long does Forster reckon he'd need to set up a co-ordinated swoop?' He pulled off one of his trainers and handed her two sheets of paper he'd folded tightly and concealed beneath the insole. They were damp with sweat. 'That's a complete breakdown of the supply network here, running from the Chapare to Santa Cruz.'

She studied it for a moment, her eyebrows lifting. 'That's incredible, Kurt.'

'How long?' he repeated. 'How long for a co-ordinated swoop?'

'To include all this – sensibly, a month of arranging and planning, but I don't feel we can wait that long. Dale will have to pull in some favours – let's say seven days.'

Mallory nodded. 'In the meantime I'll find out what I can about the European end.'

Savage nodded. 'It was a shock to hear about Miguel Castaño's visit. You realise he's Kelly's latest boyfriend?'

'Yes.' Terse. 'I met him just before I left.'

'God.' A look of abject horror was on her face. 'He didn't recognise you?'

He shook his head. 'I don't think I'd be here if he had.'

'What do you know about him?'

'Not a lot. Just that he runs an international practice from Madrid.'

'That's right, and fairly high-powered by all accounts. We've run checks on him and his company. All above board and highly respectable. Most of his business is commercial with contacts and clients in most South American countries, most of Europe and more recently the old Eastern Bloc states. Obviously I checked on his links with Kelly's father. That all appears kosher. One of Castaño's clients, a fish products manufacturer, wanted access to the Irish Sea which is restricted under EC regulations. With Joe O'More's help, Castaño's client has bought a controlling share in a Cork fishing fleet. Castaño's firm also runs a criminal division and that's one area where Miguel came in for some stick a few years back. His firm defended some Basque separatist terrorists – and lost. But some of his influential friends in government and industry were unhappy to see him assisting the ETA movement even if, as he claimed, he was just doing his job. Anyway, after that case, he kept strictly to defending more conventional criminals.'

'Like Stan Summers.'

'He's an interesting character. Born and brought up in Billericay, son of a bookmaker. Got into a spot of trouble as a kid – shoplifting, joyriding and some GBH – but he settled down in his early twenties once he had his first wife and their child. Worked on building sites, then set up renovating old houses. Then he moved on to more ambitious things, becoming quite a big property speculator in the eighties and made a killing, mostly investing other people's money and taking a good cut of the profits.'

'Anything criminal?'

'Well, there's an open file at New Scotland Yard, but nothing proven. Some complaints of intimidation of sitting tenants and suspected violence between him and a rival firm. For a while he dabbled in the porn import game. Mostly the nasty stuff, heavy SM and animals. But he dropped all that when the law was tightened in the late eighties. He's also got interests in used cars and fruit machines, so it's a fair bet he has plenty of low-life contacts.'

'How did he get involved with Castaño?'

Savage shrugged. 'At this stage the best we can establish is that they appeared to meet first at some party on the Costas about three years ago. A London villain, a friend of Summers, was celebrating because he'd just defeated an extradition request from London in the Spanish courts. Castaño's firm had handled the case.'

'And how did he get involved with Harry Morgan and that lot?'

'That's easier. Summers used to have a nightclub and he hired his bouncers from Morgan's firm. Thripp and Billy Susan were on the staff at one time or another. The rest, I imagine, were friends of friends.'

'And Summers has had no obvious connection with drugs?'

'None that's known about.'

Mallory scratched at the rough stubble on his chin. 'Something doesn't quite fit. Like there's a part of the jigsaw missing.' He smiled at her. 'Don't worry, I'll find out what it is before I'm finished.'

305

'I'm sure you will.' She glanced at her watch. 'It's nearly ten. Time I wasn't here.'

He looked at her. 'You don't have to go. Summers won't expect to see me till the morning.'

Her eyes narrowed and a ghost of a smile touched her lips. 'Is this a record? Kurt Mallory actually asking a woman to stay?'

He laughed, self-mocking. 'I must be mellowing in my old age.'

'It's over between us.'

'I know.'

'It would be breaking all the rules.'

'That's what rules are for.'

'Then you'd better pour me a drink.'

The next morning Mallory was woken by the urgent ring of the bedside phone. As he reached to answer it, he saw that there was no one on the rumpled sheet beside him; Savage had gone.

Guy Thripp was in no mood for pleasantries. 'Get your arse down to reception in ten minutes, Kurt. We're catching an earlier flight.'

'What's wrong?'

'What *isn't*,' Thripp snapped back and hung up.

Mallory took a quick shower. The room was heavy with George's perfume and he could still smell her on his skin. Her perspiration, her juices; his head was full of her, his mind floating with images of the previous night. Somehow he had unleashed something in her, a wild animal that had been caged for too long.

He threw on his clothes, grabbed his rucksack and left the room. In reception Summers was settling the bill. He was a changed man, his face like thunder. Harry Morgan and Thripp were in equally mean mood.

During the taxi ride to the airport, Summers told Mallory he'd received a message relayed from the Viper camp at Cruz de Oro in Colombia. 'The fuckin' peasants are in revolt and Billy's dead. What the sod was he playing at? Serves 'im bloody well right for being so careless.' He turned and stared out of the window, seeing nothing but his own rage. 'And wait till Bastidas hears about this! Jesus Christ, he'll go mad when he learns his precious arms have been stolen by a load of fuckin' peasants!'

The flight back to La Paz to pick up the connecting airline to Bogotá was spent in sullen silence. By the time they switched again for the internal flight from Bogotá to Bucaramanga, Stan Summers had obviously arrived at some decisions. He spent the journey huddled together with Morgan and Thripp. Mallory was excluded.

A private Piper Apache was waiting for them on the tarmac, its engines running, ready to fly them to the strip at Cruz de Oro.

As soon as they arrived, Mallory could sense the tension. Even before the props had come to a standstill the aircraft was surrounded by armed members of the late Pedro Gómez's Colombian thugs. They were wary and excitable, seemingly expecting trouble at any second as they fanned out in a defensive circle.

Derek Rutter, the Geordie, had assumed command after Susan's death and now waited for Summers to emerge. 'Am I pleased to see you, boss.'

'Wish I could say the same,' Summers retorted. 'What other disasters have happened while I've been away?'

'Nothing since Billy was shot. That was bad enough. They took all the boots from the Colombian escort and made them walk back to camp. They took the weapons they wanted from the truck and set fire to the rest.'

Summers shook his head, still not able to come to terms with it all. 'How many have you retrieved?'

'None, boss. The burnt-out ones were unusable.'

'What about those that were stolen, have you hunted them down?'

'No, boss. I didn't want to go inflaming the situation while feelings are running high. Not without your say-so.'

Summers jabbed a thumb angrily at his own chest. 'Well, *my* feelings are running high, Rutter. My feelings are in bloody ORBIT!'

Harry Morgan stepped forward. 'Look, we'd better get

307

properly organised on this. Do we know who's got the weapons?'

Derek Rutter shook his head.

'Well, who took part in the ambush?' Summers demanded. 'They must have been local, so our Colombians must have recognised some of them, for God's sake. Have you asked them?'

The man looked sheepish. 'I don't speak the lingo too good.'

'For Christ's sake, man, it's simple enough. Names! *Nombres!* Even I know that. That's all you have to ask the Colombians and they'll realise what you mean. Use bloody sign language.' He turned, exasperated, to Mallory. 'Go with him, Kurt, will you? You ask the questions. Just get me a fuckin' list. Pronto!' He thought for a moment. 'Does Felix Bastidas know what's happened?'

'Well, he hasn't radioed in, boss. So I guess not.'

'Thank God for that. At least he doesn't know how many weapons were due in. If we can retrieve *some*, we can fob him off for a few days. But we *must* find them, understand?'

That evening Mallory spent with Rutter in the bunkhouse, talking to the Colombians and compiling a list of those who had been involved. His heart sank when he was told that Father León and Victor Tafur had been leading them. And he felt a creeping horror when he learned that it was Juanita who had actually killed Billy Susan and even worse that Mario, the film sound-man, was seen leading her away afterwards.

'I should think he just happened to be around,' he said absently. 'No point putting his name down.'

'Bugger that,' Rutter snorted. 'His fault for being in the wrong place at the wrong time. Anyway, I never have trusted that film crew. Harry should never have let them stay in the area. If he was there, then he's in the frame with all the rest.'

'Tomorrow we'll decide exactly how to teach these people a lesson and get the arms back,' Summers said later. 'I'm too knackered to think. In fact, I'll just have a nightcap and turn in.'

Mallory suddenly saw his opportunity. 'Shall I put some coffee on?'

'Good man,' Summers replied. 'And don't spare the brandy. Bring it to my quarters, will you?'

Making his way to the kitchen area, Mallory put a kettle on the

Gaz ring-burner and prepared some mugs. While the water boiled he prised the false heel from his boot and extracted a small plastic sachet of powder from the recess. *Burundanga*. The plant extract that thieves used throughout Colombia to drug their unwitting victims. He sprinkled it into Summers's personal mug as he poured the coffees.

After handing out mugs to Rutter and Morgan, he crossed the yard to the hut that Summers was using. 'Excellent. Ta.'

'You'd better try it, boss. I'm a bit heavy-handed on the coffee.'

Summers sipped. 'On the strong side. Strange taste.'

'Best Colombian.'

Mallory made an effort at small talk for a few minutes, just long enough for Summers to take three more mouthfuls of the stuff.

'God, didn't realise I was so tired.' The man staggered to his feet and took a tentative step towards his bunk. 'Christ, I feel giddy. How much brandy did you put in that?' His legs collapsed under him and he began to fall. Mallory caught him under the armpits and dragged him onto his bed.

He then moved back into the office area and began rummaging through the drawers of the desk. The European network. He wanted anything on the European network. Nothing.

Summers's leather briefcase lay on the desktop. Shit, a combination lock! He moved his thumbs across the brass fittings and pressed. The clasps sprang free. Summers must have just opened it ready to do some work before he turned in.

But Mallory's rising sense of anticipation was short-lived. An electric razor, a solar-operated calculator, an international airlines timetable, air tickets and travel documents. Ah, a loose-leaf notebook. Full of calculations that meant nothing to him. Quantities and prices? Probably, but it was difficult to tell. Delivery times and routes were recorded purely as A, B, C and so on. And codewords that quite obviously referred to suppliers as well as customers. There was no doubt about it, Summers was a total professional, committing nothing of importance to paper. At least nothing that Mallory could comprehend.

Disappointed he closed the briefcase and left for the bunkhouse. It had been an exhausting few days and for once he fell instantly into a deep and dreamless sleep. He was totally unaware of the events that were about to begin even before he awoke. If he had known the orders that Stan Summers had secretly given Harry Morgan and Guy Thripp, Mallory would have killed him in his bed that night.

They struck before the first dawn light. Five targets. And six people whom the Colombians had identified as being part of the arms ambush.

Thripp personally took command of the raid on the Tafur family's hacienda. They parked the Rocsta half a mile from the building so as not to alert the occupants. Leaving the Colombian driver, Thripp led the approach with Derek Rutter and Mick Pye and the Swinyard twins from Leicester who were nicknamed Tom and Jerry. One loud and opinionated, the other quiet and darkly introspective, they were the most uncomical duo imaginable. Both had trained as Paras and both had been dismissed for violent off-duty behaviour before turning to a career of armed robbery.

Only the farm dog sensed their silent approach, suddenly alert with tail stiff and ears pricked. It gave a low growl, but the bark that followed was cut short by a single round from Rutter's silenced Ingram. The animal was slammed into the ground, its cry of alarm reduced to a pitiful whimper.

There was no sign of the film crew's Fourtrak, but the Swinyard brothers were nevertheless detailed to check the barn where they were known to be staying. Inside there were just personal possessions of little interest, but no sign of the men themselves. Tom cursed and Jerry just shrugged and spoke on the radio to Thripp, confirming that they were moving into position outside the rear kitchen door of the hacienda.

Thripp was at the front with Pye and Rutter, guns drawn.

Victor Tafur was in his bed, unsettled, turning over beside his wife, unaware that he had been disturbed by the dying whimperings of his dog. When the glass of the kitchen window shattered he was instantly awake, sitting bolt upright.

'What was that?' he asked.

His wife murmured sleepily.

Victor Tafur, clad only in his nightshirt, swung his legs from the bed and padded towards the corridor. The building was silent now. Had he imagined it?

The sound of the two rapid gunshots terrified him. His heart skipped and he began to tremble, frozen to the spot as the front-door lock shattered and dark figures appeared in the entrance.

'Papa!'

He turned quickly at hearing Juanita's voice. She was standing in her white cotton nightdress at the doorway to her bedroom. She was gesturing to him with her left hand; in her right she held one of the Kalashnikov rifles taken from the ambush.

'Papa, quick! Don't just stand there! Get back behind the wall!'

Suddenly his brain crashed into gear. He was standing in the hallway, a ready target for the shadows walking towards him. Quickly he stepped back into his bedroom. As he did, Juanita raised the assault rifle at the intruders, leaning against the door jamb to provide some cover and to steady her aim. Her finger closed around the trigger.

Then she heard the metallic click of the hammer behind her as Mick Pye thumbed it back and pressed the barrel of his revolver into the soft flesh beneath her chin. 'Tut-tut, what a naughty girl.' He jabbed the gun hard so she winced in pain. 'Put it down. Nice and easy. Ah, not with the safety catch off.' She bent at the knees, obediently lowering the weapon to the floor. 'Now put your hands in the air and walk slowly towards my friends.' He glanced at Victor Tafur, who stood, pale and still shaking, his eyes wide with terror. 'You too, old man. We've just about had enough of your family.'

Once outside, the Swinyards bound the girl and her father with lengths of rope before bundling them into the Rocsta which Thripp had called up on the radio. Tafur's wife watched from the doorway, clutching her youngest daughter to her chest, as tears streamed down her face. She was blubbering, pleading, but her confused words went unheeded.

Thripp turned to the rancher. 'Where are those film-makers tonight?' he demanded.

With difficulty the old man found his voice. 'Out on location somewhere,' he croaked. 'Filming the wild cats.'

'Then they don't know how lucky they are,' Mick Pye said, then added ominously. 'For now.'

Juanita, who had kept her head bowed and facing away from them, turned abruptly and spat in his face. 'You wouldn't do this if Mario was here! He will make you pay for this!'

Pye's hand swiped across her face, his knuckles cracking against her nose. 'Shut up, cow! You're the only one who'll be doing any paying around here!'

Just then Derek Rutter returned from the hacienda; he was grinning and cradling a bundle of five assault rifles in his arms. 'Look what I've found.'

Thripp wasn't impressed. 'That's hardly going to bring a smile to Summers's face. He'll need a lot more than those to give Bastidas.'

'I promise you one thing, Guy,' Tom Swinyard said. 'By this time tomorrow the locals will be beggin' to hand 'em back.'

Mallory only heard about the dawn raids when he arrived at the cookhouse for breakfast. Everyone appeared in jubilant mood, laughing and joking as they recounted the events of earlier that morning.

Only Doug Tallboys and Pete Stafford looked less than pleased as they sat nursing coffees at their table. 'What's going on?' Mallory asked as he joined them.

'Vengeance of the Vipers,' Tallboys murmured. 'This morning they rounded up the ringleaders behind that arms ambush – including the priest and the girl who killed Billy Susan. Stan Summers's orders. He wants an example made of them. To persuade the locals to toe the line and bring back the stolen guns.' He glared at his coffee mug as though he'd just spotted something nasty in it. 'I really don't have the stomach for this sort of thing.'

'You big, soft Scotch git!' It was Guy Thripp who'd overheard. 'I've gotta tell you, Doug, you're a right sanctimonious prick. Some of us are getting a little tired of you. Never mixing in, looking at us with your air of self-righteous disapproval, like we were

312

something unpleasant you just stepped in.'

Tallboys's knuckles tightened on the table. 'I didn't ask to be part of this.'

A thin smile appeared on Thripp's face. 'No? Well, you didn't ask too many questions either, as I recall. You're not an idiot, are you? All that money you were being paid for a secret contract in Colombia – you must have smelled a rat. Colombia, big money, drugs – every fuckin' idiot knows the connection. You can't have it both ways, sunshine.'

The Scotsman glared back, the anger he'd felt for so long coming rapidly to the boil. 'I didn't sign up for murder and intimidation!'

Thripp laughed. 'All a necessary part of the job. And if you take the devil's money, you dance to his tune.'

'Piss off!' Tallboys snapped, and Pete Stafford placed a restraining hand on his friend's arm.

Mallory was annoyed he hadn't known about the roundup; now it was too late to warn anyone. He said: 'You didn't tell me what you were going to do this morning.'

Thripp snorted. 'Why should we? Summers thought you might be tempted to tip them off.'

'What? That's stupid. I could have translated—'

'What we had to say needed *no* translation. They're getting the message. And I agree with Summers. For my liking you're too close to that bastard Tafur and his daughter. I haven't forgotten how you went running back to them with Ricardo's body. And you were very chummy with that film crew – and one of them's had a hand in all this. Stan Summers might still think the sun shines out your arse, but some of us don't. And I think he has his doubts. Look at you, sitting here with these two fuckin' pacifists. I'll be honest, I don't trust you, never have. The way you just turned up here—'

Mallory's eyes hardened. 'But Summers is the boss,' he reminded icily.

Thripp swallowed and slowly ran the tip of his tongue over his lips. 'But Harry Morgan and me have the executive powers to do whatever we see fit, Kurt. Remember that. If we don't like you, don't count on Stan to protect you. He won't.'

Any further development of the antagonism was curtailed as Harry Morgan swept into the cookhouse. 'Right, lads, time to avenge poor old Billy's death!' he announced. 'Our Colombian friends have been busy rounding up the rest of those known to be involved in the ambush. They've been taken to Cruz de Oro and you're all ordered to join the party by our illustrious leader, Mr Summers.' He smiled. 'Did I say ordered? Slip of the tongue. I mean invited. And bring a bottle.'

Mick Pye gave a whoop of approval, waving the bottle of beer in his hand. 'Right on, boss! We'll teach the bastards.' All around the gang members began laughing and speculating over the sport to come.

Thripp leaned across Mallory's table. 'That includes you three. What is it governments insist on. Collective responsibility? That way no one can point a finger later.'

Mallory smelled death in the air. Someone was going to die, and the whole White Viper gang was going to be present. Like a bizarre ritual. No one could later claim they were not involved. It was one of the oldest tricks in the book. Collective responsibility, Thripp had called it. Mutual guilt he meant. It was the best way to ensure no one ever talked.

With rising apprehension, Mallory followed the exodus to the four-wheel drives and trucks waiting outside, engines running.

'I'm getting out of this,' Tallboys hissed as he walked alongside.

'How?' Pete Stafford asked earnestly. 'You told me yourself what they did to Hal.'

'Shit. I don't know how,' the Scot returned testily. 'I'll think of something, make a break. Somehow get clean away – even if it means going into hiding.'

'It will,' Mallory warned.

'What about you?' Stafford asked.

'Life's too short. I'll stay on while the money's good. But don't worry, I'm no grass. Just don't tell me your plans. What I don't know, I can't say. Right?'

Tallboys stared at him as he halted beside a truck, waiting for the others to climb aboard. 'I can't make you out, Kurt. You're not an animal like these. Yet you killed Pedro and you blew up those Bolivians in the Chapare. It doesn't make sense.'

'You're starting to sound like Thripp,' Mallory replied tartly.

Stafford said: 'Whatever you're planning, Doug, count me in.'

It was their turn to scramble aboard the truck.

Armed Colombians encircled the little chapel on the rocky outcrop at Cruz de Oro. They stood around in small groups, chatting and laughing and smoking, weapons slung carelessly over their shoulders. They had about them the air of victors after some great battle, yet Mallory sensed it had been a grossly unequal struggle with defenceless peasants snatched from their beds. Half a dozen women watched, weeping, babies clutched in their arms and young children tugging at their skirts.

Harry Morgan climbed out of the lead Rocsta and marched purposefully towards the shut doors of the chapel, his motley band of gringos trailing behind. The line of Colombians respectfully parted to allow them through.

As he reached the entrance, one of the village women broke through the cordon, wriggling and twisting to avoid the grasping hands of the Colombian guards. She fell to her knees at Morgan's feet, clutching at his knees, half beseeching, half praying.

'For Christ's sake,' he growled. 'What's she ranting about?'

Mallory said: 'Her husband is inside. She's begging you to release him. Says she'll do anything you want if you let him go. She means you can have her.'

Morgan's nose wrinkled in disgust. 'God, she must be joking. Get rid of her. Tell her there's a price to be paid for defying us.'

As the Colombians grabbed her by the shoulders and hauled her away, Morgan angrily pushed open the ancient timber doors.

Mallory hadn't been at all certain what to expect, but it really wasn't this. Not in his most troubled dreams could he have envisaged such a macabre sight.

Shafts of sulphur-yellow light poured in from the windows on the east side; it created a suffused and unearthly glow with dust motes swirling like flecks of powdered gold, blurring shape and form and deepening the shadows.

315

He narrowed his eyes for better definition, picking out the life-sized carving of the Crucifixion on the left and on the right the row of plaster saints along the rough stone wall. His gaze was drawn between the timber pews and down the aisle to the chancel steps.

There stood Victor Tafur and his daughter Juanita, still in their nightclothes. Both had their hands bound with rope behind their backs; both were gagged and blindfolded so that they were staring sightlessly at the young men who sat in the first of the pews – the same stoic young men who had found the courage and taken the risk of joining the priest and the farmer in the arms ambush but now regretting their action as they sat with hands clenched nervously under the smug gaze of two armed Colombian thugs.

Most stared at their feet, not wanting to see what stood before their eyes, not daring to admit to themselves that this was the result of *their* folly. But others had to look, were mesmerised in shock at the sight of Father León in his black cassock standing on the altar with his arms tied, a rope noose running from his neck up and over the rough eucalyptus crossbeam above his head.

A lump formed like a fist in Mallory's throat as he followed Morgan and the others down the aisle. His heart began to thud, the rush of blood loud in his ears. He gripped his fists until his knuckle bones showed white through the skin. He wanted to turn round and run, run far away from this place, but there was nowhere to run to and nowhere to hide.

At the chancel he joined Tallboys and Pete Stafford with others on the left, Thripp, Mick Pye and Derek Rutter grouping on the right.

Harry Morgan turned to face his captive audience in the front pews. 'Right, you lot, you've had your fun. Now it's our turn.' He looked at Mallory. 'Okay, Kurt, translate if you please.'

Mallory was hardly aware of what he was hearing or what he was saying. That it was *they* who were responsible for what was about to happen to them. This was the result of *their* betrayal and non-co-operation. Blah, blah.

Morgan laughed. 'Here beginneth the first and last lesson. Thou shalt obey the White Viper.'

Mick Pye gave a frenzied little cry of glee at his boss's crude witticism.

They must have planned what happened next, discussed it in considerable detail; probably while drinking late into the previous night. Because without an order being given every one of Morgan's closest colleagues appeared to know what to do. It was that which made the whole thing doubly horrendous. The pre-meditated malice of it all.

Thripp stepped up to Victor Tafur and stripped the blindfold from his face. The old man blinked at the sudden exposure to light, his cheeks bulging against the gag that cut into the corners of his mouth. Wide eyes appealed to his captor but were ignored. It was then that the Swinyard brothers came forward, one on each side of Juanita, roughly grabbing hold of her arms so that she couldn't struggle as Mick Pye stepped in front of her. He removed her blindfold and loosened the cloth gag, letting it fall around her throat.

'So you are the little cow who killed Billy Susan,' he sneered, his face inches from hers. 'Just a skinny, smelly farmer's daughter.'

A frown fractured the smooth olive skin of her brow as she tried to follow his words. She moved her parched mouth and sought to soften her palate with some saliva so she could speak. 'Your friend, he was a bad man. He killed my husband and Comisario Pulgarin would do nothing. Your friend deserved to die.'

That appeared to amuse Mick Pye like everything did. 'Deserved to die, did he? Well, God knows what I deserve, you little cow, because I'm a far worse man than Billy Susan ever was!'

A howl of approval went up from Pye's closest friends. He turned and grinned at them, clearly pleased with himself and his wit. He wasn't expecting the pellet of spittle that hit him square in the centre of his cheek. The low howl of mirth from the captured audience was spontaneous and quickly petered out as the livid bloom of rage spread across Pye's face.

'Bitch!' he snapped, wiping the stuff from his skin. 'That's the second time you've done that today. And it'll be the last!'

He reached out and grabbed the neck of her long cotton night-dress. With one mighty stroke his hand ripped down through the vertical line of buttons. Little white discs of mother-of-pearl spun like stars, scattering over the cold terracotta tiles. The Swinyards grabbed the sleeves of the material and jerked them down over her bare shoulders.

'*BAJERÓ! BAJERÓ!*' she screamed before Pye's fist landed hard in her solar plexus and she doubled over in pain.

The men in front of her were agog, not at her nakedness, but with sheer terror at what was taking place.

'Put that gag back on her,' Pye ordered and Tom Swinyard obliged, pulling it so tight that it forced her lips into a distorted grinning sneer like a horse with a bit between its teeth. 'Open your legs.'

She didn't obey, probably didn't understand in her frozen terror, but it didn't matter because the Swinyards reached down and pulled her knees wide apart so that she was standing in a humiliating half-crouch with her long hair falling over her face.

Above them on the altar Father León tried to speak, his words muffled by the gag, until Rutter gave the free end of the noose a gentle tug so that it tightened around his throat. Juanita's father turned his head away, blinded by his tears.

For a moment the silence was stunning and absolute; those who could look were transfixed with horror. Rutter began the slow handclap and then the others started to applaud and laugh with approval.

Mallory turned his head away. God, it was never meant to be like this! If only Mario could have foreseen where his impetuous suggestion would lead!

Derek Rutter was next, then the Swinyards. Others followed, including Guy Thripp.

Mallory glared down at his arched back and all he could think was: this was the bastard who saved my life. His ineptitude got me shot, but then the bastard's first aid saved me! The thought rattled round and round inside his skull, trying to make sense of it all.

Why did that somehow make it worse? Make him hate the man all the more? Of all the people in the world he had to owe this man his life.

Again he weighed up the chances and the odds, the permutations of trying to stop what was happening. And again the answer was the same. It would be suicidal. Some twenty-five of Harry Morgan's gringos, armed, drunk and spoiling for a fight. Then a few Colombian thugs guarding the reluctant audience and a score more ringing the chapel outside. Even if he used his gun, how many could he kill before he himself was taken out? Three or four at best – and he'd blow his cover and the entire operation in the process.

He felt the phantom pain in his chest where his lung had been tingling sharply like electricity, reminding him what it was like to believe you were kneeling at death's door.

No, play it cool, a voice whispered urgently in his head. Juanita will survive this and they're just playing silly games with the priest, putting the frighteners on him and his followers. Make the wrong move for the right motives now and you'll get half of them killed in some ultimately pointless firefight.

God, he felt so helpless, so empty. Cowed and intimidated like only Brother Hermann had ever made him feel.

Thripp laughed as he zipped up his jeans. He was getting drunk now, like the rest of them. And as another bottle was handed to him and another man took his place, he looked up at the gagged priest who stood above him with eyes closed.

'Praying,' Thripp said, his speech beginning to slur. 'The bastard's praying. Who the hell does he think he is, standing up there like he's fuckin' Christ Almighty?' He grabbed a machete from one of the laughing Colombian guards, climbed up onto the altar and sliced through the fabric of the priest's cassock, ripping it away down the front to reveal the thin alabaster body and worn white underpants. Contemptuously, Thripp ran the razor edge of the blade through the elastic waist and leg hole so the garment fell away in tatters to reveal the priest's fear-shrivelled genitals.

'Don't think he fancies our little Juanita,' Pye laughed. 'Fuckin' queer. All priests are fuckin' faggots.'

Rutter turned to Mallory. 'Your turn, Kurt!' A giggle. 'Why don't you give it to 'er up the arse? Bring a smile to both their faces.'

Mallory swallowed hard, finding it difficult to think of a reply and difficult to disguise the loathing with which he spoke the words. 'C'mon, Derek, I'm not pokin' that little whore. I don't want the bloody clap.'

'Ah, forgot to bring a condom, did we?' Pye jeered. Hoots of derision rose from the rest of the gang waiting eagerly for their turn.

It was then that Doug Tallboys made his move. He'd been standing beside Mallory and Pete Stafford, staring in blind rage at the events unfolding before his eyes. He'd known his fellow countrymen and their Colombian enforcers were capable of cruel intimidation, but he'd never envisaged anything quite like this. At last, suddenly, he snapped.

Stepping forward to the edge of the altar, he snatched up the Ingram that Rutter had left there while he'd taken his turn with the girl.

'STOP IT, ALL OF YOU!' he screamed, waving the gun in the air.

Everyone stopped and looked.

Bad move, Mallory knew, but nevertheless his hand instinctively reached towards his own gun holstered beneath his jacket. Even together they would be hopelessly outnumbered unless Tallboys found a lot more allies amongst the silent minority.

'Don't be stupid, Doug,' Harry Morgan called out. 'The boys are just having some fun. Remember what these people did to Billy.'

'Billy was a cheap thug,' Tallboys snarled, 'like the rest of you!'

Another bad move, Mallory thought.

Tallboys's eyes blazed as he kept the Ingram pointed, swaying back and forth to cover the other gang members and the line of guns already aiming at him. It was obvious he was no fighting soldier, more at home with spanners than with guns.

He glanced back at Stafford. 'Well, what about it, Pete? Here's our chance!'

Mallory caught the young man's eye and gave a warning look. The Scotsman was heading for a fall. Stafford was hesitant and forced a smile. 'What's the matter, Doug, where's your sense of humour?'

Tallboys glared, feeling betrayed.

Thripp stepped forward until he stood just feet before the pointed muzzle of the Scotsman's sub-machine gun. 'That's the trouble with engineers. Good with vehicles but know sod all about guns.' He nodded towards the Ingram. 'You've left the safety on.'

Doug Tallboys glanced down at the weapon in his hands. And Thripp had him. His movement was a blur, snatching the gun with one hand and stepping forward for an over-thigh body throw that sent Tallboys slamming against the chancel steps.

Thripp looked down at the Scotsman who was nursing the cracked bone in his elbow. 'I did warn you, Doug. And you made one mistake in your reckoning. That you're indispensable as our engineer. Wrong. We've found a replacement who's far more suited to our line of work. He joins us next week. So now you've just gone and speeded up events.'

Harry Morgan joined Thripp, standing by his side. 'You know Stan Summers's favourite little saying, Doug. The boss always says those who are not with us are against us.'

Doug's pale grey eyes stared up at them as he wiped some blood from his mouth. It was almost as though he had a premonition of what was coming next. Perhaps he had, because he showed no surprise when Morgan pulled the stubby 9mm pistol from his jacket pocket. Made no protest before the single blast echoed around the little chapel of Cruz de Oro.

Mallory winced and was instantly swamped with a feeling of guilt and shame. Knowing it would have been crazy to have intervened, but still now wishing he had.

The wild atmosphere of orgiastic mayhem died in an instant, the sense of drunken revelry burst like a balloon. Morgan turned to Thripp, clearly ill-tempered at the change of mood. 'Okay, get it over with.'

Guy Thripp gave a brief nod of approval to the Swinyard twins. They knew exactly what was expected of them. Tom drew the

321

heavy sack of grain with its attached rope onto the altar and fixed it around Father León's ankles. Meanwhile Jerry scrambled up and stood behind the half-naked priest, tightened the noose and checked that the far end of the rope was now firmly anchored to a wooden beam.

He looked at Harry Morgan. Morgan nodded. Jerry Swinyard shoved the gagged priest hard in the small of the back, catching him unawares.

The audience caught its breath as Father León toppled from the altar, lurching towards them until the rope checked him and pulled him back, just as the sack of grain was kicked away. Its dead weight dropped and the rope sprang taut. The snap of the priest's spinal cord was clearly audible.

After a few seconds of involuntary twitching like a failed escapologist, the bound and hanging corpse started slowly to turn, first one way and then the other.

Harry Morgan stepped in front of it. 'Now, I'm sure you people realise you have a choice. You hand back the stolen weapons and swear allegiance to us or you are against us. Raise your hands if you are with us.' He turned towards Mallory. 'Give 'em the message, if you please.'

He could scarcely think straight. He was shaken to the core, unable to marshal his thoughts let alone his words. Making a hash of it, he translated three times before he got it right.

One by one, the hands went up. No one declined Morgan's offer to join them, to swear loyalty.

'Right,' the boss said, 'tell them to leave now, Kurt. Our men will go with each of them to bring the weapons back.'

The audience was all too eager to leave, the chapel emptying fast. Harry Morgan followed, leading his men away until at last only Mallory, the Tafurs and Pye remained, the gangster fascinated by the gently gyrating corpse of the priest in its tattered cassock.

Pye grinned. 'Always wondered if it was true.'

'What?'

'That a hanged man always dies with an enormous hard-on.'

Mallory didn't need to look. 'It's true.'

322

Something about the certainty with which Mallory said it unsettled Pye. He grinned awkwardly. 'The ultimate orgasm, eh, death? Ready to fuck the angels.' Inexplicably he began to feel hot about the collar. 'Need a bit of fresh air. Be a mate and release the farmer will you, Kurt?'

Mallory watched him scurry out of the door, before he turned back to the altar. The priest still twisted slowly on the rope, the eucalyptus beam creaking gently under the strain. Below the dangling feet lay Juanita, unmoving, her naked body still splattered with mucus, her legs open and abandoned, hovering on the verge of unconsciousness, her mind and body in shock, paralysed. Her eyes staring blankly at the corpse above her head.

He turned to Victor Tafur. The man was as still and cold as an ice sculpture while Mallory gently released the cloth gag. His eyes were strange, fathomless. Mallory slid out one of his Chinese knives.

'Going to kill me?'

Mallory could find no words to speak as he cut through the binding ropes. Nothing he could say would explain to the old man why he had been obliged just to stand by and let it happen.

'You may as well. I have seen hell on earth today. Death can be no worse.' He looked closely into the Englishman's eyes. 'I was right after all, you are no friend of mine.'

Mallory turned silently away and began the long walk up the aisle to the door where the villagers had begun to gather, whispering nervously to each other as the story began to spread. It was they who would have to cut down the dead priest and take care of Juanita and her father. It was best, and only fitting, that they should be left to look after their own.

Accusing eyes followed him as he passed. A woman crossed herself, praying for his soul.

He stepped out into the brilliant midday sun, but today its warmth didn't manage to reach him. And it was quiet. So quiet, he noticed as he walked away, that not even a bird sang.

14

It was after dark when the hooker left the dosshouse hotel in Adoración.

Her trade was made plain by the shiny pink skirt she wore. It was short and clingfilm tight, emphasising her compact and slightly muscular figure. With her flowing black hair and dark glasses, she bore no resemblance to the pretty United Nations aid official who had a short pageboy cut, wore only a hint of make-up and had arrived a few hours earlier wearing a smart chino travel suit. In fact that woman had retired early with a migraine, and was no doubt asleep in a darkened room as the hooker passed the white-painted UN Cherokee without appearing to notice it.

She crossed the street and walked past a row of adobe dwellings and shuttered shops until she arrived at El Tigre. A few scruffy local men absently eyed her up and down as she walked by their tables, but it was still too early for the business of the night to begin. Perhaps they wondered why they didn't recognise her? Had one of the regular *putas* changed her hairstyle or was she new in town? But if they did wonder, they didn't do so for long, because they had other things on their minds – rumours that something bizarre and horrendous had happened at Cruz de Oro that morning. There were whispers of massacre and rape. Someone even said that the priest was dead. But no one yet knew anything for certain.

The hooker walked through the archway and into the adjoining bordello. For a moment she looked lost as she viewed the sparsely furnished lounge where the girls sat around waiting for the first customers to arrive. They regarded the stranger with sullen and undisguised hostility.

'What do you want?' asked the girl called Lucila.

'Señora Lacera.'

'Are you the girl from Bogotá? The one who Señor Kurt asks for?' She sounded hurt.

'Yes.'

Lucila regarded her with thinly hidden disapproval. 'You don't look so special. You're welcome to him.'

Another of the *putas* joined Lucila. 'But you're not welcome here, taking our trade.'

A sympathetic smile appeared below the dark glasses. 'It's just for tonight. We used to be quite good friends. I go tomorrow.'

Lucila suppressed her feeling of jealousy for this mysterious and sophisticated whore from her customer's past. It was unusual that anyone should go to so much trouble. Invite this girl, pay her bus fare and ask Fanny Lacera to provide the bed. But you never knew with men; they were such strange creatures. Vaguely she wondered what tricks this *puta* knew that made her so special and she felt an absurd compulsion to let her know she was just as good. 'He is a nice man. In fact we are friends, too.'

The smile melted. 'Really? Good for you.'

Fanny Lacera waddled out from her office. 'Ah, the lady for Señor Kurt. I thought I heard a strange voice.' She started towards the stairs. 'Follow me, will you?'

The rickety planking creaked and groaned beneath their feet as Fanny led the way along a dark, narrow corridor to the end room. She knocked before opening the door. Mallory and Dale Forster were already there, waiting.

'Your lady friend,' she announced, enjoying the subterfuge. 'I'll bring the other two up as soon as they arrive. Don't worry, no one will overhear you. I've kept the adjoining rooms free until you've finished.'

As she left and shut the door, Forster said to Savage: 'You look good in that outfit. Perhaps you've missed your true vocation.'

'Stow it, Dale,' she retorted and pulled off the wig, shaking her hair free. 'What's been happening, Kurt?'

He was smoking and his hands had still not stopped trembling completely following the events at the chapel. 'It all went pear-

325

shaped this morning. Before he flew out, Stan Summers organised a security clamp-down on the locals in order to get their guns back. They killed the priest and raped Tafur's daughter in front of everyone.'

Savage opened her mouth in a barely audible, 'Christ.'

Quickly he described what had happened, omitting some of the messier details. He had only just finished when Mario and Goldie were shown in.

The moment Fanny Lacera left them alone, Mario pointed an accusing finger at Mallory. 'You did nothing! You watched that child get raped and you did nothing.'

Savage intervened. 'There was nothing Kurt *could* do, Mario. Be reasonable. Tallboys tried it, and look where it got him.'

'Maybe if he'd had some support . . .'

'Forget it,' Goldie said. 'It would have been suicidal.'

'But the state of that girl,' Mario said in impotent fury, tears welling in his eyes.

'You've seen her?' Forster asked.

'We arrived back at the ranch just after they did. They were both like zombies, Juanita and her old man. All the spirit has left them both.'

'Where are they now?' Savage asked.

'Staying with friends,' Goldie replied, 'on one of the outlying farms. The whole family's in hiding in case the Vipers come back for them. They've asked us to organise a lorry to load all their furniture so they can move to Bogotá.'

'That's not our concern,' Forster said. 'You're getting involved again. In fact, none of this would have happened, Mario, if you hadn't suggested they snatch the arms shipment.'

Mario glared and jabbed his forefinger upward in a gesture of defiance. 'Up yours, gringo! Something had to be done for those people!'

'But it wasn't *your* place to do it.'

Mallory intervened. 'It would have happened sooner or later. That or something similar. Father León was determined to make some sort of stand. What we need to do now is make sure none of the Viper gang escapes the net. And the sooner the better.'

326

'Four more days,' Forster said. 'That's what was agreed, and even that is pushing it for hitting Venezuela and Bolivia at the same time.'

'Then you'll miss Harry Morgan. The day after tomorrow he's flying to Medellín for a meeting with Felix Bastidas.'

The American shook his head. 'We won't miss him, Kurt, I promise you that. Georgie and I will take care of it. Do you know where he's having his meeting with Bastidas?'

'The Casa Verde, some posh restaurant for the filthy rich on Yariante Las Palmas. Bastidas likes his long lunches.'

'Then it'll be the longest lunch he ever has.'

'But you'll be back for the big day?' Mallory asked.

Forster winked. 'I wouldn't miss it for the world.'

'When do we strike?' Mario asked, not bothering to hide his enthusiasm.

'At the witching hour plus one,' Mallory replied. 'One in the morning. I'll get rid of the guard on the north perimeter fence. I'll use a green flashlight. Three for go. Five for abort. Likewise for you. Bring the bolt cutters.'

Goldie grinned. 'I'll bring more than bolt cutters, my friend.'

Later, the hooker from Bogotá left El Tigre and returned to her hotel, slipping past the unmanned reception desk to the room occupied by the female UN official.

Mallory left a few minutes after to return to the mining camp. On the stairs he passed Lucila and Thripp on the way up. He gave a nod of acknowledgement but did not stop to speak.

Lucila hesitated on the staircase and watched him go. 'And I think he is different from all the rest.'

'What?'

'Señor Kurt. I think he is a kind man, that I am special to him.' The wounded pride showed in her voice.

Thripp was dismissive. 'Him? He's just a tramp.'

'I don't think so. He has seen so much of the world, knows so much.'

'Yeah?' It didn't sound like a description of Kurt Hulse he'd recognise. No one at the camp had completely taken to him.

Except Stan Summers, of course, who valued his linguistic expertise. And Doug Tallboys, who was now buried in a shallow grave up in the *cuchillas*.

'But he lied to me. He has this friend, this whore who he pays to come all the way from Bogotá.'

That definitely didn't sound like Kurt Hulse. 'When?'

'Tonight.'

'Where is she staying?'

'I don't know.'

'What was her name?'

Lucila shrugged. 'Maybe Doña Lacera knows.' She tightened her grip around his waist. 'C'mon, I will show you just how special I can be to a man who gives me extra dollar!'

On the way up they brushed by a tall, fair-haired American coming down. Guy Thripp knew who he was. A researcher from the United Nations assessing an aid programme for the area. Thripp made a point of knowing who everyone was in the little settlement; in fact he had quite an effective network of informers, of whom Lucila was only one. Someone would know the name of the mystery whore from Bogotá.

The next morning after an early breakfast the two UN researchers left town by road for Santa Maria. Once back at the rooms they had kept on at El Imperial hotel, Forster put through a call to the private pilot he kept on retainer at Bucaramanga. Within twenty minutes the man was airborne and on his way.

Forster drove Savage to the strip. 'Will you come back before it happens?'

She nodded. 'If all goes well. I don't want to miss the big day.'

'Good luck.' He smiled awkwardly, never sure how prickly this Brit girl would be. 'Or should I say break a leg.'

There was a hint of a grin on her face. 'That's better. You're learning.'

She leaned forward and kissed him quickly on the cheek. Then, picking up her small grip, she walked out to the taxiing aircraft.

It was three o'clock when she landed in Cali. She took a taxi to the Hotel Menéndes and went straight to her room, telling the receptionist she had a migraine and didn't wish to be disturbed. Hanging the sign on the door to her room, she made one phone call before changing into jeans and a blouse and applying more make-up. The long black-haired wig and spectacles with plain glass lenses completed the transformation. Slipping out of her room, she left the hotel by the back way.

After walking several blocks and making three textbook checks to ensure she was not being followed, she found a taxi rank and told the first driver to take her to the park that ran beside the Rio Cali.

Although Jaramillo's lawyer had earlier told her that their offices were electronically swept each morning, Savage was taking no risks.

The rendezvous was at a park bench by the river, Maria Palechor as elegant as ever in a charcoal business suit, her dark hair long and wavy.

'Let's walk,' Savage said.

'Sure.' And after a few moments: 'So what is happening?'

'We're going in to finish the business.'

'Yes?'

'In three days. On the fifth.'

'That's splendid. My client will be delighted.'

'Then the final payment will fall due.'

'Everything is ready. To the bank in the Caribbean, the new arrangement.'

Savage confirmed. 'Then this will be the last time we meet.'

Palechor had an instinct for these things. 'There is something else?'

'There's a loose end and we need your help.'

'If we can.'

'The head man, Harry Morgan, will not be there. But we know where he will be and who he'll be with. I need an explosive device with a timer. Not big, no more than a pound of plastic explosive.'

'I see. When?'

'By tomorrow morning.'

There was a low whistle as Maria Palechor sucked in her breath through her perfect white teeth. 'That is tight.'

329

'And I need one of your enforcers, someone reliable and experienced to place it.'

'It could be arranged, I think.'

'It's important.'

'My client will want to know the other target, the man who is meeting with Harry Morgan.'

Savage hesitated. 'For obvious reasons I'd prefer to keep it between me and the placer. Clearly, the more people who know . . .'

'I can tell you my client will not agree unless he knows. He could be the target himself. Stranger things have happened in Colombia.'

Savage drew a deep breath. 'Felix Bastidas.'

Maria Palechor stopped walking and looked at Savage. Had she heard correctly? Felix Bastidas, the elusive young pretender to their resurgent rivals in Medellín. 'Where is the meeting to take place? My client will want to know that too.'

'The Casa Verde restaurant in Medellín. A private room is booked for lunch. Your placer will need cover and experience to talk his way in before they arrive.' Savage had never had to set up a cold-blooded execution like this before; she thought it was as awful as having to kill someone herself. Suddenly, irrationally, she was overcome with impatience. 'Well?'

The sleek lawyer smiled and tossed her hair as she looked out across the sunlit river. 'I think I can say that Ruiz Jaramillo would guarantee you heaven and earth for such a prize.'

'Are you sure?' Thripp demanded irritably. He'd been in a foul mood since he'd received the radio message relayed from Medellín. Felix Bastidas and Harry Morgan dead, blown to smithereens in a restaurant bomb blast. The news had shocked him to the core.

'I'm positive,' Mick Pye replied evenly. 'It's as though the woman didn't exist.'

'Tell me.'

'I took one of the Colombians with me to visit Fanny Lacera. She said Kurt only ever referred to the woman by name once.

330

Thought it was Martha. He said she was a special friend he'd met in Bogotá. Fanny got the impression this woman was a whore who Kurt had got kind of friendly with. Now he had a few pesos in his pocket he wanted to pay for her to come down to Adoración and stay over. He rented a room off Fanny.'

Thripp scratched at his chin. 'That strikes me as an odd thing to do. None of our other lads has done anything like that.'

Pye shrugged. 'No, but then unlike Kurt, they don't know anyone down here. Some of the Colombian gang have paid for wives and girlfriends to come and stay at the hotel in Adoración to stop relationships breaking up.'

'Where did this Martha woman stay?'

'Everyone assumed the hotel, but I checked. No one of that name or anyone resembling her description. In fact the only woman staying there was someone from the UN.' Pye warmed to his subject. 'Something else strange. We spoke to the guy who runs the café at the bus terminal. He didn't remember anyone coming or going who could have been her.'

Thripp didn't know whether to be suspicious or not, suddenly aware that the tentacles of paranoia were tightening their grip and he was unable to stop them. 'Maybe she came by taxi and no one saw her.'

'In that one-horse town, boss? You've got to be kidding. A taxi arriving is a major social event. Someone would have known.'

Thripp considered carefully. Only three people knew that Harry Morgan had a scheduled meeting with Felix Bastidas. Himself and Stan Summers and Kurt Hulse who had been in the room at the time, helping Summers with some Customs documentation written in Spanish.

Of course the leak could have emanated from the Colombian side. Whoever had been responsible for the explosion – the DEA or the Colombian anti-drugs police or a rival cartel – could have an informer on the inside of the Bastidas operation. Someone who knew the time and place in advance.

And yet – he thought again about the scruffy Englishman he knew as Kurt Hulse.

'Things only started going wrong when Kurt turned up,' Pye

said, as though reading his boss's mind. 'Killing Pedro Goméz was just the beginning. Then Billy Susan. Kurt was one of the few who knew the details of the arms shipment and he knew that film sound recordist who was at the ambush. Now this.'

'Coincidence?' Thripp murmured.

'Let's find out. Talk to him. Wait till he's asleep tonight, then grab him from his bed when he can't get to his gun or those fucking knives of his. Put the frighteners on him. I'll soon find out if this has been coincidence or not, I promise you, boss.'

'You don't like him, do you?'

'No.' The dull eyes were unblinking. 'Never have.'

'Get some of the lads together. Discreet like. Meet here in half an hour.'

Mallory knew he dared not sleep. Wouldn't have been able to anyway, even if he tried.

He withdrew his hand from the moth-eaten sleeping bag and held the luminous dial of the cheap watch to his eyes.

Midnight. Just one hour to go. One hour before he was due to slip out into the night and make his way to the northern perimeter fence. Two Colombian sentries to dispose of before he signalled to Mario and Goldie who would be out there in the darkness.

His heart began to palpitate at the prospect, the fear starting to pump the adrenalin too soon, draining his mind as well as the strength from his body. A sort of blind, paralysing panic beginning to smother him. And the fear making him sweat. He could feel it gathering in the small of his back and between his thighs.

Just how many nights had he spent like this? Almost every one since he'd arrived at the camp, but never quite as bad as this. Lying in his cot, listening to the uneven snores of the Colombians and the endless chorus of cicadas beyond the open window. Restless, sticky and frightened. Never knowing when he'd get it wrong. Make just one small mistake and alert the enemy's suspicions. Seeing shapes in the shadows. Bent figures creeping towards him, knives or machetes hidden beneath their black cloaks. Drifting faces of men he'd known and destroyed.

332

Destroyed in the name of the Father. The dark angel of revenge. How long, he wondered, before the tables were turned on him and it would be he who heard the approaching flap of wings?

He moved his head suddenly and saw it at the window. Perched with huge talons on the sill, its eyes glinting, head cocked and its beak hooked, the hunched shoulders outlined in black against the ultramarine sky and the moon. Nighthawk or vulture? Did it matter? He knew it was coming for him.

He awoke with a jolt. There was nothing at the window. No bird, no moon. Exhausted, he had drifted into the twilight world on the edge of sleep. Again he held his watch up to his eyes. Five to one. Time enough. He couldn't bear the thought of lying there for a second longer.

Sliding his legs from the sleeping bag he sat on the edge of the cot to pull on his shirt and jacket, then dragged his leather boots over his bare feet. He went silently to the window, peered out, then slid over the sill and dropped to the alleyway that ran between the huts. For a moment he crouched, watching and listening intently for any sign of movement before creeping through the shadows to the vehicle park. From there he could see that everywhere was in darkness, nothing stirring.

He frowned. Faint light showed through the rattan blind of Guy Thripp's hut. Someone else suffering from insomnia? No doubt the man had been shaken by the news that Bastidas and Harry Morgan were dead. Perhaps he sensed the end was near? Was he aware of the darkness closing in on him?

Mallory turned his head away and dipped into the deep and shadowy lee of another outhouse, keeping himself hidden by the row of Rocstas and pick-ups. When he reached the last vehicle he peered around its tailgate.

The watchtower was thirty metres away, standing beside the chain-link fence with its spiralled crown of razor wire. It wasn't very high, the observation platform built on twenty-foot lengths of eucalyptus and reached by a crude timber ladder. He could just distinguish the vague outline of the guard hunched over the rail.

A flicker of light caught Mallory's attention at ground level. The second guard was brewing a small pan of coffee on a camping stove beneath the platform, his cigarette showing as a pin-prick glow of red.

There was no time to lose. Mallory moved like a wraith, low and slow, rolling each foot silently as he closed in – the art of the stalking huntsman he had learned as a boy in Paraguay and never forgotten.

His right hand located the loop of baling twine in his jacket pocket; he transferred the other end of it to his left hand as he glided forward. A quick flick of one wrist and then the other, coiling it tight in readiness to take the immense strain of a man fighting for his life.

Just a few more feet. The shoulders hunched in front of him, the light of the stove flame glistening on the rough mop of hair. Hissing gas now audible, the smell of tobacco smoke and body odour. Mallory towered behind the crouched figure. His arms slowly raised above his head. The baling twine pulled taut. Poised. For one split second he closed his eyes. Now! Do it!

His arms dropped over the guard's head, his wrists thudding on the man's shoulders before pulling sharply back, snapping the twine tight into the soft flesh of the exposed larynx. Mallory's knee pressed into the offered back, pushing it forward at the same time as he drew the garrotte back with so much force that the muscles in his arms began to tremble. His fists crossed over each other, his forearms locked together.

Only a soft, bubbling gurgle escaped the guard's lips before the baling twine cut off his ability to speak and denied oxygen to his brain. Big hands and dirty nails scrabbled desperately at the ever-tightening necklace of death. His feet tried to shuffle but the pain was too great and the effort was half-hearted. The will to resist was ebbing, fingers falling away from his throat. Mallory heard the tell-tale rattle and felt the body go slack. The head lolled.

He stepped back, gently laying out the corpse on the ground. Still the stove hissed on unheeded.

'Gerardo!' A voice called from above. 'What's going on down there?'

Mallory's heart stopped. He took a deep breath. 'It's me, Kurt, I couldn't sleep. Gerardo's made the coffee. Shall I bring yours up.' Positive suggestion.

'Sure, my friend, my mouth tastes like a parrot's cage.' A hoarse laugh. 'Too many cigarillos.'

Mallory took the pan from the stove and poured the contents into a mug; then he began the climb.

At that moment Guy Thripp burst into the Colombians' bunk-house. Derek Rutter and Mick Pye yelled as the Swinyard brothers ran down the aisle between the cots, waving their flashlights and waking everyone.

'Kurt's gone!' Jerry shouted. 'His bed's empty!'

'He no sleep so good,' one Colombian said and pointed to the window. 'No sleep, go walk sometime.'

'Okay,' Thripp said. 'Let's find him.'

Mallory climbed to the observation platform and handed over the mug. He knew the guard, a man called Gustavo. Pleasant enough; simple and friendly until he drank too much. He sipped at the coffee and stared out into the inky void. 'So, Kurt, what do you think about the death of Harry Morgan and Felix Bastidas? A bad omen, eh? Is it going to be a problem?'

Not for you, old son.

Mallory slipped one of his Chinese knives from its scabbard. He edged up behind Gustavo, murmuring in an absent sort of way: 'There'll be problems, I'm sure, but we'll get over them. Life is full of problems.'

The man laughed. 'Some more serious than others,' he said with feeling.

'Too true.'

Mallory's left arm swung over Gustavo's shoulder and around his face, his forearm jerking back, smashing into the Colombian's mouth and cutting off his cry of alarm. Mallory's fingers scrabbled to find the man's right ear, gripped its flabby edge and pulled it forward. At the same time he lifted the knife in his right fist and held the point just below and behind the ear. Then he jabbed, hard, feeling the flesh yield under the pressure, splitting like thin silk. The blade began to disappear. One inch. Two.

Then three.

Gustavo was dead, the brain disconnected from the rest of his body. Mallory took the weight, lowering it to the platform floor. He tried to extract the knife, the blade resisting. Finally he jerked it free, wiping it on the dead man's shirt.

Then he heard the commotion. Running men and shouts from the direction of the bunkhouse. Torches flashing, beams cutting across the vehicle park, playing along the perimeter fence. He heard someone shouting his name. The voices were English, not Colombian.

'He's not in the latrines!' someone yelled. It sounded like Mick Pye.

'Then where the hell is he?'

'SOMEONE TURN THE FUCKING FLOODLIGHTS ON!'

That had been Guy Thripp, Mallory was sure of it. His heart began to race, but there was nothing he could do. He was stuck at the top of the observation platform with a corpse at his feet and a knife in his hand. And not even a parapet to hide behind, just a thin timber rail.

Suddenly the lights came on, blinding after the darkness. Shielding his eyes, Mallory looked down and saw them. Thripp and Pye and Rutter. The Swinyards were there too; all of the leading clique.

All he had now, he decided, was bluff. 'GUY! UP HERE! SOMETHING'S GOING ON, THE GUARDS HAVE BEEN KILLED!'

Malevolent eyes followed the sound of his voice, the men turning round, and he could see that they were all armed.

Pye glanced uncertainly at Thripp, but the boss's suspicions remained firm. 'Come down from there, Kurt! Real slow! And throw down any weapons – including those bloody knives of yours!'

Mallory considered his options for a moment. He could use his own automatic or even pick up Gustavo's Ingram and try and take them all out in one sweeping burst. But his chances of success were small. They were professionally trained soldiers and

336

any survivors would retaliate instantly with only one inevitable consequence. He was a sitting duck. Better, he decided, to continue his bluff and sweat it out. There was no actual proof he was the killer.

Reluctantly he threw down his automatic, Gustavo's Ingram and his two knives before climbing onto the ladder.

Pye met him at the bottom, waving a handgun. 'Hands on head and turn round,' he barked.

Mallory obeyed, protesting as the man began to frisk him. 'Hell, Mick, I'm on your side! What's going on? I've just found the two guards – Gustavo was a mate of mine.'

'Stow it!' Pye hissed.

Guy Thripp said: 'Take him to my office.'

'Give me five minutes with him,' Pye offered, 'and I'll get the truth out of him.'

'Goldie' Goldstein had been looking through the Spylux night-sight and had been temporarily blinded when the vehicle park floodlights came on.

Mario scrambled alongside him. 'What's happening?'

'They've found Kurt. In the act, so to speak.'

'God! What do we do now?'

Goldie raised a hand. 'Wait a minute. They're taking him off. Interrogation, I should think. They've replaced the guard, put a man on the tower.'

'Just one?'

'Looks like it.'

'We can handle that.'

Goldie looked uncertain. 'I'd better tell Dale and Georgie.' He reached for the radio set and called them up. Their UN Cherokee was parked off the track a mile from the compound.

Savage answered and listened anxiously to the news before passing it on to Forster. 'Goldie, listen, Dale wants to call it off. He says without Kurt's inside help you'll need more support. In a day or two he can get hold of some good freelancers.'

Goldie didn't like what he heard. 'Kurt's a prisoner, Georgie, they virtually caught him in the act of eliminating the guards. He hasn't got a couple of days. He'll be lucky to have a couple of hours if they put the heat on him.'

'Could you handle it, though?'

'Sure, with a bit of luck.'

'There's no point in putting both of you at risk too.'

'But Kurt—'

She was brusque. 'Kurt knows the score. I'd like to do something but it would be suicidal. And Dale is adamant and it's his show.'

Goldie looked across at Mario and shook his head. The Martinican's eyes narrowed. He reached across and grabbed the microphone. 'Forget it, lady, we are going in.'

'Mario? Listen, God believe me, there's nothing I'd like more. But your lives are important too. I can't ask you to put yourself in unnecesaary danger, to lose three operatives for the sake of one.'

'You're not asking, señora, it is our decision. Kurt is our friend. This is organisation business now. We go ahead as planned.' He switched off and glared defiantly at Goldie. 'Well, do I speak for both of us?'

Goldie smiled. 'We'll use the rifle, I think.'

It took five minutes to assemble the special Interarms Mini-Mark X Mauser with its skeleton butt and outfitted with an 18.5 inch stainless-steel barrel with a one-in-eight-inch twist. The nightscope was a Davin IRS 218. But what made the difference was the specialised .300 Whisper rounds from SSK Industries. Most unusually this was a low-velocity sniper round. A state-of-the-art development which could be fired effectively with a suppressor attached to a range of around two hundred metres. Basically a .221 Remington Fireball case containing 240 grains of Winchester 296 powder and necked up to .30 calibre. Capable of delivering death with pinpoint accuracy in total silence.

By the time Goldie had set up the bipod and settled down prone in a comfortable cleft between the rocks, the camp floodlights had been extinguished and the lone guard had begun his vigil.

Now was the big test. The Mauser had been zeroed and the

338

rounds perfected at a Portcullis Industries' range in England before being flown out to Bogotá by executive jet. It had been hermetically sealed with sachets of silica gel, then carefully crated and carried in the pressurised passenger compartment. But since then it had endured the rigours of cross-country travel in their Fourtrak as well as a range of temperatures, both hot and damp weather. All these factors could conspire to alter the fine-tuning of the scope. Perhaps by only fractions of a millimetre, but over a hundred and fifty metres it could make all the difference between hitting the target or missing it altogether. And there was no way of knowing because there had been no opportunity to test it.

For that reason, Goldie decided to go for a head shot first. That was safest, ensuring instant death and no warning cry. If that failed, then the totally silent operation would allow him a second chance. He cranked the bolt, lined up his eye, relaxed his shoulders. The scope's multidot reticle for one-fifty metres appeared over the dark form of the hunched Colombian guard, set against the fuzzy green background of the image-intensifier nightsight. Goldie edged the dot up, over the chest, the neck. Head now in the sight. Target not moving, leaning against the tower rail.

His forefinger eased round the trigger, feeling the weight of the one-and-a-half-pound pull. Taking up the pressure. A deep, slow breath and another. Nice easy rhythm. Sweat gathering on his back. A smile spreading on his lips. Comfortable, heart rate steady. A gentle squeeze. Simultaneously he heard the firing pin strike, the lugs locking up and then the impatient hiss of escaping gas. Then nothing. It was eerie to hear just the velvet rush of displaced air as the Whisper round went on its way.

Goldie tensed, eyes transfixed. The target didn't move. Not true. The sentry didn't alter position, but gave a short flick of his head as if he'd heard something. An insect? Or the silent flight of the round sent to kill him.

'Missed,' Goldie said, ejecting the spent case and thumbing in another round.

He settled down again, ignoring the increase in tension and the butterfly flutter of his heart. Body shot this time. And hope that the error of misalignment was minimal. Centre of the body. Navel. Up slightly. Hover. Feeling good. Squeeze real slow.

The crack of the pin and the lugs locking, the sigh of gas and the soft whistle as the bullet headed down range.

There was no mistake this time. If he'd been concerned that a body shot might allow the wounded sentry to raise the alarm, he needn't have been. Being a long, heavy round it didn't expand when it struck the man's chest, it tumbled. Goldie winced. The action ripped open an enormous cavity in the sentry's torso, creating massive tissue damage that was clearly visible through the nightsight.

'Okay, mi amigo, time to go.'

Mario collected the bolt cutters and melted into the night. Goldie continued watching the distant scene while his friend clambered down the canyon spur until he found himself at the wire fence beside the watchtower. Pressing the nose of the bolt cutters into the fence he began snipping furiously at individual strands. When the aperture was cut, he left it in place, then signalled Goldie to join him.

'So, you bastard, who was that woman you met?' Mick Pye demanded.

Mallory's shirt had been stripped from his back and he'd been bound to the straight-backed chair by rope. The Swinyards were going through his pockets, examining his few possessions. 'Martha, you mean?'

'A whore?' Pye demanded.

Mallory tried to hide the fear he felt, clenching the muscles in his rectum and in his groin. If he was going to die he didn't want the ignominy of letting them see just how afraid he was. 'She was a bit more than that.'

'Where d'you meet her?'

'Bogotá.'

'Where in Bogotá?'

'Some bar.'

'Which bar?'

'A place on Calle 13.'

'The same place you met the guy who told you about us?'

'Yes.'

Pye's face was an inch from his, his breath smelling of the sugared almonds he habitually sucked. 'You're a fuckin' liar, Kurt Hulse. *If* that's your name, which I doubt. Workin' for the Cali cartel are you? Get in here, infiltrate, get rid of Felix Bastidas? What about Harry? Did Morgan just get in the way, so your people just blew him apart like so much dog meat?'

'For Christ's sake I don't have any *people*!' Mallory pleaded to be believed, 'I know nothing about all this. How could I?'

Tom Swinyard pulled something from Mallory's jacket pocket. A length of baling twine. He let it hang free. 'Proper little Boy Scout, aren't we?'

His twin brother Jerry peered closely at it. 'Blood and skin tissue. That's one of the murder weapons, boss, the guy he garrotted first.'

'That's nonsense,' Mallory protested.

Guy Thripp gave a brittle smile. 'Unfortunately we don't exactly have facilities for DNA testing here.'

'We ought to reinforce the guard,' Derek Rutter suggested. 'Perhaps he killed them in preparation for an attack. By Cali, the drugs police, the DEA—'

Mallory tried a different tack. He didn't want anyone finding Mario and Goldie out there. 'Look, okay, I admit it. I killed those two bastards, but it was just personal. They screwed me at canasta a couple of nights back. Cleared me out, cheating scum, they had it coming.'

'I don't believe you,' Pye said. He moved his lighted cigarette towards Mallory's left nipple. Mallory flinched as the hairs of his chest shrivelled under the intense heat. 'So get talking.'

Over Pye's shoulder Mallory noticed that the hut door was inching open. Then Mario's head appeared, close to floor level, followed by the stubby little barrel of a Micro-Uzi. Pye must have noticed something in Mallory's eyes, seen the momentary distraction. He turned round. 'Shit!'

Mallory lifted his legs, bending them at the knees and thrust out with his feet, hard. He caught Pye a crippling blow in the testicles that bent him double and sent him crashing sideways into Rutter who was trying to tug his revolver from his waistband.

A window shattered at the rear. Heads turned back the other way. Goldie slipped over the sill and into the room with practised dexterity. He was an incongruous sight, thin and studious-looking with his spectacles and long, wild hair but moving with the speed and precision of the professional assassin. 'All guns down,' he ordered. 'NOW!'

He edged crabwise until he was beside Mallory. His weapon still covering, he flicked open a switchblade with his left hand and sliced through the rope bonds with one effortless stroke.

Mallory was on his feet. He picked up the nearest Ingram, checked it over swiftly and joined Mario and Goldie as they lined the men up on the floor, legs spread and hands out.

'What are you, Hulse?' Thripp demanded angrily. 'Workin' for Cali? The DEA?'

Mallory didn't answer immediately, first frisking him for any hidden weapons. Satisfied, he leaned over so that his face was only inches from Thripp's. 'Me, Guy? Me and my friends work for all those you've killed directly or indirectly. All those whose lives you've ruined or made a living nightmare. We are their vengeance.'

'What?' Thripp was scared, didn't understand. The panic raised his voice several octaves. 'Who are you, for fuck's sake?'

'I am the angel of death.'

Mario laughed.

When the gang members had been bound hand and foot with heavy-duty, self-locking freezer ties, Goldie remained guarding them while Mallory and Mario set off to deal with the Colombians on duty at the compound gate. The men were in no way alarmed at the sight of the two figures sauntering towards them from the darkened camp. It was not unusual for a friend to visit during the night hours, someone with insomnia who fancied some company, a smoke and a chat, and who was sometimes thoughtful enough to bring a hot drink or a bottle of something agreeably stronger.

It was like taking candy from a baby, Mario said later. As they approached the little sand-bagged sangar with its corrugated-tin roof and back panel for protection against wind and rain, the two compact sub-machine guns appeared as if from nowhere. Without a command being given Mallory and Mario opened up, the double hail of fire converging inside the sangar. The soft stuttering burp of the silenced rounds was incongruously gentle compared with the chaos and destruction the guns created in a mere six seconds. One man of the five was still alive when they checked; Mario slit his throat.

They unlocked the gates and swung them open and Mallory signalled with his torch. It took five minutes for the Cherokee, now stripped of its UN livery, to arrive from its hiding place.

Savage looked anxious. 'Are you all right, Kurt? I was so worried.'

'I'm fine.' He glanced at Mario. 'I am blessed with some good friends.'

Dale Forster swung out of the driver's seat. 'Any problems?'

Mallory shook his head. 'Goldie's got the ringleaders secured. The others are hopefully all asleep in the bunkhouses.'

Suddenly Savage noticed the corpses strewn in attitudes of grotesque abandon around the sangar. She winced and looked away. Never before had she seen bodies so severely shot up, had somehow never imagined it might be like this. But then, she realised now, she had never allowed her mind to dwell on the final purpose of the exercise. 'To infiltrate and ultimately destroy the gang' had seemed so neat and tidy on paper. So simple. In her mind's eye she'd visualised the buildings being burned, together with the cocaine stores and the labs. Only later, much later, had she realised that the deniable nature of the operation meant that no witnesses could be left alive. She had never been so close to a 'black op' before, and never wanted to be again. Thankfully such tasks rarely featured in the peacetime rôle of SIS.

Forster had no such qualms. By the way he eagerly took his own Micro-Uzi from the vehicle and from the glow of anticipation on his face, it was clear he was looking forward to taking part. He'd been brought up on it, almost with his mother's milk. Vietnam, Laos and Cambodia, then El Salvador and Nicaragua. He was itching to get back into the fray.

After securing the gates so no one could escape, they returned to Thripp's hut. Savage's unexpected appearance might have drawn wolf whistles from the prisoners under other circumstances, but not when she had a gun pointing at them.

'Hurry up, Kurt,' she said tersely.

He grinned at her. 'Shoot if you need to.'

'I will.' But he saw that her hand was shaking slightly.

Mario and Goldie took the Colombians' bunkhouse; Mallory and Forster went to the Englishmen's quarters. At the synchronised time of two thirty both teams struck. Two men per bunkhouse, one turning left and the other right. A long burst up one line of cots and another down the facing row, tearing through sleeping bags and blankets into the bodies beneath. Then a quick flip of the mags that had been taped together, end to end, and an almost leisurely stroll down the centre aisle, putting an end to the misery of any survivors.

Forster had some trouble, had completely missed a couple of targets in his first burst but they posed no real threat. They were still half asleep and disorientated, scrambling naked from their beds, trying to find their weapons. But it had made the American sweat for a moment.

At the other end of the bunkhouse, Mallory deliberately passed over the cot where Pete Stafford slept. Now the ex-Para sat up on his mattress, hands above his head and face drained of colour.

'Kurt, what the hell's going on?'

Forster came to his side. 'Good question, Kurt, what the shit you playing at?'

Mallory said: 'Pete's okay. He wanted out.'

The American was on a high, his eyes wide and alert, riding the adrenalin wave. 'Fine, he can have out.' And his finger curled around the trigger for a three-round burst. Stafford's chest and abdomen exploded under the impact, throwing him against the back of the cot.

'Christ!' Mallory said, turning on Forster.

'Don't be a patsy, Kurt. This is no time for bleeding hearts. No witnesses. You know the rules. This is the end game.'

Mallory met the American's steely gaze, then reluctantly turned away. He couldn't bring the boy back, and Forster was right. One witness could result in a rap for mass murder and could even result in a revenge attack on British or American installations by the hard men of Medellín.

A mirror operation by Mario and Goldie at the Colombians' bunkhouse met with similar success. Later there was a brief fire-fight at the laboratory where half a dozen Colombians had become alerted by the commotion, but they were easily out-gunned and quickly silenced.

Their corpses were taken to the bunkhouses along with those of the gate sentries. Then it was a question of dousing all the buildings with anything inflammable they could find. There was no shortage of petrol, paraffin and meths. The laboratory, the coke store, the bunkhouses, cookhouse and admin huts all went up in quick succession.

Mario and Goldie ran back between the flaming buildings to the gate where the others waited. A Toyota pick-up had been loaded with Guy Thripp and the others, Mallory waiting with Savage and Forster by the Cherokee.

'All done,' Mario pronounced.

Savage looked around at the raging pyres, the reflected flames dancing in her eyes, giving a sheen to the perspiration on her face. 'God, I somehow never thought it would end like this. It's awful.'

'There'll be no evidence left,' Mallory said matter-of-factly. 'Just charred and unidentifiable corpses.'

She looked at him, an edge to her voice. 'Don't you feel any-thing, Kurt? Anything at all?'

He grinned. 'Sure. Pleased that it's nearly over.'

It took more than an hour to drive to their final destination. There was no discernible track as such, but the route was pass-able enough. They wound back and forth up the canyon slope and beyond to another valley and another peak. Savage had no idea where she was. Completely disorientated, all she knew was that they were journeying deeper and deeper into the wilderness. To the place that Mallory and Mario and Goldie had decided on.

'They won't want to talk,' Savage said as they bumped over rough ground.

Mallory didn't look at her directly. 'No. We'll fatigue them first.'

'Fatigue? That's an odd word to use.'

'Weary them, exhaust them. Then they'll talk.'

'Yes? I hope you're right, we don't have much time.'

'Don't worry, George, we'll take care of it.'

When they finally reached their destination and killed the lights it was pitch black. The sort of dense darkness you could feel, almost touch. Savage sensed it pressing in on her. All she knew was that they were on high ground, the air chill and thin. She looked up but saw no moon and no stars. Standing on ground she could not even see was uncanny. Like being in outer space, she thought, and she longed for the cloud to lift. Marooned in nothing. Just an awesome sensation of isolation, of being far beyond the reaches of any kind of civilisation.

'We'll wait until morning,' Mallory decided. 'Then we can see what we're doing. There are some nasty drops around here.'

Forster agreed. 'And our friends will be secure enough in the back of the truck.'

'I'll take first shift,' Mario offered.

Savage shivered. 'They'll probably die of hypothermia.'

Dale Forster grinned. 'They should worry about that at a time like this. You just get some shuteye.'

She heard the hammering.

It was very distant. Workmen probably, because their house in Battersea was very rickety. Not like it had been when she'd left it. Now the ceiling had caved in, the walls leaned and the floor sloped. No wonder the workmen were in. If they hadn't been, the place would have collapsed.

She felt warm and cold at the same time. Her body warm and cosy, her face chill. Cold outside air from the broken window, she thought. A shiver ran through her. She cuddled up towards Giles,

346

reached for him. He wasn't there.

More hammering.

The picture in her dream melted instantly, from snuggling warmth to the chill reality in a split second. Visions of the dark night, the shattered bodies in their macabre poses, the blazing buildings of the camp. All came flooding back. Two bad dreams, real and imagined. And the nightmare was reality.

She opened her eyes. The sky above her head was vast, a muted and fathomless grey. A circling eagle provided the only sense of perspective and distance. Suddenly she was overwhelmed with a feeling of isolation, of panic. Sitting up with a jolt she struggled to release herself from the sleeping bag and looked around. There was no one there. Just the deserted Cherokee and the empty pick-up.

They had parked at a little viewpoint in the rocks. Any farther and the vehicles would have plunged over into a deep river valley. Rising beyond it was layer upon layer of barren mountain like the one on which she stood. Layer upon layer of spectacular three-dimensional cutouts, like brown and rusted knife blades, stretching as far as the eye could see. The *cuchillas*. The ultimate wilderness. Nothing and nobody. It was the end of the world, or the world before time began. Primeval, prehistoric. And she had never felt so alone.

Shivering against the mountain chill, she rummaged anxiously for the polar fleece jacket in her grip, pulled it on and lit a cigarette. The flame provided welcome warmth to her cupped hands. She exhaled and walked towards the edge.

Across the vast abyss she could see streams of white foam, carving deep clefts in the mountain opposite, becoming waterfalls as they gushed into the boiling rush of the river far below.

Again she heard the sound of the hammer.

What on earth were they doing? No one had said anything about them staying any length of time. So had the plan changed? Were Mallory or Forster or the others building a shelter?

She moved back to the vehicles and looked towards the source of the sound. It came from a thin copse of trees at the bottom of a gentle spur.

347

Carefully she began edging her way down, her trainers disturbing the shale, sending showers of it tumbling before her. The noise of it disguised the sound of the voices. She paused, straining to hear. Not just voices, singing voices. Unmatched and badly out-of-tune. She could not discern the words, but thought she recognised the tune. Someone else was whistling.

She hurried on down, sensing suddenly that something was amiss. The tune in her head, catchy, taunting her memory. Irritating. Irritating and silly how the name of a melody escaped one.

Then the image came into her mind. An irreverent comedy movie, a parody on Christ. The Monty Python team and their alternative gospel, *The Life of Brian*. That song? What was the name of it, that scene?

Mario's basso profundo voice was now distinct, Goldie's higher-pitched, verging on the alto, amused. 'Always look on the bri-ight si-ide of life. . !' The sounds oddly incongruous, the irony somehow not at all funny in this strange setting.

She stumbled into the tree line and saw Mallory sitting on a boulder, smoking and watching in silence. Forster stood behind him, his face an impassive mask.

Her mouth dropped as her eyes travelled across the small clearing. They were all there. Thripp, Pye, Rutter and Tom and Jerry Swinyard. All naked, all stretched and crucified between the saplings. Arms outflung, their palms nailed into the resinous timber. The tops of corned beef cans used as washers to prevent the steel tacks from tearing through the fragile flesh and finger bones of their hands.

Mario and Goldie stood before them, clapping and tapping their feet. 'Al-ways l-look on the bri-ight si-ide of life!'

'CHRIST!' Savage exploded. 'What the hell is this? You can't *do* this!'

Mario stopped whistling and turned to face her. 'It's how we do things in South America.'

'It's – it's barbaric!'

His eyes were hard. Hard like she'd never seen them before. 'A culture difference, that's all. Revenge must be cold to make it sweet, that's what we say in South America. Ask Kurt. And ask Goldie; he's learned a few tricks from the Arabs when it comes to asking questions and getting truthful answers.'

Forster looked uncomfortable. 'And we needed answers, baby, didn't we? Well, man, you've got them. This business might be unpleasant but I'm afraid it was necessary.'

Mallory climbed to his feet. 'Summers and his men are working for the IRA.'

She stared at him in disbelief. 'What?'

'You heard. The Provisional IRA. No lawyer, no policeman, no court in the world would ever have got that out of him.'

'Are you crazy?' she challenged.

'Guy's been in a very talkative mood this morning. The IRA have used drugs money for years to finance their terror campaign. So have the Proddies. But then your people must be aware of that, George. First marijuana, then heroin, now coke. They got into it through the lawyer in Madrid. Miguel Castaño and his friends in ETA. International terrorist links, hands across the sea. The IRA and ETA scratching each other's backs. You and I know all about that, don't we?

'Meanwhile Summers had dabbled independently, buying small amounts of dope and heroin in Cartagena on the north coast. Castaño met him and put him in touch with the IRA through ETA and prepared a business plan – for a percentage, of course.'

Savage shook her head. 'I can hardly believe this. I mean the cease-fire in Ulster, the peace talks—'

Mallory said evenly: 'Peace or war, you still need money for political ambitions. That's if you intend to win.'

'How certain are you about this IRA connection?'

'Thripp is certain. When Summers was introduced to Felix Bastidas in Medellín by Castaño, he realised he needed some muscle and asked Harry Morgan's security firm to put a team together. That's when Thripp got involved. He and Morgan had a meeting once with both Summers and Castaño. Castaño brought his Irish friend along. He was just introduced as Kevin.'

'And this Kevin was IRA?'

'Summers wasn't sure, but accepted at face value that he was a Dublin businessman – Thripp says he still does. Castaño said he'd met Kevin on one of his regular business trips to Eire.'

'That's how Castaño met the O'Mores?'

Mallory nodded. 'On the usual cocktail circuit. Dublin's a small place.'

'But Thripp thought this Kevin was IRA?'

'He and Morgan had no doubt. Said they could smell it, sense it. You know what it's like; they could tell by little things he said. Things that passed over Summers's head, but the other two had served as soldiers in the Province. They picked up on it.'

Savage frowned. 'It's hard to believe ex-soldiers would knowingly get involved with the Provos.'

'Two very bitter men, George. Especially Thripp. He feels he was shafted by his own after that business with us. He never forgave them when he was kicked out of the army. He was angry and resentful. What better way to get back at those who'd betrayed him? Besides, he needed the money.'

She looked puzzled.

'His son's got Down's syndrome, remember?'

'Oh, yes, of course.' But her mind was racing. 'We need to know who this Kevin character is – and the European end.'

'Castaño's the one you want for that. He holds all the cards.'

The sudden piercing scream was demented, a sound from hell.

Savage could no longer think straight. She was confused, her head feeling like it was about to burst like an eggshell. This was wrong, wrong, wrong. The cry and the chorus of singing voices was still ringing in her ears, merging now with the low moans of the dying men. She drew a deep breath, clearing her mind, and straightened her back. 'Cut them down, Kurt. Do it this instant.'

'Feel sorry for them, do you? These traders in misery?'

'It doesn't matter. Cut them down.'

'Thripp's the one with the three-nines tattoo, the one who killed Vic West and then Luz and the baby in Venezuela. He set up the rape of Juanita. These are the same men who murdered Father León and Doug Tallboys along with God knows how many others.'

'I don't care!!' she screamed.

'Well, you should do,' he said. 'We should all care. But people don't. That's why Mario, Goldie and I – and others – that's why we do what we do.'

She stared at him. 'You're actually enjoying this,' she accused.

'No. But I'm not wasting any tears over them either.'

'I don't understand you, Kurt, I really don't.'

'I know,' he replied simply. 'You never have and I don't really expect you ever will.' He turned to Forster. 'Dale, would you take George back to the vehicles.'

The American nodded, placing a restraining arm on her shoulder. Angrily she shook it free. 'Don't fucking patronise me! What are you going to do?'

Mallory's eyes were narrow like a cat's. 'Do what you want. Put them out of their misery.'

Her eyes were ablaze. 'Then do it quickly,' she hissed.

He watched as Forster walked away with her, up the slope, and disappeared from view. Then he joined Mario and Goldie beneath the hanging men. He took the gun from his friend and checked the magazine. There were four single shots fired. One each in the head of the Swinyards, Pye and Rutter.

Guy Thripp watched through misty vision, vaguely aware that his companions were being cut down one by one and carried to a shallow grave. When it was covered, they prised the nails from Thripp's palms and dropped him to the earth before tying his hands behind his back.

Mario drew the machete from the scabbard on his belt. 'Now I shall remove his right arm and his right leg,' he announced, 'and we can leave him here for the wild cats and the vultures.'

'Put that away,' Mallory said. 'Juanita won't want your trophies.'

'Is George making you go soft?' Goldie chided.

Mallory ignored him. 'Just get back to the vehicles, both of you.'

Mario resheathed his machete and glowered at his friend before following Goldie up the slope.

'Bravo,' said a feeble voice.

351

Thripp was still lying on the ground, still unable to move but obviously slightly recovered from his ordeal.

'What?'

The man's voice was weak but still had a defiant tone. 'Going to do the decent thing? An honourable execution – Soldier to soldier.'

Mallory didn't answer. He pulled the gun from his waistband, chambered a round and pointed the barrel at Thripp's forehead.

Decent? Honourable? The words struck a chord in Mallory's subconscious. Brother Hermann had used those selfsame words.

There was no remorse in Thripp's eyes, just mockery and arrogance.

Mallory thought then of his friend Vic West, of Mario's woman and their son, of Juanita and Victor, of the priest and Doug Tallboys. Even the abused little *puta* called Lucila. Given his time again, Mallory knew that Thripp wouldn't have changed a thing.

'Mario was right. Execution is too good for you.'

He lowered the barrel to Thripp's right knee and fired twice. The man's scream filled Mallory's head and echoed, wailing between the high peaks.

Somewhere, out there, the animal was disturbed by what it heard. It was the distant, answering roar of a jaguar.

Guy Thripp, on the edge of consciousness, stared down at the bloody mess of his leg, watching his life blood pumping into the dirt. Unaware that Mallory had already cut his bonds and was walking away.

'Kurt! Kurt!' But his cry was weak and feeble, barely audible.

Mallory turned back and looked up at the circling hawk. 'Just pray that *carancho* doesn't peck out your eyes before the jaguars finish you off. May your soul wander these hills for ever. And even that is better than you deserve.'

Then he turned and was gone.

Somewhere, maybe closer already, Thripp thought hazily, the cat roared again.

15

Santa Maria was still in darkness early the following morning when Mallory boarded the superbus for Bogotá.

He was nervous, sweating as he took his seat. Any one of the well-wishers gathered to wish *buen viaje* to relatives and friends, could in fact be on the lookout for him.

There was only so much he could do to disguise his appearance and there were only two routes out of Santa Maria. It was all too easy for anyone who was determined to find him. And he was certain that news of the camp massacre had reached Medellín by now and he had no doubt that the followers of the late Felix Bastidas would be baying for blood.

It was with profound relief that he felt the pullman jolt forward on the start of its long journey south.

After the execution of the gang members in the *cuchillas* the previous morning, the carefully plotted escape plan had gone into action. Using a cross-country route which bypassed the razed ruins of the Vipers' mining camp, all five members of the hit team rode in the Cherokee to a point on the main Cruz de Oro to Adoración road.

It was there that Mario and Goldie had concealed their Fourtrak, covered with hessian and freshly cut branches. They would return to the Tafur ranch, apparently back from their filming expedition, and announce that their job for the BBC was complete. Although Deputy Gilberto would no doubt complain – again – that they had gone off without him, a fat cash bonus would mollify him and ensure his silence; he certainly wasn't going to brag to the *comisario* about his incompetence. The next morning, all packed, they would set off in leisurely innocence for Bogotá.

353

Meanwhile Savage and Forster replaced the UN livery transfers to the Cherokee before driving on to Adoración in the fast-settling twilight.

A roadblock had not been entirely unexpected. The only question was whether it would be manned by *guerrilleros*, Bastidas's men from Medellín, the police or the army. As it turned out, it was Comisario Oscar Pulgarin. He could be seen in the headlight beams of the car ahead, strutting about in his polished boots and waving one of his ivory-handled revolvers while one of his deputies conducted a haphazard search.

Mallory was able to slip unobserved from the Cherokee's rear door, skirt the roadblock in the dark and rejoin the vehicle on the other side.

'No trouble,' Forster told him. 'Obviously we weren't on his list of suspects, but he's giving everyone else a hard time. I asked him who or what he was searching for, but he wouldn't be drawn. Just said he had his orders.'

Savage nodded. 'The question is, from whom?'

Mallory had no doubts. 'From his chief in Santa Maria acting on behalf of Bastidas's boys in Medellín.'

They had dropped him off before reaching Adoración as they could no longer risk Mallory being discovered in their company. While the Cherokee continued its journey on to Santa Maria, Mallory had walked into the darkened village and slipped aboard the antiquated *corriente* bus that was about to make the last run of the day to Santa Maria. He huddled in a corner making himself as inconspicuous as possible until it was filled with *campesinos* and Indians taking their vegetable produce and chickens for sale in the market the next morning.

It had felt strange arriving back in Santa Maria after so long away. The frontier town with its leafy plaza and enormous cathedral felt like the hub of civilisation after Adoración and Cruz de Oro. But it also made Mallory feel exposed and vulnerable. So many people, so many watching eyes. Keeping to the shadows he had made his way to the dilapidated La Concordia hotel where he rented a room.

Once inside he'd set about cutting his hair, hacking away several inches off the length. It was no masterpiece but it would do. Then he'd run the cold tap, the ancient pipework thudding as it spewed brownish water into the cracked china basin, and took the bottle of hair tonic from his rucksack. In fact it contained wash-in colorant. Following a quick shampoo, he rubbed the stuff in until his black hair had become a lightish mid-brown. After a shave and wearing a replacement set of nondescript clothes provided by Forster, the transformation would be complete, plain-lensed spectacles adding the final touch.

With nothing more to do, he'd lain out on the mildewed mattress, knowing he would not sleep; it was impossible not to keep one eye constantly on the door.

Savage had already arranged a seat for him on the midday Aerotaca flight to Bucaramanga the next day, booked in the name of his Harry Pike cover supplied by SIS.

However, he had long ago decided to make his own arrangements, although he hadn't told Savage or anyone else. Experience had taught him that in this game there was only one person you could ever completely trust. Yourself. And what even friends and allies didn't know, they couldn't tell. Either inadvertently or under interrogation.

So if anyone was going to be waiting for him at the strip at Santa Maria, or for the little airliner when it landed at Bucaramanga, they were going to have a long wait. Because at three thirty in the morning he had slipped out into the dark streets and made his way to the bus terminal.

The big pullman was well on its way to Bogotá when dawn broke to herald a bleak day, windy with low scudding cloud that was full of the threat of rain.

He had his last view of the *cuchillas*; they seemed wilder and more inhospitable than ever, mist drifting in the shelter of the deep canyons. He thought momentarily of Guy Thripp, his body half-eaten by mountain cats and picked over by wolves and vultures, then put it from his mind.

By late morning the pullman reached the town of Tunja, where the driver took a break for brunch and allowed his passengers half an hour to stretch their legs.

Mallory used the shops and back streets to check and double-check that he hadn't been followed. He did not intend to rejoin the bus. Instead, he hitched a lift with the driver of a *lechero* who was delivering his tanker of milk to Bogotá.

It arrived at the city just before nightfall and three hours before the departure of a flight to La Paz in Bolivia. He took a taxi to the airport and made his way to the lavatory where he extracted the passport in the name of Englishman Jim Tate from the secret pocket in his baseball cap. Then he checked in but waited for the final call before making his way to immigration.

As he approached the desk, he noticed the three Colombian officials standing to one side; two in uniform, one in smart civilian clothes. Their eyes followed as he passed.

'Señor Pike!'

Shit, shit, shit! Keep walking. His stride barely faltered before he increased his pace. He heard the footsteps behind him, the gasp of exertion. Almost at the desk, the previous passenger moving on.

'Señor Pike!' Breathless.

Ignore it, his mind screamed, ignore it!

He placed his passport on the shelf for the officer to check.

A hand touched him on the shoulder. He feigned surprise and turned.

The plain-clothes man was clearly angry, but was forcing himself to smile. 'We're looking for Señor Pike.'

Mallory looked perplexed. 'Pardon?'

'You are British?'

The two uniformed men had caught up, their sidearms drawn.

'Si, yes. Mr Tate. Jim Tate.'

The official studied his face closely, trying hard to decide whether or not he was looking at the man he wanted. 'You are not Señor Harold Pike?'

'I'm afraid not. My name's Tate.'

The desk official handed the passport to the man in plain clothes who studied it carefully. A clear expression of annoyance showed on his face. 'I must ask you to come to our office.'

'Is that absolutely necessary, officer?' Mallory knew he couldn't afford to be too compliant or too obstructive, either would land him in deep trouble. 'I'm happy to answer your questions, but I really must catch my flight. People are waiting to meet me in La Paz.'

One of the uniformed men muttered something in Spanish about fair hair; Mallory pretended not to understand, but noticed that the plain-clothes man now seemed less sure of himself.

'What is your business here?'

'I'm a tourist.'

The official pointed at the rucksack on the floor. 'Have you checked in your main luggage?'

'That is my luggage. I like to travel light.'

'Then you will not object if I look.' Without waiting for a reply he stooped and untied the retaining cord. A compact Bible dropped out onto the tiles. It was something Mallory always kept on the top of his bag when travelling in South America – with the Latin psyche so steeped in Roman Catholic belief, the mere sight of the Good Book often acted as a deterrent to the worst of criminal excesses. Reminded of the divine retribution in store, any thief fearful for his soul might well move on to other pickings.

In fact, it had exactly that effect on the agitated official. He picked it up with due reverence, obviously surprised that an Englishman should carry one. 'What is your occupation, Mr Tate?'

The idea came to Mallory instantly. 'I am a priest. I've been looking at your marvellous cathedrals and churches – their architecture is my hobby interest.'

'Oh.' The official's hand withdrew from the rucksack like a bag-snatcher caught red-handed. He smiled uneasily. 'Forgive me, Father, but you – er – do not – er – dress like a priest.'

Mallory beamed benevolence. 'And what pray, does a priest look like? Travelling by bus is a dusty and sweaty business which ruins good clothes. Besides if I dress like the locals I find it puts both them and myself at ease.'

'Of course.' He handed the passport back in an almost apologetic manner. 'I am sorry to have troubled you, Father. We are checking all British male passport holders today in order to find this man. One of my colleagues thought you resembled a photograph we have of him.' He hesitated. 'But I can see now he was completely mistaken.'

Mallory smiled, apparently unconcerned. Surely the man could hear his heart thudding like a tom-tom, could see the blood rushing to his face? 'I wish you luck with your search.'

'*Muchas gracias*, Father. I hope you've had a good visit.'

'Most satisfying.'

'*Hasta la vista*.' Then he turned and was gone.

Mallory didn't stop shaking for the entire length of the flight to La Paz. He wished now he hadn't been so goddamn smart – had taken a direct flight out of the continent to the USA or Europe, instead of taking an internal Lloyd Aereo Boliviano airline down to Santa Cruz before picking up an American Airlines flight to Miami. Taking a more leisurely circuitous route was meant to add to the smoke screen. However good the theory, it was doing nothing for his nerves – not now he knew someone was looking for Harry Pike.

Just what sort of double-cross was this, he wondered?

Only a handful of people knew his false Pike identity. Mario and Goldie, of course, but they were totally above suspicion. And then there was George and her masters at SIS who had arranged the cover and the documents. Whilst he could never fully trust them, he had worked well with them in the past and they had never let him down before. And he was certain that Savage would not stand for it anyway – assuming, of course, she was told.

Their possible motive would not have been difficult to work out. The entire venture had been totally illegal and would hardly have won the approval of the parliamentary committee whose task it was to ensure the accountability of the intelligence services.

However effective the operation had been, the good and the true, with their own reputations being their prime concern, could hardly be seen to approve of co-operating with and accepting funds from a major drug cartel. Or mass murder. While the top spooks were well-practised at parrying the questions of politicians and Whitehall mandarins, there was always a danger when freelancers like Mallory were used. Those who did not know him might consider him to be a loose and dangerous cannon. One that might rebound in their direction. Not necessarily tomorrow, or the day after, but *sometime* in the foreseeable future. Perhaps as the result of some Sunday newspaper probe or an investigating television documentary team chasing another media award.

Similarly, the Americans might have a reason to be rid of him. To hand him over to one cartel or the other to do a quick 'wet job' and dispose of the body. Or even to set him up as a scapegoat, revealing the existence of the organisation and sacrificing it to cover some politician's back.

Dale Forster, Mallory decided, was the most likely suspect. The two of them had never really hit it off and the American was well used to the murky world of black operations. On the northbound flight to Venezuela, Mallory decided on a change of plan. Suddenly a stopover in the US or a direct return to the UK through Heathrow controls did not seem like a good idea. He had a ticket for an onward flight to Miami and then a change to American Airlines for a flight to Heathrow. Instead he left the plane at Caracas and took the next available Air France plane to Paris. Once there he caught a train to Calais, boarded the Dover ferry, then took a train to London.

He booked into a cheap Bayswater hotel and spent the next few days unwinding and marshalling his thoughts. By day he walked the parks, visited art galleries or hunted in the back streets for second-hand bookshops. He found several volumes he had always promised himself he'd read. He bought a water-heating element from an electrical shop and a bag of groceries, including teabags, milk and sugar. Each night he spent alone in his room, reading deep into the night and drinking copious mugs of tea. He lived on biscuits, soup and fresh fruit.

After six days he'd made up his mind. With his cover name known to someone who shouldn't know it, his security was compromised. No question. What he couldn't know was whether it was Felix Bastidas's friends in the Medellín cartel who were after him, or if there was a more sinister explanation. He considered telephoning George at her work place and telling her what had happened. But if it was part of some kind of setup by the Americans or her own superiors to rid themselves of material witnesses, then there was a risk in making contact with her. They'd realise he was back in the country and guess, as he wasn't apprehended in Bogotá, that he was travelling under a false identity of his own. Routine legwork by the intelligence service would soon discover that Harry Pike never entered Bogotá, but a Jim Tate had on that same day. And the same Jim Tate left the country on the same date that Harry Pike was due to depart. His disappearance in Paris and re-emergence at Dover a couple of days later would hardly even muddy the water if his own people were after him.

And Colonel Oliver Maidment? Normally Mallory would have trusted the man and the organisation implicitly. But for this operation they'd held hands with the secret services of Britain and the US, so for once his trust could not be total. Maidment could be under surveillance or his phone tapped, anticipating Mallory's attempt to contact. Or Maidment could be duped by some plausible lies into betraying him, although Mallory doubted that the colonel would fall for that.

In the end, Mallory reasoned, it was best just to let the trail go cold. To disappear without trace for a while before returning to his croft. No one could wait for ever for him to turn up. Even avenging drug barons had limits to their patience if not their budgets, whilst the intelligence services suffered the opposite problem. None of his few friends knew when to expect him home. And if Savage were genuinely surprised by his temporary disappearance, she was at least familiar enough with his nomadic lifestyle for her not to be unduly alarmed.

Probably the whole thing would blow over. The incident at Bogotá airport might well be one of those strange events that would never be explained. And he hoped that was the case.

At least it was a good time to disappear. It was August and the weather was reasonably fine. He would enjoy a few weeks living off the land, getting back in touch with nature. It would cleanse his soul and lift his spirits.

His only regret was that it meant a delay in seeing Kelly O'More again. Much as he'd tried not to, he had found his thoughts returning to her time and time again. Her tumbling copper hair, those dancing green eyes and that easy smile, the languid movements of those long legs. God, he really missed her, could think only of the two of them in his mind's eye, galloping together by the surf along the edge of Miggles Strand.

He'd been a fool – or was he just mellowing into middle age? Going soft? Mallory wasn't used to feeling this way about a particular woman. Maybe it was the thing called love, that he had always dismissed as the fantasy of poets and movie-makers, far removed from the harsh realities of life. At least it had always eluded him, until now.

Seeing Miguel Castaño in Colombia had really driven it home. It was his own fault. If he'd behaved like other men he had little doubt that Kelly would have dropped everything to live with him. Would never have been tempted by the suave lawyer. Probably she was the only woman he'd ever known who would not baulk at living the life he loved on the very edge of civilisation. Well, at the first opportunity he would ask her, and see what response he got.

There was one other certainty in his mind. His old life was over, his work for the organisation or anyone else was finished. He'd done his bit.

The face in the mirror was hardly recognisable. He'd lost weight in South America, maybe a stone, living on his nerves. His cheeks were gaunt and his eyes had an unnerving haunted look about them. No, never ever again.

What was it Brother Hermann had once said? '*The last person you ever really know is yourself.*' How right he'd been, the bastard.

In the morning, Mallory paid his bill, shouldered his rucksack and set off at a brisk pace to walk to Paddington station. There, on impulse, he did something he'd never done before. He bought a postcard and a stamp and addressed it to Kelly's bachelor flat in Dublin. He wrote simply *Love you. Kurt.* And then quickly posted it before he changed his mind.

He took the West Country train, changing at Newport for Abergavenny in south Wales. The town was near the wild and

361

magnificent Sugar Loaf; beyond them lay the Brecon Beacons and, remoter still, the Black Mountain region beyond that. Plenty of space there for him to disappear, wandering and fishing by day in streams and reservoirs, melting into the woodland at night to camp rough and cook over an open fire. Nothing ever tasted as good as fish you had caught yourself, he reflected, watching the eyes whiten and the skin of the trout begin to crisp, the mouth-watering aroma mingling with the woodsmoke . . .

The days ran into one another, melting away time itself. Mostly mild and sunny, the weather was kind with only the odd shower. Mallory found himself existing in an almost trance-like state. Sometimes wandering the hills, talking to the occasional sheep farmer or rambler, exploring old villages and chapels and studying their history. Graveyards always fascinated him, the names and dates, so many untold stories buried with these people. Once in a while he would call in at a pub for a pint in the early evening. At times he would visit a bigger town and spend a few hours browsing in second-hand bookshops. On other days he'd fish or read, or set traps for rabbits, just to vary his diet. He'd rather lost the knack of trapping since his childhood, but after the second week either his luck or his skill improved.

At last the bad dreams stopped. He was at peace with himself once more.

He awoke late, having read by candlelight long into the previous night.

There was a heavy dew on his sleeping bag and there was a touch of autumn in the air for the first time. He shivered, pulled on an old sweater and climbed out to stoke the embers of the fire. Tea and a chunk of toasted bread for breakfast. Out through the tree line he could see the marching grey thunderheads of a new weather front moving in.

It was time to go home, he decided. He had been in the hills for just over four weeks, five since he'd returned to England and nearly six since the massacre in the *cuchillas*. The memory of it startled him and he realised he had not thought about it for many days now.

Rain was sheeting down by the time he reached the railway station, rucksack over his shoulders, and caught the Swansea train. He boarded the Cork-bound ferry and fell asleep on a padded bench seat in the lounge.

When the ship docked the next morning, he went ashore and hired a small car. As he did not have a driver's licence to go with his Jim Tate identity, he booked it under his own name and set off on the fifty-mile drive back towards his croft.

Carefully he timed his arrival in the area for after dark. That and the use of the hired car made it very unlikely that any of the locals would even see let alone realise he was back.

When he finally arrived, a ferocious storm was throwing itself in off the Atlantic. He could hear the surf thundering along the shoreline like a rolling barrage of artillery. He parked in a layby half a mile from the croft and picked his way down a little-used footpath towards the beach. He settled down to study the building and its surroundings. There were no lights showing and no parked cars on the turning circle. Above the howling of the wind, he could hear the nervous whinnies of the horses. Feeling happier he edged down towards the stable outhouse. Slipping under the fence he crossed the paddock to the apple trees where, sheltered by the croft's gable end, stood the row of beehives.

He moved swiftly to the second and gently eased open the lower drawer. Dozy workers crawled benignly over his hands as he unwrapped the oilskin and withdrew the 9mm Browning pistol and slid in the magazine. Closing the drawer again, he moved on towards the front of the croft. It was dark and silent, the curtains drawn, just how he had left them.

The key slid easily into the lock and he heard the tumblers click. Unoiled hinges creaked as he restrained the door from crashing open under the force of the wind.

A smell of must and stale air reached his nostrils. Cold and damp. He slipped inside and closed the door. He felt something underfoot on the mat. Dropping the gun into his jacket pocket he stooped, his fingers feeling the smooth varnished surface and hard edges of a postcard. Placing it in another pocket he fumbled towards the hallway hook where he kept the hurricane lamp. He flicked his lighter and adjusted the flame before pushing open the door to the parlour.

'AGGH!' the startled voice said. 'SWEET JESUS!'

Mallory had taken a backward step in surprise. Now he lowered the lamp and squinted into the gloom. 'Mattie?'

'Kurt?' The relief was clear in the old man's breathless tone. 'Oh, thank the Lord for that. I'm thinkin' you're them come back.'

'Who come back?' He stumbled over a pile of books on the floor. 'Wait a minute. Let's get some light in here.'

It took a few minutes to locate all the lamps and illuminate the room in a feeble glimmer. Even in the half-light, Mallory could see things had been disturbed. His numerous bookshelves were stacked differently and the furniture was not where he had left it.

'I tidied up as best I could.'

Mallory felt the chill fingers of fear on his neck. 'When did it happen?'

'About a week ago. Must have been the Saturday or Sunday night, because I didn't come into the house those days, just tended the horses. I found it all messed on the Monday night.'

'Do you know if anything was taken?'

Rooney shook his head. 'Nothing that I could tell.' Then a mischievous grin appeared amid the beard. 'But then let's face it, Kurt, you don't keep nuthin' worth taking. Except that wee bottle o' malt.'

Mallory smiled. 'Is that a hint?'

The old fisherman ran his tongue over his lips in anticipation. 'Well, you did shake my old heart up a bit.'

'So what are you doing here?' Mallory asked, fetching the bottle from an old pine dresser.

Rooney indicated his rusty old shotgun resting against the sagging armchair. 'Thought I should guard the place. They were obviously searching for something – had made a right mess. I think maybe they'll come back. And if so, sure I'd be givin' them the fright of their lives, so I would.'

'It's appreciated,' Mallory said, pouring the malt into two

chipped tumblers. He made no mention that anything to do with his work he kept hidden in the beehives. Some secrets were best entrusted to no one.

'Ah, that's lovely, Kurt,' Rooney said as he took the measure and sipped at it with noisy relish. 'I put some old blankets over the curtains. Thought it best no one could see lights.'

'D'you think these people might still be around?'

Rooney shrugged. 'I don't know. You're a bit cut off out here. But there were some strangers seen in the village last weekend.'

'Was there anything odd about the men? Were they English or foreigners? Maybe American or Spanish?'

Rooney chuckled. 'Bless me, Kurt, no. That's why I thought nothing of it at the time. They were as Irish as I am. But they were hard-looking, if you know what I mean.'

Mallory's eyes narrowed; he didn't say what was on his mind but the mental connection between the Provisional IRA and Miguel Castaño made him think of Kelly.

He asked Rooney if she had known about the break-in.

The fisherman shook his head. 'Haven't seen the wee girl in months, Kurt.' He sounded disappointed, but as his watery eyes looked up from his tumbler of malt, Mallory realised he was trying to break the news gently. 'In fact, she's not been around since about a fortnight after you left. Been travellin', so I believe.'

'Travelling?' Mallory queried. Rooney wasn't too good at lying.

'Well, I thinks she's been spending a lot of time with that Spanish lawyer feller. Sure he invited her over to Spain for a holiday.'

Mallory frowned. 'C'mon, Mattie, stop holding out on me.'

'Well, Kurt, I think maybe they've – you know.' He looked embarrassed, searching for the words. 'Shacked up together, so to speak.'

Mallory stared at him. He felt a sudden rush of anger. With Castaño, with Kelly. How could she be so stupid? Then he realised that he was mostly angry with himself. Angry that he had let her go, treated her with indifference. To her, he realised suddenly, it must have seemed like rejection.

There was something else too. He was jealous. For the first time in his life he wanted this woman all to himself. It was not an emotion he was used to. The knuckle-whitening tension and anger was like nitroglycerine deep in his gut, just itching to explode.

Rooney saw it in his eyes. 'I'm sorry, Kurt. Still, I expect she'll tire of him soon. He's not her sort, she's much too good for him. She'll come home.'

But Mallory wasn't so sure. The most sensible women could have their heads turned by flattery, attention and romantic words, however false. And some could not stop blindly loving some of the world's most evil men.

He wondered if Savage had managed to reach Kelly on her return from Colombia, to warn her about Castaño as she had promised. It certainly didn't seem like it.

He remembered the postcard he'd sent on impulse from Paddington station and wondered if it was still lying on the doormat of her Dublin flat. The thought depressed him.

Postcard? That reminded him. He reached into his jacket pocket and extracted the card that had been waiting for him.

*Dear Kurt, I'm off on my travels again on the 15th. A
little translation work in Madrid. Hoping to meet an old
friend of yours and tie up some loose ends. Love Sally xxx*

It was the organisation. Colonel Oliver Maidment's call sign. Madrid? Immediately he thought again of Kelly and Miguel Castaño. Was there a connection? Was Maidment following through on the White Viper business? Making his own agenda? It was now the 17th of the month. He was already two days late.

Mallory was tempted to tear it up and throw it in the wastebin. He'd had enough. All that was behind him now. But the words 'Madrid' and 'old friend' intrigued him. A reference to Mario or Goldie perhaps? Or Kelly? The hook was temptingly baited.

It took no more than five minutes for him to decide. He had to go. At least to see what it was about. And if he didn't like what he saw he could always turn round and walk straight out of it.

He said: 'Thanks for looking after the place, Mattie. But no more all-night vigils, eh?'

Rooney understood. 'You goin' away again? Thought you might be home to stay.'

'So did I.'

He left the croft before first light, stealing up the cliff path and along the road to where he'd parked his hire car. Before entering he checked beneath it with his torch. Nothing. But then he couldn't be too careful.

The drive to Shannon was uneventful. He returned the hire car to the same company's airport office and took an early morning flight to Heathrow. Maidment's car was in the Long Stay park, the key tucked into the exhaust.

In the glove box he found a note of instructions, an open return ticket to Madrid, a wad of peseta bills, and a hotel reservation slip. Relocking the car he returned the key to the exhaust pipe and then took a courtesy coach to the terminal building. At the Iberian Airlines desk he booked himself on a mid-afternoon flight using his Jim Tate identity. To keep one step ahead, just in case.

Although it was late summer the Spanish capital, high on the dusty Castilian plateau, was as hot and dry as ever, the sky clear and the temperature well into the eighties during his taxi ride to the centre. It was not a city that he particularly liked, full of beggars and purse-snatchers. Its parks and tree-lined avenues were too parched and arid to be enjoyable until the evenings, its fume-filled streets too choked with nose-to-tail traffic, and the innumerable cafés and *tapas* bars too full of elegant poseurs for his taste.

He'd been booked into the Carlos V, an inconspicuous three-star hotel on Maestro Vitoria, a pedestrian precinct that was sandwiched between the main thoroughfare of Puerta del Sol to the south and the lively tourist magnet of the Plaza de Callao to the north. At least it was a quiet location by Madrid standards, the small reception lobby cool and dark and decorated with a suit of Spanish armour and a Georgian wall tapestry to appeal to American tourists like those whose luggage filled the hall.

The room was drab but functional. He switched off the air

conditioning, which he loathed, and threw open the double window doors. Noises rushed up at him from below the black iron balcony: the hum of traffic, hundreds of walking feet and a street singer strumming his guitar.

Sitting on the bed Mallory double-checked the typewritten instructions before telephoning the newspaper. He asked for small ads and repeated the contact code message that would signal his arrival. *Anna, Please marry me. Yours now and for ever. Don Juan.* The woman at the other end giggled as she took it down and told him to phone her back if he was rejected before she took his credit card number for payment.

There was little to do now except wait.

He spent some time lingering over a *cuba libre* at a pavement café until the sun went down, then strolled for a couple of hours. In the back streets he came across several whorehouses, sleek coiffured beauties in tight dresses and much gold jewellery beckoning him inside. For once he was not even tempted. It seemed there was only one woman now he wanted – Kelly O'More.

He was barely awake the next morning when the telephone rang. Instantly he recognised Goldie's voice. 'I'm phoning in answer to your ad. I'm interested in buying. Could you be at the Real Jardín Botánico at eleven?'

'No problem.'

'Fine. In the Plano de la Flor. Eleven o'clock.'

Mallory replaced the receiver, then showered and dressed. He had no taste for breakfast, instead deciding to take a leisurely walk down to the rendezvous. Puerta del Sol was busy, people grabbing morning coffees on their way to work, buying newspapers, cigarettes and lottery tickets, dissolute youths hanging around the pinball *palacios*. Leaving behind the crowds, he walked along Carrera de San Jerónimo towards the Prado museum. It was blissfully cool in its lofty galleries and a good way to kill a couple of hours, distracting himself amongst the El Grecos, Riberas, Velázquezs, Goyas, Rubenses and Raphaels and their portrayals of bygone eras. Times, it struck him, when it might have been better for him to have lived. When there was no real civilisation beyond the big cities, no rules. When men lived and died by the sword.

At fifteen minutes to eleven he walked to the adjacent botanical gardens and made his way to the raised terrace at the rear. By the columns of the pavilion was an oval pond with a statue and fountain. A pair of lovers strolled by, hand in hand. There was no one else and after a circuit of the adjoining terrace he found no evidence that their meeting place was under surveillance.

As he returned to the oval pond, he saw Goldie and Mario approaching. Both looked relaxed, chatting and laughing together, dressed in slacks and short-sleeved summer shirts.

Mario's face beamed as he saw his old friend, and hugged him with a bear-like embrace. '*Mi compañero*, it is good to see you again! I had been thinking you are dead. That the Vipers kill you before you get out of Colombia!'

Mallory smiled. 'I don't think there are any Vipers left. Not after the job we did on them.'

It was Goldie's turn to step forward, as reserved as always, just that enigmatic smile of his betraying a genuine sense of relief. 'I tell Mario you will be okay, Kurt. Going to ground for a while, eh?'

'It seemed best. And you?'

Goldie shrugged. 'No, I just covered my tracks. I was keen to get back to my family.' His wife and two children lived discreetly with him in Durban. It was a good cover, his job supposedly an international salesman for a joint South African-Israeli fruit canner.

Mario said: 'I've returned to Martinique and bought a flat. I'm thinking I'd like to go back to Cruz de Oro when the dust has settled. Maybe ask that little Juanita to make an honest man of me.'

Goldie made no comment, but his eyes said it all. The Juanita they had known and loved in their own way had been destroyed in that little chapel. The girl's soul was dead and nothing they could do would ever bring it back.

Mallory glanced around the deserted terrace. 'Is the colonel coming or will you be telling me what this is all about?'

Goldie said: 'The organisation is working alongside SIS again.

369

They've asked us to finish the job.'

'What do you mean?'

'Georgie's in charge.' He nodded towards the steps. 'Here, you can ask her yourself.'

She looked good in the blue polka-dot blouse and short white skirt. Her legs were tanned and her face was lit with a wide smile. 'Kurt!' She reached up to kiss him lightly on the cheek, then stepped back to look at him, her eyes bright and moist with relief. 'I was *so* worried about you! I had a car waiting for you at Heathrow when you got back from Colombia. When you didn't show we all thought the worst. Silly, because I ought to know you by now. Colonel Maidment said you'd be all right, that it would be typical of you to break away from the plan at the end. I sort of thought that myself but, of course, I couldn't be certain.'

'I had my reasons,' Mallory said. He felt reassured enough now to tell her about the incident at Bogotá airport.

All three listened intently. When he finished talking, Savage said slowly: 'I had no idea. You really should have contacted me when you got back.'

'That didn't seem wise. Only the three of you and Dale Forster knew I was supposed to be using my Harry Pike ID. Or possibly one of your chiefs in SIS, or someone on the American side.'

Mario approved of Mallory's wisdom in creating a new identity unknown to anyone but himself. 'Amigo, you are too smart for them.'

Savage gave him a scathing glance. 'That's not how we operate, Mario.'

'It's not how *you* operate, George,' Mallory replied quietly, 'but one can never double-guess how your superiors might operate. They wouldn't necessarily tell you. Someone might want to cover every trace of the operation because it broke all the rules.'

'I don't think so, Kurt.'

'So who broke into my home? Not your people?'

'Your croft?' Her eyes widened. 'When?'

'About ten days ago. They wrecked the place.'

'Only I know where you live, Kurt. You're on my Z-file. And there's nothing kept in writing.'

370

'Then it must be the Americans. Dale Forster knew my real identity and enough about me to track down my address.'

Savage's face had paled, despite her tan. 'No, Kurt, that's not possible. Dale Forster is dead.'

Mallory's mouth dropped.

She said: 'It happened about three weeks after we fled Colombia. A boating accident off the Florida Keys. He was on a fishing holiday, just unwinding like the rest of us. It was thought that probably a cylinder of cooking gas exploded. Another yacht saw it happen, but was too late to do anything. It sank in deep water. The coroner returned a verdict of accidental death.'

'It's true,' Goldie confirmed. 'It can't have been Dale. But also I cannot think why anyone should have been looking for someone with your cover name at the airport.'

Savage added: 'Maybe Dale mentioned it by mistake when the flap was on. There was a lot of confusion co-ordinating the raids. Venezuela was a bit of a cockup. There was a tip-off from the police and most of the Colombians escaped into the jungle. But Bolivia went well. Crabtree and Beavis were killed in a fire-fight with the Leopards.' She meant the anti-drugs police there. 'All the names of the Viper gang were issued. Maybe the list was also sent to the Colombian police in case any of them got away.'

'My name shouldn't have been on it,' Mallory retorted. 'Kurt Hulse *might* have been understandable, but certainly not Harry Pike.'

'I agree, but mistakes happen.'

Mallory was still not happy. 'They even had a photograph.'

Her smile verged on the patronising. 'Kurt, even I do not keep photographs of you after false passports are made for you. I see to it personally that all negs are destroyed.'

'Can't you check things out with Dale's superiors?'

'It was a black op,' she reminded. 'It didn't happen and no one officially knows about it, so there is no one to talk to about it. His superior's Washington number is now a dead line. Dale was a freelancer gone rogue as far as any connection with the US administration is concerned. What he got up to was none of their business.' She sighed. 'As for Dale's accident and your break-in, well, I'd say they're probably just unfortunate coincidences. Did anyone actually *see* who broke into your home?'

He shook his head. 'But nothing was taken.'

She looked at him directly. 'Let's face it, Kurt, there isn't much worth taking. It was probably local kids who'd had too much to drink. An empty isolated cottage was an irresistible temptation.'

He knew she could be right, but it still left him with an uneasy feeling. There was no point in a continuing debate, because they'd probably never know for certain. So he changed the subject: 'Why did you call me here? If it's to do with the Viper connection then it must be about Castaño.'

Savage lifted an eyebrow. 'Very astute, Kurt. Mario and Goldie have been keeping him under surveillance for the past week. The thing is, your reports from the camp suggested that several shipments of cocaine were already in train to Europe, right?'

He nodded.

'Well, so far none of it has been intercepted. All we know is that most of it has passed or is passing through St Petersburg. We've got no jurisdiction there, the local Russian mafia is in total control and the police are in a shambolic state. They're underfunded, corrupt and their morale has never been so low. Our people are doing their best, but their old Cold War contacts are with politicians, journalists and the military. They've yet to penetrate the new criminal networks.'

'So?'

'Castaño's an international lawyer and he'll be the link with Europe.'

That made sense, Mallory thought. 'Did you manage to warn Kelly, tell her what he was involved in?'

'Yes. I had to pick my moment because she's been living with him.' There was no hesitation as she said it very matter-of-factly. Her eyes were without expression as though she were hiding what she really thought. You enjoyed telling me that, he decided, hardly aware of her next words. 'We kept watch for two days – until she went to the hairdresser's. She was very surprised to see me.'

'How did she react?'

'With disbelief at first, but not for long. I think the photographs convinced her.'

Mallory frowned. 'What photographs?'

'Of Miguel Castaño sharing his siesta with one of the Spanish lady lawyers in his firm. A room at the Palace hotel, no less. No expense spared. Once Kelly was over the shock, it was no problem.'

'She's gone back to Dublin?'

Savage laughed lightly. 'No, Kurt, she offered to help. She's still with him.'

Mallory couldn't believe he was hearing this. 'What? You asked her to do that – knowing he's up to his neck in the White Viper operation? You'd put her at risk?'

'No, Kurt,' she retorted. 'And I hardly needed to persuade her; she volunteered all too readily.'

'She doesn't know this game.'

'She's in no danger. Kelly is just continuing as though nothing has happened. We simply arrange to meet from time to time.'

'*That*, George, is a risk.'

'No. Hairdressers, manicurists, even lavatories. Girlie places, Kurt, where no one's going to suspect anything. I wouldn't put her at risk. She was my friend long before she was yours. But having someone on the inside is going to make it a lot easier to get to Castaño. He's always got an armed bodyguard with him and his villa is like Fort Knox. And I'll tell you something else. When she knew this case was connected to the one that you were working on in Colombia, she was really happy to think she'd be helping you. Yes, you.'

Mario grinned. 'I think maybe this Irish girl has the hots for you.'

'Stow it,' Mallory snapped.

'I want you to meet her,' Savage said. 'Sort out how you're going to catch Castaño with his guard down. It'll have to be at his villa because that's where he keeps the details of all his more dubious transactions. He has a very secure private office there. At least that's what Kelly thinks. But you'll have to act quickly because on Monday evening he's going away on a business trip with his lawyer lady friend. He says it's to Paris but Kelly has seen airline tickets for Budapest.'

'And you say she's not at risk?' Mallory asked sarcastically. 'You should have told her not to snoop.'

'You can tell her yourself. She's arranged to go alone to the bullfight tomorrow. I've already arranged the tickets for the same section. You get there first.' She handed over a bright yellow baseball cap from her bag. 'Wear this for easy identification and make sure there's a free space next to you.'

Mallory glared. 'I'm not pleased about all this, George.'

She gave a little smile and shrugged. 'Sorry. I'm just doing my job.'

The crowd was in festive mood, cheering and chanting in the dusty bowl, the energetic drums and trumpets of the little band adding to the clamour of excitement. Two horses dragged away the one ton dead weight of the corpse, trailing a thick red smear across the sand.

The lion-hearted beast had twice almost caught the matador who was becoming too slow for the sport and too fat for his embroidered bolero top.

Mallory had no problem with bullfighting. It was part of the South American culture he'd been brought up in. And he'd had enough close shaves with angry and dangerous bulls on the ranches there to appreciate the courage of both the animals and the men who destroyed them. But he was less enthralled with the spectacle and exhibitionism of it all, the arrogant strutting poses and playing to the gallery. Let me have one of these narcissistic heroes for five minutes, he mused, and we'd soon see how brave he really is. Anyway, after five kills in a row and many more to come, it was all beginning to pall. Another corpse hauled off, another lively, kicking bull ushered in; it began to resemble a the-atrical conveyor-belt abattoir.

He looked across the arena of the Plaza Monumental to the clock on the tiled roof opposite. Almost three and Kelly would arrive at any moment. There was no mistaking the small thrill of excitement in his gut. No doubt now how much he'd really missed her. He lit a cigarette. God help me, he thought, if this is the thing they call love.

The night before in his room at the Carlos V, he had pored over drawings of Miguel Castaño's villa with Mario and Goldie, examining the many photographs that had been taken with a tele-photo lens.

Finally he had outlined to them the plan that had been form-ing in his mind. The plan he would put to Kelly at their meeting, adapting it according to her response.

It had met with Mario's gleeful approval.

Goldie was not so sure. 'Georgie said nothing about that.'

Mallory had looked at him directly, his eyes ice-hard. 'And she didn't say not to. You wouldn't object if this was a straight job for the organisation, would you?' he challenged.

A shrug. 'I guess not, but it isn't. It's a joint venture. If she was here now she'd veto it, you know that.'

'Well, she isn't here. She's using us for political ends. Okay, fine. But her people are still making use of the organisation because of the way we do things. That's also the price they have to pay.'

Goldie had looked morose until Mario placed one huge arm around his shoulders. 'C'mon, amigo! Kurt is right, we all know that. We all know what will happen if it isn't done. It's why the organisation was formed in the beginning.'

The enigmatic smile had made a brief appearance on Goldie's face. 'Yeah, I suppose you have a point.'

Mallory looked up. The hand on the big clock at the far side of the bullring inched onto the vertical. Three. He turned his head, straining to see up the crowded concrete terraces to the nearest entrance arch.

And there she was. He saw her just as the band struck up to herald the arrival of a fresh bull to the slaughter and a cry of blood lust rose up into the hot afternoon sky. She looked mag-nificent, he thought, wearing a simple long white cotton dress with a square neck, the skin of her arms lightly tanned. The wild copper ringlets glistened as she held up the brim of the wide floppy sunhat to scan the rows of seated figures that descended sharply away below her.

He looked quickly back to the arena where the bull had begun trotting round the perimeter fence, seeking a way out. It was important that theirs appeared to be a chance encounter.

It seemed like minutes as he waited, not daring to turn his head. Where was she? Had she missed him? Should he look back again?

Then he caught the waft of a light perfume, heard the people near to him moving to let her through.

'Hi, stranger.'

He looked up at the wide smiling mouth and the dancing green eyes shaded by the undulating brim of her hat.

'Sit down,' he said quietly, grinning despite his effort to appear hardly to notice her.

'Ow, gosh it's hard, so it is. And rough.'

'You didn't hire a cushion?'

'I didn't know you could.'

'Have mine.'

She lifted her bottom. 'Why thank you, kind sir. What a gentleman.' She frowned suddenly. 'Is it all right to talk?'

He smiled. 'That's the reason we're meeting. Just don't look directly at me for a few minutes. Make it seem as though we just get chatting after a while.'

'This really is exciting. I've always wanted to be a spy.'

Out in the arena, the picador, looking like Sancho Panza from *Don Quixote* in his wide-brimmed hat, was lancing the bull as the enraged beast head-butted the armour-clad flanks of his horse. Kelly winced.

From the corner of his eye Mallory watched her mouth move, entranced by the generous lips and the whiteness of her teeth. He felt an overwhelming urge to just reach out and kiss her and to hell with it all.

'Well, I'm not at all pleased George roped you into this. You could get hurt.'

'She didn't ask me to; I wanted to. I thought you might be proud of me.'

'I am. But I still don't want you to do it.'

'It's only until tomorrow. And I'm enjoying it. Can I look at you now?'

'Not yet.'

'I've missed you, Kurt. I can't tell you how much.'

'What about *el torro rabioso*?'

He was aware she was wrinkling her nose. 'Well you were right about him all along. Don't gloat. I suddenly had the notion I might be able to change him. Silly me. Still, he did have a nice bum.' She risked a sideways glance. 'Come to think of it, I've never seen you in jodhpurs.'

He couldn't resist a smile at that. 'And you never will. Tell me, did you check you weren't followed?'

'Yes, well, as best I could. But there are a *lot* of people here.'

'It's not easy.'

'Anyway, Miguel has no reason to suspect anything. He's the one with things to hide. What with – you know – and that bimbo partner of his, Claudia. Funny thing is, he hates bullfights. Can you believe that? An Argentinian who hates bullfights? He's happy for me to come alone and do my tourist bit. Anyways he's got a meeting at home with Claudia this afternoon. So she's probably waving her red knickers at him now, getting him to chase her round the bedroom.'

The quick-moving banderilleros had managed to drive two long darts into the bull's shoulders. Now it looked confused and angry as the matador strutted into the arena.

'What time are they leaving tomorrow evening for the airport?'

'Around eight.'

'When is he home from work?'

'Tomorrow he says he'll be back at five.'

'And the bodyguard?'

'Emilio's always with him. He's quite nice really, rather taken a shine to me. Probably because he knew all along Miguel was screwing that brazen trollop.' She turned her head towards him and grinned widely. 'You can tell I'm not bitter, can't you?'

'Could you get Emilio away from Castaño and out of the garden at around six o'clock?'

She thought for a moment. 'I could ask him to give me a hand in the kitchen. He likes cooking and he likes me. I'll ask him to show me one of his specialities.'

'What about the dogs?'

'Jekyll and Hyde? Actually they haven't got names, but one's quite sweet and the other's a bloody werewolf. Trouble is they look the same. Rottweilers.'

'Where will they be?'

'Roaming anywhere, that's the idea. But they have a caged compound next to the garden wall.'

'Whereabouts?'

'There's an almond tree on the outside. Opposite that.'

'Could you have them put in the compound?'

'I suppose so. I can say the grocery man is making a delivery.' She thought for a moment. 'Then if the dogs do hear your approach, it's less likely to worry anyone.'

Bright girl, he thought. 'Good thinking. And what about the perimeter alarm?'

'I guess I could turn it off. I know where it is.'

'Then we're all set.'

An almighty roar went up from the crowd as the matador went in for the kill, arm raised with the sword blade pointing down, fleetingly poised between the beast's shoulders. Kelly's hand grasped Mallory's arm and she gasped as the sword was thrust in. Deep and straight. It was perfect marksmanship, plunging directly into the heart and lungs. The front legs collapsed instantly, the bull stumbling onto its knees, hawking up great clouds of blood onto the stadium floor.

Kelly turned her head away. Mallory clapped and rose to his feet with the rest of the audience. The band struck up in triumphant mood.

16

A long trail of dust across the baking landscape marked the approach of Miguel Castaño's red Ferrari Spyder.

It had been another hot and stifling afternoon under a breathlessly blue and cloudless sky. From his hide at the edge of the pine wood in the foothills of the Sierra de Guadarrama, Mallory was able to look down on the villa and beyond to the switchback trail that led to the motorway. It was little more than fifty kilometres to the suburbs of Madrid in the southeast. A mere jog for Castaño's Spyder.

Mario and Goldie had been sitting beside him on the soft bed of pine needles in the welcome shade since they moved into position at noon. From their vantage point they could see the villa with its roof of terracotta tiles and over the high, razor-wired walls to the swimming pool and sun terrace on the other side.

It was strange watching Kelly through binoculars as she swam in the blue water, then lazed on a lounger while the maid served her an iced drink in a tall glass. People rarely see friends and loved ones from a distance, he mused. To watch her like this, as a voyeuristic stranger might, he was able to confirm in his mind just how stunning she really was. Those long limbs and her easy, languid way of walking with just the slightest sway of her hips. And that smile, even distorted through the binoculars, was as magical and infectious at a distance as when standing by her side. A half-smile to herself as she swam or stretched out like a cat on the lounger; a full and gracious smile when the maid brought refreshments on a tray. She wore a bikini with a top, he noticed, and wondered if that was because she knew he and the others might be watching. Had she dispensed with such modesty when

379

she had been alone with Castaño? Probably, he decided, and the thought made him irrationally angry. The old green-eyed god of sexual jealousy began to gnaw into his mind and he wished to hell the thought hadn't entered his head.

At last the soft and throaty burble of the Spyder's exhausts reached them as the car slowed for the electronic gates to open. Some distance behind followed the sporty little Nissan 100 NX targa driven by Claudia Venachi. When both vehicles were in and parked beneath the vine-covered carport, the gates slid shut again. Castaño was the first to emerge from the shade, wearing a polo shirt and elegant silvery suit, the jacket of which he had slung casually over one shoulder. He was as good-looking and arrogant as Mallory remembered, all tan and Bollé sunglasses, teeth gleaming and black hair tousled from the fast drive. Claudia Venachi followed him, in a business power suit that was provocatively tight and teetering on heels that were an inch too high. Last to appear was the bruiser, dressed in a baggy sharp suit that barely contained his overdeveloped pectorals and biceps. Razor-cropped, peroxide-blond hair covered his squarish head which gave the impression of having been screwed directly onto his body without benefit of a neck. He walked after his boss with a rolling gait made necessary by muscled thighs as thick as tree trunks.

A few minutes later the armed day shift left; the gunman guarded the villa whenever Castaño and his bodyguard were not there. Now he was driving to his home to snatch supper with his wife before returning in time for the lawyer's departure to the airport.

Mallory continued watching the villa until Castaño appeared alone on the sun terrace to greet Kelly. It was irritating to watch the man kiss her hard and long, while his right hand idly squeezed her left buttock through the thin material of her bikini. She showed no sign of objecting, moving away only when the maid came with a beer for her master. Kelly then pulled on a terry-towelling robe and disappeared inside the villa; if all went well, she would now be distracting the bodyguard in the kitchen.

'Time to go,' Mallory decided and pocketed his two-way radio.

The position of their hide had been chosen because it was within the villa's only blind quadrant, unable to be overlooked from any of the windows. While Goldie was to continue watching and give warning of any unexpected problems, Mario and Mallory carried the long, twin-handled canvas bag between them, setting off down a dried-up gully which offered good cover to the bottom of the slope.

Once there, they were below the level of the villa garden wall and safe from being seen by anyone in the grounds or on the sun terrace. The two men crouched down in a clump of withered grass a short distance from the almond tree which marked the position of the dog compound beyond the wall.

Fishing into the canvas bag, Mallory produced a steel catapult and four thick slabs of sinewy beefsteak. These he had saturated in *burundanga*, the same plant extract drug he had used on Stan Summers in Colombia.

He aimed and fired the four pieces of meat in rapid succession; it would not do for one of the Rottweilers to gobble the lot. As the first splatted against the wall of the house and adhered momentarily before dropping down into the compound, there was a murmur of curiosity from one of the dogs, but that was all. After waiting for fifteen minutes Mallory and his friend carried the bag to the foot of the wall. It took them barely a minute to assemble the telescopic aluminium scaling ladder. Mario held it fast as Mallory began to climb. His heart was thudding, half expecting something to go wrong. Either Kelly had been unable to switch off the alarm or the dogs would be waiting for him, licking their lips. But as his head appeared over the parapet, he immediately realised the plan had worked like a dream. The two enormous animals were curled up in the shade, eyes watching but brains too doped and soporific to care, let alone move. He turned back to Mario and gave a thumbs-up; his friend grinned and handed up a large and heavy plastic carrier bag.

After cutting the razor wire, he used wistaria branches to scramble down the inside of the wall before dropping the last few feet into the garden. He went immediately to the carport, leaned into the open cockpit of the Spyder and released the catch.

Once he had access to the rear engine compartment he took a plastic Coca-Cola bottle from his bag; it was three quarters full of petrol. He fixed it upside down so that the top was just half an inch from the swan neck of the exhaust manifold. Satisfied it was secure he then produced a coil of insulated copper wire from his bag of tricks. Securing one end to the live battery terminal, he ran the other down to the manifold swan neck and wrapped it loosely around half a dozen times.

Lastly, he took out four polythene freezer bags filled with used engine oil and stuffed one carefully into each corner of the engine compartment. It was that simple.

He spoke into his radio handset. 'Okay, it's all ready. Come and join the party.'

Seconds later his friend was over the wall with surprising deftness for a man of his bulk. Together they moved down some steps into the flagstoned courtyard at the rear of the villa, ducking beneath each window until they reached the basement kitchen. A smell of herbs hung heavily in the air, wafting from the collection of earthenware pots by the door.

Mallory edged past them, his back pressed tight against the door jamb. His hand found the butt of the silenced 9 mm Browning High Power which nestled inside his shirt. The automatic had been supplied by Savage; a 'clean' weapon with no history and its serial number filed off. He chambered the first round, released the safety and peered into the kitchen.

The bodyguard was standing at the worktop with his back to the door. Mallory grinned, this was almost unbelievable. The man's jacket and leather gun holster hung on a chair back and his shirtsleeves were rolled up. The forearms were flexed and his huge hands were moving to and fro in front of him. His palms were open, his sausage fingers extended with the delicacy of a woman's as he gently rolled out the pastry. Pastry! Mallory almost choked with amusement.

Kelly sat decorously beside him on the worktop, cradling a drink in her hands. Her robe had been loosely wrapped to offer a careless display of cleavage as she plied the man with questions about his mama's favourite recipe.

She was a real pro. No sign showed in her expression as she saw Mallory's approach over the bodyguard's shoulders; she just gabbled innocently on as he crossed the floor. He kept the gun low, hidden from her view, until the last moment.

As he swung it up suddenly, she yelped. It was an involuntary cry of surprise and horror. But it came too late for the bodyguard. As his back stiffened and the cold muzzle of the silencer pressed into the back of his neck, Mallory squeezed the trigger. The blast tore into the spinal cord, instantly severing the body from the brain, the round blasting up into the cranium and exiting through an eye socket. Blood splattered over the floured pastry and the man's head pitched forward on top of it. Then slowly, very slowly he slid down to the floor.

Kelly sat, frozen, staring at the dead man, her mouth slowly starting to form around a scream. Mallory raised a finger to his lips. 'I'm sorry. It had to be done.'

'You killed him,' she said blankly. It was not an accusation, just an expression of total disbelief. 'He'd done no harm – he helped me when I asked him.'

Mallory was checking the body over for weapons. Finding none, he took the man's pistol from the holster hanging on the chair and emptied the magazine. 'Sure, and I'm certain his mama loved him. Unfortunately he kept bad company and he was dangerous. That's why your boyfriend employed him.'

'You didn't tell me you were going to kill him.'

Mallory raised an eyebrow. 'You didn't ask me.'

Mario entered through the courtyard door. 'What d'you want me to do with him?' he asked.

'Hide him in Castaño's fancy car.' As his friend began dragging away the body, he turned back to Kelly. 'Where is Miguel now?'

'In his office with Claudia. Going over details of their trip.'

'Who else is in the house? Just the maid?'

She nodded. 'Just Rosa.'

'I want you to go and find her. Tell her she can go home early. Make up any excuse you like, but just make sure she leaves immediately.'

Kelly moved towards the door. 'So you're not going to kill her

383

too just because she keeps bad company?'

Mallory turned his back and talked into his radio. 'It's me. We're in. Come and join us.'

Ten minutes later the maid was wheeling her bicycle out of the gate and wobbling off on her way to the nearest village, hardly believing her good fortune. Meanwhile Goldie had arrived, coming in over the garden wall.

Mallory turned to Kelly. 'I'd like you to wait here and open the gates for George when she arrives.'

She nodded. 'You're not going to kill Miguel, are you?' Her eyes were wide, haunted, no longer knowing what to expect of Mallory.

'Still care, do you?' he asked sarcastically and immediately regretted it.

'He doesn't deserve that. Nor does Claudia.'

Mallory said: 'That won't be necessary if he co-operates, and he'll be given every opportunity.'

A weak smile fluttered on her lips. 'You be careful too. Don't forget he keeps a gun in the desk drawer.'

'I won't.'

He looked at Mario and Goldie, both of whom now had their pistols drawn, and nodded. 'Let's go.'

They moved with practised synchronisation, one moving and two covering, then the leader covering while the last man overtook them and advanced again. The leapfrog advance-and-cover routine took them swiftly up to ground-floor level, then across the lofty, marble-tiled hallway and up the wide sweep of carpeted stairs. Goldie reached the top first and crouched by the landing, checking the corridor and doors confronting him. Mentally cross-referencing with the rough layout Kelly had drawn for them, he trained his pistol on the door he knew to be the office.

Mallory came next, dropping down beside him. Goldie inclined his head. There was little sound, just the background gurgle of the villa's plumbing as somewhere a water tank refilled. Then Mallory heard it, the gentle tapping of a computer keyboard.

The office. Their eyes met momentarily and Mallory inclined

his head. Confirmed.

Mallory was up and crossing the landing, each step taken with a slow, rolling motion. Heel to toe, heel to toe. Totally silent. Past an open bedroom door. A glimpse of the kingsize bed, satin sheets ruffled. Curtains jigging in the warm flow of air from outside. He heard the sudden rush of tapwater. Someone was in the *en suite* bathroom. Turning, he signalled the fact to Goldie and Mario who still waited at the head of the stairs.

They nodded to each other in silent agreement, rose to their feet and slipped quickly across the landing. Mario stopped beside the bedroom door, his back pressed hard against the wall. Goldie joined Mallory and the two of them moved down two doors.

Here the noise of the keyboard was quite distinct, joined by the muted chatter of the laser printer. Mallory's fingers closed around the gold-plated door handle, inching it round. The locking peg cleared the retaining hole and the door began to swing. It opened up to reveal a fitted suite of pale oak office furniture. Desks, filing cupboards and a work station facing an open window with a spectacular view of the Sierra de Guadarrama soaked in the soft watercolour glow of late afternoon. It was there that Castaño sat at his computer VDU, tapping in data.

As the door opened up to its full extent, the hinge gave a small groan. The lawyer's back stiffened slightly, sensing that someone had entered the room. 'Emilio?' He half-turned, his face suddenly white. 'EMILIO!'

'Save your breath,' Mallory said in Spanish, stepping forward to trap the man's fingers in the drawer as he reached for the gun he kept there.

Castaño squealed with anguish, pulling his hand free and nursing it. He glared up at the silenced Browning staring him in the face. 'Who the hell are you? Police?'

Mallory smiled. 'Sort of,' he said, this time in English. 'We're acting on behalf of all the poor miserable bastards whose lives you've ruined.'

The lawyer tried again. 'DEA? Are you DEA?'

'Getting warmer. Now why should you think we're DEA? Never been mixed up in the cocaine business, have you?'

Castaño realised his error. 'Coke? No, never.'

'On your feet,' Mallory ordered.

'I've met you before,' Castaño remembered suddenly, his legs trembling uncontrollably as he tried to stand. 'I've seen you somewhere.'

'Let me help your memory. Try Ireland.'

The lawyer's jaw dropped. 'Jesus Christ! You are Kelly's friend.'

Mallory grabbed his shoulders and shoved him out through the door as Goldie stepped aside. 'That's right, amigo. And we know all about you and Señor Summers and your friends at Cruz de Oro in Colombia.'

'What?'

'We were there,' Mallory said simply and pushed him along the corridor to where Mario stood by the bedroom door.

'She's still in the bathroom,' he said.

All four entered, Castaño forced to sit on the edge of the bed while they waited for Claudia to emerge from the connecting door. Mario stood behind it as she entered.

She stopped in mid-stride, agape at the sight of the armed strangers. 'What is going on?' she blurted.

Mario stepped up behind her. 'Okay, pretty one, just keep calm. Go and sit next to your boss – or is it lover, eh?' He jabbed her in the small of her back with the muzzle of the silencer.

As she sat beside him, Castaño glowered up at Mallory. 'Were you responsible for what happened at Cruz de Oro?'

Goldie gave one of his menacing little half-smiles. 'And what was that?'

'A massacre by all accounts. The police say there was a fire that swept through the camp – but no one believes that. Anyway, it hardly matters now. That's all finished.'

'Not quite,' Mallory countered. 'There are some loose ends to be tied up.'

'Meaning me?' Castaño asked. He tried to look contemptuous. 'I am just a lawyer. I didn't know what those people were doing. I thought they were in the emerald business.'

'But Stan Summers was your client.'

386

'He lied to me.'

'And you can save *your* lies for the police,' Mario said. 'They have more time to waste than we do.'

'We're interested in the destination of the cocaine consignments,' Goldie added. 'The ones you *thought* were emeralds.'

The lawyer tried to look unconcerned. 'I've told you. It's all closed down.'

Mallory said: 'There are several major shipments still *en route* for Europe.'

'If that's so, I know nothing about them.'

'So why, may I ask, are you about to fly to Budapest?'

'A holiday, a break.'

Mallory stooped so his face was just inches from the lawyer's. 'LIAR!'

Castaño was taken aback by the ferocity of Mallory's retort. 'No, no really . . .'

'There is an easy way, or a difficult way,' Goldie said softly.

Mario added: 'The Conquistadores brought a few novel techniques with them for loosening tongues when they came to South America. *Garrotte de bolas.* They found that if they tied a man's arms and legs together behind his back, they could lift him off the ground by a rope fixed around his balls.'

'But they did it real slow,' Goldie embellished, 'otherwise they tended to tear them off.' He produced a coil of paracord from his pocket and looked pointedly at the wooden ceiling beams.

Mallory glanced towards Claudia. 'Of course, we could shoot your girlfriend here. Just to prove to you we mean business.'

The female lawyer gulped, the blood draining from her face.

'Then shoot her,' Castaño challenged. 'She means nothing to me. And neither of us knows what you're talking about, so you'd be wasting your time anyway. Do you really want the murder of two innocent people on your conscience?'

'Conscience?' Mallory asked. 'Do you think we had a conscience when we killed everyone at Cruz de Oro? We had as much conscience as the *narcos* we killed there. And d'you know what? You are an even filthier scum than they were. You sit here, safe and sound, feeding off the misery of others. Getting filthy rich – your luxury apartment in Madrid, this villa, your yacht, your pretty Ferrari car. You do not even get your hands dirty and you take no personal risks. Protected by your friends in high places—' Castaño blanched at that '— Oh, yes, we know about all your politician friends, the policemen and the judges who come to your house parties. Don't talk to me about conscience, Señor Castaño.'

Goldie spun the paracord coil like a lasso. The lawyer's eyes were mesmerised as it unfurled, trailing over the beam and down to dangle inches above the bed.

Goldie looked down at the dark stain spreading across Castaño's expensive silk-weave trousers. 'Dear me, I think our friend has pissed himself.'

'I don't think the lady will want to watch this,' Mallory said.

'Why not?' Mario asked with dramatic enthusiasm.

Claudia had already seen and heard enough. She was close to passing out. 'Look, I'll tell you as much as I know.'

Castaño glared at her. 'The stupid bitch is bluffing, trying it on. She doesn't know anything, because there is *nothing* to know! You are all making a terrible mistake!'

Mallory folded his arms across his chest and regarded the lawyer for a moment. 'I knew a man once, a brother in a holy order. A saying of his was that if you told yourself a lie enough times, in the end you would believe it yourself. And he should have known because just like you, Miguel, he lived a lie. And he died for it too just as you are going to do if you do not level with us.'

'The computer!' Claudia shouted suddenly. 'Everything you want to know is on the computer next door. That is, if he didn't manage to erase it as you came in—?' She left the question hanging in the air as she turned to Castaño. His facial muscles had stiffened into a mask.

Mallory smiled. 'Señorita, I don't suppose Miguel will thank you, but he should do. You have just saved him from a very slow and lingering death.' He waved the Browning. 'On your feet, both of you.'

They walked back to the office where Goldie, the only one of the three to have any knowledge of computers, sat himself in front of the VDU. 'Right, which of you is going to talk us through?'

'Punch up the menu,' Claudia said, ignoring Castaño's continuing scowl. 'Look under Venezuela, Exports. Yes, that's it. Most of the trade is genuine as stated, but all those shipments under Invicta Trading are the ones you want. It's a shell company registered in Panama we set up for the operation. It appears a genuine trading brokerage, buying commodities from different companies, mostly Venezuelan and selling to whoever wants the goods. Timber, chemicals, canned meat or fruit, depending which is the latest way to disguise and ship White Viper coke. Most of the traffic used to be to Rotterdam via the Dutch Antilles or to here in Spain. Always we use different ships, usually small independent companies with ships registered in Panama or Liberia. But in the last six months they are often Russian.' She peered over Goldie's shoulder as he rolled the Invicta consignments onto the screen. 'See, those are the ones you are interested in. The last one left Venezuela days after the camp attack. It was already in the pipeline and Miguel and I saw no reason to stop it.'

Goldie pointed at the consignment number on the screen. 'This one? Two thousand drums of chemicals, powdered lye.'

'Yes. A highly toxic alkaline liquid containing potassium hydroxide. We have found it a great disincentive to Customs rummage crews. They have to wear special clothing and breathing apparatus to protect against eye, skin and lung burn. In that consignment, two hundred and fifty of the drums contain cocaine packages that will only be found when each drum is drained. That is the meaning of the additional line of figures which you have to read in reverse. The last number is the total quantity of cocaine. Five thousand kilos.'

Goldie gave a low whistle. Around five tons of White Viper. The amount was stupefying. And that was only one of four shipments *en route*.

'How do you know which drums contain the stuff?' Mallory asked.

'Translate the last number into an alphabetical figure, from

389

one to twenty-six. In this case it is nineteen, meaning S. The importer just looks for all drums with the letter S in the middle of the serial number.'

'Easy when you know how,' Mallory murmured.

Goldie returned to the menu and called up the importer's list, then cross-referenced it with the consignment number. 'Intransit-Global in St Petersburg. Is that the importing company?'

She nodded, but fear was showing in her eyes again. 'Yes, but I know nothing about them. I am sorry. Only Miguel knows that.'

Mallory turned to the lawyer. 'So, do we have to string you up by your balls, mi amigo?'

Castaño, sitting slumped in a chair, sighed resignedly. 'I guess you people, whoever you are, will be able to find out the rest from that. It's a front company we set up a year ago for Señor Summers and his Russian partners. Summers provided the initial capital and they basically run the show. They had a ready source of arms they wanted to sell and we had a potential big buyer in Felix Bastidas. The Russians also wanted in on the coke trade. It is not big in Russia yet, except with the spivs in Moscow, but they wanted to get established before it really took off. Meanwhile they offered to provide us with an excellent new route into Europe. Given the big mark-up on White Viper we could afford their exorbitant handling charges.'

'How much?'

'Up to twenty per cent of value.'

This was getting interesting, Mallory thought, and cadged a cigarillo from Mario to aid his concentration. 'So who is your Russian partner?'

'Actually he's Ukrainian,' Castaño replied in a slightly patronising tone. 'Uses several names. Sergei Chenko, Nikolai Khuchuk or a host of others. His *nom de guerre* is *El Capitán*. The Captain.'

'Ah,' Goldie said suddenly, turning round in his seat. 'The Sportsmen! Now I understand.'

Mallory frowned. 'What do you understand?'

'The Captain as he likes to call himself is the head of one of the major Ukrainian mafias. They are known as the Sportsmen, very droll. Many are ex-athletes from the armed forces and the

Spetsnaz. Very powerful and the Captain has his finger in many pies. My friends have quite a file on him.' By that Mallory knew he meant Mossad. 'Very wisely he controls his empire from another country where both he and his money are safe from the law and his many rivals.'

Mallory considered for a moment, the complex geography of the region forming a vague map in his mind. Then he had it. 'Hungary,' he said.

Goldie grinned. 'That is why our friend here has air tickets for Budapest. We know that the Captain operates from there with impunity and must have some friends in very high places. He has a vast estate guarded by armed men on the Buda side of the Danube. If I remember rightly, it's some six kilometres to the north of the city in a forest area between Moskvater and Huvosvolgyi.' He turned to Castaño. 'Have I got that about right?'

Castaño no longer looked complacent. Whoever these strangers were they knew more about his world than he believed anyone could. He looked pale and shaken as he nodded. 'Yes, more or less. There are few controls on the Ukraine's border with Hungary and the Captain can pull on the necessary strings. The drums are next moved to one of his warehouses where the cocaine is unpacked by men wearing special suits and breathing apparatus.'

'How is it shipped on?' Mallory asked.

The lawyer shrugged. 'I do not know. That is down to the Captain.'

Mallory leaned forward and waved his cigarillo in front of Castaño's nose. The lawyer stared at the glowing tip, mesmerised, feeling the heat on his skin. 'You're lying again. You've already said you pay the Captain twenty per cent for his trouble. That means the merchandise still belongs to you and your client and you are not going to let some gun-toting Ukrainian mafia waltz off with it. Besides, the whole idea of a high purity brand means you have to guarantee it's not tampered with. So you'll know precisely where it is at each stage of the journey. No doubt you'll even have someone of your own travelling shotgun with it.'

Claudia was becoming exasperated at her boss's reluctance to come clean. 'Please, Miguel, perhaps you have a death wish, but *I* do not want to be shot. Tell them!'

Castaño hesitated for a moment, turning his head away as the skin on his nose began to blister. 'If you punch up Transport on the menu, you will see all the routes and times. My client supplies refrigerated container trailers for overland shipments. The freezer units contain tens of feet of internal tubing which they fill with cocaine powder under pressure. Yet they can still be rigged to appear to work. These monoblock units are held in place by just four or six bolts. Undo these and get a forklift and it can be replaced by a genuine unit in a matter of seconds. The beauty of it is, no official is allowed to touch them without specialist assistance because they contain CFC gases.'

Mallory watched as the list of dates and registration numbers wiped onto the screen. 'Out by road into Austria, then into Germany.'

Goldie said: 'You can see the sense in that. Nowadays the border between Hungary and Austria is virtually non-existent. The two countries enjoy excellent relations since the fall of Communism – like a family reunited after the old Iron Curtain came down. And there is a very heavy volume of commercial traffic.'

'And of course,' Mallory added thoughtfully, 'Austria and Germany are the same country in all but name. Their border is hardly considered to be a major international smuggling route.'

'*Yet*,' Goldie said ominously with one of his sly smiles. 'One day the honeymoon will end between the countries down there. Eventually the politicians will have to accept that too many people are taking advantage of their cosy little clique.'

Mallory turned back to the screen. 'I see that some shipments terminate in Germany and others go on down to Spain or across the Channel to the UK.'

'Yes.'

'And then Stan Summers's outfit takes over, is that right?'

Castaño nodded.

'And who represents Summers's partners? Or more accurately

who is the senior partner?'

'I don't understand what you mean.'

'You understand perfectly, Miguel. You knew Summers through earlier drugs deals when you were representing the Medellín cartel and he was looking to distribute. And you knew the IRA through your contacts with the ETA separatists when your firm defended them. You brought them all together.'

The lawyer shook his head. 'I know nothing about the IRA. They mean nothing to me.'

'C'mon, Miguel, I'm losing patience. Who was the man your ETA friends introduced you to? The man behind it all, the man who is Summers's senior partner. The IRA link. A man who calls himself Kevin.'

'You mean Señor Sheehan. At least that's the name he gives. Señor Kevin Sheehan.'

'What do you know about him?'

'Nothing.'

'You knew he was IRA.'

'No. Just that he was Irish.'

'Harry Morgan and Guy Thripp knew he was IRA.'

Castaño's eyes seemed suddenly dark and fathomless. 'Then perhaps you shouldn't have killed them. Then you could ask them about this man. Although I met Señor Sheehan, Morgan and Thripp and especially Summers got to know him far more than me. I was just the safe conduit with respectable cover for routine liaison.'

Mallory realised then that they'd been subtly duped. Even under torture and facing death, Guy Thripp had managed to steer them away from the truth. Just before they tore him down from the makeshift crucifix, he had sworn that it was Miguel Castaño who had the personal IRA links. In fact Castaño had just introduced all the parties and monitored the trade from the safety of Madrid.

The lawyer said: 'Look, Señor Sheehan, or whoever he is, was introduced to me by friends of my ETA client who I defended. You do not get better credentials than that. His money was good, always arriving when he promised, cabled from one of several

Swiss accounts.' The eyes pleaded to be believed. 'You do not ask questions of such men; only they tell you if they want you to know.'

In truth Mallory understood that all too well. As in his own deadly business, it didn't pay to ask too many questions or to know too much. For years now he had been able to work on trust. If Oliver Maidment or Goldie or Mario asked for his help he knew that whatever he was asked to do might not be legal, but was in the interests of natural justice. Likewise with Georgina Savage. He did not fully trust the Secret Intelligence Service, but he had total faith in her judgement. Yes, he understood all too well Castaño's reluctance to ask questions of Kevin Sheehan. The lawyer was, above all, a professional.

Nevertheless it was worth one last effort. 'You have no photograph of this man?'

Castaño just smiled. 'What do you think, señor? All I can tell you is that he's in his forties. I think you would say a ruddy complexion with quite fair, curly hair. That is the best I can do.'

They had just about come to the end of the road, Mallory decided. It would be up to Savage now. Up to her people to investigate Stan Summers and maybe find out the true identity of the enigmatic Irishman called Sheehan. Meanwhile he was satisfied that everything they needed was on the computer disk.

He smiled suddenly and clapped his palms together. 'All right, you can go.'

Castaño and the girl stared at him blankly, then glanced at each other.

'What?' the lawyer asked, thinking he'd misheard.

'Are you deaf?' Mallory replied tartly. 'Go. We've finished with you. And don't forget your briefcase with your air tickets.' He glanced at his watch. 'If you don't waste time you can still catch it.'

From the expression on Castaño's face, the idea of catching his flight, away from this nightmare, was extremely appealing. He clearly didn't believe it, but he still needed no second bidding to stand up and start edging towards the door, watching Mallory's gun warily. The girl followed his lead.

'Mario, take their luggage down for them. There's a phone in their car, remove it.'

His friend grinned. He knew what Mallory meant. Make sure you put the two soft grips in the forward luggage hold. He didn't want Castaño discovering his bodyguard's corpse before he drove away with the evidence.

Mallory picked up his radio and spoke to Savage who was parked up on the hillside in a hire car that had been fitted with false number plates. 'They're leaving now. Come on down as soon as they've gone. I think you'll be pleased.'

And five minutes later she viewed the Spyder rocket pass the side-track where she was waiting. As soon as it had disappeared she started up her little SEAT and turned right, back up the unmade road towards the villa.

Kelly was standing by the open gates, looking distinctly subdued.

'What's the matter?' Savage asked as she climbed out.

The Irish girl gave an uneasy smile. 'I think I must be suffering from shock. I've just spent half an hour washing blood off the kitchen floor and cupboards.' She still appeared to be trying to come to terms with events. 'Naive, I suppose, but I wasn't expecting the violence. Not someone being killed.'

'Who's been killed? Not Castaño?'

'No, Emilio, his bodyguard. Kurt just came in and blew his head off right in front of me. It was awful. I was splattered in blood.'

Savage didn't seem unduly surprised. 'I'm sorry.'

'You should have warned me.'

And if I had, Savage thought, you'd have probably run a mile just when I needed you in place. But instead she gave a sympathetic smile, thinking suddenly how young and vulnerable the older woman looked. 'You're right. I should have said what could happen. Trouble is you never know. Kurt would have to have made a split second decision. He didn't have the time and resources for tying people up and guarding them, and Emilio was a very dangerous man. Besides, Kurt was probably concerned about your safety.'

Kelly nodded her vague understanding, but her face was still crumpled as she fought back the tears. 'Yes, I suppose so. Sorry, I'm being a bit of a wimp about this. Maybe I'm not cut out to be a James Bond girl after all.'

Savage placed a reassuring hand on her friend's shoulder. 'Where are they now?'

'Upstairs. I'll show you.'

They found Mallory with Goldie and Mario standing over Castaño's VDU, double-checking what they had been told by Castaño and Claudia Venachi.

Quickly Savage was brought up to date with what had been learned. As she listened, a slow smile appeared on her face. 'The Captain, Kurt, that's wonderful. The Global Issues Department has been trying to get a handle on him for several years now. The CIA and Mossad as well. Of course, it all makes sense. Until recently drug smugglers had been using Poland as the favoured new route into Europe – there was that big case in Gdansk last year. But the border between Poland and the former East Germany has got really difficult for them with the clampdown on illegal immigrants. So the Ukraine-Hungary-Austria route to Germany is ideal.'

As she talked, Mallory found that his real attention was on Kelly. She stood by the door, her eyes downcast, her posture lacking its usual confident and upright stance. He was sure the death of Emilio had shaken her badly and as he continued watching her from the corner of his eye, his mind suddenly pictured Castaño's red Ferrari Spyder lapping up the tarmac towards the airport, engine humming sweetly and exhausts purring. The two lawyers ecstatic to be alive, probably laughing together, almost hysterical with relief as their hair danced madly in the slipstream, while beneath the sleek metal, the plastic casing of the insulated copper wire around the manifold began to melt. Power pulsing down from the battery and tiny sparks spitting from the bared strands as the neck of the plastic bottle began to crumple and distort – a half-inch away from the searing heat of the manifold.

'Of course, Hungary's banking secrecy laws are legendary,' Savage was saying. 'It's even envied by the Swiss. And it's attracted a lot of hot and dirty money – Iraqi, Lebanese and Syrian as well as new Russian money which nearly all comes from organised crime.'

Goldie tapped the screen. 'There are account details here. They don't mean a lot to me, but I'm sure your experts will make something of them.'

She nodded in agreement. 'The sad thing is we won't be able to *do* anything about it. At least with this information we should be able to intercept . . .' She did a quick calculation in her head. Four consignments in transit to Europe or already there. Maybe twenty tons of White Viper cocaine in total. The scale of the operation was mind-blowing. 'The trouble is Castaño now knows that we know. As soon as he gets to Budapest, he'll organise a change of plan.'

Kelly said: 'Why don't you have Miguel arrested?'

Savage gave a small sad smile. 'I have no jurisdiction here and Castaño is one of the untouchables. A highly respected international lawyer from an aristocratic family and with friends in very high places. It would take years of legal pressure and wrangling and even with this evidence on the computer, a conviction would be unlikely. He'd just say he was acting in good faith for clients who duped him.'

'So he just gets away with it,' she said in disgust.

'Not necessarily, but probably.'

'Why not just—' She hesitated to use the word, momentarily remembering his muscular, golden body leaning over her, her hands clenching those buttocks that had looked so good in polo jodhpurs '— why not just get rid of him? Like you did Emilio.'

Savage glanced at Mallory. 'I didn't sanction that. My people aren't allowed to, not nowadays. Don't believe what you see in the movies. I can probably justify Kurt's action in terms of self-defence, especially as he had the good sense to put the body in Castaño's car. It'll be Castaño's problem when he discovers it, probably not until he returns from Budapest. My guess is he'll use his underworld contacts to dispose of it. It'll never be found or else be attributed to some low-life. Murder by person or persons unknown.'

Kelly stared hard at her, not really wanting to hear the confirmation of something she'd always believed. 'So it's all right if you can get away with it.'

It seemed that Savage had missed the sarcasm in her friend's voice. 'In the Third World, yes, or sometimes if the victim is some sort of gangster like Emilio.' She added: 'But Castaño is different, too high-profile. If ever there was a sniff of a hint of British involvement it could turn into a major political incident. No one wants to rock European unity.'

Kelly sighed. 'It seems so unfair that Miguel should continue to get richer and richer at the expense of others and never get punished.'

'I agree. But, as I said, your ex-boyfriend is one of life's untouchables.'

Even as she said the words, as the Ferrari Spyder sped towards Madrid and the airport beyond, the plastic neck of the Coca-Cola bottle beneath the bonnet finally melted, splitting open to squirt petrol onto the sparking copper coil around the manifold.

The car became an instant, moving fireball. As the bonnet and wing panels were blasted assunder, it began careering from side to side before crashing through the roadside barrier and over the embankment. For a second it was airborne like a flaming meteor, then it plunged into a field of sunflowers. There it burned with an unbelievable rage as the polythene packets of used engine oil fed the conflagration and ate its way into the fuel lines. When the petrol tank blew, the entire vehicle disintegrated, spreading debris over a hundred metres, and sent a thick coil of greasy smoke tumbling into the air. It could be seen for miles. Eventually, after a thorough investigation, the cause of the accident would remain a mystery. There would be no traces of melted copper wire, plastic or polythene. No reason for the explosion. Only the scorched remains of a bottle cap might cause a puzzled eyebrow to be raised, but probably not. The minds of the police would be focused on why a pair of famous lawyers should have had a corpse in the boot of their car.

In fact the ugly smudge could still be seen drifting across the golden eastern sky an hour later as Savage drove along the

Madrid-bound highway with Kelly by her side.

'When will Kurt be back home?' the Irish girl asked.

'The three of them have got a car hidden up behind the villa. They'll split to the four winds – well, three in their case – it's standard procedure after an operation like this. They'll drive down to Seville and drop Mario off to catch a flight. They haven't told me the details, not policy. Then I think Goldie will be dropped by the border with Gib and will fly out from there. Kurt will dump the car, take the ferry to Tangier and then catch a flight. All destinations unknown. They'll go to ground while the dust settles. I'm sure it won't be long before you see Kurt.'

Kelly nodded gravely. 'We all left in such a rush we didn't have time to talk. I don't really know if Kurt's planning to come home at all.'

'Oh, I think so,' Savage said with a smile. 'He's spending a while with Goldie somewhere, but then you'll see him. When we were planning the raid on Castaño's villa, he talked about you a lot. Well, a lot for someone who doesn't normally wear his heart on his sleeve. I even started getting pangs of envy.'

Kelly grinned. 'Really? Anyway you're a married woman.'

'Don't remind me.'

Up ahead they noticed the pulsing blue lights of the police car first. Savage felt a flutter of apprehension in her chest. Brake lights blinked on as the traffic queue started to form and she feared a police roadblock. But her anxiety was short-lived as she saw the flashing amber beacon of a breakdown truck and the ambulance parked on the hard shoulder.

'Some sort of accident,' she murmured, changing down as they nosed up to the vehicle in front.

During the next five minutes, they inched forward. The inside lane had been cordoned off and, within the tapes, traffic police and paramedics milled around, staring at the ripped-out section of steel barrier. Neither Savage nor Kelly could see the wreckage that was somewhere down the embankment, but smoke still billowed relentlessly from the site.

Kelly shivered. 'Looks nasty. And on a straight stretch of road. Maybe it was a tyreburst . . .' Her voice trailed off as she saw the vehicle debris that had been swept in behind the cordon. The buckled front fender section, which had somehow detached itself from the vehicle before it left the road, glinted in the sunlight. Its red paintwork was scorched but the number plate was intact.

Savage braked as the queue came to a standstill.

Beside her, Kelly stiffened. She lifted her sunglasses to read the registration number again, to be sure she'd got it right. 'Oh, sweet Mary and Joseph.'

'What is it?'

'I don't believe it. That car, the number plate. I think it's Miguel's Ferrari.'

'Miguel? You – you mean Castaño?'

'It's *his* car that went off the road.' A note of certainty had edged into her voice.

Oh, my God, Savage thought. Her lips closed into a thin line and she stared straight ahead. Suddenly she knew. Remembered the time she'd seen this before. In Northern Ireland. An elusive paramilitary leader vaporised by a mystery car explosion.

'What is it, Georgie?' Kelly asked, sensing something.

The traffic was speeding up again now and Savage changed gear angrily. 'It's Kurt, damn him.'

'Kurt?' Bewildered.

A bitter smile crossed Savage's face. She shouldn't really say anything, but she was too shocked to care. 'I thought the three of them were a bit quiet when I said how Castaño was an untouchable, how he wouldn't ever be brought to justice. Christ, I should have guessed!'

'I don't understand. Guessed what?'

'That Kurt had rigged the car.'

'Rigged?'

'A bomb. One of Kurt's specialities, picked it up somewhere in South America. Virtually untraceable. The police will never realise it was an act of sabotage, or at least have no evidence.'

Kelly looked back over her shoulder. 'You mean Kurt did that? He's killed Miguel and . . .' Realisation dawned. 'And Claudia? Oh, God, he hasn't?'

Savage suddenly began to chuckle softly, shaking her head

slowly from side to side. 'That's our hero. The last of the men in the white hats,' she said with heavy irony. 'How do you see him now? A Roy Rogers or a Gene Autry? Or maybe old Hopalong? Or the Lone Ranger? Hell, who was that masked stranger? Hi-oh, Silver!'

'You didn't know he was going to do it?'

'No, I didn't. But I should have guessed. It was like what happened in Colombia.'

'What happened?'

'Some other time.' Her knuckles showed white on the wheel. 'It's the problem when you use a freelance force. Especially, that particular force. They believe in people's justice, rough justice. Reaching out to where the law can't.'

Kelly still appeared confused, but other implications were now starting to become clear in her mind. 'Won't I be a suspect, Georgie? I mean if I leave just after Miguel and Claudia are killed by a car bomb. Isn't the jealous lover going to be top of the list?'

Savage considered for a moment, realising that Mallory would have already thought it through and discussed it with Goldie. 'You might be a very *unlikely* suspect, I suppose. But that's if it even occurs to the police that it could have been a bomb. Despite Castaño's friends in high places, he also had enemies – especially in the police. His company has defended ETA terrorists and as a result of Kurt's work and Castaño's computer disk, I expect our own Drugs Squad in London will eventually send the Madrid police detailed intelligence of his suspected activities. So if a bomb is even suspected, the obvious perpetrators will be a rival drugs gang or a disaffected ETA member. A jilted lawyer girl-friend who happened to walk out on him at the same time as the accident is hardly likely to be top of their priority list. At worst, in a few weeks' time your local bobby might call to take a statement on behalf of the Spanish police, but don't hold your breath. Don't forget, I'm your witness, the friend who came to pick you up after your lovers' tiff. If there's a problem, call me. My department excels in pouring oil on troubled waters and smoothing ruffled feathers.'

Kelly grinned uneasily. 'Thanks, Georgie, you're a real friend.

I just wish I could take it all in my stride like you. It had all become a bit of a game until Emilio was killed. Now Miguel and Claudia . . .' She looked down at her hands and saw that they were trembling. 'I suppose, eventually, you can get used to these things.'

Savage didn't reply. There were some things in this business you could never ever get used to.

17

Savage changed back the number plates on the rented SEAT in the Madrid 200 car park, before returning the vehicle to the hire company at the airport. Then she and Kelly took a British Airways flight to Heathrow.

There they parted company, Savage leaving her friend at the Aer Lingus ticket desk while she took a taxi back to London. On the journey she had time to marshal her thoughts, beginning to realise the favour that Mallory had done for her and her follow-up operations. With Castaño dead, the likelihood was that the White Viper consignments would continue on their planned schedule through Europe over the next few weeks. And the full details were on the floppy disk in her bag. That meant there was now a strong possibility of arrests in Germany, Spain and, hopefully, the UK.

They might even be able to put a finger on Stan Summers, the flamboyant Essex crook. So far the only evidence against him came from the operation in Colombia which could never be used because, officially, it had never taken place. And the skeletons of thirty British nationals were not what she or her chiefs at riverside would ever want to hear rattling in a British courtroom.

As soon as she reached her office in the Vauxhall Cross building she made two calls. The first was to her husband.

'Honey, I'm home!' she announced cheerily.

He was not amused. 'Home, sweetheart, is here. With me in this empty armchair in front of the fire. Home is not your sodding office.'

She couldn't blame him. Since spending many weeks in South America, supposedly on UN business, she'd hardly been back a month before disappearing to Spain. 'Listen, my favourite City whiz kid, I just have to make one call and I'm on my way. I'll pick up a takeaway and a bottle of plonk. How about that?'

'Make it a couple of bottles. Three even.'

'Something to celebrate?'

'Not exactly. I've just lost my job.'

The second call didn't exactly cheer her either. Sidney Monckton, deputy chief of SIS, was clearly in his after-hours malt whisky and a chat mood – his way of unwinding in the wake of a hard day. He interrupted her brief update of events with a jovial: 'Pop up now, Georgie-girl, this all sounds very interesting. You're lucky I've an hour to spare before I have to be off to a Mansion House dinner.'

Lucky? To find the deputy chief in mellow and reflective mood was not what Savage called lucky, not when she should be rushing home to give Giles a shoulder to cry on. But then it really wouldn't do to have them both ruin their careers on the same day. And she had seen too many who had misread the smile on the face of this particular tiger. Monckton's whims, suggestions and polite invitations were ignored at your peril, as a downward or sideways career move or posting to some godforsaken extremity of the world would surely follow.

At least she found him in genuine good humour, the tall loose-limbed body reclining in his leather swivel chair, long fingers interlaced across his chest and a smile on the remarkably boyish face.

'Sounds like a cause for modest congratulations,' he said, splashing some amber liquid into a second tumbler. 'Now do please relax yourself and give me chapter and verse.'

Not wanting to be there for a moment longer than she needed to, Savage quickly ran through the events at the villa, outlining the details of the European distribution plans for White Viper. He listened intently. His laughing eyes, magnified through the pebble glass of his horn-rims, took on a distinctly steely glaze as she revealed the involvement of the Captain in Budapest. This was a major breakthrough and she was sure Monckton was visualising the moment he broke the news to the Chief himself and maybe even headed a deputation to appear before the Joint Intelligence Committee of the Cabinet. A handsome prize and proof that there was still a vital rôle for SIS to play in the fight against drugs now that threats to national security were getting harder to come by. It might also help to stop mumblings about the millions spent on the new art-deco headquarters next to Vauxhall railway station.

'So this lawyer Castaño and one of his business partners died in a car crash?' He could hardly keep the scepticism from his question.

Savage smiled brightly. 'Very convenient for us, sir. I imagine he just wasn't concentrating. My freelancer's interrogation probably shook him up badly.'

Monckton frowned. 'And this – er – accident was nothing to do with us?'

By that she knew he meant SIS. No possibility of fallout and unpleasant repercussions.

'Sir.' Indignant. 'I would never issue such instructions. It has all the appearances of a genuine accident.'

Thank you, Kurt, she said beneath her breath.

'Then once again your man Zigzagger is to be congratulated,' Monckton said. She did not tell him the codename was now Zookeeper. 'If the Captain and the Sportsmen are unaware of our intelligence, then we must take immediate steps. There is a lot to be done. Right now.' Of course she knew he was right. This really couldn't wait until the morning. Buttons had to be pressed, people activated. God, she was tired.

Reluctantly she returned to her office and phoned her husband to give him the good news. By the sound of his slurred words he'd been hitting the gin and tonic; it was a short and unloving conversation.

Then she convened a meeting with the duty officer of Global Issues Department and the operations desk. Within the hour, the Head of Station in Budapest would have his supper interrupted. A surveillance team would have to be thrown together at short notice. It was not a major problem because SIS had always had good contacts in Hungary even before the collapse of Communism. They would have to assemble local talent because there were few SIS field officers who had ever mastered one of the most difficult languages on God's earth and most of them had retired in recent years.

With dates and locations of the transport schedule known, together with the registration numbers of the vehicles being used, it should be relatively easy to pick up the trail.

Her meeting over and the plan of action laid, she telephoned the duty desk at the Investigation Division of Customs House. Their Drugs Liaison Officer for the region was based in Prague; he would take the next flight to Budapest to co-ordinate and dovetail their part in the operation with that of the intelligence service.

There would inevitably, she knew, be problems as both organisations tried to fight for overall control because both would want to claim the eventual credit. At least her people had a head start and held the initiative.

But it was all so tiresome, being dragged into these big boys' games, especially when the real achievement would be down to an organisation that didn't even exist. Didn't even have a name.

When Savage finally left the office it was two in the morning and the lights were still burning in ops.

They came for him at eleven thirty. Four of the bastards, brick-faced Slavs in box-cut suits reminiscent of the old KGB style. But nowadays the material was sharp and expensive and they spent all their time talking to each other on portable telephones.

Kevin Sheehan was waiting for them in the lobby of the Grand Corvinus and they knew exactly where to find him. One of them spoke English but there was no need for words. Sheehan stood and walked out, flanked by two men on each side, to the waiting Lexus saloon with its smoked-glass windows.

They travelled in silence, Sheehan preoccupied with the reasons for this hastily arranged visit. He liked Budapest. Normally he would have enjoyed its architecture and old buildings, its parks and coffee shops. He would have again been amused by the Hungarian penchant for decorating their dull Ladas and Skodas with brightly coloured transfers before the ancient cars inevitably ended their days unceremoniously dumped at the kerbside with flat tyres. And he would have eyed up the girls with their dark natural good looks and liking for indecently skimpy hot pants. Girls whom he knew the Captain and others had been quick to exploit for the burgeoning porno business: naive and anxious to please, they were only too happy to perform for a fraction of the rate of their West European counterparts. The free market economy had arrived for good or ill.

But today Sheehan was blind to everything except the reasons for his visit.

They crossed the Danube and then along the embankment before pulling up outside the double-decked rotunda of the grand Gellért hotel. Its marble pillars and baroque stone walls, now festooned in ivy, had been raised in 1918 to house the reception halls and guest rooms and the public baths they now entered.

Sheehan didn't like meeting here. Citizens queued for tickets in this mausoleum of a place beneath the vaulted ceiling and stained-glass skylight dome; they stood in groups on the mosaic floor, chatting or peering at the art-deco statues as they waited for friends. Definitely too many eyes and ears for Sheehan's liking, but this was where the Captain chose to hold court.

He'd asked Nikolai Khuchuk once, why, when he had a splendid dacha with indoor and outdoor pools, he was inclined to spend so much of his time here at the public baths? The Ukrainian had looked at him as though the answer was stupidly obvious. 'It reminds me of home,' he said.

Then Sheehan had understood. In recently democratised Budapest, the public baths with their steam rooms and cold plunges and fat *babushka* attendants were the only reminders of typical daily life under the old Communist regimes of eastern Europe. For all his wealth and influence and power, Nikolai Khuchuk was homesick.

One of the Sportsmen disappeared into the door marked Thermal and Weight Room; Sheehan kicked his heels, uncomfortable, trying to keep his face turned away from any casual onlookers.

It seemed an age before Khuchuk emerged and he clearly had no qualms about being seen. Here he was king and amongst loyal subjects, untouchable.

'Mr Sheehan, what a delight!' His voice was deep and pure Oxbridge with barely a trace of accent, although he had never set foot in England; he had been taught at a KGB language school.

He was swaddled in a terry-towelling gown which added to his girth and accentuated his short stature. His greying curly hair was still damp from the steam and he was smoking a cigar. There was a tigerish smile on his broad face and a hard glint in the crinkled eyes.

'Would you like to swim?' Khuchuk asked. 'You can hire swim shorts and towels.'

'I would like to talk.'

The tiger smiled. 'Our friend Castaño liked to swim. Liked to show off to the girls.'

'Castaño won't be swimming any more. Or showing off. He's dead.'

Khuchuk's expression hardly changed; he covered his surprise by blowing a perfect smoke ring. 'I wondered why he failed to keep our appointment. And no word of explanation, nothing.'

'A car crash.'

'I'm sorry. Let's have a drink and talk.'

He led the way through the pool room with its potted palms and sunbeds and up to an open-air terrace with a stone balustrade. It overlooked the hotel grounds and the outdoor pools. Three of the Sportsmen positioned themselves nearby, ever watchful, whilst the fourth arranged for drinks.

The Ukrainian relaxed on a lounger. 'The last time I met with Miguel Castaño – a few weeks ago – he mentioned there had been a slight hiccup on the production side.'

Sheehan's smile hid his real feelings. Slight hiccup? Wasn't that just the understatement of the decade, even the century? Their entire Colombian operation wiped out overnight and the camp set ablaze – the warning tip-off of what was about to happen being telephoned to Castaño one hour too late. It had come from another cartel who'd got wind of what was happening. Rivals they may have been but in Colombia they shared several mutual enemies – not least the DEA which, they understood, had infiltrated the White Viper operation. That seemed to be supported by simultaneous events in Venezuela and Bolivia where raids on the distribution network and the supply gangs in the Chapare were co-ordinated by known DEA personnel. A total, cataclysmic meltdown.

Not for the first time Sheehan wondered if the tip-off coming just one hour too late was coincidence.

He said: 'There will be a disruption in supply.'

'Oh.' Khuchuk didn't attempt to hide his disappointment.

'For about six weeks.'

The tiger's smile returned. 'Is that all?'

'We have new partners in Colombia. They are very efficient.'

'Six weeks,' Khuchuk echoed. 'We can live with that.'

'But there is another consequence.'

'Yes?'

'During the period of – er – disruption, it is possible the integrity of current shipments was compromised. Therefore precautions must be taken.'

Khuchuk's eyes narrowed a fraction. 'Of course. What do you have in mind, a change of scheduling?'

'Yes and no. Keep to the schedule and run the allotted vehicles, but run them clean. Meanwhile transfer the product to different vehicles and run them on a new schedule. That is why I am here – to help you set up a new schedule.'

The Ukrainian tossed his cigar butt into a nearby plant pot. 'An expensive operation at this stage.'

Bastard, Sheehan thought, but he'd been expecting it. 'But necessary.'

'Our percentage must rise by five points.'

'No.' The Irishman was firm. Already the Captain was squeezing them until their eyes watered. The new east European businessmen had no idea of the give-and-take of Western commerce; if they had an advantage, they pressed it to the point of self-destruction. 'No percentage increase. We'll just cover the real-cost expense.'

Khuchuk looked unhappy.

'Before you say a word,' Sheehan added, 'remember that your outfit is our first choice, but not our only one.'

The Ukrainian didn't answer immediately. His mind went back nine months to when he'd first tried to double-cross Sheehan – to the shoot-out on the patch of waste ground beside the Danube on the city's outskirts. His men hadn't known where they'd come from – they'd appeared as though from nowhere. Without hesitation they'd gunned down three of his lieutenants. Only later was he told the men had come from Belfast and had bought their guns from a local Serbian mafia down in Szeged.

From that bitter experience Khuchuk had learned respect for Kevin Sheehan's people; they knew their way around, they had power and they weren't afraid to use it.

The beers arrived and the Captain raised his glass. 'To our partnership – renewed!'

They hit the warehouse in Brentwood at dawn. Drug Squad officers backed by armed units from PT17 and local police and investigators from Customs and Excise swooped to cut off the little industrial estate just off the M25 and isolated the razor-wired compound where the articulated container truck had been parked since arriving off the cross-Channel ferry. It had been followed all the way across Europe from Budapest, through Austria and Germany to France.

Exactly to schedule, thought Savage as she sat at the wheel of the inconspicuous green Cavalier and watched the flashing blue lights through the rain while the police used bolt cutters to snap the gate chains.

'Should be feeling proud of yourself, Georgie-girl,' Monckton said.

She hadn't wanted him here, never in a million years. Certainly not until it was sewn up for sure. But Monckton, being Monckton, had insisted. No doubt wanted to share the glory, or claim it for himself.

'Many a slip twixt cup and lip, sir,' she replied, just a touch frostily.

'But it's all to the schedule.'

Yes, she thought, to schedule. Straight off Miguel Castaño's computer disk. The right route, the right dates, the right vehicle registration. Just one thing out of place. 'I'm still worried about the driver and his mate.'

'Probably not important.'

But she'd known since the container truck had passed through Dover that their names were different from the schedule and she thought it might be important. Even very important.

'The previous names showed up, sir. These don't.'

The original driver on the schedule was a small-time Hungarian crook with previous form according to the Budapest police. His mate was from Londonderry, middle-aged with a minor unauthorised-possession-of-firearms offence to his credit. Into this Savage had read: driver supplied by the Sportsmen and the Provisional IRA riding shotgun.

Now the two new names meant nothing to her. Both were Hungarian and both, according to Budapest, were clean.

The arclights came on in the unloading bay where the giant truck stood, its anonymous red flanks caked with dust and road dirt after its journey across Europe.

Another police car joined the collection gathered outside the compound and Savage recognised the man who climbed out of the rear. He was wearing a trenchcoat against the rain and was standing between two plain-clothes officers, gesticulating in an obvious display of protest.

Stan Summers hadn't been arrested, she knew. They just called at his home in the early hours and invited him to attend a raid on one of his business premises.

He stood, hands in pockets, for the next two hours while the technical experts used a forklift to remove the freezer unit from the container. It was clean. In near desperation other officers stripped down the rest of the empty container, prising off the inside panels and the insulation. Inside the warehouse the cargo of mixed foodstuffs was examined, making it unfit for human consumption in the process.

The sun had come up to introduce a wet, grey and bleak

411

autumn morning; it wasn't looking good.

Monckton was beginning to wish he hadn't come. 'Go over and see what they've found.'

She was glad to be away from him, to be out of the stale air and stretching her legs.

Stan Summers was still there, his chubby face beaming and looking pleased with himself; quite cocky now that the initial shock had worn off. He had even been joined by his solicitor and the two of them were chatting and smiling.

Deciding how much compensation they would sting them for, Savage thought. She lit a cigarette and, keeping in the background, sought out one of her contacts from Customs.

'Any luck?' she asked.

He looked grim. 'I thought this was STI?'

Specific Target Intelligence. 'So did I.'

'Go home, Georgie, unless you like watching grown men cry.'

'I'm sorry.'

She crossed back over the road towards the Cavalier. Somehow they'd known. Or else taken precautions and just got lucky. Without STI the next stash of White Viper could be aboard any one of the hundreds of container trucks coming across the Channel that day. Or the next, or the one after. They'd lost the needle in the haystack and it was one sodding big haystack.

'It's a blowout,' she said climbing back behind the wheel. She felt deflated, as if all her efforts in Colombia and Spain had been a waste of time. They hadn't, of course, but without a result on home turf it just felt like it.

Monckton offered no consolation; he'd seen success and failure a hundred times before. 'Best get back to riverside. Work to be done.'

She turned on the engine. 'I could do with a few days off,' she said, and meant it.

'Lick the old wounds, eh, Georgie-girl.' He laughed that fourth-form laugh of his. 'Regird one's loins and prepare to rejoin the fray.'

She engaged gear. 'I'd like to get away for a while.'

'Splendid idea. Take that husband of yours away to the Lake

District, a cottage or something. Do you the world of good.'

Fuck off, Monckton! she mouthed silently and let out the clutch with an angry jolt.

He seemed to get the message; he said nothing more, which was unusual.

Mallory stretched out his legs and dug his bare feet into the sand, enjoying the sensation of it running between his toes.

It was years since he had done anything remotely like this. Probably not since his childhood. Lying on a beach along Durban's golden mile, doing nothing but enjoying the tepid sunshine of the African spring and listening to the pounding surf. The experience was not unpleasant, but it felt profoundly alien.

Goldie was lying out beside him, his body looking pale and emaciated in the baggy blue swimming shorts. He propped himself up on his elbows, his long hair tangled by the offshore breeze, and watched his wife and kids at play.

Aggie was as reed-thin as her husband but much younger. Despite her fragile build, there was something wholesome and comforting about her. Perhaps it was her disregard for make-up and fashion, Mallory thought. A combination of the very long hair, the pale lashes of those powder blue eyes and the lazy smile. He was reminded of a pot-smoking flowerchild, a disciple of free love who had made an effortless transition into earth mother. As she shovelled a plastic spade full of sand onto the castle keep, it was easy to see that nothing would perturb her, unsettle her peace of mind.

Their two naked children jumped up and down and squealed with glee as sea water rushed into the little moat. A boy and a girl, four and three.

'This could be you some day soon,' Goldie said.

'Me?'

'Family man. Changing nappies. Picnics in the park.' A sly grin. 'I saw the way she looked at you at the villa. And the way you looked at her. It was written all over your face.'

'What was?'

'The big question.'

413

'You think so?'

'I *know* so. We all need someone, Kurt, even you. I used to think that my life was my work until Aggie came along. Then the kiddies. Guess it puts things into perspective.' He stared out at the glimmering waves of the Indian Ocean as they tumbled languidly towards the shore. 'She's a very pretty girl, Kurt. Mario thought so too, and he is an expert. And a warm personality. Too good for you, my friend. You should marry her before she finds another boyfriend like Castaño.'

Mallory nodded. 'You're right.'

'So you'll marry her?'

A grin. 'I meant you're right, she's too good for me.'

Goldie gave one of his rare squeaks of laughter. 'You should let her be the judge of that, but take my advice and don't leave it too long. You're welcome to stay with us here for as long as you like, but you must ask yourself how long is *she* likely to wait?'

Mallory watched two cormorants flying high above the beach. His friend was right, had seen it in his eyes. He had been alone in life too long, keeping friends and lovers at a distance. Exactly what was it he was afraid of? It was time to change, to recognise that barely a second had passed since they'd left Madrid that Kelly hadn't been in his thoughts. He'd promised himself he'd stay with Goldie's family for a week. And yet it was now ten days and still he hadn't made a move.

He asked himself why. It wasn't that he wanted to put off the moment, his longing to be with her again was like an ache in his gut. It was something else. Something else was unsettling him. Even here, lounging on the beach in mild sunshine and with the laughter of children ringing in his ears, he felt a nagging sense of unease. But not of the future; it was a sensation he recognised all too well from his past. Events at Cruz de Oro and in Madrid had happened thousands of miles away and were fast drifting into the mist of time. Yet they were still haunting him. Even here he felt as though eyes were always watching.

He said suddenly: 'Maybe we shouldn't have come here so soon after Madrid.'

Goldie shrugged. 'We covered our tracks.'

'I always make a point of disappearing for a month or two. To let the trail go cold.'

'It's not a luxury I can afford, Kurt. If I did that I'd spend half the year unemployed. Anyway, I switch identity when I travel and I've lived here now for ten years without problems. We have good friends and neighbours, we go to dances and barbecues. No one knows who I really am or what I do. They think I'm a travelling salesman. Why not? Boxes and compartments, isn't that what the experts have always taught us?'

'No security is ever a hundred per cent foolproof. There was that break-in at my home.'

Goldie looked sceptical. 'Is that what all this is about? That incident at Bogotá airport still preying on your mind? And you still think Dale Forster's death was suspicious?'

'The boat exploded and sank without trace in thirty fathoms, Goldie. No one will ever know the truth.'

'I never had you down as paranoid.'

Mallory laughed uneasily. 'I've been in this game too long. Maybe I'm starting to think I can't still get away with it. That's why I quit before – after I came too close to getting caught out. I only came back to avenge Vic West.'

'You are starting to depress me. How about an ice cream?'

'Sure, why not?' Mallory grinned at his friend's attempt to change the subject. 'I haven't had an ice cream in years.'

'You should do. Remind yourself of your childhood and keep in touch with your soul.'

Goldie had meant it well enough, but Mallory had no desire to remember certain aspects of his childhood. That had been when darkness had first touched any soul he still had left.

The children and Aggie placed their order and Mallory trudged with Goldie across the sand towards the promenade.

'By the way, Kurt, I got a call from Mario last night. He phoned just after you'd turned in. That idiot has got no idea about international time zones! Sends his best wishes. He's now bought this little house on Martinique. He's settling down and has got himself a fishing boat.'

'Any new woman in his life?'

Goldie shook his head, struggling against the breeze as it tugged at his voluminous shorts. 'Doesn't sound like it. He's still having wet dreams about Victor Tafur's girl. Blames himself for what happened. He says he'll wait for six months or so and go back to Bogotá. See if he can find Juanita and persuade her to marry him. Sometimes that man acts like a love-sick bull!'

'Knowing Mario, he might just pull it off. He was very fond of her.' They were nearing the promenade now and could see the ice-cream van. 'And you, Goldie, what are your plans?'

'It must be catching,' he laughed, 'but I'm thinking of retiring too. Freelancing is a precarious business. My mortgage is paid off and I'm due a modest pension from Mossad.'

'What about the organisation?'

'Maybe I'll keep my hand in from time to time. Unlike you, Kurt, I am not self-taught. I was professionally trained and old *katsas* never die. But maybe for the kids' sake, I ought to just fade away.'

Mallory noticed the parked motorcycle out of the corner of his eye. It was an ancient model that had been obviously repainted by hand; two black youths wearing woollen hats and shabby nondescript clothes sat astride it, watching people walk by. Girl-spotting, he thought idly as Goldie joined the queue for the ice-cream van.

Out at sea a white haze was settling over the horizon, blending the water with the sky so that it was impossible to see the exact line where one ended and the other began.

He heard Goldie order five cones with bars of chocolate flake at the same time as the black motorcyclist began to kick-start his machine. Twice, three times the engine gave an irritating cough, as though trying unsuccessfully to clear phlegm. Mallory shared the motorcyclist's frustration himself, listening with only half an ear, absently willing the thing to start. If it hadn't started on the fifth attempt and promptly backfired, he would probably never have looked.

The loud fart of exhaust turned several heads. His eyes left Goldie, who was walking back towards him with the five cones cradled precariously in both hands, and he shifted his gaze in the other direction. The motorcycle was wobbling uncertainly into motion, the pillion passenger's legs still outstretched, coming in Mallory's direction.

It flashed inexplicably through his mind that something was wrong. But no, there was nothing wrong. But there was. Something very wrong. The young black faces had vanished, hidden behind masks of wool. His lasting impression was of the whites of their eyes, wide with apprehension at what they were about to do. Then he saw the weapon in the pillion passenger's hand. Just a glinting barrel. A revolver, an automatic, some sort of machine pistol. It was impossible to tell. The man's knees gripped the side of the machine as the gun came up, held in a double grip.

It all happened in agonising slow motion as the motorcycle passed him by, the rider crouched over the handlebars, struggling to hold it steady at a slow and even speed. The pillion seeking out his target. Mallory thinking the danger was past; it wasn't him. Then thinking, so who? And remembering Goldie, walking towards him. Trying to pirouette, raising his hand in warning, the scream coming belatedly to his throat.

'WATCH OUT!' The force of his cry tore at his vocal chords.

But it was all too late.

Goldie Goldstein had been lifted off his feet and flung back into the queue at the ice-cream van. Others were down, too. A young woman and an older man, both lying on the pavement. Covered in blood and screaming. And a child, a small boy, writhing in his death throes as his mother rushed towards him. Blobs of ice cream splattered everywhere over the red-soaked clothing.

Mallory stood and stared, paralysed, as the motorcycle backfired again and the young rider accelerated, disappearing into the stream of passing traffic.

A random killing, the policeman thought.

He was a polite Afrikaner and he chose his words carefully for Aggie's benefit. Only in his mid-twenties but his eyes bore the hardened expression of an older man who had seen it all before.

Probably boys from one of the townships, discontented that the great promise of the New South Africa hadn't lived up to their expectations, that nothing much had really changed. The police had been anticipating a backlash and maybe this was part of it. A lot of disaffected youths out there, still simmering with resentment. Gun-trained by the ANC in the old days. Some a bit unstable. Drive into a nice town like Durban and shake it up a bit. Why not? Take a shot at the old enemy, let the white trash know that not everyone with a black skin had forgotten or forgiven.

The police would find them though; the old motorcycle was a good clue. But it might take a while.

Mallory let him out. Aggie wasn't aware that the policeman had left, she was on another planet. Curled on her bed in a foetal ball, sobbing with her thumb in her mouth. Her candyfloss world shattered and her children, not yet understanding what had happened to their father, taken in by caring neighbours.

She had calmed down a little by the evening when he took her a cup of tea. Her eyes were red-rimmed and she was so shaky that the cup rattled in the saucer when he gave it to her.

'I got your parents' number from your address book,' he said. 'They're driving down from Ladysmith.'

She was still numbed. 'Dad never did like Goldie.'

'I'm sure that's not true.'

Aggie sniffed. 'Why him, Kurt? Why? Goldie of all people would never persecute anyone for their race or beliefs. His father died in Auschwitz.'

Auschwitz, Mallory thought. How many people were aware of the irony of its translation: the last laugh. Well, Goldie had had the last laugh all right. His life had been spent trying to destroy the sort of evil that had resulted in his father's death. That had been his private motivation for working with Mossad, and later the organisation, though he doubted Aggie knew that; it was the sort of thing Goldie would keep to himself.

'Sometimes these things just happen,' Mallory answered lamely.

She squeezed his hand. 'I'm glad you're here. How long will you stay?'

'For as long as you want me to.'

For the first time her eyes were clear of tears. 'I must learn to cope. That's what Goldie would say. And you've got your own life to lead. He told me you've got someone back in Ireland who's waiting for you. You must go to her. She's very lucky.'

That night, after Aggie's parents had arrived and the family were sitting up late to commiserate with her, Mallory went to the room Goldie had used as his study. There was a notepad by the telephone. Mario had phoned the previous night, his friend had said. He flipped over the top sheet and there it was. A Martinique telephone number for the new house.

He lifted the receiver and dialled, wondering how best to break the news.

It was a bad line. A strange and distorted voice answered in French.

'May I talk to Monsieur Dubois?' Mallory asked in Spanish.

The man had no difficulty in switching languages. 'Who is calling please?'

'A friend.'

'I must have a name.'

Mallory felt an uneasy crawling sensation in his stomach. 'Who is that?'

'This is a police officer. You must give me your name.'

On impulse Mallory said: 'Smith. William Smith. I am a friend of Mario's and I'm calling from South Africa. Now please put me through.'

'I'm afraid that's not possible. Señor Dubois is dead. I am the Scene-of-Crime officer. Now I must ask you for your address and telephone number for our file.'

No one appeared to be watching the bungalow from the quiet and carefully tended Durban suburb street. But it was not yet dawn so he couldn't be certain and Mallory was taking no chances.

Leaving a note for Aggie, he slipped out through the kitchen door at the rear. The small garden backed onto another and he scaled the fence into the adjoining grounds. In minutes he found himself on the sidewalk of a virtually identical parallel street.

Same clapboard bungalows in pastel colours, same pretty front gardens and cropped lawns. He began walking at a brisk pace, frequently glancing back over his shoulder. Watching the shadows, listening for footsteps – or the sound of a motorcycle.

His head was still reeling from what he had learned from the policeman at Mario's home on Martinique. Bludgeoned to death by an unknown intruder, the place wrecked in the search for valuables. The crime probably committed by a burglar high on something or other— but until investigations were complete . . .

All this had to be some kind of nightmare. Dale Forster, an accident. Goldie, the victim of a freakish random killing. Mario murdered by some dope-crazed thief.

It was too much to swallow. Mallory never had been a great believer in extended coincidence, but he couldn't be sure. He'd even been witness to Goldie's death and he still couldn't tell whether Goldie had been the specific target or the entire ice-cream queue, chosen to represent the white middle class. Was it a messily botched assassination or a deliberate massacre? He didn't even know if the killer had been after him too? Had he just been standing too far away to be taken in a single burst or had the killer flunked the job?

All he knew was that over half the team that had gone into Colombia was now dead. And if it wasn't an amazing sequence of unlucky events, then who was behind it? And what was the motive, the reason?

Only he and Savage were left now. And if the break-in at his croft had been part of it, then by rights he too should now be dead. And that would have left George as the sole survivor.

Yet the killing process – if that's what it was – had begun before the mission to Madrid when he was still working for her and her masters at SIS. It didn't make sense, although everything pointed to some sort of governmental hand behind it all. Considerable power, influence, finance and resources were required to track down so many individuals to different parts of the world and to orchestrate a series of accidents or apparently motiveless killings. It smacked of the work of some intelligence agency, but the real reason for it all still eluded him.

As he continued walking and the day began to break, he felt calmer. For the moment at least he was certain that no one was following. The streets were filling with pedestrians making their way to work, cars were coming out of their driveways and taxis beginning to ply their trade.

He picked one up at a rank and told the cabbie to take him to Durban airport. Using his Jim Tate passport he took the first available flight to Johannesburg. Rather than fly to Heathrow, he booked on an afternoon flight to Paris. It would add a day to the journey by taking a train to Calais and then a ferry to Dover, but it meant a far better chance of entering the country unnoticed.

Thirty-six hours later he was back in London. As soon as he arrived at Waterloo station he made his way to a call box and telephoned the only number he had for Savage. Her direct office line.

A man answered. 'Yes.' No extension, no form of identity.

'I'd like to speak to Mrs Hayes.' It was the cover name she'd used in Venezuela and Colombia.

There was a hesitation, the man presumably checking the list of aliases she used. 'She's out of the office at present.' His tone was abrupt and singularly unhelpful.

'How long for?'

'I really couldn't say.' The pompous response told Mallory he was asking for classified information.

'Out like in hours or in days?' Mallory snapped.

'I really don't know.' Then, as an afterthought: 'Give me a number and I'll ask her to call you when she's back.'

'That's no good. I can't be reached.'

'Then you'll have to call again.'

One more try, he thought. 'When? Tomorrow? Next week?'

'I really couldn't say.'

Like a bloody robot! Mallory seethed. Did he tell this smug jerk that he had an unconfirmed suspicion that someone, but he didn't know who, might be out to assassinate Intelligence Officer Savage but that he had no idea why?

No, he thought not. For all he knew he was speaking to the man who was arranging it. And if he left a message he'd called then it would be known he was back in the country.

He made it sound as though it didn't matter. 'Not to worry, it was just a personal call. Thanks anyway.' And hung up.

Another tack was necessary, another route. He called the number of Portcullis Industries and asked for Colonel Oliver Maidment. He was promptly put through to his personal secretary.

Her manner was the absolute opposite of the man who had answered Savage's telephone. 'I'm afraid he's away on business in Belgrade at the moment. Can I help you or take a message?'

'Would you just tell him Kurt called. I'm going home and there's an urgent contract to sign.'

He could imagine her sharp intake of breath. That last phrase was open code for there is trouble and a meeting is required immediately. At least that's what Maidment knew. His secretary, who had been with the colonel for years, realised it meant her boss must be hunted down wherever he was in the world, even if it meant interrupting a conference with a head of state, as it sometimes had. But although aware of the importance of the phrase, she would never, ever be allowed to know its true significance.

Mallory felt happier now. Either Maidment himself or some trusted intermediary would act as soon as his message was received. They could discuss the deaths of Forster, Goldie and Mario and decide what action should be taken. And Maidment had the clout to knock on the door of the Secret Intelligence Service. It would open to him.

Digging in his pocket for more change, he dialled Kelly's office number in Dublin, only to be informed that she'd taken a few days off. She was staying with her father in County Kerry.

He dialled again and waited for what seemed an age. In his imagination he could see the telephone on the table in the large and fusty hallway, its strident old-fashioned ring echoing around the ageing panelled walls. Someone running down the long corridors to answer it.

The tone stopped abruptly; it was Kelly. 'Kurt! Where are you?'

'London. I'm coming home.'

'Thank God for that.' She sounded genuinely relieved.

'Are you okay?'

'Sure, I'm fine. But I was starting to worry about you when you didn't show after a week. Georgie warned me you go walkabout, as she put it, but when I didn't hear . . .'

'Have you been to the croft?'

'Just once, last week. I saw Mattie.'

'And there are no problems?'

The penny dropped. 'Oh, you mean the break-in.'

'Or any strangers snooping around the area?'

'Mattie didn't say. Look, Kurt, when are you coming back? You could get a flight to Shannon tomorrow morning. I'll meet you at the airport. Do you have any flight times?'

He told her. 'And don't mention to anyone I'm coming.'

She sounded puzzled. 'No, okay.'

'I'll see you then.'

'Kurt, I've missed you.'

Why did he find such endearments so difficult to utter? 'And believe me, I've missed you too.'

18

The airliner came in to land under a leaden, blustery sky. Wind and rain squalled across the runway, muffling the roar of the engines as they went into reverse thrust.

Kelly was waiting by the glass exit doors. A soaked trenchcoat hung open on her shoulders, revealing her sweater and the inevitable jodhpurs; her copper hair was sodden and dark, lying flat against her head. But her grin was wide as she saw him striding towards her. 'Welcome home to sunny Ireland,' she greeted and threw her arms around his neck.

Mallory was drenched too by the time they reached her Discovery in the car park. Dumping his rucksack on the back seat, he climbed in beside her as she started the engine and ran up the blowers to clear the condensation on the windscreen.

'Five days nonstop,' she told him, shaking her head with incredulity. 'Why *do* I love this country? I must be mad.'

Within minutes they had reached the road and he found himself glancing over his shoulder to see if anything was following.

But in the drifting downpour it was difficult to distinguish more than vague vehicle shapes and the misty haloes of dipped headlights. 'Did you tell anyone you were coming to pick me up?'

'No,' she said, laughing as she spared him a sideways glance. 'I was terrified to say a word! Why all the secrecy?'

'Mario and Goldie have been murdered.'

'You're kidding!'

The car wandered over the centre line and an oncoming vehicle blasted out a warning. 'Keep your eyes on the road, will you!'

She stared ahead. 'God, you're not kidding. Of course you're not. I'm sorry, that was a stupid thing to say. What happened?'

424

He told her. 'And that's the reason for the secrecy. In all, three of the five of us who did the Colombian job are now dead. There's only me and George left. I've tried to reach her to warn her, but she's either out of the country or on vacation. I couldn't get any sense out of her office. I just hope to God she's all right.'

'Ah!' Kelly said, now understanding. 'Well, at least you've no need to worry on that score.'

'What do you mean?'

'She's perfectly safe. She's staying with me. Even as we speak she's at home with Dad. He's probably got her playing chess with him. I expect she has the right mind for it and he likes a challenge. He wipes me out every time.'

'You didn't tell me yesterday.'

'That Georgie was staying?' She gave a mischievous grin. 'Well, I might have if you hadn't run out of coins. Why don't you get yourself a phonecard like everyone else?'

He smiled for the first time with a growing sense of relief. 'How long has she been with you?'

'A couple of days. I spoke to her on the phone last week. She was quite down. Problems at work apparently – on top of her break-up.'

'What?'

'You didn't know she and that awful husband of hers have split? Would you believe it? They had a terrible row and Giles stomped off back to *his* mother's!'

'Maybe they'll get back together.' He hoped so; she deserved some happiness.

'I wouldn't bet on it. It sounds pretty final. He was jealous of her career and you know how she feels about that. Anyway, she sounded pretty wretched and jumped at the idea of a few days' break. I hope you're not going to let her steal you back from me. I won't allow it, Mr Mallory. Do you hear me?'

He grinned. 'What it is to be loved!'

She shared his good humour and laughed, but he sensed something was troubling her. Her next words confirmed it. 'All this talk of love . . . yet sometimes I think I hardly know you.'

He shrugged. 'What you see is what you get.'

425

After a pause she said, concentrating as the wipers struggled to keep the windscreen clear: 'But it isn't, Kurt, is it? Not really. There's another side to you, a side people like me never usually see. Georgie knew and then I saw it in Madrid and – and it bloody well scared the pants off me.'

'You mean Miguel's bodyguard?'

'That, yes. And the violence, the things you do. Why do you do them? I've asked Georgie but she doesn't seem to know really. She said you killed your first person when you were about twenty.'

Suddenly the confines of the Discovery seemed claustrophobic, airless. He had a feeling of being trapped, confronted by this woman who had come to mean so much to him. She was forcing him to admit something to her, something she had every right to do if he wanted to share his life with her. The trouble was it was something he'd buried deep in his subconscious long ago. Very deep and had tried to leave it undisturbed.

His voice was hoarse when he spoke. 'George told you that, did she? Did she tell you who the man was?'

'Some Mexican thug.'

He nodded. 'A murdering bully who intimidated local farmers to get his way. He was above the law and no one would do anything about it.'

'But you did.'

'Because I can't tolerate intimidation. I know what it's like – that empty dread feeling of fear and helplessness. I knew all about that when I was a kid.'

'In Paraguay.' She glanced sideways at him. 'Tell me, Kurt. Tell me what made you the way you are?'

The traffic noise from outside was muted by the hum of the blowers and the constant thrash of the wipers became mesmeric. He'd never been more aware of her presence, her closeness and the smell of her. They were enclosed in their own private world. Just the two of them, like being in the Confessional. Needing to talk and needing to listen. 'I've never told anyone.'

'Perhaps you should have. What was it like there?'

'Great for a growing boy – but primitive. The Glaubehaus had moved out there from England during the war and they'd had to build the entire community from scratch. The area had become a place of refuge for various other sects, like the Mennonites and the Hutterians. It was in the middle of nowhere, just miles of scrub grass and a few palms. They put up a church and a school-house at the centre of the estancia and a hospital eventually and three residential settlements nearby.

'I was fostered by a family who lived at Isla Madonna, the first village they erected; the old man worked at the sawmill. It was fine at first, a dream childhood. Transport was all by horse or ox-wagon. There was fishing in the Tapiraquay, orange groves and monkeys in the woods, wild jasmine and orchids . . .'

Kelly smiled. 'That sounds idyllic – even to a girl.'

For a moment Mallory was silent, lost in the sudden rush of memories.

'But it all went wrong?' she prompted.

He inclined his head. 'I was always a bit of a wild kid, but it got bad once I learned I was an orphan. I resented having no parents like other kids. It was no fun for the family who fostered me. They were religious and strict – dedicated House of Faith followers – and I must have seemed like the devil's son to them.' He paused to light a cigarette, finding it almost physically painful to haul his mind back over thirty years, to unearth what had happened. 'When I got too much for them to cope with, the couple took me to the Glaubehaus administrators to ask for help and advice.'

'What happened?'

'In their wisdom they accepted an offer from Brother Hermann to take me in and look after me. He was highly respected, but had never married. Maybe that should have made them think, but it didn't. For a year or so we got on well. He was wise in his way. He gave me a lot of personal freedom and taught me a lot. Too much in the end. I'd got friendly with some local Paraguayan kids, farmers' sons. Brother Hermann, I realise now, was jealous. That's when the abuse started. Began touching me up, made me do things to him. It all made me feel odd, dirty and bloody fright-ened. Said if I told anyone he'd have me Excluded – that's like the Amish custom of 'shunning'. You know, put under curfew, sent to Coventry and all privileges halted. Everyone was in dread of that, kids as well as adults. Then the beatings started.'

'How old were you then?'

'About nine and a half.'

'Christ,' she said quietly. He could hear the anger in her voice. 'Wasn't there anyone you could tell?'

'After a while I did. I told my foster parents. But they couldn't believe it of Brother Hermann and told me to stop making up stories and spreading lies. Then I tried some of the Glaubehaus elders – with the same result. No one believed me and no one helped. I was alone and terrified. That's why I hate intimidation, why I hate the untouchables in this life. Sorry if that sounds trite, it's just the way it is.'

Kelly was silent for a second. 'So that's why you killed for the first time?'

'Yes. And I learned the sweetness of revenge.'

'That thug in Mexico who was terrorising your friends.'

Suddenly it seemed very hushed in the vehicle, its confines pressing in on him. He looked at her, realising she hadn't understood. Couldn't have understood because he'd never told anyone, not even Savage. 'No. Brother Hermann on my eleventh birthday. That's why I ran away.'

By the time they reached County Kerry it was getting prematurely dark and there was no respite from the weather. It was hurling itself in from the Atlantic, spewing squalls across the countryside in howls of rage so fierce that trees were bending under the force of it.

'Come in for a drink,' Kelly invited as they neared the O'More house. 'I know Georgie would love to see you and Dad always used to say I shouldn't keep you hidden away.'

Mallory shook his head. 'I'd like to get back to the croft.' Now he knew Savage was safe, he really didn't want to see anyone until he'd consulted Maidment.

'You crazy man,' Kelly said. 'It'll be damp and cold. Wait till morning when the weather's supposed to clear. I've got your horses in my stable, we could ride over together.'

That made sense, he supposed. 'You've talked me into it.'

They turned in between the old gate pillars and the Discovery's suspension began to bounce; the untended potholes in the drive were even worse than he remembered.

'You've got visitors,' he observed, seeing several other vehicles parked next to Joe O'More's beloved Healey 3000 outside the crumbling portico.

'Friends of Dad's.' She allowed herself a little smile. 'Don't worry, you won't have to make small talk. I expect they'll all be in the basement playing pool, so we can keep your presence a state secret.' She applied the brake and killed the engine; in the abrupt silence the rattle of the rain seemed to increase in intensity, gusts of wind causing the vehicle to rock slightly; it was as though they were surrounded by little demons trying to break in. 'One question, Kurt. If you think your life is under some sort of threat, why come back here at all? I mean there's nothing to keep you and I'd have thought you'd be happy as a wandering spirit.'

'I had thought of going back to Paraguay,' he admitted.

'So why come back?' she pressed.

'To see you.'

She grinned. 'That's what I thought.'

They sprinted the short distance to the front door, both soaked in a matter of seconds. Dripping puddles on the cracked tiles of the lofty hallway, they removed their outer layers. The place was chill and gloomy, but at least it was out of the wind. It smelled of must and was even more dilapidated than Mallory remembered. The white paintwork had long ago faded to a uniform yellow and the once expensive wallcoverings were peeling away with damp. Kelly placed a hand on one of the gurgling cast-iron radiators and grimaced, indicating that it was barely warm. The old place was expensive to heat.

At least the dark study was cosy, logs burning fitfully in the stone fireplace and throwing shadows and patterns of light over the rows and rows of leather-bound books. Savage was curled in a leather club chair, reading under a silk-shaded standard lamp with a glass of brandy at her side.

She peered over the top of her reading spectacles. 'I didn't hear you arrive.'

'Not surprised in this storm, Georgie. I've brought a friend with me.'

'Kurt!' Savage grinned and put her book aside. 'What are you doing here?'

'On my way home, Kelly picked me up from the airport.'

'So that was what all the mystery was about.' She gave her friend a reproachful look. 'You're a dark horse.'

'It's my fault,' Mallory said. 'I asked her not to tell anyone I was back. There's been some big trouble. Have you heard about Mario and Goldie?'

Alarm showed in Savage's eyes. 'What's happened?'

Of course she wouldn't know, he realised. Mario and Goldie were the organisation's men, not hers, and even Maidment had not yet been told. 'They're dead. Mario was killed in Martinique and I was with Goldie when he was shot in Durban.'

Her mouth opened but she could find no words to express her disbelief.

'They might have been after me too,' he added. 'Or maybe the assassins cocked up, who knows? I think Dale Forster was just the first.'

'Tell me about it, Kurt, exactly how it happened.'

Kelly took her cue to retire discreetly and make some coffee, leaving the two of them alone.

When Mallory had finished, Savage said: 'It's all very strange, Kurt, but it doesn't exactly prove anything.'

He shook his head in disagreement. 'You can only accept coincidence so far. You know how professional assassinations work. You bring in a complete outsider, give him the name and a picture of his target. He knows nothing of the background, the reasons. He does the job and vanishes without trace. With no motive and no personal connection, the police are left clueless. They may have suspicions, but that's all. It is murder out of the blue. I know, I've done it enough times myself. That's why you must have utter faith in those who hire you. Be able to trust them that the target is legitimate.'

She smiled weakly, recognising the compliment. 'So you're saying that this is the pattern here, but we'll never know for sure?'

He nodded. 'I haven't forgotten the break-in at my croft. Miggles Strand is well off the beaten track. I'm convinced now I was to have been the first victim. That means you have to be at risk too.'

'You think this is all connected with White Viper?'

'It's the obvious connection. None of us had worked with Dale before.'

She nursed the brandy in her hands and shivered despite the heat from the fire. 'Confidentially, I can tell you that something about all of this isn't making sense. Five days ago we mounted a series of co-ordinated raids across Europe. In Germany, Spain and London to intercept the trucks from Budapest. I was with a raid on a warehouse owned by Stan Summers. It was clean, the artic trailer units must have been switched. Summers just stood there, grinning like a Cheshire cat. The smug bastard. I knew then we weren't going to find anything.'

'So who tipped them off?' Mallory thought aloud.

'Well, it certainly wasn't Castaño.' She gave him a disapproving glance. 'I can't pretend your action wasn't appreciated, Kurt, but I really can't condone it.'

'I'm not asking you to,' he responded more sharply than he'd intended. 'Castaño was filth. He'd built a fortune feeding off the drugs business and terrorism, yet no one could touch him for it.'

She nodded impatiently. 'I know your reasons, Kurt. But one day you're going to get caught out and the law isn't going to save you and nor is your precious organisation. I'd hate to think of you doing life for the likes of him.'

There was a gentle knock on the door and Kelly entered with a tray of coffee. 'Hope you two have finished your secret pow-wow.' A sound of male voices drifted into the room. 'Dad's finished the pool game. I hope you don't mind if he joins us with his friends.'

Savage smiled. ' 'Course not. I'd like to meet them.'

Mallory frowned. A small warning bell rang deep inside his head, but he wasn't sure why.

Joe O'More was laughing as he entered. Mallory was certain the man had discovered the secret of eternal youth; he appeared younger and fitter each time he saw him. Only the neatly brushed white hair gave a clue to the fact he was in his seventies; there was hardly a line or blemish on his lightly tanned face, just a few crow's feet around the smiling green eyes.

'Hallo, Kurt, my boy,' he greeted, looking relaxed in slacks and sweater. 'The wanderer returns, eh? Good to see you back. I'd like you and young Georgina to meet a few friends of mine.'

The man who followed O'More in was in his late forties, with hard grey eyes and curling brown hair that was greying at the temples. He was wearing a hound's-tooth check jacket and faded jeans.

'Kurt, meet Kevin Sheehan.'

Mallory was lifting himself from his seat, hand outstretched, as he heard the name.

Two other younger men entered after Sheehan. One had dark, smouldering eyes that looked far from friendly and the second was a pale-skinned blond with a fixed sort of beatific smile. Mallory was reminded of an angelic choirboy if only that smile hadn't made him feel so uncomfortable.

'Padraig O'Donnell and Sean Waterford,' O'More introduced easily.

Mallory's eyes shifted back to the door as a fourth man entered the room from the shadows beyond. His movements were awkward, slow and stiff, his arms down by his side. It took a second for Mallory to realise he was on crutches, his right leg severed above the knee.

O'More was saying, 'Oh, and I believe you two have met before. Guy Thripp.'

For a split second Mallory was paralysed with shock. Thripp was dead. High in the *cuchillas*, in the Andean foothills above Cruz de Oro. Torn apart by wild cats and his bones picked clean by vultures.

'Small world,' Thripp said.

Mallory started to pivot, to throw himself at the two younger men as representing the most immediate danger. But as he

432

turned to face them he found himself staring into the twin muzzles of two automatic pistols.

Savage sprang to her feet, her reaction slowed by the brandy and the sheer shock of Thripp's reappearance from beyond the grave.

'Sit down,' O'More snapped, the good humour gone from his eyes in an instant.

Savage fell back, the blood draining from her face, and her heart like a drumbeat in her chest as she realised she had got it all wrong. All so horribly, horribly wrong.

She turned to Kelly in a silent appeal for help, for an explanation, but her friend deliberately looked away. The man called Padraig lifted his automatic to point it at Mallory. 'Turn around. Hands high.'

'Good lad,' Thripp said approvingly. 'He's a tricky bastard. Check he's not carrying a knife on his trouser belt – or any place else.'

As Padraig O'Donnell quickly frisked his body before pushing him roughly into a chair, Mallory turned his head towards Kelly. She was standing back, her long arms folded, hugging herself with an uncertain look on her face. Not anger, not smug satisfaction at having successfully baited him into the trap. Just sadness, he thought, as she averted her eyes from his. 'You knew all about this, didn't you?' he asked.

She tossed back her hair and looked at him directly. 'I'm sorry, Kurt, it had to be done. The truth is, when it comes to it, I love my country more than you. My duty to Ireland comes first, it's as simple as that.'

'What the hell do you mean?'

But she didn't seem to hear. Still hugging herself like a disconsolate child, she stared at the floor. Her head was shaking slightly when she spoke. It was as though she was trying to unravel her own confused thoughts and mixed emotions. Trying to justify things to herself. 'I never knew what you and Georgie were doing in South America. You were vague when I asked you out of interest – you and your goddamn secrecy. It never occurred to me that it could be connected with our operation there. Not that I knew much about it; Dad and Sheehan always keep that sort of stuff to themselves. I just handled the above-board legal side for the legitimate cargoes and then the financial side for investing profits. If you or Dad had told me more of what was going on, I might have twigged.' She glanced at Savage. 'It was only when she approached me in Madrid that I realised it was all connected. God, at first I thought she'd come to arrest me. It was a bloody relief when I realised she wanted my help, I can tell you.'

Savage said: 'You of all people. Betraying Kurt and betraying me. I was your friend, dammit.'

Kelly turned on her. 'No, you were the enemy. It just so happened I came to like you. When we first met that time I realised you were something to do with intelligence. For someone in the secret service you weren't a very convincing liar. It was a challenge to play you along once I knew you didn't suspect.'

'Or was Kurt the real attraction?' Savage asked.

Kelly gave a short laugh of self-mockery. 'Yeah, well, sure maybe he had something to do with it.'

'And your affair with him was all a sham too?'

Kelly looked suddenly angry. 'No, it wasn't!' Indignant. 'But I didn't know what he did then. I should have guessed really, but I didn't. I only realised when he killed Emilio the way he did. Right in front of me, the bastard! And then Miguel. God knows that man was no saint.' She turned back to Mallory. 'But at least he wasn't a butcher, a murderer!'

O'More raised his hand. 'Okay, girls, that's enough! Don't want you scratching each other's eyes out, do we? The point is we have them both here now and it is time to conclude some unfinished business.'

Mallory turned his gaze on Guy Thripp. The man was still standing, resting easily on his crutches, clearly enjoying the expressions of fear and incomprehension on the faces of his prisoners. 'You killed Mario and Goldie, didn't you?' Mallory accused.

Thripp's grin widened. 'I had a hand in it.'

'And Dale Forster?' Savage asked.

The man nodded. 'Revenge, as I seem to recall you saying

434

once, Kurt, when you lot had me crucified on a fucking tree, is very sweet. I really didn't know just how true those words were till now.'

'How did you survive?'

'I survived, old son, *because* you wanted *your* revenge on me. If you'd done the decent thing and killed me cleanly like the others, I obviously wouldn't be here now. But you wanted me to suffer and that was your big mistake. When you left, I was found by an Indian herdsman. He took me back down to Adoración on his mule. Christ, that was one hell of a journey! I was delirious before I passed out – mercifully. But then I'm a tough old bugger – as you can see. The old Indian took me into the cathouse and they fetched a doctor from Santa Maria. It was too late to save my leg, but Fanny Lacera had me nursed by that little hooker called Lucila. I learned a lot about you from her. Then I learned a whole lot more about your operation from Lacera. Said she'd been informing for Cali and that they'd tried to warn Castaño what you and your friends had planned for us. But the warning came too late. That's when it was suggested that you and your friends could be tracked down one by one and killed.'

'Who suggested it, Guy? Who murdered them?'

There was a throaty chuckle. 'It was organised by Ruiz Edilberto Jaramillo.'

Mallory stared.

Savage shook her head in astonishment. 'The Cali cartel,' she murmured.

Their partners in the unholy alliance to destroy the White Viper gang and the resurgent rival cartel in Medellín.

Colonel Oliver Maidment pulled over to the side of the lane and stopped the car.

Outside, the wind-driven rain was obscuring the road, reducing visibility to a few metres, the wipers unable to cope with the deluge. He switched on the courtesy light and tried to focus on the fine detail of the road map of Eire.

Christ, he was tired. His eyes were beginning to water with fatigue and the strain of trying to see where he was going in the dark. Now the tiny print of the place names seemed to be floating before his eyes.

It had been a long two days, the trouble having started when his meeting in Bucharest was interrupted by a message from Kurt Mallory. The coded words sounded innocent enough, but they demanded urgent attention. Never in all the years they had worked together had Mallory ever resorted to using them before. And Mallory certainly wasn't one to panic unnecessarily.

Getting the meeting adjourned so abruptly had not been easy and he was painfully aware that it would probably result in the loss of the multimillion-pound contract for Portcullis Industries. But as always the organisation came first. Portcullis may have represented industry and commerce, big money and international power while the organisation was worth no more than the courageous individuals who made up its numbers. But what he owed them, no money could ever buy.

Forgoing lunch, he had taken the first available flight back to Heathrow where he was met by his chauffeur. He returned to the apartment which had been used to set up the operation against the White Viper gang.

He entered the office suite and used the scrambled line to call Sidney Monckton at his home. The deputy chief of SIS sounded cautiously pleased to hear his friend's voice. 'Fortuitous you should ring, Oliver. It would seem our recent plans have come to nought.'

'What do you mean?'

'In fishing parlance, let's say the big one's got away. Look, I can't say more on the phone. Could you come over for a late supper, say around ten?'

Maidment had hung up with a growing sense of unease. Was this the reason Mallory had sent his cryptic message? Unlikely on the face of it, he thought. Not for the first time he regretted involving the organisation with the intelligence service. It wasn't that he actually distrusted them, it was just that they were too used to doing things their way, on their terms.

Then he had wondered if he had made the right decision in agreeing to see Monckton. In doing so he had missed the opportunity of catching the later shuttle to Dublin. But what the hell. To have gone over now would have meant arriving just after dark and being faced with a long drive in unfamiliar territory. And Ireland was hardly renowned for its good roads and signposting in remote areas. As it was, the postal address he now had for Mallory was vague to say the least. Just the name of the croft and a nearby village. No road or street name and no district. And there was no Miggles Strand on his map.

No, he'd as well stop over in London and fly out first thing the next day. That gave him a few hours to work on Portcullis business before his supper with Monckton, but his mind hadn't settled.

Then a thought had occurred. Mallory had only finished the White Viper job in Spain some two weeks earlier; any problems he had were almost certainly connected with that. He had been spending some time with Goldstein, he knew. If anyone had an inkling about what had gone wrong, then the skinny little Israeli would.

He put through the call on the scrambler; Aggie answered.

Five minutes later he replaced the receiver, chastened. Now he knew the reason for Mallory pressing the panic button. Goldie was dead and so was Mario. And now Dale Forster's fatal accident many weeks earlier no longer looked so innocent.

And that night the light fish supper with Monckton had done nothing to quell his growing fears that something had gone terribly pear-shaped. All the White Viper drugs shipments, so carefully dated and logged as a result of the organisation's efforts, had unaccountably escaped detection. And Essex kingpin Stan Summers had waltzed free, waving the proverbial two fingers at the authorities. Somehow, somewhere there had been a tip-off or leak.

Monckton too, had been in for an unpleasant surprise. It was the first he had heard that two of SIS's freelancers by proxy had been murdered.

He had murmured: 'Sometimes that is the price of not letting the left hand know what the right is doing.'

'My guess is my man believes he'll be the next target.'

Monckton had nodded. 'Or even my field officer.'

'Surely the *narcos* wouldn't be able to reach her?'

'No, in theory. And that is assuming it is the *narcos*. Either way, we cannot be complacent.'

He had excused himself then and used the telephone in another room. He returned a few minutes later. 'I've just spoken to our duty officer. The lady concerned is on leave. My officers are supposed to give a number or contact address wherever they are. I've tried her home number and there's no reply. I've left a message on the answer machine.'

'Perhaps she's just out for the evening.'

'Let's hope so. But apparently she's had some upset with her husband, according to office gossip. That's the trouble with women. Throw emotion and affairs of the heart into the equation and common sense flies out the window.'

'What do you want me to do, Sidney?'

A shrug. 'All you can do is try and locate your man. Get the full story from him. If you think he has good reason to fear for his life, help him go to ground. If you need backup or assistance from us, well, you've got my direct line. I'll do what I can.'

It had been a welcome and generous offer. But unfortunately it didn't help Maidment now as he sat in his car, battered by a near-monsoon, and tried to read the map.

To hell with it, he thought. He'd lost several hours and still hadn't gained anything thanks to the atrocious weather. He'd spent most of the day driving across Ireland in torrential rain, getting lost several times in the process and had still ended up in the dark. In all respects. Now he was exhausted, all in. There was nothing for it but to keep going and stop at the first pub or guest house he could find. He'd resume looking for Mallory's home again at daybreak. Hopefully the rain would have stopped by then.

He selected first gear and drove on.

Five minutes later it happened. Something rushed out from the nearside hedge. A fox, a dog, a badger, maybe a small deer. He had no real idea what. Even as he instinctively stepped on the brake and swung the wheel to avoid it, the thought struck him that it could have been a hallucination. A combination of the dazzling headlight reflection in the teeming rain and the utter exhaustion he felt. A figment of the imagination, like when driving in fog.

As the tyres locked and slid over the greasy tarmac he braced himself for an impact that didn't come. The little bugger, whatever it was, had got away.

Feeling mildly shaken, he was about to steer back onto his own side of the lane when he saw it. Having veered at an angle, his headlights now shone into the offside hedge. There was a gap, leading to a track just wide enough for one car. And hidden in the brambles was a sign. *To the beach.*

If he'd been less tired and thinking logically, he'd probably never have done it. But this was the one and only visible access route he'd yet seen for this stretch of coast where he knew Mallory lived. Before he could stop himself he'd swung the wheel and was entering the track, hearing the brambles rustle and scratch on either side.

It seemed to go on for ever. In the darkness and rain it was difficult to get his bearings, but the unmade road, meandering through fields and meadows, was definitely dipping down to where he knew the sea must be.

He stopped just in time. As the track appeared to widen, he realised that it had only opened up to form a turning circle. The tyres squealed as he braked in panic, just inches from the edge where the cliff crumbled away to the shoreline.

Pulling a flat cap tight down on his head, he ventured out. The wind nearly tore the car door from his grasp. He slammed it shut and, clutching the collar of his raincoat hard against his throat, stared out at the rolling dark mass of the Atlantic battering its way into the bay.

Lightning ripped a ragged fissure across the black sky. For a second he glimpsed the beach below and the dark outline of the croft silhouetted against a pale blur of sand.

Was that it? Was this Miggles Strand? He could hardly believe he'd be that lucky, yet how many buildings were there likely to be along this lonely stretch of coast? He'd come this far, he might as well make certain. At the very least he owed Mallory that.

With the wind gusting around him and trying its best to wrong-foot his descent and pluck him from the narrow path, he made his way down to the beach. He could see no lights showing as he approached and the squat, slab-walled cottage had a distinct air of abandonment about it.

He was gasping for breath against the wind by the time he reached the shallow porch. His raincoat was soaked and rain dripped from his hat and face and hair as he banged the old brass knocker ring without much hope of a reply. After a pause he tried again, louder this time. If anyone was inside they might be asleep and it was doubtful what could be heard above the noise of nature unleashed. He couldn't remember anything like it, the stinging lash of storm-driven rain and a screaming wind that threw the ocean breakers at the shoreline with explosive venom. Seawater spray filled the air in a drifting mist until even the rain tasted of salt on his lips.

He knocked again, venting his anger. Another impatient wait, then he lifted his sodden shoe and kicked in his exasperation. Rain dripped through his collar and trickled down his back. Shit!

Then he heard the muffled sound of movement behind him. Panic struck him and he turned.

'One fucken move an' I'll take yer head off, so I will!'

He was staring at the trembling twin barrels of a shotgun. Squinting down its length was an old man in soaked striped pyjamas and a Breton cap. The crinkled eyes above the tangled beard were wide with anger or fear. Maybe both, Maidment thought in an instant. He'd disturbed a hermit, a madman who'd crept out the back door to get the jump on him.

Raising his hands promptly, he gasped: 'Please, please don't shoot! I'm trying to find someone and I got lost!' He was having to shout to make himself heard.

The old fisherman seemed to relax a fraction, reassured by the words and the pathetic sight of the drenched stranger. 'Looking? Who you lookin' for?'

'A Mr Mallory. Kurt Mallory.'

'An' who are you?'

'A friend. Oliver Maidment. Colonel Oliver Maidment. Have I got the right place?'

The fisherman waved the shotgun. 'Come round the back. Real slow now.'

Five minutes later they were settled by a smouldering peat fire that offered meagre warmth, both men shivering with damp and cold. 'Can't get a blaze going, 'cos I don't want no one to know I'm here.'

'Why's that?'

'Kurt's had snoopers awhile back. Maybe they'll come again. If they do I want to be ready for them – like I surprised you.'

'You did that all right, Mr—?'

'Mattie.'

'You're a bit old – forgive me – for this night-watchman stuff, aren't you?'

Matt Rooney's eyes narrowed. 'It's my choice. Kurt tried to dissuade me. But he's the only friend I've got, so I do it 'cos I want to.' He thrust a bottle of malt whiskey towards him. 'Have a swig of Kurt's medicinal. Looks like you need it.'

For some reason Maidment declined; he felt tired enough already without making it worse with alcohol.

Rooney snatched the bottle back. 'Well, I need some, even if you don't. Scared the friggin' life out of me, so you did!'

As he watched the old man take two generous gulps, he said: 'Kurt left a message to meet him here. Do you happen to know where he is?'

The fisherman wiped his mouth with the back of his hand. 'He hasn't showed, that's for certain.'

'I'd have thought he might have got here earlier today.'

Rooney shook his head again. 'Nope.' Then he stared up at the low ceiling as though in search of inspiration. 'But then the road back virtually takes him past the O'More house.'

'I'm sorry?'

'Kurt's a wee bit keen on Joe O'More's daughter. And if Kurt's not by himself or with me, the chances are always you'll find him with her. If he's been away – sure, maybe he called in to pay his respects.'

'Could I phone them?'

The fisherman gave a pained look.

'Of course, stupid of me. Is it far to the house?'

'About fifteen mile.'

'Could you take me there?'

Rooney looked aghast. 'In this weather?'

'It wouldn't take us long in my car and I'd consider it a very great favour.'

'Well, I suppose . . .' He stared for a moment at the bottle. 'Just one more wee mouthful first. It's a wicked night.'

Joe O'More thought it very amusing. 'I can see you're both a little bit shocked by that revelation. And very understandable, so it is. I mean Ruiz Jaramillo sought *your* help on behalf of the Cali cartel to destroy *us*.'

Neither Mallory nor Savage commented. They just watched the man in bitter silence.

'The Cali cartel was terrified of a resurgence of their old rivals in Medellín,' he continued. 'They'd hoped the death of Pablo Escobar had ended political instability in Colombia. And for good measure they'd absorbed much of the Medellín's old markets. Then along comes Felix Bastidas with his new ideas of rebuilding Escobar's old drug trade. And worse, he wanted it to fuel social revolution, linking drugs with arms funding with the socialist guerrillas. Not only in his own country, but Venezuela and Bolivia.'

'Saw himself as the heir to Simon Bolívar,' Guy Thripp added helpfully. 'God save us from revolting peasants.'

'We knew that, of course,' O'More went on. 'We in the Provisionals have a history of co-operation with others fighting for social justice and freedom against oppression. People like ETA in Spain and the ANC in South Africa.'

'You mean other terrorist organisations,' Mallory interjected acidly.

'Shut up, Kurt!' Savage warned.

O'More just smiled. 'You're a little behind the times, I think. The actions of the ANC and the Palestinians have been vindicated by the passage of time. Here, in the island of Ireland, our political arm Sinn Fein is leading the march to peace at the present time and I'm sure ETA will soon enjoy the rightful freedom for its people under the mantle of the European Union.' He paused, waiting to be contradicted. When he was not challenged he continued in his soft Kerry brogue. 'Sure, it suited us to act as middlemen to supply arms from our old contacts in the Soviet Union as well as use them as a conduit for cocaine into Western Europe. After all, two-way trade means double the profits.'

'You should have guessed you'd upset the gentlemen of Cali,' Mallory provoked.

'That's true,' O'More admitted. 'In hindsight we should have realised we'd picked the wrong allies in Colombia. But it's first-come-first-served in business and Felix Bastidas was hungry for success and he and Stan Summers were the first people Miguel Castaño introduced us to. And once we were set up in Cruz de Oro, we thought we were pretty much invincible. Such a rugged and remote place and deep in traditional Medellín territory. Friendly guerrillas in the hills and our own force on the ground that Summers set up under Harry Morgan and Guy here. We assumed that Cali would live and let live. And so they might, if Vic West had not come along.'

Mallory said: 'The Cali cartel would have found a way, however long it took. Vic West was just the first to present them with the means.'

O'More shrugged. 'Maybe. But if we forgot how dangerous these "gentlemen" of Cali, as you insist on calling them, could be, then so did you. You see, much as they hated our White Viper operation, they also envied its success. After all, the United States market was virtually saturated with prices falling, while their expansion into the lucrative European market had become stagnant. It meant dealing with the Mafia – unpleasant and greedy people – or going through old family connections in Spain. That made it relatively easy for the European police to keep tabs on them, to keep the pressure up. Recently there has been little incentive for Cali to expand massively into Europe on its own account. By contrast, we had opened up a whole network of new routes through former Communist territories not subject to high standards of law enforcement. Over the years we had developed contacts that the Cali people couldn't even begin to dream of. High volume and even higher profits, pumping the stuff into the heart of Europe with virtual impunity.'

Suddenly Mallory knew what was coming. He wondered if Savage did too, but she gave no sign as she sat impassively as though none of this was anything to do with her.

'I don't know exactly when Jaramillo first thought of it. Perhaps it was even their plan from the very start, possibly after their first meeting with Vic West.' O'More looked directly at Mallory. 'Did you ever meet a young lawyer called Maria Palechor?'

'I don't remember,' he lied.

'Ah well, you'd have remembered her. Handsome woman. Works for Cali. Anyway, I gather it was her brainwave. It was simple enough. Get Vic West's contacts – you people – to destroy our operation on the ground in Colombia, then as soon as it was over, offer themselves as replacement suppliers for our European distribution network.'

Mallory nodded. Just as he'd started to realise, they'd been set up from the very start. Destroy the Cali's rivals for them, just so they could step into dead men's shoes.

'Maria Palechor knew Castaño, of course,' O'More said. 'Well, they were both lawyers in the same line of business. She warned him just an hour before your operation to destroy us in Colombia went down. Too late to do anything about it, of course. Her line was they'd picked up whispers of a secret plot – probably DEA, she said – to close us down. Their warning was a favour, to preserve the status quo. Said if it was true and we lost our foothold in Colombia, they'd be interested in being our new suppliers. Castaño flew here from Madrid to tell me and Stan Summers all about it.' He gave a mild laugh. 'When the bad news was confirmed I didn't know what to think at first. I mean, I was livid, furious. But Summers was truly mad, especially at losing Harry and Guy. We didn't know whether to take Castaño and Palechor's story at face value or not. And as for their offer to supply, it was all too pat, too prepared, even pointing out the overheads we'd save without our men on the ground.'

He paused, thinking back. 'That's when they played their ace. Palechor said their informers had discovered the identities of your team, even had photographs. That's when Summers, Kevin here and I decided. If they wanted a deal then, as an act of good faith, they would have to track you down and bring us your heads on a plate. And that's exactly what they did.'

Now Mallory understood the incident of Bogotá. The Cali cartel had put out the word, using its network of informers and corrupt contacts in the police and immigration authorities. But they'd been looking for Kurt Hulse or the cover name of Harry Pike he'd used at his meeting with Jaramillo. No one had known about the secret Jim Tate passport on which he'd travelled. He realised suddenly that if he hadn't taken the precaution, he'd have been the first victim. Even before Dale Forster.

O'More was saying: 'In fact we soon suspected that Castaño knew about your planned attack much earlier than he let on and accepted big, let's say, bribe money from the Cali people to hold his tongue until it happened and then to swing the deal with us.'

Kelly spoke for the first time. 'That's why I went over to stay with him in Madrid. To find out exactly what he was up to. He was supposed to be working for us, not double-crossing us and feathering his nest at our expense.'

'Of course, at that time,' O'More said, 'we had no idea who was behind the raid at Cruz de Oro. Castaño told us Palechor thought it was DEA freelancers. She gave him the cover names you all used, but then they meant nothing to us. As I said, Palechor's informers had secretly photographed all of your team. She said some of the Cali people recognised Mario Dubois who was a known emerald smuggler and Forster was identified by their people in Miami as a former DEA man. Those two were easy and the American was the first target for Cali's hitmen. He was persuaded to talk before they sunk him with his boat.'

Mallory found his knuckles clenched white on the armrests of his chair; he didn't look at Savage but was certain she was sharing his anger at the revelation.

445

'Forster couldn't give them much to identify Savage, but he knew your real first name, Kurt, and where you lived. Quite a shock when we realised it was you. Caused us all quite a panic until we realised it was just a coincidence, that you knew no more about our involvement than we knew of yours. But then to be in the closed world of narcotics, such coincidences aren't that surprising, if you think about it.'

'And Goldie?' Mallory asked.

'Ah, Goldstein. He was a mystery until you all turned up again in Madrid. By that time we'd already decided to sever our connections with Castaño – Kelly had discovered by then his only real loyalty was to himself. When Savage here approached her for help, Kelly agreed to stay on for appearances. It also gave her the chance to alert me. Our plan was already set up for Mario Dubois in Martinique by the Cali people, just awaiting his return. But we had to have you and Goldstein followed when you left Spain. We lost you, but he was fairly lax. Maybe he'd just got complacent. Anyway, we still had some contacts with old fellow revolutionaries in the ANC. It was easy enough to arrange.'

'And me? Was I supposed to have been killed then?'

O'More shook his head. 'No, that might have been too obvious or got too many questions asked. Anyway there was no need. Kelly knew you'd come back here eventually and she could lure Savage over almost any time she wanted.'

So now he knew. But that knowledge gave him no comfort. None at all. Because there was only one reason that Joe O'More was telling them all this. Their death sentence had already been passed. He wondered if Savage realised.

Even as the thought went through his mind, she looked up from her chair. 'How long have you been involved with PIRA, Mr O'More?' Mallory had to smile; she sounded like a policewoman interviewing a suspect.

'Man and boy, Miss Savage,' he replied frostily. 'My father took part in the Easter Rising and fought in the early troubles and I've always followed in his footsteps. I've kept discreet links with the Provisionals since their formation in 1972. But my daughter and I have never worn our hearts on our sleeves. There are many

446

like me and Kelly in the Republic. Respectable people of wealth and influence who have understood the cause for which our people in the north have fought. For equality and justice. To drive out the invader. The movement couldn't have survived without us beavering away in the background, particularly in the areas of finance, government and the law. It has been largely a thankless and unnoticed task but necessary. And now its justification and our reward are there for all the world to see and acknowledge.'

Savage's face was a mask. 'I presume you mean by that the current peace process?' When he nodded, she said: 'Then how in God's name do you square the honour and integrity of the Ireland you so fervently believe in with narcotics and trading in human misery?' She didn't wait for an answer. 'It so happens that I recognise Kevin Sheehan from photographs. His real name is Thomas Dee and he was jailed for smuggling heroin for the IRA in the mid-eighties. That's a long association in a dirty business for the supposedly noble cause you claim you fight for.'

Well put, Mallory thought; he was proud of her.

But O'More's laugh was harsh. 'Don't try and lay that on me, lady! The movement started with its back to the wall. In order to survive we had to turn our hand to whatever made the most money fast. As you well know, fighting a war costs a lot of money, especially if you intend to win as we, indeed, now have. Every criminal gang in Britain has its finger in the drugs pie because it has to in order to survive against its rivals. For the same reasons, so must we, because we are pitched against the might and wealth of an occupying nation! We do not *cause* misery to these people, they bring it upon themselves. They are no different from smokers or drinkers – they will get their supplies from somewhere.'

Savage smiled. 'You mean if you don't supply them someone else will, is that it? Oh, yes, I understand the usual cop-out. But as you've said, you've won your war now. Your people are supposed to be entering the respectable democratic process.'

'Democracy needs money too!' O'More snapped back. It was strange to witness the transformation of the man from mild-mannered, slightly down-at-heel country gentleman to political fanatic and active supporter of terrorism. All the time it had been

447

there, just below the surface. 'We've still got a long road ahead. If the peace process doesn't collapse – and there's every chance it will – then there will be elections to be fought and won. How else are we expected to fight the big political parties with any certainty of victory? The struggle's taken too long to risk failure now.'

Kelly added: 'Too many have died for their beliefs along the way, Kurt. You must see that, surely?'

He turned on her, lifting one eyebrow in cynicism. 'So any means will justify the end, is that it?'

Her eyes met his with a flinty gaze. 'In this case, yes. Just look at the state of our house. It's falling apart because Dad has contributed all the family wealth to the cause. But it just isn't enough. I have never *liked* the fact some of our people have to get involved in the drugs business – or bank hold-ups, kidnaps or protection, for that matter – but I accept that we've had no alternative. We've been at war and in war unpleasant decisions must be made.'

'And does that include murdering Vic West, Mario and Goldie, my three best friends?'

'You're hardly in a position to be smug, Kurt! Firstly I didn't know about all that. Dad and the Army Council don't tell me everything, you know. But anyway, your friends weren't exactly killed at random. They put themselves in the firing line just like you did. And who were they? An arms dealer, an emerald smuggler and an ex-Mossad hitman. Mario and Goldie were hardly Pinky and Perky and no one's likely to have awarded them the Nobel Peace Prize. They butchered our people and their Colombian helpers. Dammit, you know because you were helping them, torturing those men in the trees. But you were worse, leaving Guy like that. God, when I heard what you'd done and saw the state of him . . .' She paused for breath, her face reddened with anger. 'My blood froze, Kurt, and I can tell you it broke my heart. To think you of all people had done that to another human being. It made me feel dirty, unclean. To think that we'd . . .'

Savage said: 'I suppose Guy told you what your angelic team did in Colombia?'

'What?'

'The murder and torture of unco-operative locals because they stood up to your thugs. The gang rape of a girl in front of the male villagers. In front of a troublesome priest who they then hung naked for all to see. But then I suppose you've always turned a blind eye to the IRA's intimidation. Regrettable but acceptable in all-out war, is that it?'

Kelly looked momentarily bewildered, glanced at her father. He, too, looked uncertain.

'They're talking bollocks!' Thripp said quickly. 'They know they're for the high jump and they're just trying to talk their way out of it.'

Mallory found Kelly looking directly at him. 'Is it true, Kurt?'

He nodded. 'That's why we have no regrets about what we did. Thripp and his friends were worse than animals. I've never lied to you.'

'Shut it!' Thripp shouted. 'You wouldn't know the truth if it poked you in the fuckin' eye.'

Sheehan was getting restless. 'It makes no difference anyway. The past is the past and we've got a job to do.'

'Where are you going to do it?' Mallory asked coldly.

Thripp allowed himself a slow smile. 'At your croft, old son. A lovers' tiff, we thought. You kill her then commit suicide. Nice and neat with no loose ends.'

Savage turned to Kelly, her voice quaking as she spoke. Somehow she had never thought that the end would come like this. 'Are you really going along with this? I don't believe it! I'm your friend – I'd never do anything to hurt you, believe me.'

The Irish girl appeared dazed, confused by her conflicting emotions. She'd been brought up from the cradle to believe in the right of freedom for the whole of Ireland and of the iniquity of the continued British occupation in the Six Counties. Although it hadn't often been discussed it was always there, like the genes in bloodline stock. It either mattered to you or it didn't – it was a belief you were born with.

In her teenage years and later Kelly had sometimes questioned the rights and wrongs of the troubles in the North, but always

449

Joe O'More and his friends could put up the most eloquent and persuasive arguments to justify it all. Many of the worst terrorist atrocities appeared to be committed by renegade splinter groups or else were the unintentioned accidents of war. Meanwhile the British acts of violence and dirty tricks were conveniently overlooked or brushed aside by arrogant politicians from an unrepentant London. Joe O'More had chapter and verse on all the true facts.

Kurt Mallory's appearance in the enemy camp had come as a devastating shock. Theirs had been a relationship of the heart and body; he had shown little interest in politics so it was rarely discussed. He clearly loved Ireland and the Irish people and had been happy enough when she sometimes strummed out rebel songs on his guitar.

So it wasn't herself Kelly saw as the betrayer but him. For the first time in her life she had now come face to face with an act of the war – the very war she had so deeply believed was honourable and totally justified. And for the first time she had to participate in no small way and face the inevitably bloody consequences. To surrender the man she loved to Irish history. It was not easy and the mounting uncertainty and confusion were tearing her insides apart.

Feeling sick and frightened, she searched for the words to answer Savage's accusation. Words of defence and justification that had churned around her head a million times in recent weeks. 'I told you, Georgie, you're the enemy. The enemy first and a friend second. You chose your job, I didn't. Like Brit soldiers on our streets, you knew the risks when you took the Queen's shilling. Sure I'm sorry it's you, desperately sorry, but I'm also sorry about the other hundreds of Irishmen and women who have died because your people refuse to leave my country.' She turned her head away.

Even as she had spoken the words she had felt her conviction melting away. Things had happened in South America that she didn't know about or understand – it was gnawing rapidly at her conscience. Mallory might be the enemy, but her heart knew he was speaking the truth. And what had happened was wrong.

Wrong, wrong, wrong.

Savage tried another tack, addressing herself to Thripp. 'Why don't you think this through? It's hardly smart to kill a British intelligence officer in the middle of peace negotiations.'

'Stow it, woman,' Thripp replied brusquely. 'It'll look like a crime of passion and nothing's ever going to get proved. Besides we could kill the bloody Royal Family at the moment and Downing Street would ignore it in their haste to wash their hands of Ulster. And, anyway, this is one treat I'm looking forward to. I haven't forgotten what you did to me after my last job in the Regiment. It was your report that got me stitched, ruined my career – bitch!'

'No, you did that all by yourself. I simply wrote what happened. But seeing the company you now keep, I'm *very* glad I didn't cover up for you.' She took a deep breath and steeled herself, glancing at Mallory with a brief, tight smile. 'Come on then, let's get it over with.'

A small glow of pride burned momentarily in Mallory's chest as he heard her words. If he had to die this day, then he would die in good company. Both with their heads held high.

Thripp turned to Sheehan. 'You and O'Donnell take the girl down to the croft. Use the Discovery.'

The man pulled Savage roughly to her feet. Mallory began to stand.

'Not you,' Thripp snapped. 'You're not going to have it so bloody easy. I owe Harry and the others that. And Stan Summers has insisted you get a taste of your own medicine. Waterford here is a bit of an expert. From the Provos' security section.'

Mallory knew what he meant, from the kneecappers of the IRA's punishment squads. For the first time he realised the sort of man he was looking at. That angelic face and blond crew cut and that effeminate mouth, the pumping-iron body in the tight leather jacket resembling a Tom Finland painting.

'We'll see just how slowly a man can die,' Waterford promised. And while he spoke the beatific smile never wavered once.

Savage tried to wrestle free of Sheehan's grip, to peer back over her shoulder. If only she could look into Mallory's eyes once more. Let him know how she felt, how she'd always felt.

As she was half-dragged and half-carried out through the door, Kelly rounded on her father. 'Dad, you can't let them do that. You said it would be a straightforward execution. Tell them, they can't!'

O'More looked uneasy. He knew what she meant. He too had thought Mallory would just be made to kneel while the bag was pulled over his head. Maybe not shot from behind, but this time through the mouth so it would look like suicide when the body was washed ashore. 'It's out of my hands, child. This is what Summers and the others want and Guy has every right to demand an eye for an eye after what Kurt did to him.'

Exasperated, she turned to Thripp. 'Don't do it, Guy. Two blacks can't ever make a white! Just take him and shoot him with Georgie. Don't make him suffer.'

But Thripp had endured enough delay and he wasn't going to be deprived of this. 'No one's asking you to watch. We'll take him out to the stables.' He turned to Sean Waterford. 'Let's go.'

19

'Just up here on the left,' Matt Rooney said. 'You can see the twin pillars by the gate.'

Maidment slowed and squinted, his view through the windscreen distorted by the near-horizontal rain. Then he saw the crumbling brick columns and the rusty iron gates.

He braked. 'Could I ask you to jump out and open them, Mattie?'

'What?'

'Sorry about that.'

But Rooney was hardly listening. 'Sure I've never seen 'em gates closed in all my days. Damn me if I have.'

Grumbling he climbed out and Maidment watched impatiently as the old fisherman fumbled about, then returned. He opened the door. 'Bless me if I know why, sir, but it's padlocked, so it is.'

'Maybe Kurt isn't here. Maybe the people are away.'

Rooney shook his head, rain dripping from the peak of his Breton. 'There's lights on in the house.'

'Is there another way in?'

'Not with your car, sir. But I'm sure we can get through the fence. Old Joe hasn't had it repaired in years!' He sounded breathless as the wind snatched at his words.

Christ, Maidment thought, this is all I need. 'Okay, Mattie, shut the door and let me pull over.'

Rooney watched miserably as Maidment drove the car past the gates and tucked it under some trees before dousing the lights. He then hurried back, clutching his raincoat collar tight against his throat.

Gaining access to the grounds was not as easy as Rooney had

predicted. They sank to their ankles in mud and Maidment ripped his trousers on a nail as he clambered over fencing that had been brought down by the gale. There then followed an undignified scramble through overgrown brambles until they eventually reached the lawn.

They were halfway to the house when the front door opened and light flooded onto the portico and the Discovery parked in front of it.

Maidment could make out two men and a woman. From that distance it wasn't easy to be certain, but neither had Mallory's stance.

'What's going on?' Rooney said, as though suddenly reading the other man's thoughts.

The woman appeared to be struggling, the men restraining her and pushing her roughly into the vehicle. It was then that Maidment felt an awful sinking sensation in his gut. God Almighty, it was Georgina Savage.

'HEY!' Rooney bawled, but his yell was muffled by the gusting wind.

Maidment pulled him off balance. 'Shut up, Mattie, they're armed! Look!'

The old fisherman stared. 'Bloody IRA,' he decided. 'They're still around, you know. Turnin' to crime, a lot of them now.'

There was nothing they could do. Maidment felt an immense sense of impotence as he watched the men climb into the Discovery and heard the engine start up.

'What shall we do?' Rooney asked.

'Wait till they've gone,' Maidment replied tersely.

Both men watched as the vehicle backed and turned. They ducked instinctively as the headlight beams arced across the lawn before settling on the drive. On reaching the gates, one of the men climbed out to open them, allowing the vehicle through. Then the gates were locked again. Someone clearly didn't want unexpected visitors.

'I don't understand,' Rooney said, scratching his beard. 'That lass is a friend of Kelly, Joe's daughter. Who'd want to kidnap her? Perhaps Joe's in some kinda trouble.'

Maidment couldn't make sense of it all, didn't know what to believe. Had they really stumbled across a kidnap? And was Mallory somehow involved? He couldn't think how or why.

Rooney interrupted his thoughts. 'Shall I be getting my shotgun from your car?'

'You brought it with you?' He hadn't noticed.

'I always like to keep it with me. Ever since someone broke into the croft. Kurt said it was a good idea.'

The colonel grinned; it would be useful insurance. 'Mattie, you're a genius.'

He waited anxiously in the shadows for five minutes while Rooney returned to the vehicle. It had been a long time since he'd had to make quick tactical decisions of a military nature and he found the logic of his thinking positively rusty. What had that bastard RSM once told him when he was a wet-behind-the-ears subaltern? 'Always make a decision, sir, even if it's the wrong one. And with you bein' an officer, it probably will be. But it doesn't matter because *any* decision you make can force the enemy to make an even bigger fuckin' mistake of his own.'

Over the years he wasn't sure he'd ever proved the wisdom of those words, although he'd made plenty of quick decisions that he'd later come to regret.

An outside light flickered on at the side of the house. Then a group of men appeared briefly in the globe of illumination. At that distance it was impossible to tell how many or who they were. He thought he could make out three of them, but then they disappeared into the shadow of what appeared to be some type of outbuilding.

'I've got it!'

Maidment jumped. Rooney's returning footsteps across the squelching lawn had been hidden by the hiss of rain.

'Right, Mattie, I think I know how to handle this. We'll assume we're not mistaken about this. That something strange is going on and that Kurt is in there, probably in danger. If we're wrong about it then the only problem we have is profound embarrassment and a lot of explaining to do.'

Rooney saw the sense of that and nodded. 'As long as we don't

455

give old Joe a heart attack.'

'Do you mind if I take the shotgun?'

It was handed over. 'Know how to use it, do you?'

'Grouse shooting is my sport, Mattie.' He checked the weapon over and inspected the cartridges. He'd have preferred solid shot to pellets, but even they could be lethal at close range. 'They've gone into that shed at the back, so maybe there's no one left in the house.'

'Them's the stables,' Rooney corrected.

'Right, okay. But the likelihood is they've left the side door unlocked. I'll slip in there while you knock at the front. They know you, so if O'More or his daughter answers they won't be alarmed. Just say you'd heard Kurt is back and wondered if he was here.'

'What if they – or whoever answers – say no?'

'There's not much you can do. But if you do get inside and there is something amiss, then you could be in danger, Mattie. If I have to use this thing, then hit the deck fast. I don't want you getting hurt. Now, have you got a watch?'

'No, sir. I just need to know sunup and sundown nowadays.'

'Well, try counting to – say, a hundred and twenty from now. Then knock.'

'Right you are, sir.'

Maidment wished him good luck, then disappeared into the darkness in the direction of the house. The old fisherman took a deep breath, remembered to start counting, and began walking towards the portico. A porch light snapped on as he approached and made him start. Of course, newfangled sensors, he remembered, but it had still set his old heart thumping. He stood by the door, muddled up his counting at somewhere around the late seventies and began again at one. He reached fifty and thought to hell with it. He tugged at the bell pull.

Voices were raised behind the door. He thought he recognised Joe O'More, apparently arguing with someone. Probably an eye was looking at him through the tiny glass spyhole. He did his best to look unconcerned and innocent; it wasn't easy. After some delay the door inched open.

It was Kelly. 'Mattie? What on earth are you doing here?'

'Getting drenched, Miss O'More.' He forced a smile. 'Someone in the village told me Kurt was back. I wondered if he was here?'

'Er – no.' She looked flustered. 'Well – er – I haven't seen him.'

Suddenly the door was pulled open, Kelly stepping to one side as Joe O'More appeared in the opening. 'Hallo, Mattie, come on in and dry yourself off.'

'No, Dad,' Kelly protested. 'You can't.'

'Nonsense, child. C'mon in, Mattie.'

He hesitated, unsure. Something most definitely wasn't right. 'Ah, well, sure thank you kindly, but I'll be on my way.'

The automatic pistol had appeared as if by magic in O'More's hand. 'I'm sorry to do this to you, old friend. Now come in slowly with your hands raised. You know, just like in the cowboy movies.'

Rooney blanched, not believing what he was seeing. He threw his hands up with almost comical speed and shuffled in. The door was slammed behind him.

'You should have just told him to go,' Kelly said. 'It's crazy to involve him.' She sounded distraught.

'He might have seen the others take Georgina away.'

She looked at the fisherman. 'Did you?'

'Sure, I've seen nuthin', Miss O'More.'

'See!' she said turning back to her father. 'This is stupid!'

O'More looked uncomfortable. 'Well, it's too late now,' he replied irritably.

'Are you going to shoot me?' Rooney asked plaintively.

'You can't!' Kelly implored.

Her father looked confused. 'I don't know. I'll have to ask Guy what he thinks.'

She glared daggers. 'We both know what Guy will say.'

They all heard the door creak behind them. O'More turned to look across the hallway and found himself staring at the twin barrels of a shotgun.

'Who the devil are you?' O'More demanded as he overcame his initial shock.

Maidment ignored him as he inched forward. 'Put that gun very gently on the floor in front of you. Mattie, pick it up will you and come and stand over here with me.' As the fisherman obeyed, the colonel added: 'I am a friend of Kurt Mallory, Mr O'More. And a friend of Georgina Savage.'

Kelly's eyelids fluttered with involuntary relief. 'Thank God for that.'

'What's happened to them?' Maidment demanded.

She made her decision and immediately it felt as though a crushing burden had been lifted. 'They've taken Georgie to the croft – they're going to kill her – and Kurt's in our stables. They plan to kill him too.'

O'More rounded on her. 'For God's sake, child. Keep your mouth shut!'

But she stood her ground. 'No, Dad, this is all wrong.' She shook her head, repeating the words. 'It's all wrong. We shouldn't be doing things like this. Not now, we've no reason, no excuse. Kurt and Georgie were right. I've been so stupid listening to you and the others, carried along. Maybe there was justification for such actions once. But times have changed, and our people haven't.'

Rooney said: 'I'll take you to the stables, sir. Before it's too late.'

'No,' Kelly interrupted, 'if you just walk in there you'll get Kurt and yourself killed. Let me go in first, it'll act as a distraction.'

Maidment shook his head. 'So you can warn them? I don't think so, lady.'

'Please – I *love* Kurt. I don't want him hurt.'

Rooney said: 'It's true they're lovers, sir. For the past two years, so they are.'

The colonel hesitated. 'All right then. But if you alert them, you'll get the first barrel.'

She gave him a strange look. 'I understand. Come on, I'll show you the way.'

Maidment took the automatic from Rooney, made sure that a round was chambered and the safety off, then handed the fisherman back his shotgun. 'If Mr O'More so much as breathes too quickly, Mattie, let him have it. Aim for the centre of the body.'

Rooney said: 'I will, sir, have no fear of that. Kurt is the only friend I have in the world.'

Mallory was ready to die. Many years earlier he'd recognised that death normally came unannounced and rarely in the way it was expected. In his curious line of business it had always seemed probable it would come earlier rather than later. During his two years of retirement he'd reviewed that philosophy; premature death was only likely to be due to a fishing accident or a drunk at the wheel of a car. Death in old age had become more of a possibility. With his return to the fray, the mental readjustment back to acceptance that it might come any day, at any moment, had not been so easy. But the murders of Vic West, Dale, Goldie and then Mario had finally completed the process. He was at peace with himself.

As Sean Waterford strapped his wrists above his head and secured them to an overhead beam in the lime-washed stable block, Mallory had fully accepted that he was going to die. Had he been alone he might have tried something in the house. Although it would have been futile, at least he could have taken someone with him as he died. But Savage's presence had robbed him of that. Any challenge would have ensured her death as well as his own. At least now she was left with a chance of escape on the journey to his croft. He knew she'd snatch at any opportunity and he felt proud of her.

No, it wasn't death that scared him, it was the dying. He was no newcomer to pain. Long before his SAS training in anti-interrogation techniques, he had developed a high resistance to pain. And pain, he knew, was so much more endurable when you accepted that you were going to die. Because if you believed for one moment that you were going to survive, the breaking of each bone was unbearable, worsening with each act of violence until you knew that your body would now and for ever be beyond repair.

Waterford had removed his leather jacket and stuffed his pistol into the waistband of his trousers. He'd stripped down to his cut-away bodybuilder's T-shirt for comfort and so that he could enjoy his work. Mallory could smell the rankness of the man's armpits as he reached up to secure the bindings, the odour mingling with that of a cheap and sickly sweet cologne. There was something sinister about the white-blond hair and the choirboy face with its knowing secret smile. Those bright and dancing eyes so full of manic imagination and that softness of touch that made Mallory cringe. Homosexual almost certainly; fully paid-up sadist without a doubt.

The archangel Waterford was clearly going to enjoy this and would probably throw in a few ideas of his own.

Meanwhile Thripp watched thoughtfully, hunched over his crutches. His eyes had narrowed like a cat's, burning with intensity as though already seeing how Mallory was going to suffer. Already relishing it in his mind. He leaned against the post where Mallory's two *creollios* were stalled and rhythmically slapped a length of rubber hose-piping in the palm of his left hand.

The mustangs sensed that something was happening, that something was wrong. Animals instinctively knew. As he heard them stamping and shuffling, Mallory realised they would have smelled his presence, have seen and recognised him. Would be wondering why he did not come to them. And they would be feeling the fear and anger in the confined atmosphere of the place.

Waterford took a step back to admire his work.

'It's your lucky day,' Thripp said. 'Fortunately for you I can't do what I'd really like. Chop your bloody leg off and see how you like it.' He slapped the hose-piping in his palm again. 'But as we've now decided to drive your car over a cliff, your injuries are going to have to be consistent. Still, that gives me a fair bit of lee-way. Broken ribs from the steering wheel, shattered knees from the dash. Even a broken neck.' He grinned then. 'Fancy your last few hours alive paralysed from the neck down, do you? And I'm sure I can arrange for the car to catch fire. If you survive the fall you can wait to be burned alive knowing you can't move a muscle.'

Mallory said nothing, just stared through Thripp to some point beyond him.

'Let's start,' Waterford said in a soft but eager voice. He reached out his hand for the piping; Mallory realised then that, much as he might like to, Thripp couldn't do the job himself on crutches.

At that moment the two-part stable door opened at the end of the passage between the stalls and the stone wall. The rattle of rain increased suddenly as though someone had turned up the volume. A tiny whirlwind rushed in, eddying strands of hay across the floor and causing the hurricane lamp to sway on its hook.

Thripp and Waterford turned round.

'It's only me.' Mallory recognised Kelly's voice but couldn't see her features beneath the waterproof jacket and hood. 'God, it's a filthy night.'

'Get that bloody door shut!' Thripp demanded irritably and turned his attention back to his victim.

Mallory heard Kelly struggle against the wind to close both halves of the door and watched as she emerged from the shadows. Why was she here? Not to gloat, surely? He'd got her wrong, that was for certain, but surely not that wrong?

'Don't try talking me out of this,' Thripp warned. He sounded angry.

Her laugh was harsh. 'Far from it. I must be going soft. For a moment back there I'd forgotten what he'd done to you and the others, and how he'd killed Miguel. No, I've come to see you make a proper job of it.'

'No fear on that score, dear,' Waterford assured.

For a moment Kelly's eyes met with Mallory's. He tried to read her expression for signs of hatred or loathing or sorrow, but she seemed oddly devoid of any emotion.

Yet there was something in the twitch of her mouth, the slightest raising of one eyebrow, as though she were trying to tell him something.

And then he realised.

'STOP EXACTLY WHERE YOU ARE!' The voice had the clipped and authoritative tone of a British Army officer.

Colonel Maidment stepped out of the shadows, the automatic

461

held in a professional double-handed grip. Mallory was astounded, wondering instantly how the man had found his way to this place and how he had managed to enter the stables undetected.

'Step back,' Maidment ordered Kelly. 'Don't want you in the line of fire.'

Now he understood: the girl had been the colonel's accomplice, had let him crawl in and hide behind the first stall while she'd been battling to close the stable door.

'Who the hell . . . ?' Thripp began.

But Sean Waterford was faster. Young, quick-witted and a veteran frontliner of the Provos, he knew better than to stand around asking dumb questions. Sizing up the situation, he grabbed Kelly before she could move away and pulled her back with his left forearm locked around her throat. The pistol in his right hand was pressed against her temple.

'Drop the gun!' he snarled at Maidment and backed towards Mallory.

'Okay, okay,' the colonel replied quickly. He lowered the automatic.

Mallory's fingers curled around the bindings above his head; he tested his grip, and pulled himself off the ground by bending his elbows.

Thripp saw what was happening and yelled to Waterford.

But he was too late. The heel of Mallory's left boot thudded into the Irishman's fist, knocking the gun from his hand. Then Mallory's entire leg followed through over Waterford's shoulder while his right leg completed the pincer movement around the Irishman's neck. He snapped his knees, closing his calves around the offered neck like a vice and dragging the body back down onto the floor. Kelly stumbled sideways, propelled by Mallory's thigh. Maidment raised his pistol again, moving and body-swerving to bring it to bear on Thripp. But Thripp had been given a split second's reprieve and enough time to tug the revolver from his own waistband.

The two shots were simultaneous. Kelly screamed and threw herself to the ground. Another shot, two, three . . . Suddenly the stable was full of smoke and the acrid stink of cordite. The horses were startled, whinnied and kicked at their stall gates. Maidment stumbled and fell back against the wall like a prizefighter going down for ten.

Thripp had fallen from his crutches and lay motionless on a pile of straw.

Waterford grabbed his opportunity. He bit into the denim-clad thigh pressed into his face. As Mallory yelped, the Irishman used the moment to wriggle free. He didn't hesitate, just grabbed his automatic from the ground, sprang to his feet and rushed past Maidment, through the passage and burst out of the door. As he disappeared into the night, the wind and the rain howled in.

Maidment sat with his back propped against the stone wall and clutched his left bicep. Blood seeped through his fingers. He shook his head like a man coming out of sleep and looked at Kelly: 'Are you all right?'

She was still crouched on the floor, gulping in surprise, unable to speak and just managing a thankful nod of the head.

The colonel gave her a painful but reassuring grin before crawling weakly across the cobbles to where Thripp lay. He turned the body over. It had no recognisable face, the nose and much soft tissue reduced to a bloody pulp.

'That's got to have been my luckiest ever shot,' he breathed. 'I never even had time to aim. All my years in the army and I never once fired in anger.'

Kelly had staggered to her feet. She glanced at the ornamental display of farm tools on the wall and reached for an old scythe. It took some fifteen seconds to hack through Mallory's bonds with the rusty blade.

He grinned at her as he rubbed some feeling back into his hands. 'I thought you were going to use that *on* me.'

She looked at him, unsure. Of him, of herself. 'For a moment, so did I.' She smiled lamely. 'I'm sorry, Kurt, I've been a bloody fool.'

By now Maidment had limped to the door. He still had the gun in his hand and his blood was up. He squinted into the squall and shouted back. 'The bastard's taking a Land-Rover!'

Then they heard the shots. Two, three, four. Mallory sprinted to the door with Kelly. They were just in time to see Waterford driving hard down the puddled drive, plumes of spray in the vehicle's wake.

Maidment said: 'The bastard's shot out the tyres on everything, including that Healey.'

Kelly said: 'He can't get away. The gates are padlocked.' Even as she spoke the twin orbs of the Land-Rover's headlights picked out the ornate brick pillars. Waterford appeared to hesitate; the vehicle slowed. Then abruptly it surged forward, accelerating in a fury of unleashed power. The noise of the impact was enormous, the crescendo of breaking glass and crumpling metal quite distinct above the moaning wind. Sparks flew in the darkness like shorting electricity as the gates were torn from their mountings in the crumbling brick and folded over the front of the Land-Rover like giant butterfly wings.

Kelly gave a gasp. Waterford crashed into reverse gear and backed off until the gates fell free.

Only Maidment realised what had happened as the indistinct figure of the Irishman was seen climbing from the Land-Rover and firing two shots at something out on the road.

'Sod!'

'What?' Mallory asked.

'He's seen my car. It's parked out there.'

All eyes went back to the gates as Waterford returned to his vehicle and drove off, swallowed up by the night. Heading in the direction of Mallory's cottage.

'He'll be going to warn the others,' Kelly said.

'They're holding George at the croft,' Mallory added. 'They might already have killed her.'

Maidment said: 'Maybe they'll change their minds.'

'I don't think so,' Kelly interrupted. 'Look, that man who calls himself Sheehan, he was waiting for Kurt to be taken to the croft before Georgie was ex—' She blushed, shaking her head as though waking from a bad dream, 'murdered. He wanted to set it up to look good for forensic evidence and to get the times of death right. But now it's all gone wrong for him. He's a hard case,

Kurt, even Dad calls him a psycho. I'm sure he'll kill Georgie anyway because she's a witness, then come back for you. Maybe even Dad and me. He's likely to kill everyone who could give evidence – enemies and friends. He's done two long stretches and he's paranoid about going back inside.' She looked pleadingly at Mallory. 'We've got to do *something*!'

Maidment looked out at the remaining cars, a Metro and O'More's Healey 3000, each with at least one tyre flat. 'Maybe we can change the wheels,' he thought aloud.

Kelly shook her head. 'Different sizes. Anyway, it'll take for ever.'

Mallory glanced across to the first stall. 'The horses,' he said as an idea began forming in his mind, visualising distances and the lie of the land between the O'More house and his croft. 'I could cut across country.'

'You'd never get there before him,' Kelly protested.

Mallory snatched up a bridle from its hook on the stall post. 'I'll just have to try.'

She understood what he meant and made a sudden decision. 'I'll come with you. There's a back way out of these grounds that'll save a few minutes.'

Already Mallory had slid the bridle and bit onto the sturdy stallion he called Sabre. 'There's no time to saddle up.'

'I can cope,' Kelly replied, already moving quickly to bridle the bay mare. 'You were a good teacher, Kurt, and Dolly's got the sweetest nature.'

Maidment was leaning against the wall, clutching his arm and fighting back the waves of nausea and giddiness. He watched as Mallory and the girl began backing the mustangs from their stall with a sense of hopelessness. 'This is madness. You'll never get there in time and probably kill yourself in the process.' He stared down at his blood-sodden arm. 'Christ, I'm going to be dead if I don't stop this bleeding and I really don't want to call an ambulance.'

Mallory said: 'Tampons. They'll expand to fill the wound.'

'There are some in my bedroom,' Kelly added, starting to move.

465

'No, no,' Maidment said. 'I'll find them. You just get down to the croft. As long as the bleeding stops I'll wait till you get back.'

Kelly handed Waterford's abandoned leather jacket to Mallory. 'Wear this against the rain; it should fit.'

He shrugged into its comforting warmth and used a stool to spring up onto Sabre's bare back. As Kelly mounted Dolly and took up the reins, Maidment handed Mallory his automatic. 'I only used one round. There's nine left in it. Make 'em count, Kurt, for Georgina's sake.'

The hooves clattered loudly on the cobbles, Kelly following Mallory as he ducked to clear the stable doorway and Sabre trotted out into the screaming night.

'GOOD LUCK!' Maidment called after them, watching for a moment as Kelly led the way towards the back gardens. Then he lurched painfully across to the house.

At the rear of the building a flagged stone path dropped away across a rough and sloping lawn, which Kelly took at a gentle canter. The sodden ground was easily torn beneath the steel shoes, giving Mallory a clear route to follow even when he lost sight of horse and rider in the sweeping sheets of rain.

The instant they had left the shelter of the stable, Mallory's hair had been flattened against his scalp and his jeans soaked, beginning to steam with body heat. Wind and rain cut into his legs, whipping like a cat-o'-nine-tails. Hard droplets of water stung his face and eyes, thrown out of the sky with such velocity that they felt like tiny steel pellets. Visibility was almost nil; he squinted through the squall, trying to follow the tracks and melting shape of Kelly and her mount as they proceeded towards the ornamental rose garden.

He ducked beneath the trellised arch and heard the reassuring clip of steel on stone as he passed the fish pond and the walled enclosure with its rows of barbed standards and straggling climbers, where the few remaining leaves had been blasted off into a scurrying whirlwind.

Ahead of him, Kelly picked her way through to a neglected vegetable patch that was running to weeds, past dilapidated greenhouses and a tool shed, the stench of compost and horse manure thick in the air. Then she and Dolly picked up speed, trotting through banks of tall withered nettles along a muddy track. After fifty metres he saw her dip her head to avoid the swaying low bough of a tree before she dug her heels in, urging the mustang on. Clods of mud flew from her hooves as the mare accelerated, her back legs sliding as she tried to gain purchase on the slippery surface. Then both horse and rider rocketed from the ground, the powerful muscles on the beast's haunches glistening with rain as they cleared the strands of rusting barbed wire.

Mallory spurred his own horse on, leaning forward to whisper harshly in its ear, knees gripping against the slippery wet pelt of its flanks. The animal recognised the instruction and reacted to Mallory's body pressures. Then they too were airborne, the wire boundary fence of the O'More estate passing beneath them. It was a good landing on the tufty grass and now the meadow fell away unseen before them, dipping towards the coast.

Kelly had stopped some distance ahead, clouds billowing from the mare's nostrils like dragon smoke as she was reined in tight, waiting for Mallory before heading off again at speed.

The two of them had never ridden so hard and fast. Even the horses seemed to pick up the vibes, their riders' sense of urgency; together they powered on, sturdy and sure-footed beasts, eager to please and seeming to enjoy the run. They leapt two dry-stone walls dividing the patchwork of farm fields before reaching a woody glade. There the trail slowed slightly as they negotiated the puddled muddy track. Out again on the far side, the ground opening up to rough pasture dropping away, ever closer to the beach.

To his left Mallory once glimpsed car headlights flickering between the roadside hedgerow on higher ground. The Land-Rover, he guessed; it was moving at speed, but it was not a road that a driver could take liberties on. Strewn with tractor mud at the best of times, tonight it would be like an ice rink with fallen leaves and slicked with surface water unable to drain faster than the elements were hurling it down. If Waterford panicked, it was a dead cert he'd skid off the road, lose it on some sharp bend. But the man was no callow youth on his first job for the movement;

he'd undoubtedly been in tighter spots before.

So if he kept a cool head – and the fact he'd troubled to shoot out the tyres of vehicles back at the house suggested he was – then he'd take it steady. And that would give the horse riders the glimmer of a chance.

Mallory heard the high-voltage crack of lightning far out over the sea. Momentarily the huge and angry waves were lit in an electric blue radiance, pounding along the shoreline to explode in foaming white wrath. Ahead Kelly and her horse were clearly defined for one fleeting moment along with the ragged tree line that shook and trembled in the gusting Atlantic blow. For a second he saw the bruised underbelly of the storm clouds pressing down before the entire landscape disappeared again, and the thunder rolled. Horse and rider charged blindly on.

He hadn't been expecting her to stop. It was Sabre who swerved to avoid his stable mate as Kelly reined her horse tightly in. Dolly rose on her haunches, fetlocks thrashing in the air.

'What is it?' Mallory shouted above the wind.

Kelly turned towards him, her small fists white as she fought to control the horse. The hood of her waterproof had blown free and her long hair was sodden and matted, her face dripping with rain and smudged grey with mascara. 'It's no good, Kurt, we can't do it!' She pointed up towards the road. Headlights were flickering through the hedgerow. 'He's ahead of us and we've got to divert to avoid the stream! We're too late!'

He knew what she meant. The stream cut a deep cleft through the rough pasture; millions of years of Irish rain pouring almost constantly off the coastal high ground had eroded a sharp-sided chasm lined with wind-stunted trees. The banks were too sheer for a horse to descend without falling and even if it didn't injure itself, it would be unable to scramble up the far side.

Mallory glared at the row of trees and bush gorse that marked its edge and cursed beneath his breath. It felt as though the gods had conspired to defeat him, had planned it all those centuries past, had decided even then that he would fail and that Savage would die. Some things were predetermined and there was absolutely nothing you could do about it.

Up on the road the lights were receding, his quarry slipping away. He was filled with an unreasonable and boiling anger. It was as though he had betrayed her as she had never betrayed him, had let her down in her hour of greatest need.

He wheeled the big stallion round and edged towards the stream. How wide was it? Eight feet? Nearer ten.

Kelly saw what he was thinking. 'You can't do it, Kurt!' she shouted. 'You'll kill yourself and the horse!'

But there was a mad light in his eyes now and his lips had formed into a thin and determined line. He circled Sabre wide once more, leaning low over the mane and whispering encouragement in Spanish. Its ears pricked in response.

'No!' Kelly warned.

His heels nudged hard into the rain-sodden flanks and he yelled at the horse, who lunged forward with muscular legs thrashing at the soft ground. His build-up of speed was impressive, his course straight and determined as he thundered towards the narrow strip of gorse at the narrowest stretch.

Mallory urged him on, leaning his body forward, chest pressed down towards the shaggy mane at the moment Sabre's hooves left the ground. It was like slow motion, flying through space, leaving solid ground behind, launching into an abyss.

Christ, you're a fool! The self-abuse spun through Mallory's mind in that one split second of lunacy. It was a ghastly mistake, one that would kill his horse for certain and probably himself. In midair he shut his eyes, his body hunched low, awaiting the stumbling crash and the animal's cry of pain and shock. Visualised the reeds and swirling, gurgling water rushing over the stone bed towards the sea. Planning to throw himself clear, praying that half a ton of horse flesh didn't land on top of him and crush his chest to a pulp.

Sabre's front legs hit the far side with a thud. The force of it nearly catapulted Mallory clear over the horse's head. But it was an untidy landing, one rear hoof missing the chasm edge and kicking wildly at thin air. The horse slid back, startled, its back leg falling down the drop, the sudden backward momentum reversing the pull of gravity. Mallory slipped quickly from the animal's back to allow it to struggle free.

'*Chico bueno!*' he shouted encouragingly. '*Chico bueno*! Steady, steady!'

When the bewildered stallion dragged its fallen back leg up onto level ground, Mallory remounted. Sparing a glance over his shoulder, he was aware of, rather than actually made out, the dark shape of Kelly and her horse amid the sweeping curtain of rain. Caught the pale blur of her wave, realised she was turning, taking the detour down to the bridge by the beach. Taking the longer, safer route and he was glad she had.

He urged Sabre on. There was no point in allowing the horse time to spook. With a whoop of triumph he spurred the animal into a gallop, pounding across the sloping pasture to a point on their right where he knew a field gate opened out onto the road. To his left he could just detect the glimmer of headlights advancing. Both horse and rider and Land-Rover were converging. It was just a case of which arrived first.

A flock of startled sheep loomed out of the darkness, breaking like a starburst to avoid the thudding hooves. By now the big stallion was breaking sweat, foam whisked from its flanks by the huffing squall that blasted in over the shoreline.

Now Mallory could see the ragged outline of the roadside hedge, saw the smooth horizontal edge that marked the gate. Barely fifty metres to go. He dug in his heels and, leaning forward, yelled encouragement, gasping for breath as the wind snatched away his words. Forty-five metres, forty, thirty-five, thirty. Another urgent kick of the heels. Twenty-five.

The Land-Rover shot past the gate.

Fifteen, ten, five.

'UP!'

Sabre launched himself skyward, his magnificent frame outstretched. Without a trace of fear, trusting his master to the utmost.

Allowing for the narrow tarmac road beyond the gate, Mallory had taken the jump at a sharp angle to give them a run-out before they reached the ditch on the far side. Even so it was barely enough. The horse was shocked by the severity of landing on the hard surface. He jolted and pulled back as his front hooves hit, then began to slide all over the place. He whinnied in pain as his legs spread and the tendons strained, the animal scrabbling like a cartoon character on ice.

'Easy, *chico*, easy!' Mallory intoned as Sabre cantered uneasily on, his head held high, alert and wary, eyes wild with fright. 'You're okay, *chico*. C'mon let's go.'

They gathered speed. Farther down the road he could see the vehicle's lights blink red, Waterford touching the brakes before the Land-Rover disappeared round another bend.

Twenty metres. No more. Mallory could scarcely believe his luck. They were still behind, but so, so close.

Even Sabre seemed to sense that his job was nearly done, that it was just another furlong to the winning post. He strode out, stretching every last sinew as though driven by a turbo-charger, reaching for his last reserves of energy and power. Rain lashed painfully in Mallory's face till he could have sworn it was drawing blood. But he became oblivious to the discomfort, his eyes and mind focused on the closing distance between himself and the Land-Rover.

Ten feet, seven, six. His heels dug in, the horse inched closer. Three, Two – Now they were alongside, Waterford suddenly noticing and swerving as he glanced back over his shoulder. Mallory might have laughed at the expression of shock on his face had he not been concentrating on exactly what to do next.

But the driver quickly recovered. He began veering deliberately to the offside of the road, trying to force horse and rider into the ditch. Steel slapped against Sabre's side, but Mallory edged him clear so the impact was minimal.

A bend loomed. Waterford had no alternative but to slow. Mallory gained the necessary inches and seized the moment. He launched himself from the horse's back, pushing his left heel into its flank to propel himself across the gap. His hands clasped around the rails of the roof-rack and his body slammed against the vehicle's side, his legs scrabbling.

Sabre trotted to a halt, muscled body steaming in the rain, his task done.

Waterford began swinging the Land-Rover violently, so much so that it began to rock, in the attempt to throw Mallory off. But the steel rails of the rack offered a firm and unshakeable grip. With enormous effort he hauled his body up until he was able to swing one leg onto the roof and roll himself over. Gasping for breath he looked ahead in the vehicle's twin beams. Despite the silvery veil of rain, he recognised where they were – just as Waterford swung the wheel to take them down the side track towards Mallory's croft. Brambles whipped viciously at his face and back as it passed through the gap in the roadside hedge. He felt his skin and the material of his jeans tear as the tiny barbs ripped free. The vehicle began to bounce violently on the rough and pot-holed surface.

Recovering, Mallory yanked the automatic from his waistband and knelt on the roof, jamming his calves hard against the metal rack for stability. Like a praying man he held the weapon in both hands between his legs, pointing the muzzle at the tin roof above the driver's seat.

He fired four times in rapid succession. The rounds spat contemptuously through the mild steel, a ragged cluster of holes appearing beneath him.

The effect was instant; the vehicle slewed left, then right and ploughed through the old wooden fence. There was a sickening accompaniment of splitting timber, shattering glass and buckling metal. The front tyres sank into the boggy ground, the fender thudded into a grassy mound and the engine stalled. Mallory lost his balance. The abrupt halt propelled him forward, just missing the bonnet. For a second he was like a man in space, bringing up his arms to protect his face, but not knowing which way up he was as he tumbled through the air.

Had it been high summer, he might have broken his spine on hard-baked ground. But the grass was long and tufty, the ground as soft as sponge. He thudded onto his back, shocked and winded, and rolled over. Pointing the gun back at the vehicle's windscreen, he gasped with relief that he was still alive. A little bruised and very shaken, but that was all.

He scrambled to his feet and half-walked, half-staggered back to the Land-Rover, his weapon pointing all the time. Jerking open the driver's door, he stepped back. Waterford's body fell towards him, the face white and lolling. The eyes were wide and staring and blood ran freely from his gaping mouth. Three rounds had found their mark. The right knee was shattered, the blood dark around the torn material of his jeans; a similar messy patch was bubbling around his crotch and the third had passed down straight through his cranium and scrambled his brains.

Mallory heaved in a lungful of air, turned away and fell with his back against the Land-Rover's side. He closed his eyes and let the sweet, cold rain devour him, sting and revive him, his mind blissfully blank for a few precious seconds.

At the sound of hooves clacking on the roadway he looked up. Kelly emerged at the junction with the track, riding Dolly and with his stallion in tow. She dismounted at the broken fence, tied the horses to a snapped post and picked her way down through the debris. She stared aghast at Waterford's body slumped out of the open door.

'God, Kurt, are you all right?' Her eyes were anxious in her pinched, rain-streaked face. Mercifully the wind had dropped a little and the rain was easing.

He stared at her. 'There speaks the woman who was happy to see me executed.'

Her eyes were very bright and clear and close to his. 'But not tortured, Kurt, never that.'

He turned away, sensing her disappointment as he rejected her. 'We've got to get on. George is still in deep shit.'

Kelly fought back her tears, tried to appear as calm and cool as her crumpled face would allow. 'She'll be okay until they get the word.' She looked at the Land-Rover. 'Is this thing drivable?'

'Probably.'

'Let me go to the croft. They'll let me in. I could tell them there's been a change of plan.'

It made sense, if he could really trust her. Mallory nodded. 'Could you lure them out on some pretext, away from George?'

'I could try.' She glanced down at Waterford's corpse. 'You're wearing Sean's jacket.'

He saw her point. The leather blouson was expensively cut, quite distinctive. 'We'll leave the horses here. They've done their bit.'

It took ten minutes to coax the Land-Rover out of its muddy bed, even with the four-wheel drive. Easing back and forth over the boggy ground to avoid sinking to its axles in the mire, Mallory finally pulled clear, circled and returned to the track. There he turned left and drove down towards the turning circle on the cliff where the Discovery was parked.

Scudding charcoal thunderheads moved like vast and godly chariots towards Ulster and the Scottish mainland. They left behind a clearing pre-dawn sky.

'I'll go first,' Kelly said, opening the door. 'You keep a bit behind, they'll have seen the headlights.'

Mallory watched her go, moving easily down the rough path. He felt a great sadness begin to swallow him. He'd built his hopes too high, built them on shifting sand. Things would never be the same again between them, could never be. Suddenly he felt very lonely.

He shivered, then plunged his hands into the blouson pockets the way he'd seen Waterford do it. Also he copied the man's light-footed manner, half-stepping half-dancing down the path to the seashore and the dark outline of his croft.

Padraig O'Donnell had been looking out from the side window. He peered through the gap in the musty felt curtaining, the barrel of his Armalite assault rifle resting on the foot-deep sill. He had spotted the headlamp beams shining like searchlights from the turning circle. Chewing on his spearmint gum, he waited for Waterford to appear from behind the rockfall spur.

'It's Kelly.' There was a hint of surprise in his voice.

Sheehan was sitting on a dining chair, riding it back to front like a horse, his forearms crossed over its back, a pistol in his right hand. He was irritable after sitting guard so long over the rope-bound girl who was slumped on the mildewed sofa. The place was so damp and cold it was seeping into his bones. He longed to light some turfs in the big fireplace, but that just wasn't on. Security before creature comforts, that was always the rule.

He turned his head towards the window. 'What's she doing here?'

'How should I know? Perhaps there's a change of plan?'

Sheehan scowled. 'I bloody hope not. We're running out of time. It'll take a while to set up the car smash and we've barely an hour before it's properly light.'

O'Donnell chuckled. 'Sean probably couldn't bring himself to stop, sadistic little bastard. Still, perhaps Guy thinks he can squeeze some new info out of Mallory and wants to delay until tomorrow.'

'I don't fancy another day in this bleedin' fridge.'

'Ah,' the other man said, 'I think that's Sean coming now. He's stopped up on the path – what's he playing at?'

Kelly knocked on the door. O'Donnell left his seat at the window, Armalite still in his hand.

Savage had been dozing restlessly. She'd tried to keep awake, but the fear had drained her and sleep had come unbidden to the rescue. But the cold and discomfort kept her hovering on the verge of consciousness. Hearing the knock, she became instantly awake, her heart already hammering in her chest.

They'd been awaiting instructions; now her time had come. So it hadn't all been a most terrible dream. God, how she wished she was curled up in her Battersea flat with Giles.

O'Donnell opened the door. 'What is it, Kelly? Come to say goodbye to your friend?'

'Very funny,' she replied caustically. 'No, Sean wants to talk to you.'

The Irishman peered out at the distant figure in the familiar leather jacket outlined on the path. Waterford was kicking his feet impatiently. 'Why doesn't he come down?'

'Why do you think?' Kelly indicated Savage. 'He doesn't want her to hear.'

'What's happened?'

She gave a brittle laugh. 'How should I know? This is big boys' talk and I'm a mere girl.'

O'Donnell smiled, wicked. 'Sure you shouldn't put yourself down.'

Kelly aimed a friendly swipe at his shoulder. 'Get on with you, Padraig. Sean doesn't like to be kept waiting.' She glanced across at Sheehan. 'He wants to speak to you too, Kevin.'

The other man climbed to his feet, rubbing his leg where the cramp had set in. 'I'm lookin' after the wee girl.'

Kelly looked at Savage's trussed form on the sofa. 'I'll keep an eye on her. Give me the gun.'

'And have you shoot yourself in the foot?' He walked past her. 'I guess she's going nowhere. Shout if she gives you any trouble.'

Damn it, Kelly thought, but at least it had been worth a try.

As Sheehan followed O'Donnell out the door, she sped to the kitchenette, took a sharp knife from the drawer and approached the sofa.

Savage froze. Anticipated the hot burning thrust of the blade.

'Don't look so worried,' Kelly reassured with a grin, and sliced through the cord at her wrists. 'Kurt's outside.'

The landscape was lightening by the minute. Inky shadows were melting to grey and there was now definition to the silky hump of the waves as they broke along the seaweed-strewn beach. Mallory stood hunched with his back to the croft. His right hand was concealed in the front of the leather blouson, his fingers around the butt of the automatic.

He heard the scratch of boot leather on shale and O'Donnell's laboured breathing as he scaled the rockpile. 'What the hell's happening, Sean?'

Mallory knew he could wait no longer. O'Donnell and Sheehan were closing, daylight was breaking and they'd see that although wearing Sean Waterford's jacket, his hair was the wrong colour.

So he turned, very slowly, casually, extracting the gun in one relaxed, fluid movement.

O'Donnell was barely ten feet away and was already drawing to a halt as he realised something was wrong. His mouth fell open, the Armalite began to rise. Mallory lifted his gun in a double-handed grip and fired two shots at the man's body centre. He was blown backwards by the close-proximity force, rolling over to land at Sheehan's feet.

The older man barely had time to register what had happened before the second two rounds slammed into him.

Echoes of gunfire reverberated out across the bay, fading gradually like dark spirits leaving the dead. The storm had passed and the first gulls of the day were out searching for food, dark and bat-like shadows against a clear pearl sky. Tranquillity had returned. The wind had dropped leaving the changing tide to slap lazily along the shoreline.

Mallory checked the two bodies before staring out at what promised to be a Canaletto sky when the sun rose. He drew deeply on the crisp and salty air with its pungent tang of bladderwrack. Suddenly he felt deeply weary and wondered if the fight would ever end.

He gave a wry smile; somehow, despite everything, he knew the answer to that. Life without justice, however rough, was meaningless. And, as he looked down at the two men who had intended to kill Savage and himself, he savoured the sweet and heady taste of revenge. For the last time? He shrugged. Some things in life you never could tell; fate had a habit of picking the right man for the job and when fate called you had no option but to answer.

As he made his way back down to the croft Savage and Kelly appeared cautiously at the door.

'It's done,' he said.

'Dead?' Savage asked.

He nodded.

Kelly pulled a tight smile. 'You weren't hurt?'

'No.'

Savage took a deep breath of resignation as she observed the grotesque postures of the two bodies; it was back to business. She took a cigarette pack from her shirt pocket, offered one to Mallory and lit them. 'You'd better make yourself scarce, Kurt. Leave the tidying up to me. Are you okay for cash?'

'Enough to get by.'

'There'll be a cheque sent to your account within the week.' She sighed, and exhaled a long stream of tobacco smoke. 'It's probably best if we torch the croft. Destroy all evidence of your existence here.'

'Sure.'

Kelly looked aghast. 'But your books, Kurt, and your memoirs.'

He smiled without humour. 'The baggage of time. I prefer to travel light.'

Savage glanced up to the turning circle. 'Is that the Land-Rover you came in?'

'Yes. Waterford's body is in the back. Shot with this.' He handed her the still-warm automatic, butt first. 'The colonel turned up at the house with Mattie. He was wounded but not before he killed Thripp.'

She had to smile at that. 'This is beginning to seem like the last act of a Shakespearean tragedy.'

'Perhaps it is.'

'Did they hurt you?'

'Only my pride.' He glanced at Kelly. 'Our friend had a timely change of heart.'

Savage made a decision. 'My priority has to be to get you and the colonel out of here. Is he fit to travel?'

'I think so, but he needs medical attention as soon as possible.'

She said: 'As soon as we get back to the O'Mores' place, I'll assess the situation and contact our man in the Dublin Embassy. He'll arrange a doctor and a safe house for you both.'

'Safe house?'

Savage gave a smile. 'As I'm sure Kelly would be only too keen to point out, Kurt, this *is* foreign soil. So the usual precautions apply.' She took a few steps forward to Sheehan's body, prised open the stiffening fingers, removed his gun and replaced it with Mallory's automatic. 'If you could bring Waterford's body down and dump it here, it'll look like a Provo shoot-out. At least that'll give the Garda something to puzzle over.'

Mallory realised time was short and set off up the path to retrieve Waterford's corpse.

Kelly thrust her hands deep into the pockets of her waterproof. Her tangled copper hair was drying into tightly sprung ringlets. 'What'll happen to Dad and me, Georgie?' She sounded miserable.

Savage regarded her with scarcely disguised hostility; she tried not to be emotional, but it was hard to forgive the betrayal of a friend. 'That's largely up to you and him. I take it it was you who tipped off Sheehan and Stan Summers and arranged for the White Viper consignments to have their routings changed?'

The other girl nodded. 'It was the obvious thing to do.'

'Then your future will depend on whether you and your father co-operate with us, help track down the consignments in the UK and Europe.' She stared out across the bay. 'Otherwise, I imagine the British Government will apply for your extradition to stand trial. Dublin's never been very co-operative in such matters, especially when it involves the IRA. And no one wants to unsettle this tenuous peace process. If I had a crystal ball, I'd say Irish Special Branch will be breathing down his neck so closely, your father and his friends will have to forget the cocaine business. That's Dublin's usual fence-sitting stance. And my people will make damn sure your career as a lawyer is over for good, one way or another. In fact I'll see to it myself.'

'Thanks,' Kelly replied stiffly. 'But I can tell you Dad would never co-operate, wouldn't raise a hand to help you Brits.'

'But you will?'

'I told you, we've won. You're not the enemy any more. I was wrong.'

Savage wasn't sure she believed her, but had no way of knowing. But then it was a well-known truism in the intelligence business that fanatics were the easiest people to convert to the opposite cause. 'Help us and we'll help you.'

'There's no future for me here. Dad will never forgive me and word will soon get out that I was involved in all this, that I became a grass. For all your professional cover-ups, there'd still be rumours and Ireland is just one big village really.'

Up above them Mallory appeared, clambering down the rocky path with Waterford's body slung across his shoulders. He dumped the corpse unceremoniously between the bodies of O'Donnell and Sheehan.

Savage turned to Kelly. 'Thanks anyway for the change of heart, for helping to save Kurt and me.'

Kelly's green eyes pleaded to be believed and forgiven. 'I'd worked for the Provisionals' cause for too long – I'd got too close to it. I went along with Dad like I always had. I just stopped questioning the rights and wrongs. Dad always seemed so sure—'

'But?' Mallory asked.

She smiled weakly. 'But now we've won. If the peace process holds, we've got what we want. We'll have a reunited Ireland in all but name and justice will have been done.'

'Hallelujah,' Mallory said acidly.

Kelly smiled at his sarcasm. 'I don't expect you to understand. But we *have* won, Kurt, and it's time to mend our ways. I can't blame Dad and the others – I'm only just recognising it myself. It's one thing using narcotics money to fight for the cause – we had no option – but not for political funding.'

'You'll have to have an IRA flag day.'

She smiled. 'I still love you.'

Savage interrupted. 'Take the Land-Rover, Kurt. We'll follow on in the Discovery as soon as I've finished here.' She found a pencil stub in her pocket and scribbled a telephone number on her cigarette packet and gave it to him. 'That's my mobile. Pick up the colonel from the house and get on the road to Dublin fast. Call me in a couple of hours for further instructions.'

'I always said you were the best.'

She ignored that, but would remember it. 'When you finally dump the Land-Rover, burn it.' She glanced towards the croft. 'Talking of which—?'

He understood. 'There's plenty of paraffin and petrol round the back. No problem.'

Kelly touched his arm. There was a look of uncertainty on her face. 'I'll take care of your horses, Kurt, for as long as you want. Whenever you want them back – or me – just say where.'

There was just a glimmer of humour in his eyes. 'And the bees?'

The Irish girl wrinkled her nose. 'Mattie can look after them. He'll miss you.' Then she added, scarcely audible: 'So will I.'

Mallory turned to Savage. For a moment she thought he was going to kiss her, but he didn't. That man would never change.

'Ciao, pardner.'

'Ciao, Kurt. Take care.'

Both watched as he scrambled back up over the rocks, leaving his life of the past three years behind without even a backward glance.

'Who was that man you called the colonel?' Kelly asked. 'Is he one of yours?'

A ghost of a smile crossed Savage's face. 'No, he's not one of ours. Just a man with a mission.'

'Kurt worked for him?'

'I've no idea.'

Kelly listened to the sound of the Land-Rover's engine growling into life up on the turning circle. 'All the time I thought I knew Kurt, I really didn't know him at all. Who is he really? Just a stranger.'

Savage felt the hot prickling sensation behind her eyes, and sniffed heavily. 'Not just any stranger. He's the last of the strangers in the white hats.'

She turned away then, back towards the croft. There were things to be done, a can of petrol to be found, a fire to be started. As Mallory used to say, a jaguar always buries its shit.

Kelly hurried to catch up with her. 'After I've helped your people, would you help me change my identity?'

'Will you tell us everything you know about the Cali cartel?'

'Of course.'

'Then the answer's almost certainly yes.' Savage paused at the door. 'Would you want to relocate?'

'I think perhaps I'd have to after all this. But somewhere I can keep the horses.'

'Any thoughts?' Savage asked absently. She really didn't care.

Kelly O'More stared out across her beloved bay, so calm and silvery in the gathering light. 'Paraguay.'

Epilogue

Stan Summers considered himself to be the luckiest man alive.

He sat in the back of his chauffeur-driven Bentley and watched the passing crowds and Christmas lights of London's West End. Then he glanced at his wife, Lynn, who sat beside him. Her rapt and smiling face pleased him – how she loved the glitz and glamour of the capital.

Blonde and blowsy, she was twenty years his junior and a former nightclub hostess. As such she appreciated the good life he had shown her, burying her earlier loss of self-esteem by becoming one of the *nouveaux riches* she had at one time so despised, before she'd ever dreamt she might become one of them.

Shopping at Harrods, eating at L'Escargot or Langan's Brasserie and dancing the night away at Stringfellows was Lynn's idea of paradise. Her enthusiasm for the opera, ballet and the theatre, he knew, was an affectation to give herself a semblance of being cultured. Nevertheless, he applauded her efforts at self-improvement and actually felt quite proud of her when she talked knowingly of Wagner, Mozart and Verdi – even if she did tend to get mixed up.

Summers himself would have preferred to have spent the evening at one of the unlicensed boxing matches in Billericay or Bermondsey, but the consolation for him of a night of enforced culture was to rub shoulders with the stars of stage and television. With his money and contacts that was never a problem. He especially enjoyed first nights like this and hobnobbing with the famous in the green room afterwards. Lynn would love tonight; that dashing young actor, destined for Hollywood, had the starring rôle. He'd have to keep a careful eye on her.

As they slowed in the traffic, he reflected that it would shortly be New Year. It had been a funny old twelve months.

He'd done nicely out of it, although not as nicely as he should have done. It had all gone wrong when his team had been wiped out in Colombia and only Guy Thripp had escaped.

But the IRA – if that's really who they were – knew their stuff. Joe O'More told him the whole thing had been some sort of black intelligence operation, probably with the DEA, using hired assassins. He reckoned the same about Miguel Castaño's mysterious crash outside Madrid, but refused to say how he knew.

No matter. They and their new allies from Cali had wreaked revenge and no mistake; he'd heard at least three of the assassins had been traced and killed.

Then there had come another shock. A shoot-out at O'More's house in Kerry and on a beach nearby. Four people dead, including poor old Guy. A clash between rival factions of the IRA, the small television news item had said. It made him sweat when he saw that, but it made sense to him. Everyone knew the peace process in Northern Ireland wasn't universally welcomed.

It had been enough to persuade Summers to sever all connections with them. He'd hurriedly packed his bags and taken Lynn off for an extended holiday in Marbella. There was a raid on the warehouse of one of his shell companies in Manchester where the main White Viper consignment was being stored. He was able to deny all knowledge and drop the warehouse manager in the shite from a very great height. Summers's solicitor told him the police wanted to prosecute, but that the CPS didn't think the case would stand up. Summers was untouchable.

The news of Joe O'More's suicide at his country home had come as a further surprise, but it no longer mattered to him. Now he had secured personal connections direct with Jaramillo through the lovely Maria Palechor and with the man called the Captain in Budapest.

Of course, without the muscle of the Irish to enforce the distribution routes, the White Viper brand couldn't be sustained. Now it was just diluted coke like all the rest. Profits weren't so high but at least it was set to run and run. And, frankly, he was quite relieved to have the Irish connection off the scene. He was happier dealing with straight criminals. Honour amongst thieves and all that. At least you knew where you stood with them.

As Stan Summers's Bentley joined the queue of limousines awaiting their turn to drop off their celebrity passengers outside the theatre, it was watched from across the street by a man called Jimmy Hardacre.

Jimmy had been a dosser for nearly ten years and was well known to both the police and the long-suffering public in theatreland. Now in his fifties, he was a failed actor. This sorry state he attributed to the cigar-chewing Jews who ran the business and the clique of successful 'luvvies' who conspired to keep newcomers out of their charmed circle. It never occurred to him that his lost career, marriage and home was anything to do with the fact that he was an alcoholic, unreliable and had all the acting ability of a ventriloquist's dummy.

'Bloody toffee-nosed tart!' he shouted from his little cardboard house in the alleyway opposite when he recognised a well-known actress glide from her limo to the foyer.

He raised his bottle – a little whisky topped with meths – and shook it in the air, but that night he was too drunk to bother crossing the street and creating his usual nuisance.

His fellow dossers ignored him, stuffed more newspapers into their clothes and sleeping bags and curled up more tightly against the cold and Jimmy's rantings.

That annoyed him. He turned to the man sitting nearest him. 'Bloody toffee-tarted nose!' he shouted. 'Don't ya think, Kermit?'

Kermit the Kraut, Jimmy had named the younger man who had only dossed here for the last three days and who at least talked to him occasionally. Had a funny name that Jimmy couldn't remember and a funny accent that sounded German.

'A lotta toffs tonight,' Kermit observed, huddling in a filthy woollen overcoat that was several sizes too large. He scratched at his thick tangle of beard. 'Must be a first night. I reckon the punters might have a few bob. Feelin' lucky, Jimmy?'

Jimmy belched; he was past feeling anything. But the talk of punters reminded him of the smart gent of military bearing who had come and spoken to Kermit for a few minutes on each of the past two days. "Ow much your Mr Blimp give you today, then?'

'Price of a cuppa.'

'Bloody liar. Not enough for a miniature Bell's?'

'Afraid not.'

'Wanna swig of this?'

Kermit shook his head and stumbled to his feet. 'Nah, thanks, Jimmy, but if I get lucky with the punters I'll split you fifty-fifty.'

Jimmy made the effort to stand. 'I'll earn my own, thank you, Mr Kraut!'

Kermit was already shuffling between the slow-moving traffic as the older man followed.

'Spare ten pee for a coffee, sir?' Kermit asked the first of the rubberneckers behind the crash barrier; he held out his soiled and battered hat like a begging bowl.

He moved down the line, getting the usual mixed response. On the opposite side of the foyer, Jimmy had far less luck, mostly because no one understood a word he said. He looked across at Kermit, envious at the sound of jingling change.

'God, cheek of the bleeder,' he mumbled.

Kermit was actually approaching one of the first-night guests, who was crossing the pavement from his Bentley with a tarty young thing in a slinky blue dress. Holding out his hat.

'Get the fuck out of my way,' the man hissed.

The Kraut had pushed his face close into the other man's, the thick shabby overcoat blocking Jimmy's view. He heard the voice; it was definitely his friend's. But he wasn't sure of the words. 'Remember me?' A question. Then what sounded like: 'I'm doing this for gold.'

Then Kermit moved away and the man stood white-faced, sort of surprised, holding his hands across the front of his tux. He didn't say anything, but began a sort of staggering walk for a few paces, then collapsed on the steps.

Heart attack, Jimmy thought.

By the time he reached the man, his girl was kneeling by his side and a circle of people had gathered around. Jimmy peered

485

over their shoulders, gaped, then suddenly drew back. Shocked.

The shaft of a strange-looking knife was protruding from the man's blood-sodden shirt. And he looked distinctly dead.

Jimmy turned round to see where Kermit was. He had vanished into the night.

Redheads were a rare sight in Cali.

Obviously a tourist, the waiter decided as he took the bottle of wine to her table. The camera and guidebook beside her plate confirmed it.

She gave him a generous smile as he poured a glass for her before he turned to the dark-haired young secretary at the adjacent table. 'Hello, Juanita. Is it the à la carte or the special today?'

'The special, of course. I can't afford those fancy prices.'

He smiled in sympathy and turned away, scribbling on his pad. Such youth, such beauty, but such sad, faraway eyes. What a shame, he thought and wondered why?

As he walked back to the kitchen he failed to observe that both women had identical Dior plastic carrier bags beside their chairs at the adjacent tables. Later he was not surprised to see that the two lonely diners had struck up a casual conversation.

'I've heard a lot about you, Juanita,' the redhead said in faltering Spanish. 'How's the job going?'

The girl shrugged. 'Tolerable under the circumstances. Maria Palechor can be a real bitch. Still, I'm grateful you got me the job.'

'Not me. Friends of friends, your friends. It took a lot of patience and planning – and luck.'

Juanita smiled. 'And time. Well over a year.'

'As long as I've been studying Spanish.'

'You're really very good.'

'Thank you.' The redhead glanced casually round the room, ensuring no one could overhear. 'Now tell me. You are sure Ruiz Jaramillo comes to your office today?'

'Yes, it was confirmed this morning. There is a big crisis. It has just been discovered that one of the Caribbean banks that Jaramillo uses was a fake set up by the British police. To track down *narco* money, I think. Over two hundred people have been arrested in America and Europe. Everyone is very worried.'

The redhead knew about the crisis. She had only recently been told how Cali had been craftily baited into using the bank, so exposing its complex laundering network. It had been a masterstroke and was reckoned to mark the start of the cartel's eventual collapse.

Years of courtroom drama was set to follow. That was the official way of things. But this was the other way. 'What will happen when Jaramillo arrives at the office?' she asked.

'As always I will show him in and as always Señora Palechor will ask me to leave my desk until he goes,' Juanita replied. 'To make coffee, run an errand or do some filing. Their meetings are always secret. I will just leave the bag in the drawer of my desk when I leave.'

The redhead nodded. 'Is there a danger to other staff?'

'No. I have an idea to empty the adjoining office. What do I have to do?'

'You'll find the device has a dial timer for up to five minutes only so that you can control the situation. You'll see a simple on-switch and an off that will override at any time in case of problems or innocent people in danger. You can then reset it.'

Juanita looked relieved. 'So I can leave it for another day if things go wrong? That is good.'

'You'll find something else in there. A lot of money in used dollar notes.'

A perplexed look appeared on the girl's face. 'Money? I don't want money.'

'It's what was due to Mario. His closest friend believes he would have wanted you and your family to have it. We look after our own.'

'I am learning that. And if I can help again in the future, just let me know.'

A few minutes later the redhead settled her bill. She picked up the bag beside Juanita's chair and rose to her feet. 'Nice chatting to you.'

The girl smiled nervously. 'I don't even know your name.'

'It's best that way.'

'Who do I ask for if I phone?'

'Just Kelly. That will do.'

Then the redhead turned and walked out. The waiter watched the languid sway of her hips and admired the long legs and the careless toss of her copper locks.

She crossed the road and, to his surprise, climbed into a beat-up old Cadillac that had just pulled up.

He shook his head with disapproval when he saw the dishevelled individual at the wheel. Looked like a tramp.

'*El vago pequeño*,' he muttered with disgust. Some people have all the luck.